...ve w...g ...y. She lives ...
...nd is definitely a cat person.

... out more, visit www.lieselschwarz.com or follow
Liesel on twitter: @Liesel_S

Praise for Liesel Schwarz:

'[Schwarz is] the soon-to-be high-priestess of
British steampunk'
The Independent

'A distinctive read, made so much better by Schwarz's
undoubted skill as a writer and story teller, creating a
world of richly layered environments ... I'm not really
sure what else you could ask from a novel: believable
characters, an engrossing plot, written by a capable author
... highly enjoyable'
sci-fi-online

'The world itself is beautifully realised, and mixes a few
well-loved steampunk staples (you can't escape airships,
for example) with some unique ideas that really

Also by Liesel Schwarz:

A Conspiracy of Alchemists

LIESEL SCHWARZ

The Chronicles of Light and Shadow

A CLOCKWORK HEART

DEL REY

1 3 5 7 9 10 8 6 4 2

First published in the UK in 2013 by Del Rey, an imprint of
Ebury Publishing
A Random House Group Company

This edition published 2014

The Random House Group Limited Reg. No. 954009

Addre____ __ ___ _____ ___i___ _h_ R____ H____ G____ ___ be

The Ra_____ _____ ____ _____ _____ _____ rdship
Co_____ _____ ____ _____ _____ _____ on
organis _____ _____ _____ _____ 'SC®-
certified _____ _____ _____ _____ rted by
the l____ _____ _____ _____ _____ ce.

Printed and bound by CPI Group (UK) Ltd, Croydon, CR0 4YY

ISBN 9780091950712

To buy books by your favourite authors and register for offers visit
www.randomhouse.co.uk
www.delreyuk.com

Not all fairy tales end with Happy Ever After. Some begin that way.

The girl who casts no shadow has become a wife. The world once again has an Oracle and the realms of Light and Shadow are in harmony.

The pact between Alchemist and Nightwalker is no more. It has crumbled to dust and rests in the ruins of Constantinople. And a bargain has been struck. Those of the Council who would harm the girl have agreed to let her be for now.

But these are all matters which some say do not fall to the attentions of La Fée Verte. For the universe is vast and I am small. For what can one do but have regard for that tiny part of it which concerns one?

I have gained my freedom, but I sometimes find myself missing Paris and the absinthe-green dreams I used to weave in return for sugar.

They have given me my own quarters in the glasshouse that leads off the breakfast room, and I have filled it with green. Angelica and anise blossom in large clay pots amongst the ferns and fancy moth orchids that were brought from far away. But beneath the wooden cladding and frames that allow me to pass unhindered, the glasshouse is still made of iron. And were it not for the stray bumblebees I invite in to stay with me, I would be completely alone in this vast grey city of smog and drizzle. It is a place I have grown to despise, despite my good fortune.

I digress. The sunrise is about to call upon the day and there is work to do. For such is the nature of the two realms that make up this world: as happiness and contentment grow in the Light, so from deep within the Shadow, the dark counterparts grow too.

Sometimes in the quiet hours of the day I sense it, and I grow very afraid.

My mistress is too immersed within her perfect happiness to sense what will come to pass and I do not have the heart to tell her. Yet.

Better to let her enjoy her newfound happiness a little longer. She will need thoughts of this happiness to sustain her. Because when the darkness comes, it will take everything.

ೲ

Chapter One

Amsterdam, 5 February 1904

The *Water Lily* creaked happily as she surged against the headwinds that heralded landfall. As she prepared for landing, Elle eased the airship to a lower altitude.

Below her, the canals and gingerbread buildings of the city came into view. Amsterdam was as pretty as a picture, but there was no time for sightseeing. Today was a day for business. The Greychester Flying Company was about to collect its first proper freight consignment. Strictly above board and legitimate.

Elle smiled with pride. Her very own flight charter business. It was almost as if an invisible hand had granted every wish she had ever had in one magical sweep. She had so many ideas about what she wanted to do with her new venture that she could hardly sleep at night. She ran her gaze around the wood and glass interior of the cockpit. The repairs and improvements that had been made to the *Water Lily* were superb. Marsh had insisted on installing brand-new navigational instruments and a state-of-the-art balloon-gas relay system. She had protested, but he had been adamant. She was secretly thrilled though. In fact, one would never have thought the *Water Lily* had been riddled with bullet holes and dangerously close to being scrapped just months before.

Bought with his money, not yours... the voices whispered to her.

'Oh, do be quiet you old crones!' Elle spoke out loud. The voices who spoke were the Spirit of the Oracle. An amalgamation of fragments from the souls of each woman who had, over the centuries, held the position. Elle knew that when she died, a little part of her would rise up to join them too. And as much as she hated the fact that they were always watching her, it gave her comfort to know that somewhere within that patchwork of souls that made up the nebula she came to know as the voice of the Oracle, was a bit of the mother she never knew. It was just a pity that they were such a bunch of busybodies who always chose to interfere at the most inopportune times.

Never forget who you are, child, the voices said in answer to her thoughts.

'Yes, yes, I am the Oracle, the source of wisdom; the one with the gift of sight; the force that holds the many folds of the universe together; the one who channels power to those who are deserving.' She recited the mantra they had taught her in a bored singsong voice. 'Trust me, if there is one thing I cannot do, it's forget who I am. Now please leave me alone to enjoy this moment, would you? Today I am flying and I want none of this Oracle business spoiling it.'

As you wish... the voices faded away.

Just then, the communications console started rattling and spitting out a ribbon of tape, clearing her for landing.

Elle brought the airship round portside and lined her up, ready to dock at one of the platforms that lined the docks on the western district. With a shudder and hiss that sounded almost like a sigh of contentment, the *Water Lily* berthed.

'There you are, my dear,' Elle said to her ship as she turned the crank handle that released the tether ropes. 'All safe and sound.'

Almost as if in answer to that, one of the boiler tank valves opened to release some engine pressure.

Elle opened the hatch and let the ladder rope drop to the ground. With practised ease, she climbed down and stepped on to the wooden docking platform.

'Miss Chance, I presume!' A tall man with a shock of white-blond hair that was thinning at the top waved at her.

'Ah, Mr De Beer.' She smiled at him.

'Welcome to the fair city of Amsterdam.' He spoke in an accent that was a touch heavy and rounded on the vowels.

'Thank you. It's so nice to finally meet you,' she said as she shook her new Dutch docking agent's huge hand vigorously.

'And the same to you,' he said graciously. 'It is an honour to be working with the famous Eleanor Chance.'

Elle didn't have the heart to correct him on her new surname. Simply being Elle Chance for the day, not Lady Eleanor or Viscountess Greychester, was a bit of a relief, if she was honest with herself.

She loved her husband Hugh with all her heart, but

the pomp and ceremony involved in becoming part of his world over the last few months had been more than a little overwhelming.

'I have the papers ready here, to sign if you will. Once it is completed, I will tell the men to start loading the freight. I have told them to be extra careful with our precious tulips.' Mr De Beer pointed to the crates of bulbs which were stacked on wooden pallets and tied down with coarse rope. They were indeed ready to be loaded into the hull and destined to brighten the gardens and huge glasshouses of Kew that summer.

'My men shouldn't take too long. Sign here, if you please,' he said as he handed her a wad of papers.

Elle felt a pang of sadness when she signed the docking papers and charter before handing them back to Mr De Beer so he could tear off the counterparts. Patrice, her old agent, had been such fun.

In the old days, before Constantinople, Patrice would have taken her to some exotic disreputable bar or café for a drink while they waited for the freight to be loaded. He would have had her in fits of giggles with his lumbering charm and silly jokes. Despite his betrayal and all the terrible things he had done, Elle found herself missing his massive moustache. She had been told afterwards that very few bodies were ever recovered from the Constantinople earthquake that had killed almost every living alchemist and a large percentage of the Nightwalker population. They had all been gathered in an underground amphitheatre when the vortex that their leader, Sir Eustace Abercrombie, had created, collapsed, bringing a large part of the city down with it. The last memory Elle had of Patrice was of him hanging on for dear life at the edge of a spinning vortex of complete darkness…

She closed her eyes at the awful memory. Patrice had simply been sucked into oblivion, never to be seen again. She did not think that a funeral had been held for him and the thought of it made her sad. Such a wasteful and futile quest for absolute power…

'Miss Chance, is everything all right?' Mr De Beer asked. He looked concerned.

Elle blinked herself back to the present. 'Yes, all is well. I was just remembering something. Silly, really.'

She shrugged off her dark thoughts. Patrice had betrayed her, and he had betrayed her husband too, by working as a double agent. Even if he were alive today, she did not think she could forgive the fact that he had sold her to the alchemists as if she were nothing more than a means to gain a profit.

But this was the beginning of a new era and she wouldn't allow dark thoughts to taint things. 'Say, do you know where the pilots' mess is?' she asked De Beer.

'Ah, yes, it's just over there. Upstairs in that building with the green roof.'

'Thank you.' She smiled at De Beer. 'Take off in three hours?'

He doffed his flat cap. 'Will see you then, Miss Chance.'

The pilots' mess room was exactly where Mr De Beer had said it was, on the first floor of one of the administrative buildings adjacent to the landing docks. The smell of meat stew mingled with the odour of tired bodies hit her right in the nostrils halfway up the stairwell. It was a familiar smell that made her feel warm inside. It was the smell of freedom.

The mess was really nothing more than a large, slightly grubby warehouse that had been converted to serve as a canteen and waiting area for pilots and crew between flights. The wooden floorboards were scuffed and grey paint flaked from the walls, in the way that utilitarian buildings seemed to do, but this did not seem to bother anyone.

She walked up to the canteen counter and ordered a coffee. It came in a tin mug and had a faint blue-grey film on the surface that hinted at the hours it had been brewing behind the counter.

She had just picked up her coffee when someone called her name. 'Ellie!'

Only her father and one other person called her that.

She spun round to greet the young man who was, at that moment, bounding up to her like an over-eager Labrador.

'Ducky!' She hugged him with genuine affection.

'Or should I rather bow and say, good afternoon, my lady?' In one quick move, he converted her hug into a half-nelson that would have made any wrestler proud.

Elle started laughing and dug her fingers into his ribs to tickle him. This was a practised manoeuvre she had perfected while they were in flight school. Richard 'Ducky' Richardson was the brother she never had.

Ducky, so called because of his prowess on the cricket field, let go of her. 'My word, it's good to see you. What on earth are you doing here?'

'I'm flying.' She smoothed her hair back into its customary low knot at the back of her neck.

'Is that old tub of yours still in the air?' he said with amazement.

'The *Water Lily* is not a tub. And she's just had a complete overhaul. I'd bet she'd outrun your rickety old ship any day of the week.'

'Ha! Now that's a wager I'd like to take.'

'Just name the day and I'll be there.'

Ducky grinned at her. 'Oh, Ellie. It's so lovely to see you. I'm so sorry I missed the wedding, but I was in Japan and I couldn't get back in time. You did get married awfully quickly,' he said with naughty smile. 'I would have thought you would be busy planning christening breakfasts at the moment.' There had been more than a few finely arched eyebrows raised at news of her sudden marriage to Marsh and the gossipmongers were all watching eagerly to see if their suspicions were correct.

'Oh stop it!' Elle felt her cheeks grow warm. 'When you know something is right, there really is no reason to wait. And besides, you know I'm not the type of girl who fancies elaborate weddings.'

'Come, let me introduce you to the crew,' Ducky said.

On the other side of the canteen, a group of men had halted their game of cards and were watching her intently as Ducky steered her over to them.

'Lads, I'd like you to meet my very dear friend Mrs Eleanor Marsh, or, rather, Viscountess Greychester to be precise,' Ducky said. 'Elle, may I present the crew of the *Iron Phoenix*.' He made an over-elaborate sweeping gesture.

Chairs scraped as the crewmen all rose to their feet, nodded awkwardly and mumbled 'my lady', in gruff tones. All except one. He was dressed like her, in a white shirt and brown leather coat.

'Gentlemen, do sit. Today I am simply Elle, the pilot. There really is no need for formalities, please.'

'By all means, join us.' The man who was still seated spoke with a soft drawl that immediately placed him from somewhere in the New World, America perhaps, she wasn't sure.

She studied the men. Ducky was the embodiment of a clean-cut Englishman. Apple-cheeked, bred from solid stock and good to his bones, his only flaw was his natural sense of adventure. Despite his family's best efforts, he absolutely refused to settle down. It was also one of the things she loved best about him.

Sandy was the word that first came to mind when her gaze slid to the American. He had the gravelly, freckly look of a man who had spent the majority of his life outdoors. He wore a fedora, pushed back on his head, which he had not bothered to take off indoors. She stared at his hands that were resting on the table. Broad palms, strong fingers. The hands of a man who knew hard work. A soldier's hands, she decided. He was far too suspicious-looking to be a farmer.

He gave her a quizzical look. 'Well, are you going to sit down or not?' he asked.

Elle realised that she had been staring. 'Why, thank you,' she said sweetly. She set her coffee mug down on the table and took the seat Ducky offered her. As she sat, she shoved her new leather holdall between the legs of her chair. The strap was new and stiff and she had to wiggle it around a few times before the finely stitched brown leather would settle.

The holdall had been a gift from Hugh. He had spotted it in the market in Florence on their honeymoon. 'For the one that I didn't manage to save in Paris,' he had said when she had unwrapped it from the tissue paper.

They had spent that afternoon curled up in front of the massive medieval fireplace in their room while the grey winter rain slipped down the windows outside. A honeymoon in the middle of winter did have its advantages, for it was far too cold to be traipsing about outside sightseeing for too long.

'Do you play cards, Mrs Marsh?' The American spoke, interrupting her thoughts.

Elle looked straight into the bluest eyes she had ever encountered.

Without thinking, her fingers went to the place between the buttons of her shirt to the slim hilt of the stiletto she carried inside the laces of her corset.

'I've been known to play the odd hand,' she said.

She lowered her hand unobtrusively, feeling silly at her sudden reaction.

He smiled. 'Well, then. Mr Richardson, why don't you deal us a fresh hand. The rest of you men have three hours' shore leave. And don't make me have to come and collect you later.'

'Aye, aye, captain,' Ducky said and picked up the cards as the remainder of the crew took the hint and went off on their own business.

'Captain?' Elle looked at Ducky.

He laughed. 'Dashwood. Logan Dashwood. He pilots our crew. I am first officer on the *Phoenix*,' Ducky explained.

'At your service, ma'am.' Dashwood touched his hat. He wore no collar and she noticed that his shirt was unstarched and unbuttoned at the top. A long strip of leather darkened from wear was wound loosely around his neck. A small amulet carved from what looked like black stone was threaded through the leather, just visible above the place where the buttons met. Elle could feel the dark hum of power from the Shadow side emanating from it.

There was something odd about this man, but she could not say what. 'Well, Captain Dashwood, let's play,' she said, dismissing the thought.

She picked up her cup and took a sip of the lukewarm liquid. It tasted tinny and so foul that she could not help making a face.

'That coffee looks like it could strip-clean the tanks of a spark engine,' Ducky said.

'You are not wrong.' Elle put the mug to the side. The wedding band she wore on her left hand glinted in the watery light of the mess hall.

Dashwood's smile broadened. He reached over and took her hand in his. 'Not married that long then, I see?'

'Long enough,' she answered, drawing her hand away.

'That wedding band is still very shiny. Does your husband approve of you gallivanting around the world in the company of men, Mrs Marsh?'

Elle glared at him. 'I am not gallivanting. I am

working. There is a big difference between the two, Captain Dashwood.'

He held up his hand. 'I was just trying to be friendly. No need to be so prickly.'

She could tell that he was laughing at her, but she was no stranger to the reaction. She had spent years fighting the perception that she was some spoiled rich girl who took to flying because she was bored.

'So, Ducky, how was Japan? You must tell me all about it.' She turned to her friend, ignoring Captain Dashwood entirely.

Ducky's eyes lit up. 'Japan is like nothing you have ever experienced. Had to get out of there in a hurry, though. All the signs are that there is serious trouble brewing out there.'

'It's all over the London papers,' Elle said. 'Such a worry, isn't it?'

'I found myself without a commission. That was until I heard that the good captain over here was in need of a first officer, on account of a slight problem with crew...'

Ducky broke off what he was saying, for Dashwood gave him a very stern look.

'And so Mr Richardson found himself stationed on the *Phoenix*. And a finer first officer no captain could hope for.' Dashwood finished Ducky's sentence for him.

Ducky swallowed and picked up the deck of cards. From the looks of things, they had been playing that American card game called poker, which had recently become all the rage.

Captain Dashwood placed a small stack of matchsticks

in front of her. 'Shilling a stick? Or is that too rich for your blood?'

'Wager accepted, Captain Dashwood.' Elle gave him a slow smile. Her friend the Baroness Loisa Belododia had taught her how to play when Elle and Marsh had stopped by to visit her at her winter castle in the Carpathian mountains. Loisa was an excellent card player and Elle had learnt a few tricks from her.

Ducky dealt the hand for them.

Elle felt the soft hum of magic from the amulet around Captain Dashwood's neck the moment she checked her cards, but she said nothing.

He won the first two games easily as Elle observed him play. Each time she looked at her hand, the amulet strummed with an energy that could not be ignored.

So the good captain was cheating. Well, she had a few aces up her sleeve too.

'Another game?' He sat back in his seat with arrogant satisfaction.

'Why not? You seem to be on a winning streak, Captain.'

He laughed softly as Ducky dealt again.

Elle closed her eyes and thought of two cards that would make up a bad hand on the table. Carefully she reached out with her mind and sent the image along the trail of energy back to the captain. His eyes narrowed for a fraction of a second and then he gripped his jaw with glee.

Elle glanced at her cards again. She had an ace.

She added her matchsticks to the growing pile in the centre of the table. The game was on.

Expressions grew serious as they concentrated on the cards.

Ducky bet. Elle took another card.

Dashwood drew a card and bit the corner of his lip.

Ducky placed his cards on the table, face down. 'That's as far as my bravery allows me to go,' he said shaking his head at the small fortune in front of him.

Elle and Captain Dashwood stared at one another for a few long moments and Elle felt the crackle of energy from the Shadow side course through her.

'What about you, Mrs Marsh?' the Captain said.

'Oh, I am still very much in the game, Captain.' She added more matchsticks to the centre of the table.

'Hmm, a woman with gumption. I am impressed. But let's see what you are made of. I raise you,' he said as he pushed all of his matchsticks into the centre of the table. Then he looked up and gave her sly smile.

Elle felt the strum of his amulet and fought against it.

'Very well, Captain.' She put all her matchsticks on to the pile. 'What else have you got?'

Dashwood scratched his chin and a look of uncertainty flashed across his face. 'What did you have in mind, Mrs Marsh?'

This time it was her turn to give him a sly smile. She leaned forward and pulled the docking papers out of her holdall. 'The *Water Lily* for the *Phoenix*. Winner takes both ships.'

Dashwood's eyes widened in surprise for just a second, but it was enough to tell her that he had not expected her boldness.

'Elle, no! Dashwood never loses.' Ducky put his hand on her arm to stop her.

'There is a first time for everything,' she said without

taking her eyes off the captain. 'What do you say, Captain Dashwood?'

'Very well then, if you are so eager to part company with your ship. I'll take that wager. Perhaps you could even ask your husband to buy it back for you later,' Dashwood said.

Elle kept her features neutral, but she was sorely tempted to put him in his place. The arrogance of the man was absolutely incredible. And to think, he had been cheating all this time without anyone knowing.

'Show us what you've got,' she said.

'Full house,' he said as he laid the cards down on the table. 'Three aces and two kings.'

Elle stared at his cards without saying anything.

He hooted and lifted his arms in the air. 'I win, and you, madam,' he pointed at her, 'owe me a ship.'

'Perhaps you celebrate a mite too quickly, Captain,' she said.

He sat forward in his chair. 'What do you mean?'

'Well, you see, there are four aces in a deck of cards. And I happen to have the fourth one right here. Along with a king, a queen, a jack and a ten. Of hearts.' She laid the cards out one by one as she named them.

'Blimey,' said Ducky before he burst out laughing. 'I think they call that a Royal Flush. Is that right?'

Dashwood blanched. He stared at the cards before him. 'How is that possible?' he muttered.

Elle shook her head. 'Well, Captain, I would recommend that you check whether your opponents have special abilities before you start cheating at cards.' She waved her hand over the table. 'See?' she said.

Even in the harsh spark lights of the canteen, Elle's arm cast no shadow on the table. It was one of the many peculiarities that being the Oracle brought, for she was the one who walked between the two worlds.

She turned to Ducky. 'Ducky, how would you like to come and work for me? I suddenly find myself the owner of an extra airship in need of a pilot,' she said sweetly.

Ducky gawped at her.

'You dirty cheater!' Captain Dashwood slammed his fist down on the table with such force that it made the matchsticks jump.

'Oh no, Captain. It is *you* who are the cheater. I just happened to spot that little mind-reading amulet the moment we sat down. You really should be more circumspect about these things. Now, if you'll excuse me.' She gathered her holdall and rose from the table. 'Ducky, will you bring the *Phoenix* to Croydon? Greychester's rented a hangar there. Take on whichever crew members you consider to be good men and necessary in order to fly her home safely. I will ask Mr De Beer to arrange the papers for us.' She turned and inclined her head at Dashwood. 'Good day to you, sir.'

Ducky rose and gave Dashwood an apologetic shrug. 'A wager is a wager, Captain. I'm sorry.'

Dashwood said nothing, but just stared ahead of him as Ducky followed Elle downstairs.

Mr De Beer looked up from his desk when Elle strode into his office with Ducky at her heels. 'The *Iron Phoenix* is now part of the Greychester Flying Company Fleet,' she said.

'Is she now?' Mr De Beer said in surprise.

'She is indeed,' Elle said with a little nod. 'Can you arrange her papers for Croydon please? Mr Richardson will pilot her as soon as she is cleared for take off.'

'But what about Captain Dashwood?' Mr De Beer said.

'What about him?' Elle said.

Her docking agent dabbed his thinning hair with his handkerchief. 'Captain Dashwood is not a man I would like to have for an enemy, madam. Are you sure you want to do this?'

'We had a bet and I won. Fair and square. Now the ship is mine and I make no apology for it.'

Mr De Beer shook his head in dismay. 'Very well, then. I will arrange it. You had better get ready for cast off, Mr Richardson. As luck would have it, I have a departure opening right after the *Water Lily*. You had better take it before the captain decides to change his mind. We don't want any trouble, now do we?'

'I think that is an excellent idea, sir,' Ducky said. He too was looking slightly out of sorts. Elle noticed him glance over his shoulder at the direction of the mess as he spoke.

'Come, Ducky, you had better show me my new acquisition.' She smiled in triumph as she left De Beer's office. Today was truly a great day for the Greychester Flying Company indeed.

Chapter Two

Ingolstadt, 5 February 1904

The icy winter fog swirled and spilled along the cobbled streets, rendering the stone-clad buildings slick as they stood firm against the biting cold.

Clothilde crouched silently on the roof amidst the slow-crumbling gargoyles that guarded the city. She watched as day fought night and the darkness dissolved into a murky dawn.

It followed her wherever she went, this fog. Ever present, ever swirling. She lifted her head and sipped the air. It would rain soon, as it always did.

Below her, a single lonely bell tolled, telling the good people of this place that the sun was about to rise. There were dark creatures afoot at this early hour. And she was one of them.

In anticipation of the icy rain that would soon fall, she tightened her cloak around her, making sure that the hood covered her extraordinary hair. As white as sea-bleached bone, it reached down to her knees. Her skin was pale and fine; her features perfectly moulded as if from the finest porcelain. Her lips were bloodless and sculpted, the face of a marble statue.

She knew many glamours of disguise and so she could change her appearance as she pleased, but in her unguarded state, Clothilde was almost entirely devoid of colour except for her eyes, which were a startling shade of sea green.

She was one of the last of her kind: *La Dame Blanche* – the Lady in White.

The promised rain started sifting down, pinpricks of sleet, soaking everything before freezing into a black shell that covered everything.

Clothilde was used to waiting in cold places, for that was her lot in life, and most of the time she welcomed the numbness that it brought. But this morning she had an appointment to keep and so she dared not tarry.

She had chosen the roof of the great cathedral with care. The apex of the dome was a powerful crossroads between the realms of Shadow and Light. Far below her on the floor was a fine mosaic circle, its Shadow purpose cleverly disguised by the religious symbols of the Light.

This was ironic, because here, high above this city of learning and enlightenment, were all the Shadow elements she needed in one place.

She closed her eyes and reached out to the barrier that held the two realms apart. The barrier was everywhere, visible in the shadows that are cast by every single thing here in the Light. But here, high above the circle, the portal lay open, ready for anyone who had the skill to tap into it. How stupid these humans were. Thinking that a few puny rules enforced by *Warlocks* could stop someone like her.

The energy reacted to her touch as if it were alive. Some said the barrier had assumed a life of its own after all this time and Clothilde was inclined to believe that. It was certainly unusual for a Shadow creature to touch the void from the Light side. Unusual and highly illegal. The penalty for being caught was instant death. Or so they said. But Clothilde had lived for a very long time and she cared little for the rules imposed on her by men.

She braced herself for the next step. It was big risk to take, reaching into the divide like this – back to front – but she was hungry and the need for nourishment strong, so it was a risk she was willing to take. She took solace from the fact that no one was watching. No one would know.

Carefully, she reached in between the folds of space and time. It opened up before her – a small rent in reality, fringed with gold. She rooted around until her hand closed around the pocket of trapped energy that hung suspended between the realms, ripe for the picking. The energy pulsed against her palm with a warm life of its own and the sensation sent a delicious shiver through her entire body. Unable to contain herself, she slipped her fingernails into the soft metaphysical membranes. It took only a second, the space between heartbeats, before the magic slipped through the fissure she had created. The sensation was like biting into a ripe, exotic fruit – lush and exquisite. Clothilde could not help uttering a low moan as she felt herself fill with power.

No man could ever match the sensuousness that tapping into the void could evoke.

She was young, measured against those of her kind, but she had spent more than one lifetime searching for a man who was strong enough to withstand her voracious appetites, but they all shrivelled up and died, crumbling to dust between her fingers. Such fragile creatures, such a pity.

Sated, she stood and straightened her cloak. A gentle psychic tug caught her attention and she stared in the direction of the university. The pull she felt was the desire of men. She could feel herself being summoned.

The entrance to the small wing in the engineering faculty of Ingolstadt University was through a heavy door made of pure iron. Clothilde wrapped her fist in her cloak to lift the knocker, flinching at the sting of the metal through the fabric.

A young man opened the door for her. He was impeccably dressed in a fine suit, his hair still damp from where he had washed it this morning. The only sign that indicated his association here was the discreet little silver medallion he wore pinned to the lapel of his jacket. His eyes lit up with lust as he took in the full impact of her presence, but she stopped his thoughts before they could go too far. He would be such easy quarry, but this was no time for seduction.

The young doorman frowned with a disappointment he did not fully comprehend before his sense of duty took over. 'This way, miss. They are expecting you.'

He led her down a chilly corridor. From the cobwebs that hung in the high corners of the ceiling it was clear that this was a place few visited.

The metal doorframes briefly crackled with a glimmer of blue electricity as she walked by and she had to stop herself from wincing at the protective spells they held as she passed each one. All these precautions, while understandable, were most annoying.

She was led into an opulent room, decorated with heavy baroque gilding and filigree. A bright fire crackled in the oversized fireplace and filled the room with warmth.

A group of men were seated around a long table that was placed perpendicular to the entrance. They were all dressed in black and each man wore a white mask tied at the back of their heads with a black satin ribbon. Apart from their hair and a few bald patches, the masks completely obscured all recognisable features of the attendees.

This was the Consortium: a group of international financiers who controlled the financial markets of the world.

The power that emanated from the group assembled around the table was almost tangible. But this was a power that had nothing to do with magic. This was the power of the Realm of Light, the power of money and influence.

'Miss de Blanc. We are pleased that you answered our invitation. Apologies for meeting so early, but our members are all busy men and we thought it would be more discreet if we assembled out of sight.' She was not sure which one of the men had spoken.

'Thank you for inviting me. It is an honour to be in such auspicious company.' She made a slow, careful curtsey.

'We have been watching your progress at the medical faculty here with great interest. Your intellect coupled with your other talents makes you truly unique.' He paused for a moment. 'A most extraordinary achievement. And a woman too.'

'I thank you, sir,' she said. A shiver of arousal passed through the room as the men reacted to her low voice, but Clothilde felt nothing but contempt for them.

The chairman cleared his throat. 'As mentioned in our invitation, we believe that you are ideally suited to the task we have in mind.'

'I am flattered by your praise,' she said. None of the masked members moved. It was most disconcerting.

'It is correct that you are familiar with spark monasteries?'

'Yes, I briefly lived in one as a foundling many years ago.' Clothilde kept her face impassive. She was far older than any of the men she faced. Older even than their grandfathers, for she had lived with the electromancers in the days before the men of the Realm of Light had found ways to use the spark they made to power their machines. It was a fact she would keep to herself, for no man wants to be reminded of the fact that women age. Instead, she smiled sweetly. 'The electromancers found me and I stayed with them until they sent me to the convent. I think they always sensed that my talents lay in the workings of the human body, so when I was old enough they sent me to the sisters at a convent that specialises in the healing arts. I worked as a healer in the hospice until the world had changed enough for me to enrol here at the university to study.'

'Splendid.'

'I live to serve.' Clothilde murmured the mantra of the electromancers and inclined her head. 'But tell me, what would you have me do?'

'Well, we are most interested in the experiments you

have been conducting in the field of galvanism. Most scientists had dismissed the theories long ago, but you have persevered.'

'I am not most scientists,' she said with a little smile. 'I have always been most interested in the application of spark electricity to flesh and the reanimation it brings.'

'Well, yes, and we understand that your findings have been most extraordinary.' One of the masked men motioned to a leather attaché case that lay on the table before them. 'Your instructions are contained therein. You are to burn the papers once you have read and memorised them.'

'I understand,' she said.

'Inside you will find a folder with the necessary letters of introduction. You are to show these to the abbots on the list who are designated to assist you. And most importantly, you will contact us with news, by means of the method described in the instructions once each stage of the process is completed.'

'I understand,' she said again.

'And you are to follow these instructions to the letter. No exceptions, is that clear?'

'Clear, sir.'

'And Miss de Blanc, we are well aware of your... weaknesses. If the electromancers did anything noteworthy in this regard, it would be that they taught you temperance and control. We do expect that you exercise this at all times. The weather, well, there is not much one can do about that, but we absolutely forbid the seduction of any men for the duration of this contract. Have we made ourselves clear?'

'Yes. No sorcery apart from that needed to complete the task.'

One of the Consortium motioned to the young man who had been waiting discreetly in an inconspicuous corner. He stepped forward with a writing tray complete with pen and ink.

'Then sign the contract please.'

Clothilde picked up the pen. A thick contract lay before her on the tray.

The young man flicked the pages over and showed her where to sign.

She scribbled her name without even looking at the document. There was no point, for there would be no negotiation with the Consortium and, besides, she would be long gone before any of them would ever be able to do anything. But if it made them happy, then she would oblige.

She inclined her head in a gesture of subservience when she put the pen down, but inside she felt her emotions roil at their arrogance. In answer, the windows lit up with a flash of lightning and, outside, thunder rolled as rain lashed against the roof.

'Very good,' the man who had spoken first said. 'You are to leave for London without delay. We have booked you a first-class passage on an airship that leaves tonight. We are told that the factory is installed and ready to start up.'

The young man stepped forward and handed her a wallet that was thick with bills.

'You should find enough in there to cover all expenses,' the member of the Consortium said.

'Thank you,' Clothilde said.

'The war between Russia and Japan has created an opportunity for us to move our plans forward sooner than we had envisioned. This venture is therefore an imperative. The emperor is awaiting his first consignment as per the specifications in the papers.'

'War with Russia and Japan?' Clothilde said.

Someone laughed. 'Yes, we expect war to be declared at any moment. And we look forward to it with great anticipation. The dawning of a new era.'

'I am honoured by the faith you have placed in me,' she said.

'It has nothing to do with faith, Miss de Blanc. We will be watching your every move. There is no room for error. Do you understand?'

'Yes, perfectly,' she said sweetly.

One of the masked men leaned over and whispered something. The one he had spoken to inclined his head.

'Furthermore, we have an additional task for you.'

The man who had whispered nodded and stood up from the table. He walked up to Clothilde and presented her with a wooden case. As she took it from him, she thought she could hear a faint ticking from within.

'We want you to find suitable candidates for these. They need to be strong, as we will be testing this new invention for future use. One of our members known only as the Clockmaker will send you all the additional equipment you will require for this experiment. It must be conducted with the utmost secrecy.'

'I will do my best,' said Clothilde.

The men at the table grew silent. 'We do not want

your best, Miss de Blanc. We demand your complete and utter compliance with our every request. Any questions?'

'No. I understand completely,' she said. Outside, more lightning flashed, filling the room with white light, followed by another rumble of thunder.

The masked man reached into his pocket and pulled out a brass key on a piece of string. He presented it to her with an air of reverence. 'The master key for the hearts,' he whispered. 'Take care of it.'

As she touched the key to put it round her neck, she felt a tremor of thaumaturgy pass through her. The strangeness of it made her shiver. This was very strange magic indeed.

'Very well then, you may go,' one of the men said.

Clothilde gathered up the satchel and case, carefully tucking the wallet inside the folds of her robes.

She gave the Consortium another low curtsey, pausing for an alluring moment before rising and leaving. But as she turned to leave she kept her face turned to the floor in order to hide the slow smile that spread across her face.

These men had no idea who they were dealing with. And enlightening them was going to be such fun.

Chapter Three

London

Elle was still smiling when Neville drew the car up alongside the house in Grosvenor Square. The townhouse was an imposing Georgian building with carved sandstone pillars on the facade. A row of camellia trees grew near the black railings outside the front steps. At the moment they looked dark and bare, but Elle knew they would be glorious in spring when they bloomed. This was where she lived.

Marsh was waiting for her at the front door when she reached it from the street.

'I'm home!' Elle kissed her husband as he helped her out of her coat.

'Did you have a good flight, my darling?' he said.

'Oh Hugh, it was simply wonderful. And I have such exciting news!' she said over her shoulder as she went into the house.

Elle flung herself into the leather Chesterfield in the library with a sigh. 'Oh, it's nice to be home. I could murder a nice cup of tea right now. Ring the bell, would you?'

'Well, what is it?' Marsh said as he rang the bell-pull and sank into one of the wingback chairs opposite her.

The fire had burnt down in the fireplace, but the room was lovely and warm after the crisp cold of the February afternoon. The library was one of Elle's favourite rooms in the house, mainly because it was so utterly dominated by Marsh.

She smiled at him with glee. 'I got a new ship.'

Marsh frowned. 'How on earth did you do that?'

Elle sat forward in her seat. 'I won her in a card game. The same game we played with Loisa when we visited on the way back from the honeymoon.'

'You gambled?' She watched her husband's expression darken. 'I knew I should have come with you. What if you had lost?'

'I wouldn't have. The captain of the ship was cheating. He had an amulet around his neck which made him able to see what cards the other players held. But I stopped him from seeing my cards. When I had a good enough hand, I made him think I had worse cards than I really had and so I won. Serves him right for trying to cheat,' she said in one excited breath.

Marsh's frown deepened. 'Shadow magic,' he said. 'What if you had been discovered?'

'Oh, don't be such a worryninny. I was very careful and the captain of the ship didn't guess who – or should I say what? – I am. Besides, I bumped into Ducky in Amsterdam and after I won the ship, I hired him to pilot her home. He's busy berthing the *Iron Phoenix* in Croydon as we speak. We need to book her into Farnborough for an overhaul though. She's a bit rickety.'

'Eleanor!' Marsh thundered.

Elle jumped. Marsh only called her Eleanor like that

when he was angry with her and they were about to have an argument.

'What?' she said, squaring her shoulders.

'I will not have my wife gambling with ruffians. Do you not understand how dangerous that is? You promised you wouldn't take any unnecessary risks.'

'They were not ruffians. Well, not terribly bad ones, if you have to be completely precise. But it was only an innocent card game in the pilots' mess. I told you I wouldn't leave the airfield, and I didn't.'

Marsh ran his hand through his dark hair, worn just a little too long for society. 'Innocent card games do not end up with people losing their ships to one another.'

'Don't you think you are overreacting ever so slightly?' she said sweetly.

He strode up to his desk and grabbed the newspaper that lay neatly folded on its broad leather-topped surface. 'Look!' He thrust the newspaper at Elle.

She took the paper and opened it.

'There.' He jabbed at the news report in the right-hand corner of the page, right underneath the headline that spoke of the trouble between Russia and Japan.

The heading read: SKY PIRATES SPOTTED OVER THE ENGLISH CHANNEL.

'I have been pacing up and down all day worrying and waiting for you to come home safely.'

'Oh,' said Elle. 'But we saw no pirates.'

'There could very well have been. I can manage the thought of you flying the *Water Lily* because she is small and not worth bothering with. But with two ships you are a – a fleet!' he spluttered.

'Oh Hugh, you are being utterly ridiculous,' Elle said.

Marsh sighed. 'I love the fact that you are so bold and fearless, my darling, but you really do need to be more careful.'

'But I was careful,' she said. 'Hugh, you can't wrap me in cotton wool. I need to take risks if I am to turn this charter company into a success.'

Marsh closed his eyes in exasperation. 'How do you suppose I can allow that?'

Elle felt herself grow angry. She hated it when he condescended to her. She rose to her feet. 'Hugh, flying and airships are my business and I was flying for years before you came along, so please stop interfering.'

This was not a new argument. It had taken all her powers of persuasion to stop him from coming along to watch over her.

'Elle, you can't keep the ship. You have to return it to the airfield in Amsterdam. Surely you of all people must know that.'

She didn't want to admit it to Marsh, but Captain Dashwood had looked awfully angry the last time she had seen him. And yet, despite her rather rickety short-comings, the *Iron Phoenix* was a beauty. She was a big freighter, with a hull almost seven hundred feet long. With it, Elle would be able to take in bigger, longer charters for larger fees. And with larger fees she would be able to pay back the money Marsh had lent her to start the company.

His money, the voices suddenly whispered out of nowhere. That was enough to make her decide.

'No. I am keeping the *Iron Phoenix*. My mind is quite made up. The captain knows he lost the bet fair and square. And I am hiring Ducky to pilot her for me. I could use the help, to be honest.'

'I think that is a tremendously bad idea,' Marsh said.

'Well, I don't.' She crossed her arms over her chest. 'The situation would have been very different if you had been the one doing the winning. You are only saying this because I am a woman.'

'I am not going to change your mind, am I?' Marsh rubbed his face in resignation.

She smiled and put her arms around his neck. 'No, you are not. I want my charter business to grow and be successful and an extra ship is precisely what I need.'

'You know I would have bought you another ship. All you had to do is ask,' he said.

'But that wouldn't be the same,' she said.

Marsh put up a hand in defeat. 'Do you have any idea how hard it is to stay here and wait for you to come home every time you take to the air on some adventure?' His dark eyes pleaded with her in a way that told her he was serious.

Elle felt a rush of affection for him and kissed his cheek. 'Marsh, we have spoken about this at length. You know you can't come with me on flights, because flying is something I must do on my own. We are both strong-willed people. And if we impose on one another, we shall end up despising each other over time. You have to leave me be on this topic.'

'I don't like it. Sometimes I think I shall go out of my mind with worry,' he grumbled.

'Well, now you know how the wives of soldiers and sailors have felt for centuries,' she said.

Just then, Edie the maid rolled in the tea trolley.

Elle clapped her hands in delight. 'Ah, just what I need. And with strawberry tarts as well!' The little tarts filled with jam were Elle's favourite.

'I think I need something stronger than tea.' Marsh walked over to his drinks cabinet. He selected one of the decanters. It was filled with bright green liquid that could only be absinthe.

'Speaking of which, where is Adele?'

'Oh, she's in the greenhouse. No one is allowed in there. She is driving the staff to distraction with her demands. Who knew that one so little could make so much trouble.'

Elle laughed. 'Well, she *is* an absinthe fairy.'

Marsh turned and smiled at her. 'So, could I perhaps persuade you to forgo your tea and join me in a drink?' he said.

Elle gave him her most alluring smile. 'You might. And if you'll bring mine to me upstairs in a little while, who knows? I might even invite *you* to join *me*.'

Marsh gave her a wicked grin. 'Invitation accepted, but don't blame me if Mrs Hinges is annoyed because we're late for dinner.'

Chapter Four

An almighty crash followed by a high-pitched scream greeted Elle as she came downstairs one morning, a week after her flight to Amsterdam. Edie came tearing up the stairs. Elle caught her by the upper arms and brought her to an abrupt halt that almost made them both tumble back the way the poor girl had come.

'Edie, what on earth is wrong?' Elle said.

'Begging your pardon, my lady, but it's the fairy. She's absolutely impossible!' Edie rubbed her tear-streaked face. 'I cannot attend her any more. I simply cannot.'

'What happened?'

Edie started sobbing into her apron. 'His lordship is downstairs,' she said between sobs. 'I think you had better ask him, my lady.'

Elle drew the girl's face out of her apron. 'Why don't you take a few moments to calm yourself? And once you've washed your face, go and ask Mrs Hinges for a sweet cup of tea. It is the best remedy after an upset. I know this from personal experience.'

'Yes, my lady.' Edie bobbed a quick curtsey and wiped her nose with the side of her hand. 'Thank you, my lady.'

Elle watched the maid hurry downstairs before continuing on her way.

She stopped at the door to the breakfast room. The place was in a complete uproar. Chairs lay overturned. The tablecloth had been dragged off the table and lay in a heap on the floor amidst the broken breakfast crockery.

In the conservatory the stacked terracotta pots had toppled over. Shards of pot and soil were spilled all over the floor. Someone had trodden mud all over the black-and-white chequered marble floor and Turkish rug of the breakfast room.

On the table in the midst of all the chaos, stood Hugh, holding what looked like the extended ribs of an umbrella stripped of its canvas. The ribs were attached to a cascade of copper wires, which snaked all the way to the floor where they fed into what looked like a very poorly sealed tank of spark. Globs of the bright blue liquid had sloshed on to the carpet and were creating alarming sparks and acrid puffs of smoke.

Adele hovered at the entrance of the conservatory with her arms crossed, blocking the way of anyone who dared enter her domain.

And, if that wasn't enough, someone had strewn enough sugar on the floor to sweeten the waters of the Thames.

'Hugh, what on earth is going on in here?' Elle said, surveying the whole muddy, sticky, smouldering mess.

'Elle!' Hugh turned and smiled at her. 'I think I've devised a machine that will allow humans to converse with fairies. Adele has been helping me. Look.'

He put the umbrella down and dusted some sugar off

a set of rough-drawn plans. A few scrunched-up balls of paper, also flecked with sugar, rolled off the table and landed on the floor.

'I see you have been busy,' she said drily. 'You do know that Mrs Hinges is going to have an apoplexy when she sees this.'

The copper wires started buzzing from lying too near the spark and they set a bit of the tablecloth on fire.

Marsh ran over and started putting out the flames with his hand.

'Don't you mind Mrs Hinges. She will understand,' he said between pats.

Elle crossed her arms and leaned against the doorframe. 'Good heavens, I think I've married my father,' she murmured. Since Marsh had given up his power and become an ordinary mortal, he was becoming more and more like the professor by the day. It was a most alarming thought.

'Adele and I have invented a new game,' Marsh said, entirely unperturbed by Elle's icy stare.

He picked up one of the balls of paper and threw it into the air.

'Go on, fairy, fetch!' he said.

Adele dashed into the breakfast room and started zooming around at a speed faster than the eye could follow. Round and round she went in an attempt to create enough updraft to keep the paper afloat in the air. Her flight path made everything in the room rattle and even more sugar and paper scattered across the table and floor.

'Oh, and before I forget, your father telephoned to say he is coming down to London this evening for dinner.

I have some questions to ask him about aether con-
ductors.' He beamed at her. 'I never knew how much fun
inventions were. I would have given up my position on the
Council years ago had I known. I thought that binding
my Warlock power would be difficult, but this is fun.'

'Oh, Marsh, you didn't invite my father, did you? We are
supposed to be going to the opera with Lady Mandeville
and her daughters tonight. I cancelled a charter especially
so I could go.' Elle closed her eyes in frustration.

'That's no bother. You go with the ladies and I'll stay
here with Adele and your father. Mrs Hinges will look
after us.'

'What makes you think that I want to go to the opera
with the Mandevilles by myself? I only accepted the
invitation for your sake and because we had no option
but to say yes. Did you not think to ask me first?'

Marsh pulled the wires out of the spark tank and the
sparks that were emanating from the umbrella stopped.
He walked over to her and put his hands on her shoulders.
'You weren't here to ask. You, my dear, were too busy
stealing airships from other pilots while I, your poor
husband, was left alone to my own devices.'

Just then the doors of the library burst open and
Professor Charles Chance, followed closely by the
housekeeper Mrs Hinges, burst into the room. 'Ah,
Eleanor! There you are, my girl. Couldn't sleep, so I took
the early train. Hope you don't mind. Thought I'd catch
one of those moving pictures at the cinema theatre while
I'm here.' He kissed the top of her head as he walked past.
'Oh, what a display of supra-kinetic energy. I say, old
chap, you and the little green one have been hard at work.'

'Papa…' Elle started to say, but the professor had already pushed past her and was staring at the paper balls, which Adele had now managed to suspend in the air in a pattern that resembled a solar system.

'Wonderful, dear boy. Simply wonderful,' the professor said to Marsh as he shook his hand.

'Good heavens! Look at the mess. It's like the gates of the underworld have opened up in here,' Mrs Hinges exclaimed.

'Mrs Hinges—' Elle started saying, but Mrs Hinges also pushed past her and started waving her arms at Adele. 'Put those papers down, you little green minx. Don't make me fetch the broom!'

In response, Adele screeched and started aiming the paper balls at Mrs Hinges like missiles. Mrs Hinges, unused to random aerial attacks by absinthe fairies, let out a most undignified squeal of surprise before setting off after the fairy while waving her hands in the air, but Adele simply darted up and perched on the chandelier, out of harm's way.

Mrs Hinges stopped before Elle, slightly out of breath. 'Eleanor, my dear, we really need to talk about…' She stared pointedly at Marsh. 'It's too much for the staff to cope with. And my nerves cannot take it. They cannot, I say. Very soon, no one will want to work here and you will find yourself without help.'

'I know, Mrs Hinges—' Elle started to say, but just then Adele dashed off to one side, knocking a vase of flowers and the row of bric-à-brac from the mantelpiece. The whole lot came crashing to the floor in a cloud of papers and grains of sugar and dust.

And all the while, the professor and Marsh continued their discussion about the umbrella carcass, utterly oblivious to the pandemonium that was unfurling around them.

'*Enough*!' Elle shouted at the top of her voice.

Everyone stopped and stared at her. In the silence, a small porcelain dog, the last ornament standing, slid off the edge of the mantelpiece and smashed on the floor where the bits rattled for a moment.

Elle walked up to the cabinet and pulled out the bottle of absinthe. She yanked the cork out and held the bottle aloft. 'Adele. Inside. Now.'

The fairy obeyed and wisped into the bottle. Elle fastened the cork, sealing the fairy inside with a tad more force than needed.

She took a long, deep, steadying breath. 'Hugh. Go upstairs and ask Neville to go to town to see if he can get us an extra ticket for my father for this evening. I'm sure Lady Mandeville would love to meet the professor.'

She turned to the housekeeper. 'Mrs Hinges, take my father to the drawing room. Prepare the blue guest room for him and ask Neville to see that the professor's tails are pressed. He is going to the opera.'

'Yes, my lady,' Mrs Hinges said, for once without comment.

Elle turned to Neville who had appeared in the doorway, but, on seeing the commotion, had tried to be as inconspicuous as possible by hiding behind one of the ferns which stood in copper pots on stands by the doors. This was proving to be an impossible task, given that Neville was almost as tall as Marsh, with a shock of dark-blond hair that stood up no matter how much he combed it.

'Neville, there you are,' she said. 'Please go and find Caruthers. Ask him to assemble the staff. Volunteers for this clean-up get an extra half-day wages as compensation.'

'Yes, my lady.' Neville nodded and disappeared from the room as quickly as he could.

'And Mrs Hinges, I was going to wait to discuss this with you, but I think it would be better for everyone if you went home with my father when he returns. He needs you more than we do at the moment.' She gestured at her father who appeared to be dressed in an unstarched collar and shirt that, despite his best efforts to hide it behind his waistcoat, had clearly not been pressed. Judging by the angle of the collar, it looked like he had done his buttons up wrong.

Mrs Hinges put her hand to her throat in shock. 'I do say,' she started mumbling, 'I've never been spoken to like this in all my life. If there is anything wrong with my work, I would that you say so, but to be dismissed like that—'

Elle turned on her, eyes blazing. 'Oh no you don't. You know very well that this has nothing to do with the quality of your work.'

Mrs Hinges closed her mouth, sealing off whatever she was about to say.

'And you two!' Elle turned and pointed at Marsh and the professor. 'No more spark experiments in the house.'

Neither of them answered and Marsh guiltily kicked a stray ball of paper under the table.

'And now I am going upstairs. When I come down

again, I don't want to see a single thing out of place. Do I make myself clear?'

Everyone mumbled various forms of the affirmative.

And with that, Elle set the absinthe bottle down on the top of the cabinet, turned upon her heel and marched upstairs.

Chapter Five

Later that evening Marsh came to her as she was putting the finishing touches to her hair and face. She was, at this stage, still in the process of looking for a proper lady's maid as befitted her new rank and station. But Elle had always prided herself on her self-sufficiency, and with the exception of enlisting Edie to help her with her laces, she managed quite well on her own. She had been so busy that hiring a maid to dress her had been fairly low on her list of things to accomplish.

'You look lovely,' Marsh said. He rested against the doorframe of Elle's dressing room.

'Thank you.' She smiled at him in the mirror. 'Although I always did think it a little silly to get this dressed up only to sit in the dark for a few hours.'

'You have such a strange way of looking at the world. But I have something for you. To wear in the dark.' He sauntered over to where she was sitting and produced a flat velvet box from behind his back. 'For you, my dear wife.' He opened the box with a flourish.

She gasped. A diamond-and-emerald necklace along with a pair of matching earrings nestled inside its cushioned interior. 'Oh Hugh, they are magnificent. But aren't they a little much for an evening out with the Mandevilles?'

He laughed. 'And don't forget dinner at Simpson's. Everyone is going to be looking at the breathtakingly beautiful Viscountess Greychester this evening. And what kind of a husband would I be if I didn't drape my wife in the most extravagant jewels money could buy?'

She touched one of the earrings and it twinkled back at her.

'I asked the bank to withdraw my mother's jewels from the Greychester family vault when we got back from our trip. I was planning to give these to you for your birthday, but you were so cross this morning that I thought these might cheer you up.'

'I'm sorry about that,' she said. 'I may have overreacted a little.'

He shrugged. 'You were right. Things had become a tad out of hand by the time you arrived. Seeing you so angry this morning made me pause to think. It has been a very long time since there has been a Lady Greychester in this house and even longer since anyone wore these jewels, so I thought it was high time to do something about it.' He set the box down on the little table behind him and lifted up the necklace. 'I asked Edie what you were wearing tonight and when she said that it would be this dress...' He motioned to the ludicrously expensive Worth creation she was wearing. It was layer upon layer of gold and ivory silk and lace with a subtle floral pattern woven into the fabric. '...I thought the emeralds would be perfect.' He draped the necklace around her neck and gently placed a kiss on the back of her neck, just below the clasp.

Elle felt a shiver of pleasure at his touch. 'They're beautiful,' she murmured.

'Better keep away from Adele when you are wearing them, though.'

Elle laughed. The last time Elle had worn diamonds, Adele had used them to escape from the café in Paris where she had been forced to work.

'Shall I help you with your gloves?' He raised an eyebrow at her.

'Hugh, you are so naughty,' she said but handed him the long ivory-coloured gloves with the satin-covered buttons. Who was she to deny a gentleman his pleasure?

'Is my father ready?' Elle asked as she slipped her hand into the first glove.

'Yes, between Neville and Mrs Hinges, they have worked miracles. The professor is a new man,' he said as he slid the fabric up her arm, sending little shivers through her.

'Sometimes it is hard to distinguish who is the parent and who is the child when it comes to my father. It was wonderful fun when I was a child, but as I grow older, I do worry about him,' Elle said, trying to keep her thoughts on mundane matters, but finding it increasingly difficult.

'The professor is quite capable of looking after himself. You worry too much about other people, my darling,' Marsh said as he started doing up the tiny buttons.

Elle sighed with pleasure and she felt herself flush as his fingers caressed the buttons. He closed the last button and placed a kiss on the delicate skin that was left exposed on her upper arm between the sleeve of her dress and the top of the glove.

'And you spend far too little time on yourself,' he said in a low voice that suggested that they were definitely going to be late for the opera.

Elle cleared her throat. 'It takes so much work to run a household. I had no idea. Life was so much simpler when—' She broke off her sentence when she realised what she was about to say.

Marsh frowned.

'It's just that I never considered the possibility of getting married and having my own home, let alone all this.' She gestured at the opulence of the room around her. 'It's so very different from how I had thought I would end up in life.' The words were coming out all wrong and she watched the hurt spread across his face as she said them.

'I'm sorry you feel that way.' He lifted the second glove, his touch suddenly perfunctory and matter-of-fact.

'That's not what I meant,' she said, trying to mend the damage she had done.

He looked away. 'This isn't enough for you, is it?' He finished buttoning the second glove. 'What more do I need to do, Elle? Tell me.'

'Nothing, Hugh. I want to be here and be your wife, but I also want to fly and be my own woman. Is it so hard to understand that I need both things in life to be happy?'

He ran an exasperated hand over his face.

Elle stood and put her hand on his arm. 'Thank you for the jewels. They are beautiful and I'm sorry if I've upset you. I don't think I am expressing things quite the way I mean. And I certainly don't want to argue with you and spoil our evening, I just want you to understand.'

He pressed his lips together. 'Fair enough. Let's not argue then. Lady Mandeville and her daughters are fine gossips and the last thing we want is for them to start spreading rumours.' He gave her a tight little smile and offered his arm. 'Shall we?'

She picked up her fur-trimmed opera cape and took his arm. 'Monsieur Puccini's *La Bohème* awaits.'

The light from the Royal Opera House spilled out of the brightly lit windows and on to the cobbled street below, illuminating the evening fog and rain until the air looked like a fine sheet of spangle.

The streets around Covent Garden were congested with carriages and steam cars attempting to deposit their occupants as close to the entrance as possible.

Footmen with large umbrellas stepped on to the cobbles to help glittering ladies in evening gowns and furs negotiate the puddles. Their evening dresses stood out in the gloom around them like exotic pastel-shaded flowers. London society had come out in full force to see Nellie Melba, the world's greatest soprano, perform Monsieur Puccini's exquisite work.

'Good heavens, how do you think she manages to breathe between sentences?' Elle whispered to Marsh, below the relentless chatter of Lady Mandeville and her daughters to Professor Chance, as they made their way through the gold trim and red velvet of the grand foyer. Lady Mandeville was a rotund woman in her late forties. Her two daughters, despite valiant corsetry, looked to be heading the same way. And although Elle was about the same age as the Mandeville girls, she found it very difficult to maintain conversation with them. Their minds were filled with the type of feminine frippery and frivolity that Elle hated. They were also quite clearly in complete awe and envious of the fact that she was married to London's former most eligible bachelor. To make matters worse, they swooned and giggled each time Marsh paid them the slightest bit of attention.

Above them, huge crystal chandeliers shimmered brightly. The light caught and intensified the glitter of diamonds and other precious gems on the people below.

'I honestly don't know,' Marsh murmured back. 'I think your father is starting to regret his decision to join us.' They both watched the professor with amusement as he tried to stem the tidal wave of verbosity aimed at him.

'Just look at the diamonds on the duchess,' Miss Mandeville the elder whispered to Elle.

Elle looked over to where she was indicating.

'Paste,' she whispered back. Elle was an expert at spotting costume jewellery.

'Are you sure?' Miss Mandeville looked scandalised.

'Almost as sure as I am that we are both standing here,' Elle said. The big diamond draped round the neck of the lady in question was most definitely polished glass. The real one would be far too valuable to wear out in public like this. But she did not bother explaining that to Miss Mandeville, who was at that moment whispering furiously at her sister.

She smiled up at her husband. Marsh was every bit the handsome viscount in his formal top hat and tails, and Elle had caught more than one lady studying him surreptitiously from behind a strategically placed opera programme or fan.

'Everything all right?' he said.

'Everything is more than all right,' she said with a rush of pride.

'Have I told you how beautiful you look tonight?' he murmured. 'I keep thinking about dragging you into one of these dark little recesses so I can have you all to myself,' he said. 'We have some unfinished business that started with those gloves of yours.'

Elle felt herself blush. 'Behave, or else I might take you up on the offer.'

He made a strange growly noise, which told her she had scored a point.

At that moment, she caught her father's eye. He stared at her with all hope of rescue.

'We had better save my father,' she said.

'The performance will force them into silence for a little while. Until intermission that is.' Marsh placed his hand on the small of her back. 'Let's escape while we can. I believe our seats are this way.'

And so it was, with no small measure of relief, that Elle sat back in her seat as the lights dimmed to signal the start of the performance.

'Thank goodness for that,' the professor muttered a little too loudly in the moment of silence before the orchestra started up.

Elle heard Marsh snort and shudder with laughter, which he did his best to disguise as a cough.

Then the music filled the theatre. Elle pulled her new

brass opera glasses from her reticule and slowly adjusted the gears in order to bring into focus the famous tenor who had just stepped on to the stage for the first act. She became so enraptured by the sad story of Mimi and Rudolpho that she barely noticed when Marsh took her hand in his as they sat together in the dark.

Suddenly, the world shifted. Elle gasped as she felt the barrier between Shadow and Light lurch violently.

'What is it?' Marsh asked, suddenly concerned.

'It's nothing,' Elle whispered back to reassure him.

She sat forward in her seat and adjusted her glasses again. They were the latest in spectral optics, guaranteed to allow the viewer to see in extremely fine detail. She felt the shift again. This time, the lurch of energy was so strong it had made her feel quite out of breath. It was almost as if someone was manipulating the divide between Shadow and Light right here, in the concert hall. And they were not being particularly careful or discreet about it either. She scanned the rows of seats below them. She could see nothing out of the ordinary. The audience sat, entranced by the beautiful music that filled the air and quite oblivious to the workings of the Shadow Realm.

She felt the movement again and this time she followed it, as one would do with sound. Her gaze fell on a woman who sat in one of the side seats. She was wrapped in a dark cloak. All Elle could see was the side of her fine white cheek. But the woman must have sensed her presence, because she suddenly turned and looked straight at Elle.

In that moment, Elle felt a gush of energy surge through her. She gasped with shock and almost dropped her glasses. The woman was definitely channelling power, in a public place, without even trying to hide it.

The thought filled Elle with such outrage that she half rose from her seat.

An expression of surprise briefly crossed the woman's face and, in that instant, Elle felt the flow of power cease. Then the woman rose and slipped out of her seat. She moved silently down the aisle and melted into the shadows cast by the velvet drapery.

'What is it?' Marsh said again.

'I told you, it's nothing,' she whispered. 'I need a bit of air, it's very close in here. I won't be a moment. Stay and make sure the Mandevilles don't follow.' She was out of the stalls before Marsh had an opportunity to stop her.

As quickly as she could, Elle ran up the stairs. She wanted to catch up with the woman before she got away but was hampered by her skirts.

Watch out, dear heart. Beware! the voices of the Oracle urged.

'You are not helping,' she said to them. 'I only want to know who or what the woman is. And if you were better teachers, then I wouldn't need to be running after her like this.'

The voices did not reply. Elle was not sorry, for she needed all of her concentration to run up the red-carpeted stairs in her evening gown and fine-heeled slippers. Behind her the aria rose to a dramatic crescendo.

She reached the side entrance staircase and paused for breath. Running in a tightly laced corset really was most unpleasant, but before she could catch her breath properly, a soft flutter of fabric caught her attention as the hem of the woman's dark cloak disappeared around the corner.

'Wait! Stop! I only want to talk to you!' Elle called after the woman, but she did not stop.

The woman's escape was conveniently halted by one of the door ushers. Elle caught up with her as she struggled to push past.

Elle put her hand on to the woman's sleeve. 'Wait! Who are you?'

The woman swung round and glared at her.

Elle took a step backwards as she took in the sight of her white hair and stark sea-green eyes.

'Leave me be!' the woman hissed in what sounded like a heavy French accent. She turned and smiled at the usher. The man went all cross-eyed and swept the door open for her.

'Wait! Stop!' Elle said, but the woman slipped out from under her grasp and disappeared into the dark night and the rain.

'Did you see that?' Elle stood at the door next to the speechless usher.

The usher slowly shook his head and blinked at her. 'May I help you, madam?' he said.

'Um, no. Thank you. Sorry for the trouble,' she murmured. 'I just needed a breath of fresh air.'

'Would you like me to escort you back to your seat?'

'Thank you, that's very kind, but I can manage on my own. Good evening,' she said politely.

Back in the stalls, Elle did her best to slip into her seat as quietly as possible.

'What was that all about?' Marsh whispered.

'It was nothing. I thought I recognised someone, but I was mistaken,' she said.

'Don't go running off like that. You had me worried,' he whispered. 'I know I no longer have my powers, but even *I* could sense the Shadow back there, Elle. I was about to raise the alarm.'

'I told you, it was nothing. She ran off before I could speak to her, so no harm done.' Elle closed her eyes in exasperation. His overprotectiveness was smothering her, but here was not the place to raise the issue.

'Let's enjoy the rest of the performance, shall we?' she said to him.

He gave her a long look, but said nothing. Instead they turned their attention to the remainder of the opera.

Chapter Six

The Black Stag was not very big or impressive as far as public houses went. It was a squat wood-framed building that had been clinging to the bank of the Thames since Tudor times, much in the same way a tick clings to the side of a beast. The place was mostly frequented by dockworkers. They were hard men with big hands and unwashed bodies who poured mother's ruin into their pints and drank to forget the bleakness of their existence.

Only the toughest bangtails and gin fairies survived here and they clung to the crooked beams and low-slung doorframes, where nothing escaped their gaze.

'Did you bring the money, sir?' Art said.

Henry gave a small nod. 'Under the table.'

Art leaned over and eyed the portmanteau at their feet. 'Very good, sir.'

Henry lifted his hat as if to put it on his head but changed his mind. He placed it back on the ring-stained table in front of him. The fine beaver felt appeared very much out of place against the cheap sticky wood.

'There is no need to rush now, my lord. We've got the

whole evening yet. They'll be along any time now.' Art took a sip from his glass.

'Are you sure we have the right place?' Henry said.

'I am sir. The Black Stag. Two hours after sunset. I'm sure they'll be along soon.' Art sounded slightly annoyed. He spoke as if he were placating a petulant child.

'Sorry,' Henry said. He took a deep gulp from his own glass. The ale was thin and tepid and he was sure he could see a fine greasy film over the top. He shuddered quietly and looked around him. What a squalid place. And was that a real Nightwalker brooding in the corner? This certainly was not the type of establishment he would normally frequent, but desperate times called for desperate measures. And he was a very desperate man indeed.

Art sat with his hand round his glass, his eyes trained on the door.

Henry noticed for the first time that the stubble on his companion's chin was tinged with grey. How old was he? Did he have family? Henry realised that in spite of the fact that Art had been in service with them for most of his life, he knew almost nothing about the man before him. Thinking back, he couldn't recall a single incident where the two of them had been alone together for more than a few moments. He wondered if he should make small talk to pass the time, but somehow it seemed inappropriate.

Just then, a man walked in and went up to the counter. The peacock feather in the band of his hat drew a few hostile looks.

'Bloody travelling folk. Bringing the Evil Eye in 'ere. Take that thing out of here!' the landlord growled. He gave the counter an extra wipe in the direction of the man with the feather almost as if to wipe the bad luck away.

Someone near the counter cursed and spat on the floor.

The man with the peacock feather in his hat ignored them. Instead, he scanned the room until he spotted Art. His dark eyes rested on them for a moment. Then he nodded and walked out.

Art let go of his glass. 'Come along then, sir,' he said to Henry as he stood up from his chair.

Henry took a deep breath and smoothed his hands down his waistcoat. 'Right then,' he said. He gathered up the bag from under the table and stumbled after Art, tripping over the loose floorboards as he went.

Outside, it was really dark. Henry paused under a spark light for a moment to find his bearing. In this part of the East End streetlights were few and far between, but this one flickered bravely against the inky fog.

'Art,' he said looking about in a moment of panic, not sure why he was whispering.

A hand gripped his upper arm. 'It might be best to get out of the light, sir. We don't want to attract too much attention to ourselves, do we? The fellow went that way.' Art's breath was sticky and strangely intimate against his neck.

'Right then,' Henry said again, gathering himself.

They walked along the alley that led off from the pub. A miasmic stench rose up from the river tainting everything within a half a mile from the water. It was so thick and potent that not even the relentless drizzle seemed to be able to quench it. The streets were clogged with mud and dirt, and the patina of squalor stuck to everything.

Someone moved up ahead and Henry caught the slight movement of a peacock feather bobbing up and down as the man they followed passed through a patch of grimy light that spilled out from between a set of ill-fitting shutters. His footfall sounded on damp wooden planks that had been thrown on to the squelchy street to serve as walkways.

'Hurry. Don't lose him,' Art whispered. They walked on in single file for a while. The buildings turned to dockyards and the fog grew thicker. Henry shivered inside his good wool coat.

Art stopped and gripped his arm again. 'Wait a moment, sir,' he whispered. Henry felt his heart thump against his chest as he strained to see, but his efforts were in vain. The fog had him almost completely blinded.

Near them, someone struck a match and a lantern flared into life. The form of the man with the peacock feather took shape in the flickering light.

'Come,' was all the man said. He pointed at Henry and the illuminated side of his face curled into a smile. 'This way.'

Henry took a step back and bumped into Art, who gripped his shoulders with his large hands. 'Steady on, sir. I think they want you to go in alone. I'll be waiting right here if you need me.'

'Don't leave me here on my own,' Henry said to Art with an imploring look before he followed the man with the peacock feather round the corner.

A horse snorted and suddenly the lantern revealed the

shape of a covered wagon. The only sign of life that could be discerned was a thin strip of orange light that leaked out from underneath a crack in the door.

Henry stumbled again, this time over uneven cobbles under his feet. 'Sorry. I'm sorry,' he mumbled under his breath.

'No need for sorry,' the man with the peacock feather said smoothly. 'This way, please.' They climbed the steps and entered through the little door of the caravan.

Inside it was very warm. Glass-covered candles whispered a gentle welcome to those who came in from the cold, and strange flickering shadows around the inside of the wagon spoke of the magic that went on in there.

'This is Florica,' the man with the peacock feather said.

Florica looked up and smiled at the man. They had the same eyes, Henry noted, the colour of ripe juniper berries. She said something in a language he did not understand. The man with the peacock feather smiled and rested his hand on her shoulder for a moment before he sat himself down in the corner.

He took a hunk of half-dry meat that sat wrapped in a piece of cheesecloth from the shelf next to the stove, pulled out a long knife and started carving small slivers from it. The man offered him a piece of meat, which he held out to him between thumb and blade.

Henry did his best not to shudder. 'N–no, thank you. I've already eaten,' he said as politely as he could. The ruby-dark meat looked dubious and he was not about to take any chances.

'Please, make yourself comfortable. My brother

Emilian watches over me while I work.' Florica gestured for him to sit.

So Mr Peacock-Feather has a name, Henry thought as he sat down on a wooden bench. He clutched the portmanteau on his lap.

The inside of the wagon was lined with floral-print curtains which seemed inappropriately cheerful in the circumstances.

Florica's heavy brass earrings rattled as she lifted her shawl from her hair. Henry stared in fascination as some of the fronds of the shawl caught on one. She shook her head to free the shawl and met his gaze. 'So you seek my help.'

'I–I brought the money,' Henry nodded and held up the bag.

Emilian leaned over and took the bag from him with surprising speed. He unclipped the latch, peered inside, and smiled.

'Good,' Florica said. 'Now. I can tell that you have come about a woman, no?'

'Yes. They say you are able to heal people,' Henry said.

'You have something that belongs to the woman?' Florica said.

Henry reached into his pocket and pulled out a silver locket. 'My fiancée. Emily. Her portrait and a lock of hair.'

Florica ran the silver locket through her fingers. 'And she has been ill for how long?'

'Six months. We became engaged just before she became ill. Now, we don't know … we don't know if we'll ever…' Henry's voice trailed off.

'Ah. Yes. Love. It is a powerful thing. A lot of things come from the heart,' Florica said.

She opened the locket and tipped the curl of blond hair into her palm. She held her hand to her face and sniffed.

'Yes. I can feel it. Your love for this woman is strong.'

'Yes,' Henry said. His breath caught in his throat. 'Please say that you will be able to help her.' Sweat beaded on his forehead as he spoke. 'The doctors say that there is nothing that can be done. Her heart is dying. I'll do anything, give anything, to have her whole and well again.'

A slow smile spread over Florica's face. 'Anything is a very heavy price to pay,' she said. 'Are you sure you can afford it?'

Henry leaned forward, his eyes bright. 'I love her. Please do something. Anything.'

Emilian grinned from the corner and sliced off another sliver of meat.

'So it shall be done,' Florica said.

'You mean you will be able to help her?' Henry said.

Florica nodded slowly. 'That I will do. But the price is steep. Are you sure?'

Henry nodded. 'I'm sure. Just do it, for heaven's sake.'

She leaned forward. 'Swear it,' she hissed.

'I swear,' Henry said.

Florica reached behind her and picked up a battered tobacco tin. Carefully she measured out a fine powder, weighing it into her hand, before tipping some of the contents into the candle before her. The caravan filled with a fine fragrant haze. It made Henry's eyes water and his head swim.

'First you need to relax. Close your eyes,' she whispered.

'Very well, then. I am relaxed.' Henry straightened his spine and slouched again in an attempt to convince her.

She laughed softly. 'No. Not like that.' She looked at her brother. 'Lie him down on the bench.'

Emilian gripped Henry's arm and pulled him round so he was lying on his back on the bench. The wood was hard and the edges dug into Henry's shoulders. Before he could protest, he felt cold manacles click around his wrists. Emilian pulled them tight and suddenly Henry found himself trussed up like a Christmas goose.

'Wait. Hang on. This can't be right ... stop!'

'Hold still,' Florica said.

'What do you mean "hold still"?' Henry said. 'I demand that you explain the meaning of these shackles right now.' Henry struggled against his bonds.

Emilian laughed. It was only a little chuckle, but it sent cold shivers down Henry's spine.

Florica rested her head on Henry's chest. 'You have a good one. Not very brave, but loyal. It beats strong. I will do this thing for you because I pity you, poor man. You give your heart to your lady and *our* Lady will give you one of hers.'

'What on earth are you talking about? Stop this right now or I shall call for help!' Henry said.

'Silence!' Florica hissed. 'The bargain has been struck and there is no going back now. You are one of the lucky ones. One of the special ones. The Lady's army needs leaders and you shall be one.'

She looked up at Emilian. 'The box,' she said.

Emilian handed her a polished wooden case.

Henry watched with growing horror as she lifted a metal contraption out of it. It had gears and a handle that made the mechanical bits whirr. The front bit clawed and rattled as she turned the handle.

'N–no, please,' Henry tried to say, but Florica placed her hand over his mouth with surprising force. Large tears started running out of the corners of Henry's eyes.

'Better round the servant up from outside. We can add him to this evening's catch. They can deal with him along with the others at the factory. The Lady will like it if we bring her more than she asks for, I'm sure,' Florica said.

Emilian nodded and disappeared out the door.

Florica turned and looked down at Henry. 'Now, hold nice and still and this will only hurt a little,' she said.

'Promise me she'll be better,' Henry wheezed from under her fingers.

'I promise by the Shadow that the strength that lies in your heart will go to hers this very night, and she shall be healed,' Florica said. In that moment her eyes filled with compassion for him. 'I am very sorry,' she murmured.

Henry closed his eyes and gritted his teeth. 'Anything to save her – just be quick about it.'

The last thing he remembered was the sensation of someone unbuttoning his waistcoat, which was also the last thing he felt, before he screamed.

❦

The Clockmaker sits hunched over, eyes trained on the tiny cogs and gears before him. Around him the walls are alive with faces and pendulums that tick and click and whirr. Carefully, with the measured precision that comes only from years of experience, he lowers a small brass part into the heart of the casing. He raises up the tweezers he holds and caresses the spring as the little piece falls into place. The tiny counterweight pauses, fighting momentum as it strains to slip into motion. And then, soft as a breath, the device clicks and comes alive.

Gently the Clockmaker eases the casing over the finely machined innards and with a deft twist of his screwdriver he tightens the little screws.

The clockwork heart whirrs and shivers as it lies in his palm. At the centre of his little miracle lies a tiny crumb of carmot, no bigger than a grain of sand. No more is needed to give the heart life.

The Clockmaker smiles. 'You will be special,' he murmurs. He lifts a key that hangs from a string around his neck and eases it into the heart. The clockwork heart jolts and starts ticking.

The Clockmaker smiles again. 'Yes, you will be special.'

Then he lowers the heart into a wooden case that lies before him. The box is already half full with ticking hearts, each one nestled inside a little hollow lined with purple velvet.

Satisfied, the Clockmaker turns back to his workbench. With infinite patience, he selects a new casing and one by one he selects cogs and springs and eases them into place.

'Special,' he murmurs. And the clocks on the wall tick along in applause.

ॐ

Chapter Seven

Elle sat up in bed with a gasp. The sight of the strange woman and the roar of power that flooded through her had upset her more than she cared to admit. She had spent the night wrapped in Shadow nightmares, running through a labyrinth of dark passageways, with the terrible sound of clocks ticking surrounding her.

It was still dark outside and she could just make out the soft clinking of people at work in the kitchen as the staff readied the house for the day.

'What is it?' Marsh mumbled beside her.

'Nothing. I think I just felt something shift. It's probably nothing, but I had better make sure.'

She slipped out of bed and walked over to a slim brass lever, which was set in the wall next to the mantelpiece. She pulled it and, with the sound of carefully greased cogs and gears, a panel slid open to reveal a hidden chamber behind the fireplace.

She lit one of the thick candles that were held in a series of sconces in the wall. The flickering light revealed the most eye-catching thing about the little room: the circular mosaic floor, set with lapis lazuli, jade, red jasper and onyx.

Elle looked at the finely inlaid pattern of maidens and ancient symbols with mixed feelings. This was a Delphic circle, the type used by the Oracles to divine and speak. Marsh had built it for her as a gift, so she could attend to her duties as the Oracle within the comfort of their home. But, despite her efforts to make the best of things, these duties were something she was still not entirely happy about.

'Anything?' he said from the other room.

'Not yet. But I won't be a minute,' she said with a little smile as the panel slid shut.

There was no fireplace in this room and the floor beneath her bare feet felt cold.

She took a deep breath to ready herself before stepping on to the mosaic. This circle was sacred; it was a portal – a place where one could access the barrier that held the two realms of Shadow and Light apart. The multitude of layers that made up the universe lay before her.

She closed her eyes and focused, reaching into the metaphysical space that opened up before her to reveal the great divide. It unfurled in sheets of golden, gossamer light. The realms of Light and Shadow lay like mirror images of one another: Light and Dark; Yin and Yang; Alpha and Omega. The divide had been placed there by the Council of Warlocks in an attempt to restore harmony to the worlds after the terrible wars that became known as the Dark Ages had ended. On the Light side lay the world of man. It was a place of progress, enlightenment and science: the modern world. The Shadow side was of ancient magic, where creatures spoken of in myth and folklore dwelled for evermore.

And, like the spine that holds the many pages of a book together, she – Eleanor Marsh, née Chance – was the binding force that held everything together.

Gently she reached out to touch the sheets of energy on either side of her. Right for Light, left for Shadow.

Allowing her mind to run along the divide was not unlike running one's hands along sheets of finely woven silk. It had been only half a year since she had ascended to this strange place of power, and now she did it with practised ease, all the while keeping an eye out for any knots or snags that might cause trouble for those who dwelled on either side of the barrier. All seemed smooth and peaceful. There certainly was no sign of any clocks or clockmakers.

Elle considered stepping across into the Shadow, to make sure that nothing bad was lurking close, but decided against it. She always seemed to run into inconvenient things when she did that. Her knowledge of creatures of the Shadow was less than perfect, so it was always a bit of a risk. And she did not have time for taking risks this morning. She had work to do.

Carefully, she shifted out from between the worlds and opened her eyes. All was well with the barrier, and the Shadow would have to wait until later.

'Everything all right?' Marsh asked as she stepped out of the secret chamber and bundled herself back into the warmth of the bed.

'All is well,' she said, snuggling up against him.

'Good grief, your feet are like icicles.' He flinched, but kissed her again, running his hands over her shoulders, willing her to sink into the covers for a little while longer.

'I had such a strange dream this morning that I actually thought something was amiss in the Shadow, but it's nothing.'

'Then stay,' he said.

Elle moved out of his embrace and sat up. 'There will be plenty of time for that later, oh amorous husband of mine. I have to get to the airfield before they ship the *Phoenix* out.'

He sighed. 'Yes, I know. Flying always first.'

She slipped out of bed and walked across to the darkened doorframe that led to Elle's pride and joy: their newly installed, state-of-the-art, spark-powered en-suite bathroom. It was a miracle of copper pipes and brass taps over inlaid marble designed to create maximum comfort and pleasure. The bathroom even had a built-in lavatory installed beside an imported Huber's Gegenstrom rain bath unit that blasted out a cascade of heated water to bathe under.

Much to their amusement, Mrs Hinges called the shower apparatus the work of Beelzebub. She also believed that dousing oneself with hot and cold water was a practice that was extremely Continental.

'Stay with me,' Marsh said, leaning against the doorframe. 'Forget about the new ship. We can take the day and do something fun.'

'I can't. I promised Ducky I would oversee the estimates for the repairs. The engineers are coming out specially to see the *Phoenix*. You know I need to be there.' She turned on the taps of the Huber.

He looked disappointed and Elle felt her resolve falter. Marsh had sacrificed so much to marry her and suddenly the thought of abandoning him made her feel churlish.

She steeled herself and shrugged off the thought. Marsh could be very persuasive when he put his mind to it and if she gave in now, today would become tomorrow and the next and, before she knew it, flying would be something of the past. And as much as she adored her husband, Elle needed to fly more than anything in the world. Her passion for taking to the air was so intrinsically part of her that to prevent her from flying would be like preventing her from breathing.

Besides, she thought with just that tiny bit of resentment that never quite seemed to go away, she had to make sacrifices too. She certainly did not volunteer for the cursed position of Oracle.

Marsh ran his fingers through his hair. 'Very well then, you win. But get Neville to collect you from the airfield in the motor. I don't want you out in the dark hours of the morning all by yourself. It's not safe.'

Elle sighed from behind the lacquered screen where she was busy slipping out of her nightdress. 'Oh, for goodness' sake, Hugh. When are you going to stop acting like I'm some delicate flower? I am perfectly capable of looking after myself.'

His gaze darkened. 'You are my wife. And you are the Oracle. And that makes you vulnerable to all manner of threats. I will never stop worrying about you, as long as I live.'

'But don't you see? Those are exactly the reasons why I must carry on as before. If I allow myself to become a shrinking violet, then they will have won. And I absolutely refuse to do that. Ever,' she said as she secured the belt of her silk bathing kimono and tied her hair up.

The room was filling with delicious billows of steam from the shower water. She stepped out from behind the screen and closed the tap. Her ablutions would have to wait until after this discussion. She did not like to think about the Alchemists and their vortex of evil or the fact that she had been chained to a wall in that dark dungeon in Constantinople just months before. She still woke up in a cold sweat some nights, dreaming about it.

Marsh pressed his lips together and she could see the little muscles in his cheek flicker as he clenched his teeth. This was an argument that neither of them ever seemed to win, because neither of them was entirely wrong about the matter.

And she hated to admit it, but had Hugh and her father not arrived in that underground amphitheatre when they did she probably would have died there.

She turned away from the shower and put her arms around her husband. 'I will be careful. I promise.'

'You know as well as I do that they are still out there, Elle,' he said in a low voice.

Elle sighed again. Her husband had the most annoying habit of being completely and utterly right at the most inconvenient points in her argument. 'We haven't heard a word from the Council since you saw them in Venice. And that was months ago. They have no reason to come after us as long as we keep our side of the bargain.'

He put his arms around her and kissed her hair, but she could feel the tension in his body. 'I do not like it.

And I definitely do not trust the silence. We cannot let our guard down, Elle, not for a single moment.'

'Good morning, Adele,' Elle said as she sat down opposite Marsh at the table in the morning room.

At the sight of Elle, Adele shucked up her shoulders and turned away in displeasure.

Elle grimaced. It was going to take a lot of apologising before she was restored to the good graces of the fairy, it seemed.

Edie appeared, carrying a small tray with a telegram, which she set down on the table.

'Thank you, Edie,' Elle said.

The maid gave Adele a wary look and the fairy hissed at her.

Edie retreated as fast as decorum allowed.

'I see it's war on all fronts then,' Elle said to the fairy as she opened the telegram. Her eyes flickered over the message and, in an instant, her face opened up with excitement. 'I have a telegram from Mr De Beer. I have a new charter. To Singapore!'

Marsh folded the paper up carefully and put it on the table.

The headline read BATTERSEA ELECTROMANCERS HALT SPARK PRODUCTION. SHORTAGES FEARED.

'I think I shall take the *Iron Phoenix*,' she said.

'Are you sure that's wise? What about the urgent repairs that could not wait this morning?' There was a dangerous edge to his voice.

'Oh, I'm sure we can make do. Would you like to come along? I'm sure we could do with an extra crew member.'

'I thought this was something you had to do on your own,' he said stiffly.

'And I thought you were bored and worried waiting for me while I am away.'

His face tightened. 'I wouldn't want to smother you or anything.'

'Oh, Marsh. When did you turn into such a boring old fopdoodle?' she said.

'How dare you call me that!'

Adele fluttered off the table and settled herself on the mantelpiece. She crossed her arms, waiting for the spectacle that was sure to come.

'Fopdoodle,' Elle said, and this time her voice held its own dangerous edge. 'You promised that you and I were going to have a life that soared high up in the sky. Instead, you lurk in your study by day and when you emerge, it's only to wreck the house with one of your insane inventions.'

Marsh grew very still.

'Is that what you really think?' he said in measured tones.

'Yes, it is. You have changed, Hugh. You are not the man I married.'

'I have only changed into the man you wanted me to be, my dear,' he said bitterly.

'Have you now? Perhaps the man I thought you were was nothing but a lie. Shall we look at all the lies you've told me in the time we've known one another?' She laid down the challenge between them. This was dangerous ground, for he had indeed been somewhat economical with the truth about her status as the Oracle and all it entailed when they had met.

'I am sorry you are so disillusioned and that life with me is such a disappointment for you,' he said.

'And I am sorry you did not keep your end of the bargain. You said that we would be able to go on as before. You promised, Hugh.'

His face went very still. 'Well, forgive me for being the only one to take this marriage seriously,' he said smoothly. 'You really don't see it, but everything is always about you, my dear. One moment, it's "Oh Hugh, I have to do this by myself". The next I am invited to come along as if I am a lapdog. I am expected to come running when you whistle.'

'That's not true,' she shot back.

'You forget, my dear, that I am the one who has made the sacrifice here. Hundreds of years of my life, gone. All so I can be with you and then you are never here.'

'And I haven't made sacrifices? This, my duties as the Oracle; it's everything I chose not to become in life, yet here I am.' She waved her arm in a gesture that encompassed the room, her life. 'You lied to me in Venice to get what you wanted. And now you have broken your promises to me again.'

'Stop it!' He held up his hand. 'Just stop it. I cannot bear any more of this fighting, Elle.'

Elle bit her lip, her retort unsaid.

'Do I really make you that unhappy?' he said. 'Are you so smothered that you feel the need to run away at every opportunity that presents itself? Is this what marriage has done to you? Tell me, Eleanor, I need to know.'

She shook her head. 'Please understand,' she whispered.

'No, my dear, I think you are the one who needs to

understand. There is a vast difference in our ages. I have lived more than one lifetime. Time for me moves at a pace most people cannot comprehend. I accept that. I have made allowances for that. But you need to meet me halfway. I cannot maintain this marriage on my own, while you run around hell-bent on proving to the world that you can do anything.' He ran his hand through his hair in exasperation. 'I wish you would realise that you don't have to do all that. You can just be yourself and happy, here. With me.'

She looked away, hands folded in her lap.

'You need to decide where your priorities lie, Elle. Are you with me, or are we to be like all those other couples who live in separate worlds?' Marsh stood up from the table and walked over to the door of the conservatory.

She did not answer him.

He stared at the plants, as if to draw strength from them before he spoke. 'I must be clear on this. I am not happy about the way you acquired your new ship and I will not have my family's name associated with gamblers and cheats. A woman's place is beside her husband, wherever that may be. It is her duty and she must comply with that duty over and above all the passions that may drive her.'

'But, Hugh, it doesn't have to be that way. Why must I stop being my own person before I can be your wife?' she said.

He stared at her for a long time before speaking. 'I cannot make that decision for you, Elle. And if you cannot find it within yourself to accept things as they are, then you and I are heading for some serious difficulties in the years that are to come.'

She swallowed. 'Are you asking me to give up flying?'

'Don't oversimplify this. You know perfectly well that I am not asking you to do that,' he said.

'What will you have me do then?' she said.

He did not answer her, and the silence ticked along between them as they stared at one another from opposite sides of the breakfast room.

'I–I think I need some time to think,' she said.

'I agree. So do I.'

Elle felt her throat constrict. So it would boil down to a choice between being happy or dutiful. Suddenly she felt overwhelmingly sad.

'Then I shall go to Singapore and fulfil the charter,' she said slowly.

She saw him stiffen slightly, but he stood very still, eyes trained on the lace-fine heads of angelica plants before him.

'You are welcome to join me,' she said again.

'No.' His answer was so final that it left no room for compromise. 'Now if you'll excuse me, I have some correspondence to attend to,' he said.

She swallowed down the lump in her throat that was about to cut off her air.

'Will you be here when I get back?' she said.

He frowned. 'Of course I will. I am your husband. I will always be here for you.' Then he picked up his newspaper and walked from the room.

※

Fairies have long memories. We are a people slow to forget when we are wronged, but we are not without compassion.

The girl sat down at the table and covered her face with her hands. She sat like that for a very long time, not moving.

I fluttered down from my hiding place to sit next to her. I could not help her with this problem, but I could show solidarity. And so I did.

'I'm sorry I yelled at you for making a mess,' she said to me. I nodded.

'I'm making a right mess of things myself, aren't I?' she said.

I nodded again. There was little I could say to deny it.

'Will you stay here and look after him while I'm gone?'

Then, in a gesture that surprised even me, I rose and embraced her.

When we embraced, the fizz of my small absinthe magic met with the roar of the force that was the Oracle. She did not realise this, but I was only a mere trifle compared to her shining light. But in a tiny way, as we touched, I hoped that she was comforted.

※

Chapter Eight

Clothilde shrugged her shoulders to loosen the stiffness that was building between them. She had been meditating on the roof of the monastery in the soft drizzle for most of the night. She spent the time in a deep trance, absorbing tiny fragments of energy off everything around her. She dared not seek to reach into the void for nourishment now. The encounter at the opera house had been too close for comfort. It had all started so innocently. She was an elemental born of air and water – always drawn to music – much like the sirens and kelpies of the sea – and so she had decided to treat herself to a performance. While she was listening, the urge to feed from the barrier had come upon her. She had started feeding in public when she realised that Light dwellers were completely oblivious to her appetites. The fact that there was someone present who could tell what she was doing was utterly frightening. She knew nothing of the young woman who followed her, except that she was extremely powerful. Revealing herself had been a silly mistake to make, one that the Consortium would be deeply displeased to hear about. She would have to be careful from now on.

But dawn was breaking and there was so much work to do. She sighed and stood to climb the narrow stairs off the roof.

The Battersea Spark Monastery now lay within her power. This was the place where the electromancers practised their craft. Here, much in the same way that bees worked in a hive, they harvested lightning and other forms of static electricity which they combined with their shadow magic to turn into spark: the blue liquid that powered the steam engines, which in turn ran the world.

She let out a cynical laugh. When she had arrived at the monastery she had expected discipline and devotion as she had seen in the monks of her childhood. A time when spark had been used for healing and light. That had been a time before the brothers had sold themselves into servitude to the Light. A time before the steam of huge engines covered the earth. But the industrial revolution had come, and now she found nothing but laziness and repose while machines did all the work. These little men had become complacent. They were so shut up in their own little world that they were utterly oblivious to their importance. But that was all changing, thanks to her.

Emilian was waiting for her downstairs with a dry set of robes. The peacock feather in his hat bobbed as he inclined his head when she stepped out of the shadows.

'Everything all right, *madame*?' Emilian was not one for airs and graces and his 'madame' had a touch of impertinence about it.

'Why wouldn't it be?' Her voice held a deep throaty resonance that men found irresistible. All men except Emilian.

'How was last night's catch?'

'I think your ladyship will like what we brought you.' Emilian flashed her a satisfied smile as if he was harbouring a special surprise for her.

'And why would that be, pray tell?'

'Big fish. I think you will be pleased.'

'Is that so?'

Emilian nodded. 'We prepared him, like you said we should if we found a special one.'

Clothilde was immediately intrigued. She smiled at Emilian. 'Well, then we had better go see this fish of yours.'

The monastery lay quiet in the early morning cold as she strode across the courtyard. The monks had been highly affronted by the Consortium's directive. Even though the Consortium owned and financed the running of the monastery, the monks had protested at her taking command.

There was so much muttering and disquiet that she had had to step in and take action. The abbot had been dispensed with quickly. She did not like the idea of mutilating a monk, but sometimes an example can be most persuasive. He had made an excellent test subject – the first of her special ones. Since then, the monks had obeyed her, but she could tell that they did not approve of her work. Some things never changed, she thought bitterly. Even as a child they had showered her with disapproval. Now they just stared at her in cold condemnation, which made her hate them even more. She wished she could feed them all into the machine, but the pleasure of seeing them transformed was forbidden, along with the other pleasures she craved each day. It had been so long since she had held a man utterly and completely in her thrall. The need for power and seduction made her ache inside.

She shook her head to clear her thoughts. It was most unfortunate that she needed the electromancers to produce the spark she needed for her work. Life would be so much simpler without them.

A single novice held the door for her as she swept inside. His hands trembled as he took her damp outer wool cloak from her.

'Bring the special one to my laboratory when you have herded the others into their pens,' she said over her shoulder to Emilian.

Clothilde wrinkled her nose as she walked along one of the narrow corridors that led off the main hall. Acrid spark magic seemed to ooze out of the very walls of this building. It made everything smell like the metal and burn of electricity. The pure energy that bonded high up in the clouds and struck the earth as lightning flowed through her. She found the crude thaumaturgic amalgamation of static electricity and the power of the Shadow that the electromancers made these days, and which humans called spark, distasteful.

In the middle of the monastery was a cavernous space the monks called the spark turbine hall. It was in this hall that the Consortium's machinery had been installed. A wide conveyor belt ran along half the length of the hall and into a huge machine. The machine was connected to giant spark tanks that supplied it with energy. The whole system was operated from the console in the mezzanine level that overlooked the hall.

She noticed a few bloodstains on the brass pipes that ran alongside the India rubber of the conveyor belt and she curled her lip in disgust. Those lazy little men were slipping in their cleaning duties, it seemed. She flicked her long hair over her shoulder and walked on, resolving that there would be words about the matter later.

She strode though the hall and up a flight of stairs to the control room from where she could watch the processing.

Behind the machine was an array of blue-black metal and shiny brass pipes that ran from the machine to the lighting collection chimneys. This hall was the place where the electromancers took static electricity and combined it with power from the Shadow Realm to make the spark that fuelled the steam engines of the world.

Whoever held control of one of these machines, held control over the world – the world she would command someday. But right now, it was wise to keep her plans to herself. Access to privately financed and unlimited reserves of spark and steam was most convenient. And she was going to need vast amounts of energy to complete the task she had in mind. But she was not worried, for this was the first step in her plans. She would not need to bend her head to the Consortium for too much longer, for soon she would have an army all of her own.

Clothilde revelled in the frisson of power that surged through her at the thought. She flicked on the switches and the machine hummed to life, emitting a crackle of blue sparks that ran from the metal pipes and into the machine in the middle of the floor.

The dials on the machine started dancing and great

puffs of steam rose up from its diabolical pistons. Clothilde waited a few moments until all the dials on the console were at the right level before she gave the sign. It was time to begin.

The double doors at the end of the hall opened and a group of people were ushered inside by her strongmen, each armed with a spark prod.

These were the dregs of humanity – drifters, prostitutes and vagrants. People taken off the streets after dark or harvested from prisons and workhouses. For a small fee their minders were only too happy to be rid of a few more mouths to feed.

These were the members of society that no one cared about. The ones no one would miss once they were gone. They were the people who would change the world forever.

'Ladies and gentlemen!' She spoke into the speaking tube that made her voice boom across the cavernous room. 'You have been selected for a very special task. Today your meaningless lives will be transformed into something useful. You should be grateful for this gift!'

The group of people before her looked around uncertainly, blinking in the bright lights that shone on them. Some of the women were crying and a few of the men who had not quite been subdued by the spark prods were still struggling with the shackles that held them.

Clothilde held out her arms. The resonant notes of her voice filled the room and everyone turned to look up at her. She felt their awe as they took in the sight of her shimmering white resplendence and she smiled as she watched her magic take control of those before her. It did not matter if you were male or female, because very few people were immune to the magnetic power of seduction that her kind could wield.

Electromancers entered from one of the side doors. Their grim faces contorted with anguish when she clenched her fist to tighten the spell that held them to her will. Their resentful acquiescence gave her even more pleasure. There would be no rebellion from these little men today. She would make sure of that.

'Brothers in lightning! We have work to do,' she said.

The electromancers turned to her and bowed. 'We live to serve,' they said.

'As do we all!' she answered. It was the mantra these men had used for centuries, as well as the low humming song they sang while they worked.

She gave the signal and, in unison, the electromancers raised their arms in the air.

'I give you the lightning you need!'

Outside, thunder rumbled and lightning cut through the sky, linking up with the fine metal rods posted across the roof like poisonous spines. The very air around the electromancers started crackling as they commenced with the ritual they called simply, 'The Making'.

Giant bolts of lightning struck the roof of the monastery.

The monks started humming. It was a deep sound emanating from the back of their throats. Energy surged up through the metal pipes in the console. The gargantuan glass receptacles in the hall started filling with blue spark.

'Let the production begin!' Clothilde gave the signal.

The prisoners were now lined up in an orderly row. She pulled a lever and a row of what looked like black metal meat hooks started moving in a circular motion from an overhead trolley that fed into the machine. Her henchmen started attaching the straps and shackles that held the prisoners to the hooks. In some cases, where the prisoners were unshackled, they simply allowed the hook to catch on the flesh of shoulders and necks.

Clothilde braced herself for the sheer panic that invariably rose up from the floor at this point in the proceedings.

In a swift move, each startled individual was hoisted in the air. A woman started screaming as the hook slipped into her shoulder before the hot iron that branded each arm with a number sank into her flesh. One by one each person was laid flat on to the conveyor belt, ready to be fed into the machine. The air filled with abruptly silenced screams and the smell of blood and burning skin.

She was the Lady in White. A witch; a ghost. That most malignant of beings that haunted men in their dreams. She could control lightning, and storms followed her wherever she went. Standing at crossroads, her kind had seduced and enslaved the unwary for centuries – gorging themselves on the life force, leaving only husks. But she was different. For Clothilde was ambitious. Merely taking one or two victims at a time was not enough for her. So she had used her intellect and her abilities. She had studied science and medicine. She had read about the art of seduction and how one should manipulate. She had become the most powerful of her kind.

She gave a satisfied smile. Physically these people were

entirely under her control, yet it did not stop them from screaming as soon as they realised what was about to happen to them.

She wished she could find a way to shut them up, for at times the sounds of their anguish haunted her in her dreams.

She leaned over and pulled another lever, and the giant piston in the middle of the machine started stamping up and down. Each time it came to rest on the chest of a person. In one swift move it extracted their still-beating heart and replaced it with a mechanical one. The hearts were deposited into glass jars filled with the liquid formula she had invented, then the machine sealed the jars and gently placed them on another conveyor belt that took the jars to her laboratory.

There the hearts would be kept in rows on shelves, neatly catalogued. They were essential for her control over the project.

On the other side of the machine, each new soldier for Clothilde's army was fitted with a brass muzzle, and a chest plate was riveted in place to cover the clockwork device that newly beat inside the bleeding chests. In the centre of the chestplate was a keyhole. A universal key was inserted which wound the newly installed clockwork device before each soldier was deposited and left to wait in neat silent rows for her every command.

The entire factory huffed and hissed through a series of tubes and vents that would put any cathedral organ to shame. Clothilde watched until every last one of the new recruits were complete before she turned off the machine. The factory fell silent before her.

'Take them to the holding stalls and see that they are fed,' she said to her strongmen. 'Electromancers, you may commence the clean-up. And make sure you polish every bit. I don't want to see streaks of blood on the machine. Do I make myself clear?'

'We live to serve,' they mumbled.

'As do I,' she said, suddenly feeling weary.

She wanted to retire to her rooms for a rest, but there was work to do. For in her laboratory was a young nobleman, a special new recruit awaiting her attention.

Chapter Nine

They come in the night when the fog is at its thickest. They shuffle along softly in broken shoes while the city sleeps. For the most part, they are silent. The only thing that can be heard as they pass is the ticking of their insides and, to those who know how to listen, the soft insistent hum that comes from the hunger that drives them.

These creatures have a new type of hunger, unlike anything seen or created in the world of Shadow. The stench of the strange new power that oozes from them causes the very barrier between the two realms to shiver. For these are amalgamations of science and magic that should not be.

And yet the new creatures come, bringing death to those who encounter them on their way. They are abominations, who carry within them the very essence of greed and destruction that will ultimately bring the world, as we know it, to an end.

And far in the distance, the Clockmaker sits back and watches with glee. He does not care for the horror and misery he has created. To him these creatures are his children. And as he gazed upon them, he saw that they were good.

Elle snorted rather inelegantly and sat up in her seat. She rubbed her eyes and listened to the discordant thrum of the ship's engines in the background. The left engine sounded dangerously out of tune, which was most worrying, given that they were high up in the sky and thousands of miles from anywhere.

Around her, the *Iron Phoenix* creaked and groaned as if it were almost too much effort to stay afloat. She had once been magnificent, but years of neglect had turned her rickety. Not for the first time, Elle tutted at Captain Dashwood's slovenly ways.

'It's a good thing I rescued you from that oaf when I did. Just look at what he's done to you.' Elle always spoke to her ships as if they were alive.

The only thing of beauty the *Phoenix* still possessed was her iron figurehead. She had the body of a shapely, bare-chested woman and the head of a fierce bird. The spirit of the phoenix sat proudly at the prow, her long wings spread open, trailing down the side of the ship behind her, as if she was about to take flight.

Elle rolled her neck to release the tension that had accumulated there from sleeping in a strange position. She and Ducky had been flying for almost three days now, taking turns in shifts at the helm, but somehow the journey wasn't getting any shorter.

Elle was thoroughly bored and restless. With all this time and silence to do nothing but think, a dark sense of unease had settled over her. And every time she closed her eyes those awful things haunted her dreams.

'Ah, you're awake,' Ducky said, coming up from the galley below.

'Ducky, how could you let me fall asleep at the helm? That's so irresponsible of you.'

'Oh, don't be silly. I had the old girl well under control,' he said. 'And besides, you looked like you could do with a jolly good nap.'

He sat down in the worn leather seat next to her and opened the tin of Mrs Hinges' excellent biscuits he had found.

'What's wrong, Bells? You are not the kind of girl who goes wandering around with dark shadows under her eyes.'

Elle smiled at his use of her nickname. He used to call her *'ells Bells* or, later, simply Bells for short. 'It's nothing.' Elle rubbed her face and looked away. Ducky had a way of being utterly on point. There was no hiding the truth when he was around.

'That new husband of yours had better be treating you well. Or else me and the boys will give him a jolly good thumping.'

'It's not that,' she said in a soft voice.

'Well, something has spooked your horses up into the hedges. I've been watching you for three days now and in all the years I've known you, I've never seen you this out of sorts. Come on, out with it.' Ducky put the biscuits down, sat back in his seat and pulled out a cigarette.

Smoking inside the ship was a habit Elle disapproved of most strenuously and she gave him a look of displeasure. But Ducky simply ignored her and carried on tapping the end of the cigarette against the tin, as he waited for an answer.

'I haven't been sleeping well lately,' she admitted.

'And why is that?'

'I've been having these strange dreams. I can't really explain them, but they feel so real. It's like I'm watching things happen.'

'Hmm,' he said. He stood up and opened one of the small windows and lit his cigarette. He took a long satisfied draw and blew the smoke out into the freezing night air.

Elle shivered. 'Each time I close my eyes, the dream comes. Each time, it's the same thing, but in different aspects.'

'Sounds like you should lay off the after-dinner brandies, my dear,' Ducky said.

'No, it's not like that. I know it's a message and I am supposed to do something about it, but I don't know what. I'm telling you, Ducky: when I'm dreaming I feel like I am there.' She wondered briefly if she should confide in him, tell him the truth about her newfound abilities, but she decided against it. Ducky was a pragmatic man on whom the nuances of the Shadow would certainly be lost. He would not understand. Even the fact that she had demonstrated to Dashwood that she had no shadow had passed largely over Ducky's head.

Elle wrapped her arms around herself, rubbing her shoulders against the draught that came in from the open window.

'I'm sorry, but I don't believe you. The Eleanor I know would not be daunted by a few silly nightmares. Good try, though,' he said.

She sighed. 'And it's Marsh.'

'I knew it. What's he done?'

Elle gave him an admonishing look. 'I really should not be discussing the intimacies of my marriage with you, you know.'

'Ooh. Intimacies. Now you've got me interested. What, is the old boy not up to scratch when it comes to opening the batting?' Ducky said.

'Ducky!' Elle blushed. 'It's nothing like that. It's more about me, really.'

Ducky flicked his cigarette butt out the window, shut it, and sat down opposite her. 'Tell me. Your confidences are safe with me. You should know that.'

'I think he wants me to give up flying,' she said.

Ducky burst out laughing. 'Oh, come on, Elle. Really?'

She nodded. 'Seriously, he's always talking about a wife's duty being beside her husband and such things. He's desperately unhappy about me taking this charter. We had a frightful row over it.'

Ducky opened the cubbyhole and pulled out Elle's half-jack of brandy. He opened the bottle and handed it to her. 'Marsh is right, you know. It's not just about you any more. You have to think about the both of you now. And perhaps more than just the two of you, in time to come.'

'But why do I have to be the one who blinks out of existence though?' Elle said.

Ducky shook his head. 'Do you even see how ridiculous you are being? I mean, look at the facts. He bought you your own flight charter company and financed your business. For heaven's sake, Elle, the man even put his name on the board outside and all you do is pout about the fact that you are not flying as much as you used to!' Ducky folded his arms. 'If you were my wife, I'd put you over my knee and spank you for being a brat.'

Elle stared at him. 'How can you say that?'

'Think about it,' he said, taking a swig from the bottle.

The *Phoenix* suddenly bucked and groaned as they hit a pocket of aether turbulence. Elle felt her stomach do a backflip as the thrusters righted them.

'Either I am finally losing my mind, or something is telling me that I shouldn't have taken this charter,' Elle said once the rattling of the ship had died down.

Ducky put the cork back into the brandy bottle and strode over to the helm of the *Phoenix*. With a deft hand, he spun the wheel and the *Phoenix* groaned and tilted to the side as the thrusters slowly started turning the ship about. Like the war galleons of old, it would take about a mile in distance for her to make the wide half-moon turn through the air.

'Ducky, what are you doing?' Elle said.

'I'm changing course,' he said.

'But we've only just cleared the Arabian Desert.'

'Exactly! And if we hurry, you can be back in London in a few days.'

'Ducky, no! What about the charter?'

'The charter can wait. Or they can hire someone else. We'll send them a message to say that we were having mechanical difficulties. Which, by the sound of things, isn't that far from the truth.'

Elle stared at him, not sure if she comprehended.

'I am taking you home, Lady Greychester, whether

you like it or not,' he said. 'You have a husband at home waiting for you who requires an apology.'

'I suppose I did rush off without thinking things through properly,' she said reluctantly.

'You should always trust your instincts. You need to find your place beside Marsh before you start thinking about flying. Otherwise you will spend the rest of your life regretting it.'

He's right. You must go home, the voices suddenly spoke inside her.

'The ship does sound like she needs to be pulled up into the ground docks for a proper overhaul and service. I'm thinking the repairs might be more than she's worth, if the sound of that engine is anything to go by.'

As if in answer, the *Phoenix* listed slightly and two of her engines backfired, releasing a greasy cloud of spark-laced steam into the night air. 'Surely Dashwood could have taken a little bit more care with his ship. I mean, honestly,' Elle said.

Ducky laughed. 'You don't know Captain Dashwood. And I wouldn't worry too much.' He patted the helm. 'This old bird is unstoppable.'

'I don't think I want to know Captain Dashwood any better, given what I've seen.'

Ducky just laughed as he kept his eye on the horizon.

Elle sat back in her seat. 'I am outvoted, it seems,' she said drily.

'Not for long, Bells. Not if those Suffragettes get their way,' Ducky said, oblivious to the other presence on board.

'When did you suddenly become so wise?' she said to him.

'Oh, I've always been a fount of wisdom,' he shot back. 'You've just never noticed.' He set the steering lock into place once they were back on course and came to sit next to her. 'I've seen the two of you together and if there is one thing I know, it's that Lord Greychester loves you.'

'And I love him too, Ducky. Very much,' Elle said.

'Well then, don't mess it up, you silly thing.'

Elle rubbed her face. Perhaps Ducky was right. She was being extraordinarily silly. There had to be a way to make things work and running away was not the answer.

'I need to think things through,' she said.

Ducky smiled. 'Well, don't look at me. Up here there is very little else to do but think. Perhaps this is why I am so wise.'

Elle laughed and rose from her seat. 'I am going to make some tea. Would you like a cup?'

'Yes, please. And perhaps also a nice sandwich to go with it,' Ducky said with a cheeky smile.

Elle shook her head and went down to the galley to make the tea. As she filled the kettle with water, the cloud that had been hovering over her lifted a little. There really was nowhere else in the world where she wanted to be more than at home, with Marsh. What did she really have to prove to anybody when all she needed in life to be happy was right before her?

And so the *Iron Phoenix* trundled and backfired her way on a high-altitude course back to England.

Chapter Ten

Marsh drummed his fingers on his upper lip as he contemplated the letter he had just opened. Around him, the Greychester house was as quiet as a mausoleum. The only sounds that reached him here in his study were the relentless patter of rain against the window casements interspersed with the ticking of the grandfather clock in the hall. It had been four days since she'd left in the airship. Four days of worrying and waiting and the silence was slowly grating away at his nerves. He was constantly surprised at how she filled his life with noise and activity. For one so small, his wife certainly had a way of making a large impression. He cursed his own stubbornness again for not going with her on the charter. It had been unfair of him to put her on the spot like that. Forcing her to choose would only drive her away from him. He needed to give her space to find her own way.

He glanced at the letter again. Police Commissioner Willoughby had invited him to luncheon at his club. The invitation was certainly tempting. Goodness knows it was dull enough around here without Elle, but he could not help but wonder about the sudden gesture of friendship.

It was true that he had met the commissioner on a

few occasions, but he certainly would not count the man within his circle of acquaintances. What could Willoughby want with him?

He shifted in his chair to release the crick that had formed in his back. Giving up the Shadow was proving to be more difficult than he had thought. He was certainly not enjoying the twinges and aches that were starting to plague him. It reminded him daily of his new mortality and the fact that time was ticking by. Most Warlocks were oblivious to time, for they lived lives that were ten times longer than those of mortal men. They went through life in a state of perfect fitness and health until the end. Then their powers simply faded until they blinked out of existence. But that was no longer his chosen path. He was going to have to endure the slow, steady decay into a gout-ridden rheumatic old age.

An ember popped in the fireplace sending a burst of sparks up the chimney. Marsh stared at the glowing coals as he thought things through. The Council of Warlocks had not been amused when they received his resignation. Threats and admonishments had flown; it had taken all of his control and influence to walk away from them. But he did not mind, because he was doing it for her.

For Elle.

Marsh felt his heart constrict at the thought. She was slipping away from him. He could feel the distance between them widening – every day a little more. No matter how hard he fought to keep things as they were when they had first met – the way she smiled at him in Florence when they stood huddled in a doorway to take shelter from the rain – it was like trying to hold on to desert sand.

He sighed and rubbed his eyes at the thought. He should never have let her go off to Singapore like that. And with Richardson of all people. The chap was decent enough but he could not fight his way out of a paper bag. What on earth could he do to protect her if they ran into trouble?

He sighed with frustration. Why did she have to go running off at every opportunity? He knew the answer to that, for he too was driven by the same passion for adventure. But at least he was able to control his urges. Suppress them for her sake. Why could she not do the same for him?

Marriage. Him. It wasn't enough for her, and the thought made his insides quiver. Perhaps it was because she was so young, but even after all they had fought for and all they had survived, she simply refused to acknowledge how vulnerable she was.

He had nearly died a thousand deaths when she had run off after whichever Shadow creature had been in the audience at the opera the other night. The very thought of it made him grow cold.

That's it, he thought. Sitting alone in this house brooding was not going to help anyone. So perhaps Elle was right. Perhaps he needed to get out of the house. He would meet Willoughby to see what the man had to say.

He knew it would take almost a week for Elle to get to Singapore and that she would be unable to contact him until then, but he found the silence was almost unbearable. The distraction would help the time pass.

He picked up Willoughby's invitation from his desk.

Yes, he would go. At the very least he would have an amusing story to tell her when she finally did come home. He stood and rang the bell pull for Neville to bring round the car.

Willoughby's club was a small obscure Georgian building hidden in an alley off Dean Street in Soho. Marsh hitched the collar of his grey wool coat up higher to keep the drizzle off his neck and knocked on the door.

An elderly footman with extremely old-fashioned powdered hair greeted him. 'May I help you, sir?' he said raising an eyebrow at the scuffed and slightly frayed top hat Marsh wore. He had deliberately dressed in his simpler street clothes today. They were the ones he had worn when on Shadow business for the Council. He liked the anonymous, comfortable feel of the worn fabric. It made him feel unobtrusive, as if he blended into his environment.

Marsh handed him the invitation and his visiting card.

The doorman scanned the card and glanced back up at Marsh. The only indication of surprise the man gave was another slight rise of his carefully plucked eyebrow. 'Please, do come in from the rain, my lord. May I take your lordship's coat?'

The doorman snapped his fingers and a footman appeared from behind the counter to assist.

'Thank you.' Marsh shrugged out of the soggy wool and handed it to the man.

'Right this way, my lord,' the footman said as he led Marsh up the narrow stairs that led into the main sitting room of the club.

Commissioner Willoughby looked up from a table

where he was reading the newspaper near the window. His spider-veined face split into a smile when he saw Marsh. 'My Lord Greychester, so good of you to come.' He half rose from his chair in a gesture that created the impression of exceptional rudeness given that Marsh outranked him considerably and should have therefore been the one to speak first.

'Police Commissioner, how do you do?' Marsh said, ignoring the slight. Willoughby had always been a brute with ideas above his station in life.

'Please, sit. Do make yourself at home. Would you like a drink?'

'Don't mind if I do,' Marsh said. 'A nice brandy to banish the cold perhaps?' He settled in the leather-covered Queen Anne chair opposite Willoughby.

'Ah yes, a good brandy. Just the thing for a day like today.' Willoughby nodded at the waiter who had appeared by their side with a tray. 'I am pleased you decided to join me.' Willoughby's smile did not quite reach his eyes as he spoke.

'I thank you for the kind invitation,' Marsh said. 'But I must admit that I was somewhat intrigued by your letter.'

'Yes. I thought we might meet here where we could speak in relative privacy as the matter is a delicate one.' Willoughby picked up his pipe and set about preparing a smoke. 'You see, I am in need of a man with your unique talents,' he said after a few moments.

'And what talents are those?' Marsh said lightly.

'We at the Metropolitan police make it our business to know other people's business, my lord. We know of your history with the Council of Warlocks.' He paused for a moment. 'Let's just say that you were recommended to me as a man who might be able to help.'

'And who, may I ask, would be making such recommendations?'

Willoughby gave him an oily smile. 'Oh, I don't think I'm at liberty to say. But they spoke very highly of the excellent work you did for the Ministry while in service of the Council. How is your lovely wife, by the way?'

'The viscountess is well. Thank you for asking.' Marsh kept his expression neutral. Willoughby knew more about his personal business than he was entirely comfortable with. But Marsh was a seasoned negotiator and he would not allow this man the pleasure of seeing his discomfort. 'With such a recommendation, how could a man refuse?' he said instead. 'But first tell me what this is about and then, perhaps, I might be able to confirm whether rumours about my work are true.'

Willoughby gave a little short bark of laughter. 'Well played, my lord.'

Marsh inclined his head slightly.

The waiter served the brandies. Marsh picked up his glass and swirled the brown liquid, feeling it warm in his palm.

Willoughby took a sip of his drink and wiped his moustache. 'Lord Henry Alcott, the heir and seventh Earl of Mallory, disappeared four nights ago.' Willoughby struck a match and held it up to his pipe. 'His family have been beside themselves with worry. We have commissioned a search, but my men have found nothing. The boy has simply disappeared into thin air.'

'I see,' said Marsh.

Willoughby sucked on his pipe. 'We've had word that the newspapers are going to publish news of his disappearance any day now and they are not going to be kind about the police.'

'And how is this my business? I'm sure young Alcott will turn up.'

'Yes, well, this is where the problem arises. The earl does not want news of his son's disappearance to be made public.' Willoughby looked uncomfortable. 'Let's just say that the lad was last seen in less than polite company.'

'Who hasn't gone missing for a few days after a night out at his age?' Marsh said.

'Well, he was involved with a girl who was entirely unsuitable. Well bred, but poor, weak and sickly. They did all they could to discourage the affair, but the lad was hell-bent on finding a way to save her. He was in search of a cure for her when he disappeared, along with the earl's valet.'

'I see,' said Marsh.

'And well, we suspect that Shadow creatures were involved. He was last seen following one of those gypsy folk out of the Black Stag. It's in the docklands. I don't expect you know it.'

Marsh flinched at the commissioner's use of what was a rather pejorative term, but for the first time since he sat down he felt his interest piqued. 'But the travelling folk are not necessarily connected to the Shadow. And besides, creatures of Shadow can only cross into the Realm of Light if they speak a binding oath to do no harm.'

Willoughby nodded. 'Yes, that may be so, but there are reports of strange things going on in the dark of night.'

'Such as?'

Willoughby reddened and took a quick sip from his glass. 'Perhaps another time. We are here to discuss the business of the Mallorys.'

Marsh frowned. 'In almost all cases, a broken oath would mean instant death to the creature in question. Of course the Nightwalkers, wolves and other half-shadow creatures who were created on the Light side are the exception, but surely you are not insinuating that someone has found a way around the decree?'

Willoughby held up his hands. 'No. Not in so many words. I am simply sharing my suspicions.'

The last sip of Marsh's brandy burned his throat as he swallowed it down. He was starting to see why Willoughby had called on him. It was true that Shadow creatures did no harm in the Light, so their usual modus operandi was to abduct victims to the Shadow side where anything was possible. Usually these attempts failed, but if someone or something out there had found a way around the barrier, there could be trouble.

'This is really a matter that should be reported to the Council. They are more than equipped to deal with situations such as these,' Marsh said. 'And you know well enough that I am no longer a member of the Council. I am finished with the Ministry. Retired.'

Willoughby coughed. 'We were hoping that we wouldn't have to create an international incident by notifying the Council. Matters are so delicate politically at the moment. We were hoping that you might agree to make a few discreet enquiries. See if there are Shadow creatures out there that are up to no good. At least that way we will know what we are dealing with before we sound the alarm.'

Marsh nodded slowly. He felt a profound sense of worry unfurl in him. Had the incident with the alchemists in Constantinople upset the balance of things that much? But Elle said that there was nothing wrong with the divide. She performed her duties as Oracle when they arose as she had promised. Not that she actually cared for the cause or even appreciated the sacrifices that had been made, he thought in a surprise moment of bitterness.

'Tell me what you know.' Marsh sat forward and spoke in a low voice.

Willoughby nodded. 'We've had an increase in complaints from people who have had loved ones go missing over the last week. One or two of the workhouses have been found empty. It was as if someone had gone into the building and cleared everyone out overnight. These people had simply disappeared, leaving everything as it stood.'

'Is that so?' Marsh said.

'It only happens when the fog is thick. People go out into the night and simply never come back. It's a most curious state of affairs. And then there are the rumours...'

'Rumours?' Marsh said.

'Something about creatures people are calling the Tickers. It's all probably just idle gossip, but apparently groups of two or three of these so-called Tickers are prowling the streets at night, stealing people away. But none of my men have ever seen one, so it probably is just mass hysteria. You know how people can be when there's a good story doing the rounds.'

Marsh pressed his lips together. 'All right, Willoughby, you have my interest,' he said. 'I will have a look round for you. If I find evidence of Shadow creatures being involved, I will need you to report this to the Ministry, who will in turn refer the matter to the Council of Warlocks. If not, then you may rest assured that Henry's disappearance is nothing more than a silly boy who got more than he bargained for on a night out.'

Willoughby's face lit up with relief. 'We would be ever so grateful, my lord,' he said.

'But I work alone. And I do not want people bothering me at home about this. You will hear from me and not the other way round. Is that agreed?'

'As you wish. You may commence the investigations at your earliest convenience.'

'Agreed,' Marsh said.

Willoughby inclined his head and smiled. 'You might find, my lord, that this is the beginning of a most rewarding mutual arrangement. Our department is at the forefront of the world when it comes to investigating crime and I can see that a man like you would be most useful to our endeavours.'

'Perhaps,' Marsh said with a tight smile. 'Now if you will excuse me, I think I had better be on my way.'

'Thank you for your time. I look forward to hearing from you further.' Willoughby rose from his seat. Marsh shook the commissioner's hand briefly before taking his leave.

Downstairs in the foyer, the doorman held up his coat and hat, which had both been dried and brushed while he had been upstairs.

Marsh lifted his collar and stepped back into the relentless rain. The mud in the streets was making life miserable for both men and the poor carriage horses who clopped through the city. He stopped and dropped a handful of coins into the hat of a clutch of shivering children who were sat huddled together in a doorway. London was truly gripped in the misery of what was surely the wettest, coldest February in living memory.

Marsh bunched his hands inside his coat pockets and walked on. There was something Willoughby was not telling him. This was a clever ploy because it only made him want to investigate the matter more. And he had not considered Willoughby a cunning man. He had been wrong.

Not for the first time, Marsh felt himself yearn for the piece of mandrake root bound in linen that was buried under the ancient yew tree in the gardens on his estate. For in that sacred place and in the light of the full moon he had performed the ritual that had sealed away his powers. On that clear, cold night shortly before his wedding day, Marsh had become an ordinary man. At the time it had seemed like a good idea, for he would rather die in one lifetime having loved Elle, than spend centuries on his own. That was the sacrifice he had made. The question now was whether it had been a decision he would live to regret.

❧

Outside the front door of the house, the fog swirled. It parted briefly like stage curtains for the Warlock to slip through and out into the waiting night. He left alone, without telling anyone where he was going.

I must admit that I did not want to go out in the dark of the night where it was cold and raining, but I had promised my lady that I would look after him. A promise is a promise and so I followed, for I could tell that there was an ill humour in the air. It spoke of darkness and demise. It was a foulness that the Warlock with his new blunted senses did not notice.

In spite of the weather, he chose to walk through Hyde Park. The trees sighed as he passed. They always lamented when they sensed magic that was lost. I've often wondered if there were trees that wept for me somewhere.

In the darkness I could sense them waiting. They were many – an army, completely silent, but for the synchronous ticking of their hearts.

Outside the Serpentine gates, the Warlock paused to hail a cab. A sleepy steam cab driver, perched atop his converted hansom, trundled up.

'The East End,' the Warlock said.

The cabbie grunted and I could tell that he, too, was unhappy about being out on a night like this. But the cab shuddered to life and, under cover of the noise and steam of *the engine, no one noticed me slip on to the back of the parcel rack.*

We travelled for quite a while through the gritty rain-slicked streets. The only signs of life were yellow and orange lozenges of light that shone from unshuttered windows. Those with any sense were locked away indoors, sheltered from the cold. For only the very stupid or desperate would brave the wet and the unexplained things that roamed these streets at night.

The Warlock told the cab to stop near a public house. It was an old, shabby place with very little that was beautiful about it. I do not like these places, for they remind me too much of the servitude I had left behind in Paris.

No matter where one goes in the world, there are the places where Shadow creatures ply their trade. I knew I would not be welcome here, for Shadow creatures do not like competition.

But I held my nerve and followed the Warlock inside, unseen.

The Warlock ordered a pint from the counter and sat down at one of the tables. He took a resolute swallow of the ale, grimacing as he contemplated the rings that stained the wood. I made myself as small as possible and found a place to sit on one of the grimy sconces near the ceiling.

The Warlock did not wait long before a man wearing a hat with a peacock feather strode up to the table.

They spoke and the man nodded.

The Warlock pulled a portrait photograph from his breast pocket and slid it across the table. 'This man. Have you seen him?' he said.

'I might have. It's hard to say,' the other said.

The Warlock narrowed his eyes and slid a coin across the table. 'Perhaps this might help you remember.'

His companion picked up the shilling and held it up to the light. With nimble fingers and sleight of hand, he made the coin disappear. 'I seem to recall seeing someone of that description. But it is not safe to speak here. You will have to come with me.'

'And where might we be going?' the Warlock said.

A small smile flickered on his companion's face. 'To see someone who remembers better than I do.'

I strained to listen more, but my attention was drawn away, for I sensed the danger moments before it materialised next to me.

Gin fairies. I could smell the perfume of juniper on them.

'Oi, Frenchie. You ain't got no right to this corner. This here is our place,' one said. He had beautiful eyes, the colour of summer at midnight.

'I'm not here looking for business. I am just watching over a friend,' I said.

The biggest of them snorted. 'I can't say as I care. Business or no business, we don't like your kind round here.' The three fairies circled around me in a rather menacing way.

One of them caught my eye. He was a handsome fellow with a face that was gentler than the others. He gave me a long, sad look that spoke of regret and the hope that things might be different.

'I'm sorry. I'm…' I started to say, but I glanced over to the table where the Warlock and the peacock-feathered man were and I gasped with dismay. The table was empty.

'Forgive me, I did not mean to offend,' I said as I pushed past the fairies and flew out the door before we could come to blows. I wish I could have stayed to make friends, for I had missed others of my kind. But a promise made is one to be honoured and my path lay in pursuit of the Warlock.

Outside was only the street in all its ordinariness. I could see no one through the swirling mist.

At a dark lamppost I paused, looking left and right. The Warlock's scent clung faintly to the cold metal, but it was melting in the mist. It would not be long before all traces of him would be gone. I flew in the direction his scent drifted from, but the buildings in this place formed a labyrinth that was almost impossible to navigate.

I flew this way and that, ever more confused until I was completely and utterly lost. I became very afraid, for London was a dangerous place for someone as little as me. And all the while, the rain sifted down, soaking into my wings with an iciness that was almost debilitating.

Eventually I came to a small clearing that sat dank and forlorn beside a bridge. In the darkness a small fire burned. I could smell the scent of incense and horses. Travelling folk. These people were usually sympathetic to creatures of Shadow. I was sure they would let me rest here a while until the sun came up.

I sighed with relief as I settled on the steps of the wagon. I was sure the good mistress who lived here would not mind.

And, true to my predictions, it was not long before I sensed someone behind me. I looked over my shoulder, just in time to feel a large bell jar clamp down over me. I groaned inwardly, for there were few things in the world I hated more than being captured in glass jars. Yet once again, here I was. At the mercy of someone who did not understand who I was or what I could do.

The face of a woman appeared outside the glass. She lifted the jar and placed it on the table inside the wagon.

'Hello, sweetling,' she murmured. Her voice was gentle but

oddly distorted by the curvature of the glass. 'I am honoured that you have come to my doorstep. Please feel welcome here.'

I shook my head and started throwing myself against the sides of the jar in the hope that I might be able to escape. My efforts were in vain, as they always seemed to be. For it is the lot of my kind to be forever bound. Never free.

The woman laughed. 'Oh, not so happy then, I see.' I noted that she was far younger than I had first thought. Her face was fresh and unlined with the plumpness of youth. But it is so difficult to tell the age of mortals, for they die so quickly.

'Well, I am sure we might be able to fix this,' the woman said. 'If you don't want to be in the jar, you should simply agree to behave. This will only take a moment.'

She reached for her sewing basket and drew out a skein of bright red silk – the kind fine ladies used for their embroidery.

She started singing in a soft, low voice as she unwound the thread. As she sang, I felt the amber tendrils of her magic surge up and envelop me. It was so thick and strong, like wood smoke from a damp fire, that it almost suffocated me.

Hoping to find a means of escape, I looked about frantically for any bottles of liquor. Brandy, whisky, even gin – anything that might help me slip into spirit form so I may leave this wagon. But I found none, for the wagon was spotlessly clean and furnished simply with no signs of any vice.

Very slowly, the woman lifted the lid off the glass jar. She dropped the silk inside and slipped the little noose she had knotted around my ankle. I wanted to protest, but before I could fight her, I felt the magic tighten around me with sickening certainty. I was caught, like a rabbit in a snare, with a bright red bit of silk

'There you are. Now you are mine. It really wouldn't do for

you to go wandering about in the night like that. It's dangerous out there and you are almost half frozen. You should be glad that I found you and took you in.' She unrolled the silk and tied it to a brass ring that was set in the wood of the inside of the wagon.

Then the woman opened a cupboard and pulled out a bottle of absinthe and a bowl of sugar. *'With this silk you are bound to me now, but there is no reason why you should be deprived.'* She set both down in front of me.

'Please. Eat, rest.' She uncorked the bottle. *'I am very sure that you and I are going to have wonderfully sweet dreams together. I really do mean you no harm.'* She smiled warmly at me. *'I hope you will be my friend.'*

I tried to fight it, but the lure of the liquor and friendship was too strong. I knew I had to keep searching for the Warlock, but my kind never really has much of a chance resisting the call of absinthe. And so against my better judgement, I slipped back into the cool green oblivion that would forever be my prison.

ॐ

Chapter Eleven

Elle hopped out of the front seat of the motor and bounded up the stairs before Neville could walk round to open the door for her.

He had been remarkably quiet on the way home from the airfield, but she had not really paid him much heed because she was too excited to see Marsh.

She hoped he had received the telegram she had sent from the airfield in Dieppe, just before they made the crossing over the Channel.

The spark lights outside the front door cast a welcoming glow for those coming out of the early February darkness.

Elle paused under them to smooth down the skirts of her new dress. She had purchased it on impulse on her way back from the telegraph office. It was a pretty shade of the lightest blue and trimmed with lace. It softened her features and highlighted the colour of her eyes.

The thought of seeing Marsh again sent a flush across her cheeks and a cloud of butterflies swirling up and down her insides. She wasn't about to admit this too openly, but she had missed her handsome husband more than she had thought possible.

She had done a great deal of thinking on the way back

after her discussion with Ducky and there was so much she wanted to tell him.

She threw open the front door and dumped her holdall on the mahogany table with the China vase in the entrance hall. Today it held a large bunch of white lilies and the cloying sweetness of their scent made her nose prickle.

'I'm home!' she called up the stairwell as she took off her oversized hat and dropped it on top of her holdall.

Only silence greeted her.

'Mrs Hinges? Caruthers?' She strode through to the library, sure that Marsh would be sprawled on the sofa, but the room was empty and dark. The fireplace was cold.

She turned and walked through to the drawing room. The wooden heels of her smart new shoes made a hollow sound on the old floors.

Just outside the drawing room, She ran into the butler. 'My lady, welcome back.' He looked somewhat flustered.

'Oh, hello, Caruthers,' she said.

The butler gave one of his solemn bows. He was a tall man in his early sixties with a stern face that came from years of following proper decorum. But Elle was not fooled by his restraint. Below those bushy eyebrows were fiercely intelligent bright blue eyes. Caruthers was a man who smelled of silver polish and peppermint; a man whose fierce scrutiny missed nothing, so she regarded him carefully. Something was very wrong in this house and she needed to know what it was.

'Did you have a pleasant journey, madam?' he said, without batting an eyelid.

'Yes, thank you. But where is everybody? Why is the house so quiet?'

Caruthers paused, with a pained expression on his face. 'Perhaps your ladyship should come into the drawing room and sit down for a moment.' He opened the door and gestured for her to enter. Elle noticed that he was struggling to meet her gaze.

Elle went cold. 'What's happened?' she said.

'Please, this way, my lady.'

Inside the drawing room, Mrs Hinges was perched at the very edge of one of the occasional chairs. She rose the moment Elle entered, her hands fluttering to her throat in the way they did when she was upset.

'Mrs Hinges, what's wrong?' Elle said.

'I'm so sorry. We have been out looking all night,' she said.

'Searching for what?' Elle felt her heart race.

'Eleanor.' The professor spoke in a quiet voice behind her. He had been sitting so still in one of the wingback chairs that Elle had not noticed him until now. He looked tired.

'Papa, for heaven's sake. What on earth is going on? I thought you would have gone back to Oxford by now?'

'There is no way to say this gently.' The professor rose from his seat as he spoke. 'Hugh hasn't come home.'

Elle felt the air leave her lungs as if someone had punched her in the stomach. 'What do you mean Hugh hasn't come home?' she said.

'He went out late yesterday afternoon, just after sunset. He didn't say where he was going and until now he hasn't returned. I'm so sorry, my dear,' Mrs Hinges said as gently as she could.

'I saw him take his carriage cloak and a rather frayed-looking top hat, ma'am,' Caruthers said. 'I tried to recommend that he take his good hat, but he was out the door before I could finish my sentence. He went out alone and did not say where he was going or when he was to be expected back.' Caruthers looked contrite.

Elle felt herself grow even colder. The carriage cloak and a frayed top hat were the same clothes he wore in Paris on the day they had met. Marsh wore those clothes only when he did not want anyone to recognise him; when we was about his business as a Warlock for the Council.

'I don't think we need to worry quite yet,' the professor said. 'Perhaps he is running an errand or something.'

'Errands don't take all night, Papa,' Elle said. 'Where is Adele? Perhaps she knows something. I told her to watch over him while I was gone.' Elle rose and walked to the conservatory.

In the atrium the ferns waved a gentle hello in the air she stirred up as she strode into the glass room. Everything was silent. Today there were no bees droning against the glass. Adele liked to invite lost bees into the atrium where she offered them sanctuary in return for visits to her plants. Where she found willing bees in the dead of winter was one of the many mysteries that shrouded the fairy.

'Adele?' Elle said.

There was no answer. She started peering through the plants, lifting fronds out of the way. At the back of the atrium was a pretty wooden fairycote they had bought for Adele shortly after they moved to the house. It was a miniature dollhouse, complete with wooden doors and shutters. Each room was decorated with exquisitely crafted miniature furniture. The outside of the dollhouse was decorated with intricate fairy patterns. Marsh and Adele had spent hours copying these from a book he had found in his study. Adele was indeed one of the few absinthe fairies in this world who had her very own mansion house.

Elle peered in through the doors and windows, but all the rooms of the dollhouse were empty.

'We haven't seen the fairy either. She has disappeared too,' Neville said. The whole household – the professor, Mrs Hinges and Caruthers – were all with Neville in the breakfast room behind her.

'Shall I send someone to draw you a bath, ma'am? You must be cold and tired from your journey,' Caruthers asked.

Elle shook herself out of her reverie and blinked at the concerned faces who were watching her closely.

'Yes, of course. I'll be along in a moment,' she said flatly.

She could not afford to go to pieces. She owed them all at least that, but right now all she wanted was to be alone and so she allowed herself to be herded off to her rooms, like some fragile creature in need of care.

In the privacy of the bathroom, Elle sank into the warm bathwater. She turned the bar of rose-scented soap over and over in her hands and watched as it turned the water cloudy around her, in much the same way absinthe taints water with its touch.

They had been so harsh with their words to one another the last time they had spoken. Where was he? Had he gone back to the Council? And if he *had* gone back to the Council, where did that leave her?

'Oh, where is he?' she asked the voices, but for once they were utterly silent.

She sat in the bath until the water cooled, until Mrs Hinges tactfully tapped on the bathroom door to enquire whether she needed anything.

'I'll only be a minute,' Elle called. She rose from the water, shivering, and started towelling herself dry.

Mrs Hinges was waiting for her when she stepped out of the bathroom. 'Elle, my dear, why don't you sit down?'

Elle sat on the stool in front of the mirror in her dressing room. She felt cold and numb and in no mood to take on the formidable Mrs Hinges.

'I know it might not be my place to interfere, but I have noticed that things haven't exactly been perfect between you and his lordship.' Mrs Hinges picked up one of her hairbrushes and started brushing Elle's long auburn hair, like she had done when Elle was a little girl. 'I'm only mentioning it because I care about you both as if you were my own children,' she said.

If it had been anyone else who said these words, Elle would have been outraged at the impropriety of the comment, but Mrs Hinges was the closest thing to a mother she had and her concern touched Elle deeply.

'I know, Mrs Hinges, and now he's not here. What if he's left me?' Elle felt her throat constrict at the thought.

'Now, don't go finding thoughts which have no right

to be in your head. He has only been gone a little while. Men sometimes need a little bit of space. And there may be a very good reason for all this.'

'And what if I've given him too much space?' Elle said. 'Goodness, I've been such a horrible wife.'

'Oh, his lordship does not strike me as the kind of man who would abandon his duty,' Mrs Hinges said.

Duty. There was the word – all ugly and constrictive.

Elle rested her hand against her forehead, suddenly deeply tired.

Mrs Hinges put her hands round Elle's shoulders. 'I think you should get into bed and get some rest. I will bring you some dinner in a little while. Neville has said that he will go out again this evening to look for him. If anyone knows all of Lord Greychester's haunts, it is Neville. Who knows, things might look better in the morning.'

For once in her life all the fight and anger went out of Elle and she allowed herself to be tucked into bed like a child. The cup of warm milk Mrs Hinges fed her later was laced with nutmeg and something bitter she could not quite put her finger on. But eventually, the warmth lulled her into an exhausted sleep.

The morning brought no relief. Elle glanced back from the window when the maid brought in her morning coffee.

She had been sitting on the windowsill in her nightdress for hours, just watching the street outside.

She poured herself a cup and continued her vigil at the window. Outside, the relentless drizzle sifted down, turning everything outside into a state of mushy dampness. In fact, the morning was so grey that it was hard to tell where the low clouds ended and the fog that rose from the ground began. So much for an early spring, she mused.

Sighing, she left the window seat and wandered across to Marsh's wood-panelled dressing closet. This was her husband's inner sanctum, a place she almost never entered and never on her own. The dressing room was immaculately clean and tidy, for Neville was a good valet and he kept Marsh's things in excellent order.

Elle ran a hand over a cufflink box. And the row of neat brushes Neville used on his coats.

Then, quite on impulse, Elle opened Hugh's clothes press. Inside, his jackets, coats and trousers hung in neat rows. She wrapped her arms around the clothes and buried her face in the cloth in order to inhale the scent of sandalwood and him.

The familiarity of the fabric against her skin brought both anguish and comfort in equal measures, before something rustled against her cheek.

Elle looked up from the clothes with a little frown. There was something in the pocket of one of the coats she had just gathered up. She started feeling about until her fingers closed around a folded piece of paper. She drew it out and took it over to the window where she opened it. The paper was crumpled and had disintegrated in one of the corners as if it had had somehow become wet. But the neat copperplate writing was easy to read. It was a letter from the Office of Police Commissioner Willoughby inviting Marsh to meet him at his club. It said nothing about why, but gave the date as the day before he disappeared.

Elle's forehead crinkled with worry. What had Marsh been up to while she had been away?

He had sworn to her that he wanted nothing more to do with the Shadow politics, but here he was being summoned to meet with the police commissioner. Unwelcome thoughts of their argument sprang to mind once more. Had he really been bored and frustrated enough to start working again without telling her?

Elle stared at the letter in her hand. She hated to admit it, but she was going to need some help in order to sort this mess out. And while she generally hated asking anyone for help, she knew just the right person for the task. Someone who would be on her side and who would be able to talk some sense into Marsh.

Still holding the letter Elle strode over to her bureau and pulled out one of the telegraphic message transfer forms she kept there for emergencies. Quickly she scribbled a note, pausing only to make sure that the message conveyed the urgency but gave away no information to prying eyes.

She put the folded form into an envelope and rang the bell pull. When Edie appeared, she thrust the note into the startled girl's hand. 'Take this to Caruthers. Tell him to go to the post office immediately to transmit the message. It is urgent.'

'Yes, my lady.' Edie bobbed a curtsey and headed for the door, looking somewhat alarmed.

Elle looked at herself in the mirror and let out a startled laugh. Dressed in her nightdress with her hair escaping wildly from her braid, she did look rather like a female version of her father when he was in one of his intellectual frenzies. But none of that mattered right now. She finished her coffee in one gulp and set the cup down with determination. She was going to find her husband and get to the bottom of things.

But first, she needed to get dressed.

Chapter Twelve

'Here is fine, Neville. I shan't be too long,' Elle said as they pulled up outside the red-brick buildings of New Scotland Yard.

'I will find somewhere to wait for you, my lady,' Neville said as he hopped out of the driver seat to open the door for her.

The police station was crammed with people of all shapes and sizes thronging just inside the main entrance.

The distinct miasma of unwashed bodies saturated with gin hit Elle square in the nose as she collided with a gaggle of women who were shouting at the hapless police officer who was trying to round them up.

Elle sidestepped the women and walked straight into a wall of muscle that belonged to a very determined-looking man. He growled at her and stepped on the hem of her dress. Elle heard a most worrying sound of ripping fabric as he pushed past her, shoving her to one side. Elle was suddenly most grateful that she had decided not to wear one of her wide-brimmed hats this morning. Defiantly, she shoved the man aside and wrestled her way into the thronging queue of people waiting to be served at the counter.

Behind the counter a harassed constable was doing his best to help those in the queue. Judging by the redness of his nose, which at that moment he was wiping with a grubby handkerchief, the poor man looked like he needed to be in bed with a basin of soup and a hot water bottle rather than here, fighting the surging tide of humanity before him.

'Next!' he shouted hoarsely.

Elle fought her way forward and righted herself against the wooden edge of the counter. 'Viscountess Greychester. I would like to see the police commissioner please,' she said in a low voice.

The clerk's eyebrows shot up as he took proper notice of her. She was dressed in a fine charcoal wool skirt and jacket, which she had paired up with a velvet-trimmed coat and lady's bowler hat. She lifted the little black net veil attached to the hat that covered the top half of her face. 'It's extremely urgent, sir,' she said.

'Um. Perhaps you should come this way, my lady,' he stuttered as he opened the fly door to the side of the counter. A few of the people in the queue voiced their objection to the constable abandoning his post but the man ignored them steadfastly.

'Make way, please,' he croaked as he ushered Elle into a waiting room that was situated down one of the little corridors that led off from the main entrance. 'Would your ladyship please wait here while I go to find someone to assist?' he said. 'I will send someone along to collect your ladyship in a moment.'

'Thank you,' Elle said.

'We are extraordinarily busy this morning, so please

excuse the delay,' he said apologetically before he scooted off, closing the door behind him.

The waiting room consisted of two wooden chairs and a table. Grateful for the respite from the crowd, Elle breathed in the institutional smell of carbolic and floor wax, willing herself to remain composed.

Minutes ticked by and no one came to collect her, so she waited.

And waited…

…and waited.

Elle was not a woman blessed with unending reserves of patience, and after what seemed like a respectable amount of time, she opened the door and peered out.

Outside the door, chaos continued unabated. In fact, it looked like the crowd of complainants had grown thicker.

The cold-riddled constable was back behind the counter, trying desperately to direct people to various areas, but without much effect. Some of the people were waving portraits and photographs in the air. Others were shouting at the top of their lungs, demanding action.

And to add to the general mayhem, a gaslight troll was actively resisting arrest for fighting in the street. Not known for their intelligence, trolls could be relied on for brute strength and the ability to perform repetitive tasks without growing bored, no matter the weather. Because they were tall and had long arms and knobbly elbows, trolls were especially gifted at lighting lamps. The only problem with them was the fact that they had very short tempers and were extraordinarily strong. And from the look of the three officers it took to subdue the current troll in question, the charges were not unwarranted. The creature was braying at the top of his lungs and thrashing wildly as he was shackled and led away.

Elle frowned. She was not in the habit of waiting at police stations, but even she could see that something very strange was going on here. The question, though, was what.

She sat down on one of the chairs and glanced at her little silver pocket watch. She had been waiting for nearly two hours and midday was approaching. As if in answer, her stomach growled in protest. If the police commissioner was anything like most gentlemen she knew, he would be departing for lunch soon. And if lunch was followed by cigars and brandies, there was no way of knowing when he would be back, if at all.

Elle stowed her watch and straightened her jacket. It was time to take action. She was not going to allow herself to be treated like a problem that might go away if ignored for long enough. It was time to take matters into her own hands.

Carefully, she opened the door and slipped out of the little room into the corridor. To the left was a flight of stairs that led to the upper floors. And if she knew anything about official buildings, the commissioner's offices would be upstairs and as far away from the hubbub as possible.

She lowered her head and strode purposefully along. One or two people stepped out of the way for her, but no one stopped to question her presence. It was a trick Patrice had taught her. Walk with purpose and look like you know where you are going and people will assume you belong there.

You must forget about Patrice, the voices interrupted her. *To him, you were nothing but a means to an end. You should never have trusted him in the first place.*

'Oh, do be quiet,' Elle hissed at them as she walked along. 'You are never there when I need you and when I don't, you interfere. Your constant whispering is enough to drive anyone round the hat shop. I have no privacy. No room to think. Even when I'm with my husband, I feel like you are peering over my shoulder. I wish I could banish you away forever.'

If you ask us, we will go . . . we had wanted to wait to tell you this, but the power to command us lies within you.

She suddenly felt the strangest surge of anger-fuelled energy rise up within her. No more could she stand these voices intruding on even her most private of thoughts. They were always there, watching and whispering; judging her every thought and action. In fact, she had not known one moment of solitude since they appeared almost half a year ago. She had even heard them whispering on her wedding night. And Elle was tired and overwrought with worry. 'Fine! Then please go away and leave me in peace. I am better off without you,' she said.

The voices did not answer.

The large bubble of frustration and resentment that had been building up in her chest for the longest time finally burst. Before she could stop herself a stream of words formed in her head. 'Voices of the Oracle. You are hereby and for evermore banished from my presence. Turn your eyes away from me and do not trouble me ever again.' It was the strangest sensation, because it was as if she was speaking to them inside her own head.

Two officers looked at Elle as she had stopped in the middle of the hallway and when she found herself again, she realised that she was staring into space as if she were simple. She ignored their puzzled glances and walked on.

You have ordered us and so we must be away. Are you sure? For when we are commanded to go, we may not return.

'Yes, I am sure. I am sick and tired of you haunting me. I just want you to leave me alone!'

But you need us . . .

'No I do not. All I want is for you to leave my head. Immediately. Enough is enough.'

If that is your wish, we will obey. Farewell, our dearest one. You are forever in our hearts . . .

Elle didn't answer the voices as they faded from her. Annoying, useless things. They were always too melodramatic anyway. But fear not, they would be back soon enough. The interfering busybodies would not be able to resist for long.

Elle gathered her thoughts. Right now was not the time for daydreaming. She needed to concentrate on where she was going, because the inside of New Scotland Yard was a maze of corridors and offices and there was no more time to waste. After a few false turns she eventually found a door with a brass plaque that read COMMISSIONER on it.

She was wearing a pair of black kid leather winter gloves and she rapped on the door sharply with her knuckles.

'Come!' a voice said from within.

Oh good. He *was* in, she thought with a small measure of relief and opened the door.

Police Commissioner Willoughby was a man with

highly impressive whiskers. They sat on the side of his head like a pair of stately caterpillars, all combed and trimmed in their lush and silver glory. He looked slightly surprised as she entered, but good manners won out and he rose from behind his desk.

'Madam,' he said.

Without giving him a chance to enquire, Elle held out her hand to greet him. 'Lady Greychester. How do you do, sir?' she said.

'How do you do, my lady? Please do sit down. And to what do I owe the pleasure of this visit?' he said smoothly.

The hair on the back of her neck rose as she noticed his gaze narrow ever so slightly when she sat. She would have to play her part carefully if she was going to get anything out of this man, she realised.

'It's my husband. The viscount,' Elle said.

Willoughby shifted in his chair. He looked like the kind of man who was not entirely at ease when it came to dealing with women. Perhaps that was the way to approach him.

Elle fished out a small lace handkerchief from her reticule. 'You see, he's been missing for almost two days now. And I really don't know whom to turn to,' she said, keeping the pitch of her voice slightly higher than normal.

'Well, we are here to assist, my lady. But perhaps it might be better if I called for one of our inspectors to take down a statement.' He gestured towards the brass speaking apparatus on his desk. It was the latest aetherographic voice transmission set. The system constituted a private telephony system that connected to other handsets in the building via its own spark-powered telephony exchange.

It involved a series of high-frequency wires inside ribbed rubber tubing, which made it a frightfully expensive system. She wondered how the police might afford such things.

'My inspectors are much better equipped than I for this kind of situation,' he said.

Elle grabbed his hand, suddenly grateful that she had not taken off her gloves. 'No. Please, Commissioner, this matter must be handled with the utmost discretion. You see, my husband and I are often the subject of gossip in the society pages. People might start rumours that my husband has deserted me. And I would not be able to bear the shame of it,' she said. Somehow Elle managed to muster just enough emotion to make her bottom lip tremble.

'But of course, my dear. You may rest assured that the matter will be dealt with most discreetly.' He rose and made a gesture at the door, which looked suspiciously like he was trying to herd her out of his office.

'And there is also the other matter,' Elle said, this time more firmly. It was time to call his bluff.

Willoughby's eyebrows drew together in a frown. 'And what other matter would that be?'

'I have the invitation you sent my husband asking him to meet with you at your club on an important and delicate matter. You, my dear Commissioner Willoughby, were one of the last persons outside of our household to see my husband before his disappearance.'

Willoughby gave a short bark of laughter. 'My dear lady. Surely you can't be serious? While it may be so that I met with your husband on Tuesday at my club, I can assure you that he was quite well when we parted company. Hugh Marsh is an old acquaintance of mine and there was nothing untoward in us meeting.'

Elle sat back in her seat as she regarded the commissioner for a few long moments. 'Mr Willoughby. I think we are at the end of this dance, so I will be blunt. I know my husband was working for you. I know that after your meeting, he set out on the following evening on what I can only assume was the business you discussed.' She folded her hands in her lap. 'But what I don't know is why. Or what he was sent to do. And I can't start looking for him until I know these two things. So could we please dispense with the niceties so you can tell me what I need to know?'

Her gamble to be direct seemed to pay off because, in response, Willoughby turned very red. 'Your allegations, madam, are quite preposterous. The viscount was not working for this police department. And even if he were, I would not be at liberty to disclose such information. Especially not to a . . . a lady.'

He stepped out from behind his desk and took Elle by the upper arm, lifting her out of her seat. 'Now if you'll excuse me, there is a rather urgent crisis developing downstairs.' He hauled Elle to the door. 'I regret that we simply do not have the resources at the moment to deal with recalcitrant husbands. I'm sure he will be home soon. So I shall bid you good day, madam.' With that, he shoved her out of his office and closed the door firmly in her face.

Elle gasped with indignation when she heard the lock click as he turned the key. She started banging against the door with her fist. 'This discussion is not over, Commissioner. I am not leaving until you tell me what I need to know!'

'My lady?'

Elle spun round. Behind her stood a slightly embarrassed-looking constable. He cleared his throat and rubbed the back of his neck. 'Apologies, madam, but could you please come with me.'

She held up her hand. 'Tell your commanding officer that this matter is far from resolved.'

'This way, please.' The constable gripped her by the elbow and started marching her down the stairs. At the bottom, he turned right instead of left, leading her away from the direction of the entrance.

'Isn't the entrance that way?' she said pointing in the opposite direction.

The constable blushed. 'I'm sorry, my lady, but you have to go this way.' They started walking along a long intimidating corridor that was painted white and green. The walls became barer and more uninviting as they went along.

'Now, hang on just a moment. Where exactly are you taking me?' she said.

The constable did not answer but instead he started walking faster, dragging Elle along until they came to a metal door. The constable pulled out a bunch of keys and opened the door.

'Are you arresting me?'

'I'm sorry, ma'am. Could you step inside, please,' the constable said.

'But I haven't done anything,' she shouted.

'Charges are inciting civil unrest, threatening a police officer and conspiring to commit acts of violence with the Suffrage movement,' the constable mumbled. 'Commissioner said not to charge you with breaking into his office. But I am at liberty to do so if you continue to resist. If you would come along quietly, then things will go better for you.'

'Suffrage?' Elle felt the first vestiges of panic rising up within her. 'What on earth are you talking about? I came here to speak to the commissioner about my missing husband.'

'I'm sure you did, my lady,' the constable said without conviction. 'Every woman we bring in here says something like that.' They had reached another heavy metal door. The constable rang a bell and another guard appeared and opened it for them.

'Put this one in with the others. No special treatment. Orders from the top,' he said as he passed Elle through the gate.

'You can't do this. I've done nothing wrong,' she said as the new guard took hold of her.

'Nobody ever does, madam,' he laughed as he dragged her down the corridor.

'Wait! This is a mistake.' Elle tried to struggle as he turned the long key in the lock of what definitely looked like a cell door.

The guard, however, seemed quite adept at keeping hold of reluctant prisoners with only one hand while negotiating locks and keys with the other, and before Elle could protest much more, she was shoved into the gloom of the cell. The door shut behind her with a resonating clang.

'Let me out of here this very minute, you brute!' She banged on the door with her fist, but the iron was so thick that her protestations were ineffectual. All she heard were the receding sounds of footsteps down the corridor. Undeterred, Elle kept knocking.

'There's no point in shouting. You'll only end up hurting your throat. Best to keep up your strength,' a soft voice said behind her.

Elle spun round. There were four other women in the cell, each of whom was watching her gravely.

'Please, do sit down and join us.' A slender young woman in a grey dress spoke. She gave Elle a small smile and gestured at the other end of the bench. 'There is space enough for one more.'

Elle abandoned her attempts to gain the guard's attention and sat down on the bench. 'Thank you,' she said. The shock and mortification of being slung into the clink had made her knees a bit wobbly.

'I like your hat,' she said. She gazed at Elle's outfit with open admiration.

'Thank you,' Elle said. She righted the little net veil that had suffered the brunt of her scuffle with the guard and held out her hand. 'Eleanor Marsh. Call me Elle. How do you do?' she said.

'Christabel Pankhurst. How do you do?' the woman in grey said. 'And these are my fellow Suffragettes,' she said as she introduced the other women.

'How do you do?' Elle said politely.

'And there really is no need to pretend you are someone you are not, my lady. I went to school with the Mandeville girls and my father knows your husband.

We've all seen pictures of you in the paper,' Christabel said.

Elle shook her head. 'I'm sorry. I wasn't trying to create false pretences. It's just so hard to know whom to trust these days,' Elle said.

The other women all murmured in agreement.

'Quite right.' One of the older women spoke. 'We understand your fears, sister.'

'And I'm still getting used to using my new title. Nobody seems to understand that I don't like the fact that it feels as if I blinked out of existence the moment I tied the knot.'

Christabel smiled and took Elle's hands in her own. '*We* understand. All of us object to being treated as if we were nothing more than chattels.'

Elle shivered. Christabel's hands felt like ice. She suddenly realised that the poor girl had on nothing more than a thin linen dress and she was doing her best not to shiver from the cold.

'Been in here long?' Elle said, trying to take her mind off the awful situation she found herself in yet again.

'A few days. But my mother and sister will be along to collect us soon, I'm sure.' Christabel bit her lip.

Elle took off her coat. It was good lambswool, finely woven in a grey tweed pattern with a fine thread of purple and green running through the fabric. 'Would you mind looking after my coat for me for a little while? I'm dressed for outside and this cell is so close, I feel like I can hardly breathe in this old thing.' She handed the coat to Christabel.

The girl hesitated.

'Please. I insist,' she said. 'And feel free to borrow it if you wish.'

Christabel took the coat and wrapped it round her slim shoulders. She gave Elle a grateful smile. 'This is the first time I've ever been arrested. I shall remember to dress more warmly next time.' She looked at the sleeve. 'These colours are lovely.'

'Well, then ladies, I suppose I had better do my best to settle in. There is no way of telling how long I might be here.' Elle fished around inside her reticule and pulled out a tin of her favourite lemon-flavoured boiled sweets. She always carried a small tin with her. Preparedness was the mark of a good pilot. She opened the tin and handed them round. 'Nothing like a lemon drop to keep one's spirits up.'

'We are supposed to be refusing all food. On principle,' said one of the women. She stared at the tin of sweets longingly.

'Oh, don't be silly. Lemon drops are not food. And besides, no one will ever know.' Elle gave her a conspiratorial smile. The Suffragettes gratefully accepted her offer and soon all the women except Christabel were chatting and licking the white powder from the lemon drops off their fingers.

After what seemed like hours, there was suddenly a loud clang and the crunch of metal on metal as the door opened. Elle grabbed the sweets and shoved them into the pocket of Christabel's apron just as the heavy door swung open.

'Someone's come to collect you, Lady Greychester. Time to go,' the guard said.

'Well, ladies, it has been delightful to meet you all. I wish you all the best in your endeavours.'

As Elle stood to go, Christabel reached into the other pocket of her apron and pulled out a flyer. 'Do join us. Deeds, not words,' she whispered as she pressed the pamphlet into Elle's hands. 'And if you ever need anything, just ask.'

Elle inclined her head. 'Take care of yourselves. Stay strong, ladies.'

Christabel gave a brief, brave nod as the guard escorted Elle from the cell.

'Best stay away from that one, my lady. She may look all innocent, but she is nothing but trouble,' he said as they walked along the corridor.

Elle refrained from giving the officer an acidic retort. She'd spent quite enough time on the wrong side of the law today and insulting the police officer that held the keys to one's freedom might be a step too far.

Outside, Neville was waiting beside the car. 'Thank goodness you are safe, my lady.' He looked utterly relieved to see her. 'When you didn't come out of the station for ages, I went inside to ask. They told me you had been arrested, so I went home and we had to tell the professor. He called your uncle, Lord Geoffrey Chance, who managed to sort things out.'

Elle groaned and slumped her shoulders. Calling Uncle Geoffrey was never a good idea and she could just imagine what he was going to say the next time he saw her.

'I didn't know what else to do.' Neville shrugged apologetically.

Outside, the light was fading and the cold fog was starting to curl through the streets.

'Not to worry, Neville. You did the right thing. But I tell you what, let's go home, shall we?' Elle shivered and rubbed her arms to warm herself, suddenly missing her lovely warm coat.

'Right away, my lady.' Neville touched the brim of his hat and opened the door for her.

Elle had spent the entire afternoon behind bars and it had left her feeling tired, hungry and chilled to the bone. She did not want to think how wretched things were for the poor Suffragettes who were still in the cells. Rumour had it that when they refused to eat, the guards force-fed them cold semolina with a funnel and a rubber tube. She shuddered at the thought. She also resolved that she would make enquiries about joining the movement as soon as she found Marsh and all the misunderstandings were cleared.

With a sigh of gratitude, she sank back into the familiar leather seats as the car pulled off into the gathering murk.

Chapter Thirteen

Clothilde had not been in her chambers for ten minutes when Emilian knocked on the door.

'What is it?' she said without bothering to conceal her irritation.

'We have kept the big fish separate for you,' he said.

'Oh yes, I almost forgot. The surprise. Another big fish,' she said somewhat sarcastically.

'He is powerful, this one. He wouldn't submit like the others. Has magic in him, my sister says.'

Clothilde turned to Emilian in surprise. 'Magic, you say?' She pursed her lips.

'That's what we think. But go and see for yourself. He's downstairs, in the jar room.'

'Please wait for me outside. I won't be a moment,' she said as she stepped behind the painted screen that stood in the corner of the room. Disregarding the risks, she closed her eyes and slowly reached out through the barrier. Gently, she eased open another pocket of energy and allowed herself to drink from it, indulging in the sheer luxury of the power as it washed through her. The effect was almost immediate and she instantly felt stronger. She had to admit that the intensity of the energy in London was far stronger than anything she had ever experienced. Once this task was over, she was considering settling here permanently.

Refreshed, she stepped out of her chamber and smiled at Emilian who was patiently waiting for her. 'Well, I suppose I had better go and have a look at your new fish, hadn't I?' she said. 'Might as well check on the new batch of hearts while we are there.'

Her footsteps made almost no sound as she descended the stone stairs that led to her laboratory.

In the room at the bottom of the stairs, Clothilde stopped and stared. Before her was a man chained to a chair that was too small for him. His dark hair was a little long in the front and flopped down over his forehead. But it was his eyes that held her transfixed. They were alive with a passion and intelligence she had rarely encountered before. 'Leave us, Emilian,' she said. 'I wish to be alone with this one.'

Clothilde swallowed as she felt a shiver of anticipation run through her. Emilian's pathetic little sister had, for once in her life, been right. This was no ordinary man.

'Let me go,' he growled as soon as he spotted her. He glared at her with so much anger that she had to resist the urge to take a step back.

She smiled at him. 'Letting you go wouldn't be any fun at all, now would it?'

'Who are you?' he said. His broad shoulders flexed as he strained against his bonds and Clothilde felt her mouth go dry at the sight of all that muscle and pent-up anger.

He was tall, too. She could tell from the way his legs

folded underneath the chair. Had she finally found the one she had been looking for all her life?

'Speak, I say!' he barked.

Clothilde gave a little start, but composed herself. She was the one who was in charge here, after all.

He was definitely dangerous, though. She could smell very old magic on him. It was faint and intermingled with the smell of sweat and sandalwood, but it was undeniable.

She sashayed over to the man and placed a hand on his shoulder.

He flinched and tried to shake her off.

'Be calm,' she murmured, allowing a few moments for her manipulative powers to wash over him.

He resisted and shoved her power back at her with a jolt. 'I said unhand me, witch! Right now. Before I become really angry.'

She let go of him. My, but he really was strong. And there must be knowledge of how to use that power within him too. She had never encountered anyone not of the travelling folk like Emilian and his sister who could resist her influence like this.

She started playing with his hair, gently probing his mind for information with her touch.

He pulled his head away. 'Don't you dare touch me, Shadow-whore,' he spat.

The insult stung and she lifted her hand away. He was making her angry. Angry and excited. She felt the darkness starting to swirl inside her. 'I would be careful about how you address me,' she murmured.

The man met her gaze. 'And if I were you, I would start running, because once I am out of these shackles, you will regret ever having crossed paths with me!' He yanked against the wrist manacles that bound him and the wood of the chair made an ominous cracking sound.

Clothilde felt a slight frisson of fear. What if he got loose? This man would surely overpower her. Images of them wrapped in an embrace flooded through her mind, both fearful and thrilling at the same time. Could she afford to take such a chance to see what he would do? She bit her lip in a moment of indecision.

Did she need to tell the Consortium about this one? He could be hers forever. Just think of the sweet magic they could make together once he submitted to her will.

Almost in answer to her thoughts, the man roared and yanked at the chains again. One of the spokes of the chair gave way and shattered.

The violence of his struggle galvanised her into action. Yes, he would be hers. She would keep him all to herself. He would be her little secret.

Another chair spoke broke as the man struggled and Clothilde watched on, her mind whirling with possibilities. He needed taming. Allowing him free rein while her plans were still forming would not do. But later might be a different matter. Yes, later, when all she had set out to do had been achieved, this man would rule by her side. That was certainly why he had been sent to her like this.

Quickly she stepped up to him and placed her hands on the sides of his temples. She was suddenly grateful for the little bit of extra power she had taken before coming down here.

'Now hold still and this will all go better for the both

of us,' she said. She summoned all she had within her and plunged her energy into his head. The impact of their spirit-selves colliding was like running face first into a rock wall. She gasped and reeled, but took a breath and plunged back into his psyche again.

He roared and she felt him straining against her. Another chair spindle cracked and they both fell to the ground.

Then quite suddenly, she broke through his defences. And in an instant, they were both swirling inside his mind. But this was no gentle, graceful dance. Everywhere she looked, he slammed against her, blocking her view.

He was protecting something, hiding it from her, and it was taking all his strength to do it, she realised with a growing sense of excitement.

She peered past his swirling barriers, deeper and deeper into the dark recesses of his mind. She had never encountered a man whose psyche was so layered. It was utterly breathtaking.

He was a Warlock, she noted, with equal measures of apprehension and excitement. And his power seemed to be bound and tightly strapped down by a very strong spell.

Clothilde gasped as she watched him struggle to release his power from its restraints. He was fighting her with every fibre of his being, straining with raw effort of will against the magical bonds that sealed his power.

It's an effort to hold him with his power bound, she thought. What would happen if he freed himself? And why would one so powerful seek to do this to himself? It was a mystery she had no time to unravel.

The remainder of the chair cracked again and he rolled

over, partly covering her with his body. She wasn't going to hold him for much longer. But she wanted him. The thought of him belonging to her was utterly irresistible.

She wanted to lose herself inside his mind where he would reveal all his secrets to her, but she daren't wait any longer.

She let go of him and returned to her physical consciousness to gather herself. Outside, thunder rumbled and bolts of lightning coursed through the building.

Clothilde reached up for the lightning, which had been steadily building up around them, and focused all of her power on him.

There was an almighty flash of purple light. She felt the Warlock's mind fill with the darkness she sent. Black and viscous, like hot tar, it slid through him, obliterating all thoughts and memories before it. And then, just before everything inside his mind went dark, Clothilde thought she caught a glimpse of an image of a woman, but it was gone before she had time to take it in.

His body went limp; all that had made up this man was extinguished.

Gently she rolled him on to his back. His handsome face was pale but relaxed, as if he were asleep. The only detectable sign of life was the gentle rise and fall of his chest.

'Hush now, my dearest. It will all soon be better,' she murmured against his cheek.

'Emilian!' she called.

He was in the room within moments, as if he had been waiting just outside the door.

'Help me get him on to that table,' she said.

Emilian helped her lift the unconscious man on to her operating table.

'Make sure he is strapped in properly,' she ordered. She was not going to take any chances. Not now that she had found him.

'Leave us now,' she said to Emilian once the man had been secured. 'I don't want to be disturbed. Is that understood?'

'Yes, mistress.' Emilian bowed and closed the door after him as he left.

Clothilde found herself humming softly as she started unbuttoning the man's collar and shirt. As she had hoped, the wall of chest that was revealed under the layers of waistcoat and shirt was broad and strong. Gently she ran her fingers over the fine sprinkling of chest hair that adorned it. Yes, it was a fine chest that would hold its new heart beautifully.

She allowed herself one more lingering look at the beautiful angles of his face before setting to work.

'You were made for me, dear one,' she murmured. 'And yet, I do not know your name.' The man did not – could not – answer. 'But you will be mine. And when you awake we can both choose new names for ourselves. Just you wait and see.'

She walked up to one of the cabinets and unlocked it. Inside was the polished case that the Clockmaker had given her. She opened the case and carefully selected one of the clockwork hearts nestling within the purple velvet.

Back at the table, Clothilde carefully lined up her surgical instruments in a row on the table next to her. For once, this was going to be a labour of love and she wanted to take her time. She would make sure that all the incisions were perfect.

'Yes, you will be beautiful afterwards. Not like the others,' she murmured.

Slowly the scalpel slid though skin and muscle, separating bone and cartilage. And as she worked she started humming to herself. It was a lonely, sinister tune from her childhood.

'Just think of all the beautiful dark magic you and I will make together one day, my love,' she whispered. 'All we need to do is free you. And once you are free, we will be together forever,' she said as she raised her bloodied hands in order to complete the next step. 'I will be the only one who holds the key to your heart.'

And all the while, the thunder and lightning roiled outside.

Chapter Fourteen

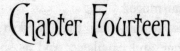

Elle sipped the nutmeg-laced milk Mrs Hinges had brought her as she stared into the fire. Outside, the rain sifted down in soft relentless sheets into the inky blackness. Tonight's storm was fiercer than usual. The skyline of the city was illuminated each time the lightning flashed across the sky.

She shivered as the draft from one of the casements whispered against her skin. There was something ill in the air tonight. It was something dark and ominous, she couldn't quite put her finger on what, but it was there all right.

'Is anything the matter, my dear?' the professor said. They were in the small drawing room.

'Apart from the fact that my husband is missing and that I was arrested today?' Elle said with a little more force than was necessary.

'Oh, you know what I mean,' the professor said.

'Sorry, Papa. It's been a fraught day. I did not mean to be short with you.'

'Never you mind, my dear. But do tell me what is on your mind. Sometimes it helps to discuss a matter. You know, two minds are more likely to find a solution than one.'

'Police Commissioner Willoughby is definitely hiding something,' Elle said. 'And there is nothing as dangerous as a powerful man with a secret.'

'You are not wrong on that count. But was it really necessary to antagonise him enough to arrest you?' the professor said gently.

'But that's exactly my point, Papa. I did nothing to provoke him. Locking me up was nothing more than a warning. He wants me to understand that he won't stand for me interfering in his business.'

The professor sighed and puffed on his pipe. 'Your uncle was not amused.'

'Well, I am not amused by Uncle Geoffrey either. He's so . . . so judgemental,' Elle said. 'And if the truth be told, I don't even really care about the commissioner's business. The only thing I am interested in is finding Marsh.'

'It's possible that Willoughby may really know nothing,' the professor said.

'I very much doubt that.' She set her cup down on the mantelpiece. 'I have some business to attend to. Please excuse me, Papa.' She kissed her father's cheek.

'Where on earth are you going at this time of night?' the professor said with a look of alarm.

Elle smiled. 'I shan't leave the house, I promise.'

'That is exactly what I was afraid you might say.'

'I have to look for him. I cannot just sit here doing nothing,' she said.

The professor sighed. 'Very well. Go and do what you must. Just remember that we are all here to help. Don't shut us out.'

'I won't, Papa. I promise,' Elle said, pausing at the drawing-room door. 'Goodnight.'

'Goodnight,' the professor said.

Upstairs, Elle opened up the secret room and set about lighting the candles in the chandeliers and sconces. Soon her sanctum was glowing in a soft warm light. She picked a velvet cushion off one of the benches and placed it inside the mosaic circle. No one said anything about discomfort being a requirement for being an oracle and the pillow would help against the chill of the stone floor.

She stepped out of her kid leather slippers and into the circle.

Around her the voice of the Spirit was silent. So her prediction had been wrong. They had not returned. The voices of oracles past were clearly not happy with her either. 'Well, you are simply going to have to join the queue of people who are displeased with me. Right behind my uncle Geoffrey, my husband and that pilot who lost his ship to me,' she said.

There was no answer.

She took a deep breath and focused herself as she settled down on the cushion. She concentrated for a moment until she found the barrier that divided Shadow and Light. Her breathing slowed and she felt the first stirrings of her Shadow-self separating from her physical body. She frowned and concentrated on maintaining the connection, but she was apprehensive, skittish even. She had never done this completely on her own before. Marsh had always been just outside the door, keeping guard over her while she was vulnerable. He always seemed to be there for her. Wasn't it strange that she had never noticed that about him?

The last thought fled from her mind as she was met by a sudden rush of aether. Quicker than a thought, she was propelled through the barrier and into the Realm of Shadow.

Around her was only darkness. She concentrated on imagining the place she wanted to visit and she felt herself shift with alarming speed until she landed with a thump on the ground.

The last time she was here, she had not been alone.

On their wedding night, once they were alone in the dark, Marsh had pulled her into his arms and together they had slipped into the Shadow. A golden meadow had risen up around them almost instantaneously.

'I've been wanting to come back here for the longest time,' he said to her.

She felt her heartbeat accelerate. 'So have I,' she whispered.

'And this time, there is no need for restraint. What do you say, Mrs Marsh?'

She gave him a wicked smile. 'I should say that I agree.' The last time they had met in this place, they had not been married. And there were many things that held them apart. This time things were very different.

'I have something for you.' Marsh raised his hand.

Elle looked up at him in surprise. On his palm lay a wedding band. 'I thought you said that we were to wear no wedding bands,' she said.

'I may have told a small lie there. I know it's not quite the fashion for men to wear wedding rings, but I want the whole world to know that we belong together, so I have one too.' He opened his other hand and there, on his outstretched palm was a second larger ring, almost identical to the first.

Both rings appeared to be made from a white metal that shone brighter than silver. When she looked more closely, she saw that his ring was actually made up of many fine strands, intricately woven together to form a band. The smaller ring had tiny sparkly stones threaded on to the metal.

'It's beautiful. I don't think I've ever seen anything like it,' she said.

'I asked for one of the wyrd-weavers to give me a strand of silk. Yours has flowers from this glade woven into it. I thought they would be pretty.'

'Wyrd-weavers?' she said.

Marsh laughed 'The three sisters. Three women; half maiden, half spider. One weaves the future, one the present and one the past. Together they weave and spin the intricate web that determines the fate of each and every living thing. Adele helped me find a goldsmith who would forge these for us. You would be amazed if you knew some of the acquaintances that fairy has.'

'Nothing about Adele would surprise me,' Elle said.

'These rings are forged from the same strand of silk. Even though they are two circles, they are forever joined as one. Just as our fates are. Look.' He held up the two rings and Elle saw the fine strand shimmering between them.

'When worn with intent, the wearers are joined together and nothing, save their decision to be severed, can ever break that bond.' His expression grew serious. 'I never want to lose you,' he said.

She smiled up at him. 'I never want to lose you either.'

'This is to show you that no matter where we are in the world, we will always be able to find one another. What do you say?'

Elle lifted the ring off his waiting palm and slipped it on to the ring finger of her left hand. As it slipped over her knuckle, she felt the faint tremor of Shadow magic move through her as the ring fastened itself to her. 'Together forever,' she whispered. 'I love you.'

Marsh slipped the bigger ring on to his finger and as he did so, Elle felt the strange sensation of something locking into place.

'The bond between us is now sealed. And it is more permanent than any promises that may have been made in the Realm of Light.'

Elle simply nodded, for she was too caught up in the moment for words.

'Forever,' he whispered as he lifted her hand and kissed it.

'For as long as we both exist,' she answered, finally finding her voice. Then she lifted her mouth to kiss him.

Elle's entire body shook from the sudden pain she felt at the memory of that night. It ripped through her with a physical force that dragged her back to the here and now.

She sat up and blinked. The candles had burned out and she was lying on the floor with her arms around the velvet pillow.

She sighed and rubbed her face. So much for her search efforts. Somehow she had managed to direct her powers into the past rather than into the future. This was certainly something new. Not very helpful, mind.

Somewhere deep inside the house, she heard the clock chime. She counted the sounds silently until it reached seven. Was it really seven o'clock in the morning? She felt as if she had closed her eyes only a few moments before.

Elle stood up and slipped out of the secret chamber, taking care to close the panel behind her. She was cold and her muscles ached from sleeping on the cold floor.

Outside, the darkness had made space for the first murky light of dawn. This morning the swirling fog was so thick that she could hardly see the street down below.

But through the shadows, she spotted a funeral carriage with two perfectly matched black stallions pulled up outside the house. Elle squinted through the murk. The doors of the carriage bore the red insignia of two dragons facing one another with a sword between them.

Elle let out a little squeak of delight and ran to her dressing room to find some clothes. Thanks be to the wonders of speedy modern travel, she thought.

The Baroness Loisa Belododia had arrived in London.

A commotion had already erupted outside the drawing room by the time Elle reached the bottom of the stairs.

'Madam, I must insist that you go to your rest now,' she heard Caruthers say.

'What nonsense! Do you see any sunlight? Yes? No? Because all I see is fog and rain in this place. Now get out of my way before I lose my temper and decide to have you for my lunch,' a woman said in an accent that was a tad heavy on the Rs.

Elle opened the doors to find Loisa Belododia standing in the middle of the big drawing room, hands on her hips. She was dressed entirely in the most exquisite black crêpe de chine. The hem and sleeves of her dress were artfully ragged with wisps of delicate handmade lace. In addition, she was covered from head to toe in a long black veil of the sheerest chiffon to ward against any stray shafts of sunlight.

'Loisa!' Elle rushed up to her and hugged her friend. 'You came! But at this time of day? How on earth did you get here so fast?'

Loisa waved a dismissive hand that made her veil ripple. 'Yes, it is disgustingly late, but here I am. I was en route to Paris to do a bit of shopping when they telegraphed your message to me on board, so I took the first berth to London that I could find. It was third class too.' She shuddered. 'See, these are the things I do for my friends.' The baroness pressed her shrouded ruby lips against Elle's cheeks, once on each side. Then she looked over her shoulder at the maid who was hovering by the windows. 'Oh, for goodness' sake, girl. Close those drapes. Do you want me to turn to ash? If I do, you are the one who will have to sweep this beautiful Aubusson.' She tapped the rug with her fine silk slipper.

Poor Edie quailed. Elle let go of Loisa and set about orchestrating the closing of the heavy drawing-room drapes to seal out the faint light of the drizzly morning outside.

She lit the spark lamps just as Loisa raised her veil.

The Nightwalker looked tired and there were smudges under her beautiful dark eyes, but she was smiling.

'So what is so urgent that you bid me to come to London at this most wretched time of year? That infernal passenger airship nearly went down over the channel with the high winds.' Loisa took off her gloves and hat and handed them to Edie who curtseyed and left the room as fast as she could. 'Darling, you look pale. Have you been sleeping properly? And where is Hugh? I need to have a word with that man for mistreating you like this.' The Nightwalker spoke in a steady stream of sharp questions which was very unlike her usual charming and composed nature. Elle noted the slight look of worry in her eyes.

'Oh Loisa, it was so good of you to come. I didn't know who else to turn to.' Elle sat down on the divan before the fire. 'Let me ring for refreshments. There is much I need to tell you and most of it is not good news.'

Loisa settled herself in the chair opposite Elle and folded her perfect white hands in her lap. 'Well, out with it then,' she said.

Elle took a deep breath and proceeded to tell Loisa everything that had happened, pausing only to pour the tea, which had arrived shortly after she had rung the bell pull.

'*Mon Dieu!*' Loisa muttered. 'This is dark sorcery indeed.'

'He has now been missing for three days and so far I have not been able to find even the slightest clue as to where he might be,' Elle said.

'Then we have no time to lose. Where shall we start?'

Loisa looked around the room as if for inspiration.

'Dearest Loisa. You must be exhausted. Perhaps you should get some rest. I will have something sent up to you for your dinner. Your coffin should be upstairs now, so please do go to ground.' Elle put her hand on her friend's arm and smiled. 'Mrs Hinges has Caruthers and Neville out looking by day. I will call you if there is any news. As soon as the sun sets tonight our search can begin in earnest.'

Loisa pressed her hand to her mouth and stifled a yawn. 'Perhaps you are right. But what are you going to do all day while I rest?'

Elle smiled at her. 'I think I have an idea. I'll tell you whether it worked when you rise.'

Chapter Fifteen

Back in her room, Elle got out of her morning dress and slipped into a set of comfortable silk robes. She had given instructions to Mrs Hinges that for the duration of the baroness's stay they would all switch to nocturnal hours. There were a few startled looks, but the promise of double wages to make up for the inconvenience seemed to placate the staff who were by now accustomed to the odd goings-on that pervaded Greychester House.

This was just as well, for Elle did not want to be disturbed. She pulled the brass lever and stepped back inside her secret chamber.

This time, she paused only to light the one fresh candle she had brought with her from downstairs. Last night's foray into the Shadow Realm had not been particularly successful, but now she was ready to try again.

She closed her eyes and stepped into the circle.

Almost immediately, she felt the power caught in the barrier surge up and envelop her. She released her hold of it and within seconds she was crossing the divide with a speed and force she had never experienced before.

Light and shadow swirled around her until she landed

on the ground. She was back in the golden field, but the place had lost all its vibrancy.

The tiny jewelled flowers had dried and withered until they were completely drained of colour and the light around her had turned from gold to bronze like the sepia of an over-exposed photograph. She did not pause to marvel at the changes in the place though, for time moved differently here and she could not waste a moment of it.

Elle twisted her wedding band round her finger and composed herself. 'Well, Hugh, let's see if these rings really work.' The world of Shadow swirled around her, brushing up against her skin. Ever so gently, she allowed her energy to reach out and find the fine thread that ran from her hand. There, under her fingers, the fine silk stretched out far off into the darkness.

Carefully, she lifted the thread and followed it, gently winding it around her fingers as she walked. The thread seemed to disappear into her own ring the moment it touched her hand and so she walked on. The question as to who was the fish and who was the fisherman was one she did not really want to consider.

She walked for what seemed like hours. The path wound through the strange and undulating landscape. Everything was completely silent, except for the sounds of her footsteps crunching on the dry ground underfoot.

As she walked, the brown sepia tones around her grew darker and the world changed to monochrome. Black-limbed trees grew thicker and thicker, their branches clawing at the sky, until she found herself in the middle of a dark forest.

Every now and then, she caught the flicker of eyes

glinting through the thick mist that shrouded the trees. She was not alone.

The path through the forest twisted and wound itself this way and that. Elle tripped over tree roots and slid on slimy rotting leaves but she kept moving. Her only guide was the fine silver thread that stretched out before her.

After what seemed like days of walking, Elle stopped and rested against one of the trees. She was exhausted and close to despair. The fine strand stretched out before her, with no end in sight.

She studied the rotting stump under her foot. It looked exactly like the rotting stump she had tripped over a while before, but there was no way of telling whether this was the same stump or not. She was normally an excellent navigator, but in the Shadow all sense of direction was different and with a growing sense of dread, Elle realised that she might be lost.

And being lost in the Realm of Shadow was a very bad thing, because in this place it meant never getting out again.

The little creatures in the trees chattered and hissed, now closer than before. One dropped down from one of the branches. It was the size of either a very large, hairless rat or a small dog, depending on which way you looked at it. Elle flinched at the sight of its leathery skin and disconcertingly monkey features that were almost human. It hissed and chattered its razor-sharp teeth. Her despair was making them bold. They could smell her fear.

She lifted the silver thread and tugged it gently. It yielded and came towards her without any resistance. Was Marsh even on the other side of it? She sighed and rubbed her face. For all she knew, she could have been following nothing.

'Lovely evening for a walk, don't you think?' Someone spoke from the darkness to the left of her.

Elle felt the hairs on the back of her neck rise up. 'Who's there? Show yourself,' she demanded.

She heard a soft rustle and an old man in a cloak stepped out of the mists.

'Who are you? What is your name?' she said.

'Those are bold questions to ask of a stranger,' he said. Carefully he opened his cloak to reveal the rather old-fashioned lantern he was carrying. The golden light that flickered behind the glass was warmly mesmerising in this miserable place.

'Doesn't hurt to know who one is dealing with,' Elle said, dragging her gaze away from the light.

The old man nodded slowly. 'Well, I suppose it doesn't. The name is Old Jack. How do you do?'

He was short in stature with a shaggy beard. The dark cloak that hid the lantern fell all the way down to his feet. And when he moved, his shadow rippled in the same way light refracted off the sheen of a soap bubble. In the Realm of Light, shadows were dark. Here, in the Shadow, it was the opposite.

Jack stood perfectly still as if he was waiting for her to say something.

'Eleanor,' she said.

He laughed. 'Well, now that we have both lied to one another, I think the game may begin, girl-with-no-shadow.' He pointed at the ground to where her own shadow should lie, but there was none.

'There is no game and I shall be on my way in a moment, if you don't mind,' Elle said.

He laughed and shook his head. 'My dear girl, anyone can tell that you are completely and hopelessly lost. Are you not?'

'And what if I was? It is no business of yours, surely?'

He smiled at her and his face crinkled into a mosaic of wrinkles and bad, yellowing teeth. 'Oh, I don't think that is entirely correct. You see, these are my woods and so anyone walking in them would be my business.'

'I am merely passing through here. And I am not lost. I know exactly where I am going.' She moved her hand behind her back so he would not see the strand.

But it was too late. 'Ah yes, a strand of wyrd silk. I haven't seen one of those in many years.' Old Jack looked down at her hand. 'The dip-dibs told me someone was chasing a strand of light through here. But one should never listen to a dip-dib. They are all terrible liars. Will do anything to sink their little teeth into your flesh. Only fresh blood will slake their thirst.'

'Thank you for the advice,' Elle said drily.

'Are you sure of the love of the person who is on the other side of that?'

'Of course I am,' Elle said.

'And are you sure that you feel the same?'

'Absolutely.'

'Hmm. I hope for your sake that this is true, because unless your intentions are equally matched, the magic that binds you will not draw you together.'

Old Jack lifted his lantern so the light could follow the fine white thread that disappeared off into the darkness of the trees before them. 'I don't mean to be rude, but I have to say that your little thread looks a bit slack to me. I wouldn't rely on this love if I were you, my dear.'

Elle stood up and straightened her robes. 'I'm sorry, sir, but that really is none of your concern. Now, if you would excuse me, I shall be on my way. Thank you for allowing me the little rest here.'

Old Jack lifted his lantern and peered at her in the yellow light. 'You shouldn't be so hasty. I think you and I have much more to discuss before you go.' He smiled at her in a most sinister manner.

Elle took a step away from him. 'If you don't mind, I really am in a frightful hurry. So tell me truthfully: what is it going to take for you to leave me alone?'

'Oh, it's not that simple, my dear. As I said before, these are my woods and you are trespassing. And if I order it so, you will wander round and round in circles here until you collapse, wyrd silk or not.' Jack scratched his shaggy beard. 'And these woods are full of creatures who hunger for the flesh of the freshly dead. Don't you, little dip-dibs?'

The air filled with the sound of hissing and chattering in answer to Jack's question.

Elle sighed. 'All right, what will it take for you to give me permission to walk through your wood?'

Old Jack's smile broadened. 'Well, seeing as I am in a good mood, I will make it worth your while. I will let you pass unhindered, but in return, you must allow me a little holiday on the Light side. It's been such a long time since I've been able to visit.'

'You know the rules,' Elle said.

'Yes, I must promise to do no harm. But what does that really mean? And how can you expect to do no harm when you are a creature whose very existence depends on it?'

Elle shrugged. This discussion was far too philosophical and Shadow creatures were notoriously illogical when it came to such things.

'How about this as a proposal?' she said. 'Let me out of these woods and show me the way to the other end of this thread and I will agree to meet with you at another time to discuss a visit to the Light. I cannot promise that I will be able to find a way around the oath you will need to take in order to cross the barrier, but I can promise to see what I can do.'

Old Jack nodded. 'A fair offer. It is wise to refrain from promising things that do not lie within one's gift. But what you propose is not enough. Your end of the scales is still too light, my dear.'

'It is all I have to offer at this stage,' Elle said.

Jack shrugged. 'Well, making sure that people get lost is so much in my nature, I am not sure I will be able to overcome it for your sake.'

'What else do you want then?' she said.

'Hmm, now there is a question I am not often asked,' Old Jack said. 'A holiday to the Light side where I can do what I will, unfettered by rules and oaths. If that is not possible, you must agree that you owe me a favour. A favour I can call upon at any time.'

Elle considered his words. It was definitely a trick, but right now she was in no position to bargain. In her blind haste to find Marsh, she had foolishly wandered into the clutches of a Shadow creature and he could keep her here as long as it took to get what he wanted.

'There really is no point in delaying the inevitable,' Jack said as if he had read her thoughts.

'Very well, I agree that I shall owe you a favour,' Elle said.

She could deal with this later. And who knows, the Fey had such a distorted view of time, that he may even only decide to call up the favour a hundred years from now, when she was long dead. All in all it was not ideal, but it was the best bargain she could make right now.

Old Jack's smile grew wider and he held out a gnarled hand. 'Then let us shake hands and be friends.'

Elle took the old man's hand into hers and shook it calmly. She felt a little tickle of magic in her palm that told her that the bargain had been sealed. She let go of Jack's hand as fast as she could.

'Come along, then.' He lifted his lantern and gestured towards the darkness. 'It's not far.'

They walked along through the forest in silence. The light from the lantern cast an eerie yellow glow on the path before them. And although her travelling companion was slightly odious, not tripping over things in the dark was certainly an improvement on before. As they walked, the trees grew thinner and shafts of light poured down to the ground.

Jack stopped walking and held up his lantern. 'This is the end of my domain, Lady Oracle,' he murmured. 'Walk on and be on your way. We shall see each other soon to discuss our bargain.'

'Goodbye Jack, and thank you for your help,' Elle said, but he had already disappeared.

She turned to survey the landscape. Before her lay a bleak open plain where the sky and the ground were both the colour of bleached bone. The only other thing inhabiting this place was a tiding of very large and scruffy-looking magpies. They sat, huddled in the white branches of a dead tree. The sun and the shadow magic reflected off their mother of pearl black feathers, interspersed with the white. The magpies gazed at her with their unblinking, beady eyes.

'Dark! Dark!' One of the birds let out a rasping squawk that echoed across the emptiness. The sound made Elle jump, but she bit her lip and pressed on, all the while holding on to the filament she hoped would lead her to Marsh.

Apart from the magpies, there was nothing but the whistle of lonely wind. But as she walked, the wind brought with it a strange ticking sound.

Suddenly, the magpies startled. They rose up, as one, from the tree in a mass of black and white feathers, squawking wildly as they flew.

The ticking grew louder and louder, a macabre metronome that echoed across the landscape. Eventually it grew so loud that it felt as if the noise was resonating in her very bones. Elle looked around to find the source of the sound, but around her was nothing but bleakness. Jack's wood was far away now.

The ticking was an unwelcome reminder of the awful dreams she had been having of late.

Elle swallowed down her fear and walked on, hoping

desperately that she would find Marsh before she ran into whatever it was that made that sound, but they appeared on the horizon all the same.

At first, the figures were nothing more than a few smudges of dark and light on the horizon. Elle squinted in the bright, eerie light but it was almost impossible to make out anything more.

Time and space worked differently here in the Shadow and in the blink of an eye, they had crossed the dry shimmering distance that separated her from them.

They stood very still, in a huddle, not looking at anything. And all the while, the sound of ticking rose up from their midst. It was a terrible sound of mechanical unison. Un-human. Un-dead.

With a growing sense of horror, Elle realised that her fine silver thread led straight into the middle of these creatures.

She walked up as close to the huddle of blank bodies as she dared. They did not move or acknowledge her in any way. Slowly she reached up to touch what looked like the outline of a shoulder, but her fingers slipped right through the image. These creatures were nothing but incandescent mirages. They were nothing.

How strange, she thought. Did that mean that these were not creatures of Shadow? Was their presence here simply an imprint of what was happening on the other side of the barrier?

This was so far beyond the reaches of her knowledge of these things, that she had no idea.

Gathering up all of her courage, Elle pulled at the filament between her fingers. The flock of undead wavered like sea grass under water. Some of the creatures turned and looked at her, but their faces were nothing more than blank spaces. It was as if the essence of whoever these people had once been was stripped from them, leaving only an empty husk behind.

She felt resistance give between her fingers and pulled again, this time with more force. The bodies moved again, and, from their midst, one of the creatures stumbled. Its left arm was extended as if it had been lassoed.

Despite herself, Elle let out a small cry of despair. For there was no mistaking the height and dimensions of the body she knew so well. She had found her husband. Or at least she had found what was left of him.

The outline tilted his head to one side and reached out to her. In that moment, Elle wanted to wrap him in her arms and take him home, but she knew she could not. The infinite barrier of Shadow and Light that lay between here and home separated them. And with a growing sense of despair, Elle realised that there was nothing they could do but stare at one another from across the divide.

In the distance the magpies sounded the alarm. She saw them circle round and round as the sky overhead darkened.

Thunder rumbled and, in the distance, bright flashes of lightning split the sky.

'Run! Run!' the magpies squawked as they flew past.

Elle spun round. The horizon had turned gunmetal grey. Angry clouds boiled and multiplied with sinister speed. Something was coming. She felt the weight of it on her chest, threatening to push the air from her lungs.

Elle started shivering and with a growing sense of apprehension she realised that she was unarmed and vulnerable in this strange place. Whatever was coming was powerful and obviously very dangerous.

The bank of cloud was almost here.

Elle looked about. There was nowhere to run and nowhere to hide. Going back to Jack's wood for shelter was not an option either.

Wishing herself home in an instant was possible, but also a bad idea. The last thing she wanted was for the thing that was making the cloud to follow her to the portal she used regularly.

In that moment, Elle realised she would not be able to take Marsh with her. 'I love you. And I will come back to find you,' she whispered. Slowly, she started unwinding the thread that held them together.

The wind whirled around her and Marsh disappeared into the waiting herd of shadows.

The storm was upon her now. The clouds were so low that Elle ducked and threw herself to the side, narrowly escaping a bright bolt of lightning as it struck the place where she had been standing.

Whatever was in those clouds, it wanted her away from here. More bolts of lightning rained down around her. She smelled the crackle of spark in the air and realised that she needed to run.

In a moment of desperation, she reached into the barrier that divided Shadow and Light. This was a very dangerous thing to do, but she had no choice. She felt the energy give and space opened up big enough to slip through. This practice was tightly guarded and controlled, but then she cared little about what the Council thought at the best of times.

Stepping inside the barrier felt like plunging into cold water. She held her breath and peered through the distortion. On the one side she could see the brightness of the Realm of Light and on the other the greenish-brown murk of the Shadow side. As carefully as she could, she swam across to the Light side. Through the shimmering ripples she could see the inside of a cavernous warehouse. She could see rough-brick and iron pillars. The glass-paned roof vault stretched high overhead and even here, in this place of nowhere, the ominous sound of ticking resonated through her. The frisson of danger was almost palpable and she shrank away from it. This place on the Light side seemed as dangerous as the one in the Shadow she had left. The ominous shapes of the undead materialised from the gloom. And while they seemed quite harmless in the Realm of Shadow, she was not so sure that the same would be true in the Realm of Light. And there was no way she was going to risk running into those creatures on her own.

There was nowhere to run and she was running out of breath.

Elle closed her eyes and plunged back to the Shadow side. She felt the barrier give and then she landed on sand, spluttering and gasping for air.

The sky above her had turned bone white again and everything was silent.

'Gone! Gone!' the magpies shouted from their tree.

Elle looked around. She was all alone in this desolate place. Marsh was gone and there was nothing she could do about it.

Looking about one more time to make sure she was safe, Elle closed her eyes and willed herself home with all her might.

She felt a wave of energy flood through her and in a single breath she was back on the mosaic floor in the little room behind the mantelpiece. Gasping and utterly exhausted, she crawled from the room and on to the bed, where she finally fell into an exhausted sleep.

Chapter Sixteen

Loisa was waiting for Elle at the bottom of the stairs when she came down for dinner that evening.

'My dear, you look so tired,' Loisa exclaimed. 'What on earth have you been up to while I was asleep?'

'We need to speak,' Elle said.

'I thought as much. Let's go to the library where the others won't hear us,' Loisa said.

Elle led her friend through to the library and there, by the comforting light of the fire, told her about what she had found in the Shadow that day.

'That was a very big risk to take.' Loisa's perfect black ringlets bounced as she shook her head in amazement. 'It sounds to me as if you got away just in time.'

'I think you might be right.' Elle twisted her wedding band around her finger as she spoke. 'And there is the matter of the bargain with this Jack creature.'

Loisa pursed her lips. 'I would keep an eye out for that one. The Fey are notorious tricksters. Speaking of which, where is that little splash of green you keep as a pet?' Loisa looked around the room to see if the absinthe fairy was listening.

Elle sighed. 'Adele disappeared around the same time as Hugh did. No one has seen her.'

'Such a pity. She would have been most helpful right now. But that's their way. Around when you don't need them; away the moment you need them most.'

Elle smiled to herself. Nightwalkers and fairies were notoriously adversarial. It was a dislike that went back more centuries than anyone could remember.

'He's definitely here on our side of the realms. I say we go and look for him,' Elle said.

Loisa tapped her black satin slipper against the rug as she considered the matter. 'You said he was in a large building. Perhaps a factory or a warehouse?'

'It certainly looked that way,' Elle said.

'Perhaps we should start looking for him in these. Surely there can't be too many cavernous warehouses in London, no?'

'That is exactly what I was thinking.' Elle was not as confident as Loisa. It seemed to her that there were a great deal of warehouses in London, but she did not want to diminish Loisa's enthusiasm.

'And you are sure that the police will be of no help?'

'Very sure. In fact, I wouldn't be surprised if the police commissioner himself was involved. We can trust no one.'

Loisa stood and straightened her gown. 'Well, then. I would suggest that you and I go for a stroll after dinner.'

Elle hugged the Nightwalker. 'Oh Loisa, thank you.'

Outside, the relentless drizzle sifted down across streets and grey slate rooftops. Loisa shook her black parasol to rid it of the wet. The weather did not bother her physically, in fact Nightwalkers preferred the cold, but she did object to it ruining her hair. 'Nothing is worse than London drizzle for ruining ringlets,' she said to Elle as they walked.

Elle was wearing one of Marsh's hats to accompany her usual 'work' outfit of jodhpurs and calf-length leather coat. The hat was a terribly modern fedora he had purchased on a whim. It was a little too big for her, but it kept the rain off her face, which was what mattered.

'I think that getting our curls wet is probably the least of our worries right now,' Elle said. They were trudging through the muddy streets around Limehouse. It was three o'clock in the morning and the place was completely deserted.

'None of these warehouses look even remotely familiar,' she said. 'And there are so many of them along the Thames, we will never find it at this rate.'

'Oh, don't exaggerate. At the very least, we now know he is not in this place,' said Loisa trying to sound cheerful.

Elle bit down on her teeth to stop them from chattering. They had been walking for so long that the wet had seeped all the way through her coat in the way that only London drizzle could. Her boots and jodhpurs were splattered with mud and the linen shirt she wore stuck to her skin in a most miserable way. The rim of her fedora hat drooped under the weight of the drizzle. Normally her outlandish outfit kept her warm, even in the coldest of high airstreams, but here on the ground, her clothes were proving to be less than waterproof.

'You are cold,' Loisa said in a matter-of-fact tone. She was not looking all too dry and composed herself.

'A b–bit,' Elle said. 'But let's keep walking and I'll warm up.' She was not about to let Loisa show her up in this endeavour.

'But I think we should make a start for home. It is only a few hours until sunrise and I don't want to be caught by the sun.'

'Good idea,' Elle said. Even though she wanted to keep searching, she had to admit that the prospect of being warm and dry was very appealing. 'Let's take the road that leads along the riverside.'

As they walked, Elle scanned each of the riverside warehouses to see if any of them was the one she had seen from the Shadow. Some were too small. Others were the wrong shape. Some were made of wood. Some were clearly so derelict that not even the undead would consider living in them. None matched the place she had seen.

They trudged along in the dark in miserable silence. The squelchy muck covered their boots and stained Loisa's sodden skirts. Their search so far was proving to be most miserable and unsuccessful.

Suddenly Loisa stopped and looked over her shoulder. She motioned for Elle to stay still. Then she turned and walked on.

'What is it?' Elle whispered.

'I'm not sure. I thought I heard footsteps. I think someone might be following us.'

Elle unclipped the Colt 1878 Frontier revolver she carried, but left it in the holster attached to the custom-made corset she wore over her shirt. There was no telling who would be out at this time of night, but if Loisa was on alert, then it was wise to be prepared.

At Waterloo Bridge they stopped to rest. Spark lights sat in proud iron holders all along the length of the bridge. They glowed an eerie shade of blue in the night fog. Elle rested her elbows on the sandstone railings and peered into the darkness. Until recently, the authorities had been charging people a penny to cross, but this had proven to be so unpopular that they had stopped it. Below her, a barge trundled by. It let out black puffs of steam as it chugged along. Here, so close to the water, it was even colder. 'It's no use, Loisa. We have walked for miles tonight and we have found absolutely nothing.' She hung her head in weariness.

An icy wind, chilled even further by the freezing water of the Thames, rose up from below and blasted them. Elle's teeth chattered. 'I t–think I n–need to get warm soon. I d–don't know how much more of this cold I can t–take,' she said.

'Shh!' Loisa held out her hand. 'Listen.'

Elle tried to listen but she was so cold she could hear nothing over the sounds of the wind and her own shivering.

'Get down. Don't move.' Loisa motioned for Elle to crouch next to one of the columns that anchored the balustrades.

Quiet as a whisper Loisa spun round and disappeared into the shadows. Elle counted her breaths as she waited for something to happen. Her knees ached from crouching, but she held still.

Elle heard the faint whisper of crêpe de chine and then a man shouted out in fright.

She rose, Colt at the ready, only to see that Loisa had

grabbed their pursuer by the throat and was now holding him firmly over the edge of the bridge so that his feet dangled in the air.

'Now, sir. Please kindly explain why you are following us,' she purred.

'Please, I meant no harm!' The man flailed about, but he was powerless in Loisa's grip.

'Speak! Or I shall drain you and drop your lifeless corpse into the water below. Or would you prefer the paving next to the water?' Loisa's fangs glistened in the light of the spark lamps. 'And it has been a long, cold night so I am rather hungry.'

'Please, don't kill me,' the man whispered. 'I'll tell you everything you want to know. Just please put me down.'

In one graceful move, Loisa hauled the man up over the edge and deposited him on the cobbles before her.

'I suggest you start talking, sir,' Elle said, coming up from behind Loisa. She pointed the gun at him. 'Why are you following us?'

'I wasn't following you. Well, not really.'

'Then what were you doing?'

'I was looking for *them*.'

'Them who?' Loisa hissed.

'The Tickers. I...I spotted you earlier this evening looking about the warehouses, so I assumed you were also enthusiasts. And...and you looked like a man with the hat and trousers, you seemed like you knew where you were going, so I started following you. I did not realise that you were out hunting. I meant no harm, I promise.'

'What do you mean when you say "the Tickers"?' Elle

said, ignoring his comment about her attire. The Colt glinted in the light of the spark lamps. 'My friend here might be compassionate, but if you are lying, I will shoot you where you stand.'

'No. Please don't shoot!' The man cowered. 'The Tickers. You must have read about them in the papers? The strange creatures who wander the streets at night?' The man wiped his hands on his trousers and made an awkward bow. 'I'm Jasper. Jasper Sidgwick, by the way. How do you do?'

Elle looked at Loisa who just shrugged.

He reached into his pocket and Elle raised her Colt. 'Slowly. And don't try anything,' she said.

Mr Sidgwick pulled out a little card and handed it to her. 'It might be a little hard to read in the dark, but I am a member of the Society for Psychical and Otherworldly Research. At the moment, our society is all in a whirl about the new phenomenon. We are trying to discover where these new creatures hide, as they only seem to come out at night.'

Elle peered at the card in the light of the spark lamp. It had the man's name on it. 'I've never heard of your society,' she said.

'Oh, we are more involved in séances and investigations into those who have passed on to the afterlife. We meet fortnightly, but our society is a select one. We prefer to conduct our investigations discreetly.'

'And why are you so interested in these Tickers, as you call them?' Loisa said.

'Well, they are dead in a way, but still alive. Almost like tangible ghosts and so this is of interest to us. We could learn a lot from them. And some of our members have actually seen them.' Jasper straightened his coat. 'Members post their sightings in the newspaper. Look up the advertisements for Mrs Sidgwick's clairvoyance services. It will state a date, place and time. This is a log for others to note.'

'I see,' said Elle. 'And then those who know the code can track their movements. That's quite a clever system, Mr Sidgwick.'

'I thank you for the compliment. And if you really are enthusiasts, you are welcome to join us at our next meeting if you wish,' he said shyly. He pulled out a pair of wire-rimmed glasses and put them on. It was hard to tell in the dark, but Elle realised that he was probably not much older than she was.

'Thank you. We might just take you up on the invitation,' Elle said as she uncocked her revolver and slipped it back into its place by her side.

'And do be more careful next time you follow ladies in the dark of night. They may not be as friendly as we are,' Loisa added.

Jasper gave Loisa a nervous smile as he put on his bowler hat. 'Well, then, I had better be off. It was nice to meet you. And please do call. You have my details on the card. We meet on Wednesday evenings at the pub below the Savoy Hotel. From about eight o'clock onwards.'

'We will be sure to bear that in mind,' Elle said.

'Goodnight, then.' Jasper turned and walked off into the mist.

Loisa and Elle looked at one another as they listened

to Jasper retreat. After a few moments, his footsteps sped up considerably to a shuffling run.

'What an odd fellow,' Elle said.

'Very odd indeed.' Loisa stifled a yawn. 'I vote we find a nice dry cab to take us home.'

'Motion seconded,' Elle said, suddenly deeply grateful for the miracle that was modern transport.

Chapter Seventeen

Elle found the advertisement for Mrs Sidgwick's clairvoyance services in the back of the newspaper the very next evening.

'It seems to be saying that there have been sightings near Aldgate. Do you think it's worth a try?' she said to Loisa.

Loisa sipped her cup of blood-laced chocolate and stared off into the distance as she thought matters over. 'I can't see how it could do any harm. That boy was so frightened that it didn't even enter his mind not to tell the truth.'

'We were a bit harsh with him, I think.' Elle held the little card between her fingers.

'What on earth have you two been up to?' The professor looked up from the book he was reading.

'We bumped into an undead enthusiast last night. I think Loisa put the fear into him right and proper though.'

'I really don't think you should be out wandering the streets like that,' the professor tutted.

Elle gave him a warning look. This was an argument that had been raging for years. 'I know you worry about me but this is something I have to do. I must find my husband,' she said.

'I know, I know, my dear.' The professor held up a conciliatory hand.

Just then there was a commotion at the front door. Elle and Loisa rose as Mrs Hinges, dressed in her best winter coat, burst in.

'Mrs Hinges?' Elle said.

'Oh, my dear!' she breathed. 'I am so very sorry to barge in through the front like this, but I have news!'

'What on earth?'

'Oh, I couldn't sleep this afternoon, so thought I would make a few enquiries myself. You know, ask about a little. But the weather is so awful that it took forever to get home on the bus.'

'Oh, Mrs Hinges.' Elle felt a surge of deep affection for her.

'Listen to this,' Mrs Hinges said. 'I spoke to Mrs Barrett, she's the housekeeper for number fourteen. Well, she says that she heard from one of the maids in number twenty, who does extra laundry for her on her days off, that the Earl of Mallory's son has disappeared.' Mrs Hinges unwound her scarf and took off her hat. 'Terrible scandal brewing. You see, *he* was engaged to this girl. Terribly sickly and entirely unsuitable. But he would hear nothing of it.'

Elle and Loisa stared at her, uncomprehending.

'Don't you see?' said Mrs Hinges.

'Not really.' Loisa shook her head.

'The young man set out to find a cure for his lady. Because if she were well, there would be no objection to them marrying. He went out of a night and never came home. Just like our dear Lord Greychester.'

'Are you sure?' Elle said.

'As sure as I stand here. Disappeared into thin air along with his father's valet. Set the whole house on its head.'

Elle sat back in her seat and thought it over for a little while.

'Mrs Hinges, thank you for taking the trouble, but you really will catch your death if you go running about like that,' the professor said. He looked most concerned.

'Oh, don't be silly, professor. I am made from sturdy stuff.'

That set off a debate between the professor and Mrs Hinges which had been raging even longer than the one he had been having with Elle. Amid the discussion, Elle and Loisa escaped from the drawing room and went upstairs to ready themselves for the resumption of their search. It was still early but, it being February, the sun had gone down and it was pitch dark outside. Perfect conditions for Nightwalkers.

'Look at you!' Elle said when her friend joined her a few minutes later. Loisa was dressed from head to toe in black. She wore a pair of fitted black leather trousers – the type favoured by the cowboys of the wild west – knee-high boots, and a wool jumper over a fine lacy blouse.

'I absolutely ruined my favourite dress last night with all that mud so I thought I would take a leaf from your book, my dearest,' Loisa said as she pulled on a black leather coat that fell to just below her knees. 'Do you like it?'

'I think it's fantastic,' Elle said. 'So much more

practical than skirts. But where on earth did you get all these clothes?'

'Ah, well, some of these things I brought with me.' She gestured at her leather coat, which did indeed look very Transylvanian. 'And I sent someone out to the dressmaker I retain here. She is used to strange requests.' Loisa gave her a little suggestive smile and placed a finely fitted top hat with a delicate lace veil on to her curls to complete the ensemble.

Elle held up her hands. 'Fair enough. And maybe tonight, we won't be stalked.'

Loisa laughed. 'I think we should go and visit Jasper, just to see the look on his face. I think his society might positively die if they found out who you are,' she said with a wicked gleam in her eye.

Caruthers coughed discreetly. 'Your cab has arrived, ma'am.'

And so, suitably wrapped up against the biting cold, Elle and Loisa set off into the darkness.

The steam cab stopped just outside the arches of Leadenhall Market. 'This is as far as I go, ladies,' said the driver. 'There are too many strange things that go bump in the night these days and a man can't be too careful. No offence, madam,' he said nodding towards Loisa.

'That's fine, but please wait for us here. There will be an extra fare in it for you if you do,' Elle said.

'Will do,' said the cabby, although Elle was not so sure he would be a man of his word.

Elle and Loisa started walking towards Aldgate. Even though it was still early, the streets were eerily quiet. The only noise they could hear and light they saw spilled from the pubs that squatted along the street.

'We had better head for the water. That's my guess,' Elle said as they walked down Fenchurch Street. Around them, church bells tolled ominously in the mist.

'There is something ill in the air. I can taste it,' Loisa said.

'I feel it too, it's making my skin crawl,' Elle said. She had the eerie feeling that they were not alone.

'Let's go east, towards the Tower,' Elle whispered. They walked on, boots echoing against the damp cobbles.

It was Loisa who heard them first. She stopped and put her hand on to Elle's arm, turning her head just a fraction to catch the faint sound of ticking, like a watch buried deep within a pocket.

'This way,' Elle whispered. Without making a sound, the two women stepped into the shadow of a doorway.

The sound of ticking increased, now accompanied by a soft scuffling and scraping. Elle held her breath as she watched the small cluster of undead lope past them. None of them looked right or left. Instead, they seemed utterly intent on reaching whatever destination they were seeking.

'Phew! That was close.' A man spoke from the other side of the alleyway.

'Who's there?' Loisa leaned forward and peered into the shadows.

There was a slight movement as Jasper Sidgwick stepped out of the shadows.

'Mr Sidgwick!' Elle said. 'You nearly gave me a heart attack.'

'Good evening, ladies. I knew you would find them. And what a sight they were!' He strolled up to them, beaming from ear to ear. 'There are a few of us dotted about the area, searching, but none of us have ever managed to get so close. Did you hear that ticking?'

Elle and Loisa stared at Mr Sidgwick.

'I am so glad I bumped into you.' He bowed politely. 'Perhaps now you might honour me with the particulars of your names?'

'Eleanor Marsh. How do you do?' Elle took Mr Sidgwick's hand and shook it firmly. 'This is my dear friend, the Baroness Loisa Belododia. She is visiting from the Continent.'

'Delighted to meet you. Please, call me Jasper.' He took Loisa's hand and bowed over it most gallantly as the Nightwalker looked on in bemusement.

'So, what do we do next? Those Tickers seemed quite determined to go that way,' Elle said.

'Well, I'm not sure, to be honest,' Jasper said. 'We normally only wait for them to pass. Observe statistics like numbers and group size, male or female and such things, and then go back to compare and compile the collected information. It's more of an observation than a participation really.'

'We need to get closer,' Elle said.

'Oh, do say I can come with you,' Jasper said.

'This could be extremely dangerous,' Elle warned.

'Then you need a gentleman to escort you,' he said.

Loisa rolled her eyes. 'We are wasting time,' she said in a low voice.

'Very well, but stay back and don't get in the way,' Elle said to Jasper.

They walked eastward through the eerie lanes, past the Tower of London and the entrance of the newly completed Tower Bridge, which straddled the Thames. The spark lights on the crossbeams of the bridge made the structure glow eerily in the night fog.

'This is St Katharine's Dock,' Jasper whispered. Elle could hear a slight tinge of fear in his voice.

Around them, the sad wood-fronted buildings of the docklands slum huddled close to one another. A gust of wind rose up and swept through the gaps and chinks in the houses, damp and bitterly cold. It made the loose planks and sheets of corrugated iron rattle mournfully. The only warmth in this place was the flickering light of the spark lamps which the city had installed a few years before in an attempt to make the area safer. They now merely stood as a silent testament to the failure of that endeavour.

'Not the most agreeable of areas, I'll grant you that,' Loisa murmured as she sidestepped a pile of soggy horse muck.

In the distance they could hear water sloshing against the wharf and the mournful ting...ting...ting sound of rigging against boat masts. And below it all, just barely within the reach of normal human hearing, Elle felt the relentless rhythm of the ticking, like a pulse beating too hard for comfort.

'They are close.' Elle felt a sudden surge of energy from her wedding band. It coursed through her and made her left hand tingle. Even here in the Realm of Light, she and Marsh were bound. 'Over there,' she said, pointing into the dark distance.

Carefully they crept up to the edge of the little square that framed the docks.

'Gosh, I've never been this close,' Jasper whispered when the sounds of grunts and shuffles became audible over the sound of the ticking.

The fog parted slightly and they stared in amazement.

Before them, huddled in a tight group under the light of a spark lamp, were about forty undead. Men and women with their clothes hanging grotesquely off their emaciated frames. They stood with their heads and arms at haphazard angles, like resting marionettes waiting for their puppeteer.

And each one had a brass mask that covered the bottom half of their faces, clamped and tightly bolted over the jaw, as if to prevent them from biting and tearing at things. The muzzles were intended, it seemed, in much the same way as one would muzzle a vicious dog.

But it was their eyes that were the worst: milky white and devoid of the iris, they stared blankly ahead of them, even as they moved and stumbled about.

To the side of the group of undead was a tall man. Like the others he was without a hat or coat. He stood perfectly still in the midst of the shuffling. His slightly-too-long dark hair hung in greasy streaks over his pale face. And when Elle spotted him, her heart lurched in her chest.

Loisa turned to look, and uttered a small shocked cry.

They had found Marsh.

Chapter Eighteen

'If you go round the other side to distract them, I can move in and see if I can grab him,' Elle whispered.

One or two of the undead grunted and moved at the sound of their whispers.

'That's one idea,' said Loisa.

'Well, do you have a better one?'

Loisa shrugged. 'I suppose not.'

'And take Jasper with you. If we lose one another, then let's agree to meet where the cab is waiting in Leadenhall.'

'Be careful,' Loisa whispered. 'Jasper, come,' she said before she slipped away into the dark with the grace that only a Nightwalker could muster.

Elle counted the long seconds as she waited for them to execute their distraction. While she waited, she kept her eyes firmly trained on Marsh. He had not moved since she had first spotted him in the crowd.

Above them, the skies opened up and a fine spray of freezing cold sleet started falling. The drops of ice stung the skin and soaked into clothes with merciless cold.

Elle said a silent prayer to whoever might be listening

and held her breath. Surely Loisa would have come up with something by now?

In the distance, a loud crash and the sound of glass breaking broke the silence. A flame flickered in the dark and Jasper stepped forward, banging loudly on a piece of corrugated iron roofing, which he held before him like the shield of some Medieval Templar.

'Oi! Here! Come and get me, you ticking bastards!' he shouted, and banged on the metal.

Elle smiled with surprise. She did not think gentle Jasper would be capable of using such peppery language.

The undead turned, transfixed by the noise and light. The collective rhythm of their ticking became faster and slowly the group started shuffling towards Jasper. Elle had no doubt that Loisa was lurking somewhere in the shadows, ready to pounce.

Then she spotted her chance. In the shuffle, Marsh had fallen to the back of the group. Elle sprinted up to him as fast as she could and grabbed the back of his coat. She spun him round and looked into his blank eyes.

'We need to leave this place. I need to take you home,' she said to him.

He did not respond. There was not even the slightest flicker of recognition in his eyes. Gently she tugged his arm for him to follow her, but he did not move.

'Oh, what have they done to you?' she whispered, close to despair.

She dragged at his arm, but all he did was lean into the movement as if he had suddenly become rooted to the spot.

Elle closed her eyes in frustration. The other creatures

had moved off about ten paces now and all it would take was for one to look back for her to be in serious trouble. They might be muzzled, but they were still capable of carrying her off to wherever it was that they went. And that was not a place she wanted to be.

'Damn it, Marsh, move!' she hissed.

He turned his face towards her and a slight crinkle in his brow made it look as if he was trying to understand, but it was like trying to move a fully grown oak tree.

'Stop!' a man shouted, off in the distance.

Elle felt her heart sink as two burly men stepped into the light of one of the street lamps.

'Oh bugger,' Elle blurted out. The undead were not alone. Instead, they were accompanied by four or five large guards.

'Stop where you are or I'll shoot,' the man said again. Elle caught sight of a large and dangerous-looking shotgun which one of the men raised and pointed at her.

'And stop that racket!' another man said. He started walking towards Jasper, but Loisa leaped out and grabbed him by the throat. In seconds, her Nightwalker grip had him out stone cold. Despite her delicate appearance, Loisa was very old and very strong.

Jasper's shouting and banging was becoming more frantic as the undead advanced upon him. It wouldn't be long before he would have to abandon his post.

She heard the sickening sound of metal upon metal as the guard cocked the shotgun.

'Jasper, run!' she shouted, just as the first shot rang out. It missed but the shotgun pellets pinged as they went through one of the corrugated iron walls behind her.

The sound had made the undead turn and stumble in the direction of the gunfire. Elle pulled out her Colt and briefly considered returning fire, but she would be shooting in the general direction of Jasper and Loisa which was not good. No, escape and evade was the sensible way forward here and she was suddenly deeply grateful for the rain and fog. In sheer desperation, Elle reached into the barrier and felt for the filament that bound her to Marsh. She stood, left arm up to her elbow in the Shadow Realm, and pulled with all her might.

Marsh moved. He stumbled a few paces and grunted.

She took his hand and held it in hers. To her astonishment, she felt the tingle of the bond trickle down her arm, over her wrist and into him.

'Now, walk,' she said as she pulled him towards her.

Marsh grunted and moved a few more steps before faltering.

Another shot rang out and the spark light above them went out in a spray of broken glass.

Elle tugged at Marsh again, willing him to break with whatever was keeping him rooted to the ground. He shuffled forward again.

'Good. Now a few paces more, my darling,' she said, trying not to let her desperation show.

The other guard suddenly cried out in surprise and Elle prayed that Loisa was the cause.

Marsh stumbled a few more paces towards her.

'That's right, keep going,' she coaxed.

'Round them up, I'll go after the girl,' a third man said.

She could hear footsteps in the dark and the sound of

shuffling as they rounded up the other undead charges. Whoever survived Loisa's attack would be upon her and Marsh within a matter of seconds.

Just then, Loisa leaped out of the dark, hissing like a very large, very dangerous cat. The guard cried out in surprise as Loisa pounced upon him.

Elle had no time to lose. She took a deep breath and dragged at Marsh with all her strength. 'Move! Damn you, Marsh. Move!' she said between gritted teeth.

He grunted and suddenly Elle felt a surge of energy. It crashed over them, enveloping them like a tidal wave. For a few moments, they stood shrouded in the space between the realms of Shadow and Light. The light contorted and wisps of grey and black moved all around them. From where they were standing, the shapes of the buildings seemed as if they were under water. Marsh threw back his head and groaned as if he was in terrible pain and took a few shuffling steps in her direction before stumbling after her. With all her strength, Elle dragged Marsh towards what looked like a timber-covered alleyway.

The muffled sound of a shotgun rang out again and, far away in the distance, she heard Loisa squeal in pain. She heard the sickening sound of flesh and bone hitting cobbles. 'Please let Loisa and Jasper be safe,' she prayed.

'After them! They went that way,' she heard one of the men shout.

'Walk, just a few steps,' she said to Marsh who was still dutifully holding her hand. He made a small shuffling motion, obeying her command.

'Yes, my darling, that's right, one step at a time,' she said.

Above her, thunder rumbled and clouds dark as soot boiled in the sky. Elle shuddered again as she felt the wave of energy ripple through the air, every bit as foreign and horrible as it had been in the Shadow Realm. Who – or what – had chased her the day before was now most definitely on its way here too. They dared not remain in this space for too long.

She took another few steps and this time it was easier for Marsh to follow. Elle tucked herself under Marsh's armpit and held his arm over her chest. Her touch seemed to galvanise him into moving more and he leaned against her as they shuffled on ahead.

Elle did her best to ignore the cold edge of the muzzle covering his jaw that was pressing in her hair. She had lost her hat somewhere back in the dark, but that did not matter right now. Together she and Marsh walked a little further until they were outside the docks.

By this stage, Elle was panting with stress and exertion. Hot-slick sweat coursed down her body, wetting her clothes from the inside and chilling her even further. But she could not stop, because the only way for them now was forwards.

Gently, she nudged Marsh along through the murk of the barrier until they were standing near what looked like a mucky side street lined with more clapboard houses. Gathering all her strength, she plunged back into the Realm of Light.

'All right, big husband, we've managed to give those oafs the slip for the moment. Now let's see if we can get you home,' she said in a tone that was as jovial and optimistic as she could manage. To her relief, he started moving after her in a gentle shuffle. And so they set off through the narrow alleys that led away from the docks.

Behind her, she could hear the sound of footsteps, but Elle did not need to look back to know that they were being followed. She needed to hurry, for it would only be a matter of time before they were spotted.

The Tower of London loomed up in the dark to her left. Its battlements looked like the broken teeth in the jaw of some ugly beast. She briefly considered the possibility of hiding inside in order to escape the guards and the undead on her heels, but the doors would be locked at this time of night. She had no option but to run.

Marsh grunted and flailed his free arm in acknowledgement of their pursuers.

'Hush now. Don't look,' she said to him.

He dropped his arm and shuffled along obediently.

The wind picked up and with it came fat, cold snowflakes that splashed against her face. She gasped at the cold wind, but pressed on.

They rounded the corner and started up the street known as the Minories, which ran all the way up the hill back to Aldgate. The dingy shops and narrow houses were all closed and boarded up for the night, although here and there she could see the faint flicker of lamps behind the sackcloth and shutters covering the mean windows.

They walked until they passed the bright light of the Three Lords pub, but there was no one hanging about outside in this weather. They would see no help from kind strangers tonight, for no one would risk life and limb to help the awful creature she was dragging along with her. So she kept walking all the way up the hill that led into the city.

Marsh stumbled once on the now icy pavement, almost dragging her to the ground, but she managed to steady them against a wall. She was numb from cold and bone-tired from dragging Marsh along, but there was no time to rest. She looked over her shoulder into the darkness behind them. The footsteps were getting louder, but it was so hard to tell through the muffling blanket of white February snow. It would not be long before the undead chased them down.

On impulse, she turned left into Jewry Street and on to a wooden-clad entrance, marked simply as Saracen's Head Yard. The low overhang of the buildings offered some shelter from the driving wind and snow and Elle allowed herself to rest for a moment with her head against a sign that read COMMIT NO NUISANCE.

Marsh grunted and looked up in the direction they had come. She heard the jingle of keys and the muffled sound of footsteps.

'Do you see them?' one guard asked the other.

'Nah. They must have given us the slip further down. I told you we should have looked inside that pub.'

'There is no way she would have taken him into the pub,' the first said. 'The regulars would have thrown him out straight away.'

'Let's try that way anyway. I could do with a quick drink.'

'Not a bad idea, my son,' the first guard said. 'We can leave this lot in the little square outside.'

'And besides, we are going to need a drink in us to

fortify us for the explanation her highness is going to want once she hears what's happened.'

The first guard grunted.

Elle held her breath and listened to them round up the other undead before heading back the way they came. She stood there for what seemed like an age until the only noise she could hear over the wind and the drifting snow was the ticking sound that her husband made.

'Come on then,' she said to Marsh, as she dragged him out of the alley and towards upper Leadenhall Street. She stumbled along in the dark, all the while thanking the Fates that she was good at navigating.

Elle nearly cried with joy when, like a benediction, the bells of Old St Botolph's church tolled to her right. They had made it to Aldgate. Marsh grunted and turned towards the sound of the bell.

'This way, we don't have much further to go,' she cajoled as she turned left, using the momentum of their movement to pull Marsh along.

The walk from St Botolph's church back to Leadenhall Market is not particularly long or difficult, but to Elle it was one of the longest of her life. Her back ached and her arms were burning with the effort of holding on to Marsh as they stumbled along, skidding and slipping on the sludge and ice. Around her, the snow sifted down mercilessly, icing over everything it touched.

When they finally stumbled in under the red and cream painted arches that made up the market she let out a small sob of relief.

Leadenhall was closed for the night. A few of the meat hooks and chains that held foodstuffs during the day swung and squeaked eerily in the cold draught that blew through the market.

With agonising slowness, Elle dragged Marsh onwards until she found the cab.

The driver sat hunched up in his coat, but stirred when she approached.

'Where are the others?' she gasped.

The driver squinted in the dark as he took in the sight of them. 'The woman in black paid me an extra shilling to wait for you. They said to tell you that they would meet you at the house. No amount of money is worth staying out in this weather, I tell ya,' he grumbled.

'Please can you take us back to Grosvenor Square?' she pleaded. Marsh stumbled into the light behind her.

The driver took in the brass muzzle over Marsh's face. He blanched and recoiled in his seat. 'I don't know what games you are up to, missus, but I ain't playing. That thing is not going in my cab,' he said.

'No, you don't understand. This is my husband. He can't hurt you and he needs help. Please, we can pay,' she said.

'Well, show me the money then,' the cabbie said.

Elle felt about in her pockets and pulled out all the money she had, well in excess of the normal fare home. 'Here, take this,' she said as she shoved the money at him.

The driver took the coins and pocketed them. 'That's a start, but I think that pocket watch would just about even things out. I am taking my life into my hands here.' He pointed at Marsh's waistcoat. Amazingly, his pocket watch was still pinned to the buttonhole of his waistcoat.

Elle felt her temper flare. If there was one thing she

detested, it was when someone took advantage of those more vulnerable than themselves.

Before the cab driver could say anything else, she opened the cab door and shoved Marsh inside. He grunted and rolled over in the seat. 'Stay,' she told him firmly before slamming the door and locking it.

'Oi, what do you think you're doing?' the cab driver said.

Elle pulled out her revolver and pointed it at the cab driver. The man's eyes widened as he took in the sight of the barrel of the gun. 'Now, look here—' he started to say.

'No, you look here, sir,' Elle interrupted. 'This has not exactly been the best of nights. I am cold, I am tired and my husband needs help. I have paid you more than the required fare. So now either you are going to drive us home or I am going to shoot you where you sit and take your cab. There are plenty more undead ticking things lurking about in these parts. And if they smell blood, they will rip your body apart so comprehensively that not even your own mother would recognise you,' she said in a low voice. 'Do I make myself clear?' She had made up the bit about the limb-tearing for effect, and it seemed to work.

'All right, madam. Please, let's go,' the driver said as he fired up the spark reactor. 'No use in hanging about,' he muttered faintly.

Mercifully, the boiler was already hot and the cab started moving. Elle jumped up on to the seat next to the driver and pushed the gun into his ribs. 'Grosvenor Square. And with a dash of speed,' she said between clenched teeth.

The cab driver did not wait to be asked twice. He set off into the snow-slick streets at a speed that was not entirely safe for the prevailing conditions, but Elle did not complain. At least they were going home.

Their journey passed in a daze. Elle felt her knuckles grow cold and stiff as she kept the revolver pointed at the driver. Icy blobs of snow splattered into her face and hair. And as she sat, she did her best not to let her teeth chatter. Fortunately, the old cab was rattling so much, she didn't think the driver noticed.

Elle had never been so relieved as she was the moment they pulled up outside Greychester House.

She jumped on to the ground and unlocked the cab door. Marsh was still lying on his side in more or less the same position he had been in when she shoved him in there. It took all her strength, but somehow she managed to drag him up and bundle him out of the cab without too much difficulty.

Marsh's legs buckled under him as they reached the ground but Elle dragged him up on to the first step when the front door opened.

The cab driver did not hang about to see what might happen next and roared off into the night.

'Caruthers, please help me. Anyone, help!' Elle called out. She was close to the end of her strength.

'Already here, my lady. We've been waiting for you,' Neville said. She noticed he was holding a cricket bat. 'The baroness arrived about three-quarters of an hour ago. Mrs Hinges is tending to her and the professor is waiting in the drawing room.'

'Thank goodness for that. Would you mind giving me

a hand? He is ever so heavy,' she said. Elle gasped as her knees buckled when she stood.

'Good heavens!' Neville paled when he set eyes on Marsh. 'Caruthers! You had better come out and lend us a hand!' he said.

'Let's see if we can set him down in front of the fire in the drawing room. Grab his other side,' Elle mumbled. Her lips were so cold that they did not seem to work that well any more.

Together, the three of them manoeuvred Marsh into the house and on to one of the wingback chairs next to the fire in the main drawing room.

Marsh sank into the chair with the groan of a man who had been standing for a very long time.

Elle stood shivering and wet in the middle of the drawing room as the household stepped into action. The fire was stoked, tea was made and someone rushed off to fetch the doctor. Someone wrapped a warmed dry blanket around her and handed her a hot drink that was both tart and bitter on her tongue.

Another pair of hands led her to a seat. After that, she must have dozed off, because all she could remember of that night were snippets of conversation which drifted past her.

'... how extraordinary. He's completely immobilised... I wonder what makes that thing in his chest tick,' she heard her father say.

'... find some dry clothes for her ladyship, before she catches her death.' The comforting voice of Mrs Hinges drifted into focus.

Elle came back into awareness when Marsh groaned

and tried to rise from the chair, but Neville had tied him down with a pair of leather straps. Even immobilised, Marsh craned his neck as if he were trying to sense where she was. His face turned from side to side while his milky eyes remained completely blank.

Loisa appeared in her line of vision. 'Eleanor!' She patted Elle's cheeks.

'Loisa, thank goodness you are all right. What happened to Jasper?' she slurred.

'He's safe and at home. But I think we need to get you warmed up and dried off before you contract pneumonia,' Loisa said and she nudged her towards where Mrs Hinges was waiting for her.

'No, I must hear what the doctor says. We have to fix him before it's too late,' she mumbled.

'The doctor will speak to us tomorrow,' Mrs Hinges said. 'There is nothing that can be done this evening. But you, on the other hand, need to look after yourself. I don't think I could manage both of you at death's door at the same time.' Mrs Hinges chatted to her all the way to her room and helped her undress as her fingers were so numb that she could not undo her own buttons.

The last thing Elle remembered before she closed her eyes was the warmth of her comforter that enveloped her as Mrs Hinges tucked it around her.

Chapter Nineteen

Elle sat up in bed with a start and looked over at the clock on the mantelpiece. It was half past ten in the morning. Mrs Hinges must have put something in her tea last night, because she felt puffy-faced despite the fact that she had been asleep for hours. She groaned and struggled out of bed. Every muscle in her body ached and she was so stiff she could hardly move, but she managed to dress nonetheless.

When Elle came downstairs Loisa was in the entrance hall, ostensibly examining one of the pot plants. Her beautiful porcelain doll face was hollow-eyed and grey in the half-light of the hallway.

'Loisa, have you rested?' Elle said with concern.

Her friend shook her head with a nonchalance that belied her fatigue. 'I was just on my way up.'

'What happened last night? It's all such a blur.'

Loisa looked grave. 'I tried to kill the guards but they were wearing charms or amulets, which sapped my strength, and they fought me off. So when the undead and the guards set off after you all we could do was follow behind. But there were too many of them for me and Jasper to take on alone, so we circumvented them and went to the rendezvous as agreed. We waited and waited, but you did not appear. We feared the worst when a few stray undead started appearing and in the end we had to run or face being captured. We told the cab driver to wait for you. We caught another cab near Liverpool Street that took us to Jasper's home and then came here. It was quite an adventure.'

A series of grunts and cries, followed by the frantic whining of a gramophone record player wound too fast, came from the drawing room.

Loisa put a hand on her arm. 'Prepare yourself. Seeing him in the light of day is not going to be easy.'

Elle closed her eyes as the harsh realities of last night came flooding back. Her eyes felt swollen and gritty and she had to blink a few times to get rid of the sudden surge of wetness that blurred her vision.

Neville and Caruthers had manoeuvred her husband into a wicker bath chair and they were both on their knees on the carpet securing the wheels. Marsh was grunting and straining against the canvas sleeves of the straight-jacket that bound his arms. Slivers of drool were escaping from the brass muzzle that covered his jaw. Mrs Hinges stood beside the professor who was in one of the wingback chairs; together they seemed to be directing operations.

Elle let out a small sob that had formed unnoticed in her chest. 'Is that really necessary?' she said over the noise of the gramophone. She walked over to the machine and lifted the needle off the record. The room stilled, save for the grunts and groans.

'The music seems to calm him, my lady,' Caruthers said.

She walked over to the chair and put her hands on her husband's knees. 'Shh. There you are. It's all right, be still now,' she murmured. She felt the thin filament between them draw tight and Marsh stilled. He turned his greyed-out eyes to her, as if he could see her somehow.

She rubbed his knee. 'There now. See, that's better,' she said. Marsh grunted and closed his eyes.

Elle pulled her handkerchief from her pocket and carefully started wiping the drool from his muzzle. As she worked, Marsh suddenly turned his head and tried to snap at her hand. The sound of tooth upon tooth was horrible and the bath chair wobbled under his weight.

Elle recoiled in horror.

'I bet you he's just hungry,' Loisa said. She had come into the drawing room and was standing quietly behind Elle.

'Have you tried to feed him?' Elle said.

'Well, I wouldn't even begin to know what he eats now,' Mrs Hinges said.

Despite the utter horror of the situation, Elle could not help but smile. For once in her life, Mrs Hinges was completely at a loss when it came to catering. Elle did not think she had ever encountered someone Mrs Hinges could not feed.

'Perhaps we should experiment,' said the professor. 'I'm sure we can undo that horrible muzzle once he's properly secured in the chair. Let me just go and fetch my tools.'

'How about some porridge to start or some meat broth? See what stays down,' Mrs Hinges suggested.

'No porridge,' Loisa said. 'This is necromancy. The

undead usually crave living flesh. He needs meat. Raw and as fresh as possible.'

'I'll see what I can do.' Mrs Hinges did her best not to shudder.

'Neville, what about those cast-iron statues of the lions at the bottom of the stairs? I'm always stubbing my elbows on them and they weigh a ton. See if some of the lads downstairs can give you a hand to get them in here,' Elle said.

The professor smiled. 'An excellent idea, my dear. Iron should modulate the thaumaturgic energy fields and, if my theory is correct, it should dampen his strength a little.'

'I will get right on to it, my lady,' Neville said.

'Caruthers, I am placing you in charge of the gramophone. Only soft gentle music to calm him,' Elle said.

'Right away, my lady.'

Loisa was leaning against the mantelpiece, pale and fragile in the light of the fire. Elle turned to her. 'Loisa, we have much to discuss, but first you must rest. We can't have you turning to dust here on the rug, hmm?' Elle said.

Loisa smiled at her affectionately. 'I think I might have a short nap,' she said.

'Dinner is at seven. We will see you then.'

The baroness looked decidedly grateful as she swept from the room.

Elle heard the sound of Marsh's teeth clicking together near her hand again. While she had been speaking to Loisa, he had leaned towards her, his teeth working furiously as if he was trying to chew through the muzzle to get to her hand.

More slivers of drool were swinging from side to side as his head moved. The sight of him filled Elle with such anguish that she had to look away.

'Perhaps we might find a way to put the muzzle back once we've fed him. We don't want him injuring some unsuspecting passer-by,' Elle said softly.

Just then, the deep gong of the doorbell reverberated through the house.

'The doctor is here,' Caruthers announced.

Elle turned to the drawing-room door. 'Well, let's see what he has to say.'

Dr Miller was a skinny man with a rather large, beak-like nose that, along with his propensity to stoop, made him look very much like a carrion bird. This was rather unfortunate, given the fact that he was a physician and a good one at that.

'Most extraordinary,' said Dr Miller as he leaned forward to examine Marsh. 'I don't think I've ever seen anything quite like it.'

'We think we can remove the muzzle, but I'm not so sure about that thing in his chest,' the professor said in an attempt to be helpful.

'Hmm. I wonder. Are those brass screws holding the muzzle in place?'

'I think I have a screwdriver that would work very well for that,' the professor said as he started rummaging through his toolbox.

'I will of course need to bring him to the hospital so

we can examine the device further,' Dr Miller said as he examined the source of the ticking with his stethoscope. 'And if I might say so, I do believe that he would make an extraordinary subject for a medical paper. This type of science is far more advanced than anything we have seen. The person who invented this is a genius. There could be real benefit for medical research.'

Elle stood very still, biting the insides of her cheeks as she did her best to control the emotions that were storming through her. 'No. I am not going to allow that. Lord Greychester is still a person, regardless of what you might think. And he is still my husband. He is not to leave this house so he can be poked and prodded by strangers.' Everyone seemed to be regarding her husband as if he were some oddity that needed to be gawped at like an animal in a zoo or a circus performer.

She looked down at her hands. Her left ring finger felt numb and had turned a deathly white colour, just above the metal band. When she moved her fingers her hand ached with a strange dullness.

'My lady, there simply is no other way to establish whether we can remove the device. We have no option but to do more invasive investigations and those simply cannot be done except within the controlled environment of a hospital. He will be perfectly safe, I'm sure,' the doctor said.

'I said no!' Elle's tone was a bit too loud and the doctor's eyes widened in surprise.

'I say,' he muttered, 'I am only trying to help, you know.'

Elle took a deep breath. 'Dr Miller, I'm very sorry but it has been a most unhappy event. Whatever happened to my husband, it was metaphysical. There are strange forces at work here that have nothing to do with modern medicine. And I will not let Lord Greychester out of this house until I have more answers.'

'Perhaps we might continue this discussion when you have rested a little,' the doctor said kindly. 'Would you like me to give you a sedative?'

'No, thank you. My mind is quite firmly made up. I will not have you and your colleagues poking and prodding my husband as if he were some freakish medical phenomenon. I will not.'

'Of course, my lady. I meant no offence,' the doctor said.

'Now, tell me about that mechanism in his chest.' Elle pointed at the opening in Marsh's shirt which the doctor had been examining. It looked like someone had taken a large apple corer to the centre of Marsh's chest. And there, slightly to the left, exactly where his heart should be, an oblong brass mechanism had been inserted. It had a small glass dome and, inside, Elle could see what looked like a mechanical heart. The cogs and gears of the device whirred and moved in simulation of a human heartbeat.

The doctor rubbed his chin. 'Well, yes. It is quite something, isn't it? As far as I can tell, it looks as if his heart has been removed and replaced by this clockwork device. And without it, or his heart, in place there is no demonstrable way to keep him alive.'

'And taking the machine out and putting his heart back? Is that possible?'

Dr Miller shook his head. 'I honestly don't know. See how the skin around the device has been cauterised.'

He pointed at the puckered, greying skin adjacent to the device. 'In my considered opinion, unless the heart has somehow been preserved, there would have been a definite deterioration of the heart tissue, making it impossible to be restored. I mean, we don't even know where the heart is.'

'But if they did preserve it, do you think you could put it back?' Elle said.

'That sort of surgery is beyond my expertise. I could ask my colleagues who specialise in surgical procedures, but I suspect it's most unlikely.'

'And the undead-like state? Is that linked to the device?'

'I would have thought so. But how much of the actual person remains is very hard to say. From the looks of things, not much.'

'But he will remain alive as long as the device keeps ticking?'

The doctor looked at Elle seriously. 'In a manner of speaking. If you define his current state as not dead, then I suppose you could call whatever he is alive.'

'He is alive in there, I can feel it,' Elle said, undeterred by the doctor's pessimism.

The doctor took her hand. 'My lady, I'm afraid that your husband's very survival depends on the faultless operation of that device. And I am very concerned about the fact that there is a keyhole in the centre of it.'

'Yes, I noticed that too,' the professor said, looking up from his toolbox. 'If that heart works like any other clockwork device I know, then it will need winding. And that can only be done by whoever currently has the key.'

Elle chewed her lip, which felt flaky and dry under her tongue. 'How long do you think he has before time runs out?' she asked.

The doctor sighed. 'There is simply no way of knowing. What do you think, professor?'

The professor scratched his head. 'Judging by the size and dimensions of the heart, measured against standard clocks with winding mechanisms of that size, I would say about a week.'

'So we have about a week to find the solution,' Elle said.

'In theory, yes,' the doctor said. 'But I am completely stumped. This type of medical procedure is beyond anything I have ever encountered and I honestly cannot guarantee that we will be able to put things to rights.'

'Well, gentlemen, it seems that I have one week to find the key to my husband's heart,' Elle said. She folded her arms with grim determination. 'We had best get on with it then.'

Chapter Twenty

'Such a tragedy. My poor Hugh,' Loisa mused as she sipped her tea. They were sitting by the fire in the small drawing room after dinner.

Marsh was sleeping in the cot they had set up for him in the library next door. After the visit by the doctor, the professor had managed to modify the muzzle by fitting a release latch. They could at least now open and close it in order to feed him, if they were very careful.

Marsh had, true to Loisa's recommendations, consumed almost two pounds of raw liver once they had brought him under control. Elle was grateful that she did not have to witness him feeding because it was, by all accounts, a rather grim event.

Mrs Hinges had looked tired and drawn when Elle had found her in the kitchens earlier that evening. The strain of looking after a Nightwalker and a master who was hovering between the living and the dead was starting to show.

Outside, the rain whooshed against the window-panes with relentless monotony. A storm had rolled in during the late afternoon, complete with more thunder and lightning. It was truly the type of dark and stormy night so favoured by writers of melodramatic prose.

Elle looked up from the evening paper and set down the magnifying glass she had been using to examine one of the photographs on the page. The headline that had drawn her attention read: MYSTERIOUS TICKING MONSTERS SIGHTED IN HYDE PARK.

'We found him near the docks, so let's see if we can pick up a trail from there. Enough people have seen these Tickers to make it into the evening papers. Surely someone would have seen which direction they went.'

'In this weather?' Loisa looked at the windows. 'We'd be lucky not to lose ourselves out there, let alone find some unknown enemy.'

Elle sighed. 'Loisa, I can't just sit here and do nothing. Every minute that passes is a minute wasted.' She felt her breath catch. 'At the very least, we need to find the key that winds up that thing in his chest. Surely they must go somewhere when the sun comes up? And I'm willing to bet that we will find the keys and the answers to this mystery there.'

Loisa nodded slowly. 'I believe this to be the work of a necromancer.'

'Conjuring of the dead.' Elle nodded gravely. 'That seems logical, but how does this help us?'

Loisa shrugged. 'At least we have an idea of what we are searching for. But finding a necromancer's lair is easier said than done. And even if we did find it, how would we go about approaching it? It's not as if we will be invited for tea and cakes upon our arrival.'

'I don't care,' Elle said. 'I am not going to let him die, Loisa. I will not.'

Loisa's expression softened. 'None of us want him to die. I know you love him, my darling. But we need to be clever about this. Taking on a necromancer is not something one attempts lightly. Personally, I don't mind so much. I have less to lose than you do. But you might well end up as one of these ticking things. And that is not something we can afford, *Madame Oracle*.'

Elle looked up at the ceiling in frustration. 'And somehow we always end up back at the infernal business of being the Oracle. Some days I wish I could just tear down the barrier that separates the two realms and be done with it.'

Loisa smiled. 'As do all the Shadow creatures, but we both know that this is not something that can be. Too much chaos. And you would have the blood of all those who would die on your hands. But while we are speaking of it, how fares the great divide?'

Elle stared out the window into the darkness. 'The barrier is fine. I have sensed a few odd wobbles lately, but nothing too serious.'

'Odd wobbles?'

'I don't know. Like someone was prodding the barrier. Sometimes people or creatures attempt to cross and mostly the effect is the same as running headfirst into a large, very firmly set jelly pudding. Whoever tries it simply bounces back. I feel the impact because I am the force that holds it all together. But these wobbles were different though. They felt a bit like someone was pushing into the folds – as I can do.'

'Do you think there is another oracle?'

'I doubt it. The Council of Warlocks would have found her by now. Trust me: nothing would make them happier than to find someone else to fill that position.' Elle gave a cynical laugh. 'I would have been swiftly relieved of my duties by now if there were someone else.'

'Perhaps someone who would be capable of assuming the powers of the Oracle?'

Elle shrugged. 'I honestly don't know. There was an incident the other night at the opera. I thought I saw a strange woman and she was affecting the barrier, but she got away. Perhaps the two matters are related, but who knows? The woman could be anywhere.'

Loisa frowned. 'I know of very few creatures of Shadow or Light for that matter who could break the barrier.'

Elle sat forward. 'Do you think a necromancer could?'

Loisa shrugged. 'I am not a scholar. My knowledge is very limited, but I don't see how.'

'Perhaps we might go and see someone who could help,' Elle said. 'Do you know any occult scholars who might know?'

Loisa sat back and thought for a while. 'We could try one of the sectarians, but they have their spies and I'm not so sure that we want the Council of Warlocks to know about Hugh. Who knows what they might do if they found out?'

Elle shivered. As usual Loisa had hit the nail squarely on the head. Marsh was her only protection against the nefarious plans the Council had for her. These included, among other things, a scheme to lock her up in a cave while they drained power through her until she died. If they knew Marsh was indisposed, or dead for that matter, they might decide to take action. And that would be a very bad thing indeed.

'You are right, Loisa. That is a bad idea.'

'Hold on a moment.' Loisa gave her a sly smile. 'What about our new friend, Jasper Sidgwick?'

'Do you think we can trust him?' Elle felt her excitement grow.

Loisa shrugged. 'I don't know. But he is a hopelessly ineffectual occultist with a magnificent collection of books. I had the pleasure of listening to him recount the catalogue all the way from Leadenhall to his house yesterday.'

'And you think he might have something?'

'Undoubtedly. And yet he seems to know nothing of the Council. It is quite extraordinary that someone so educated could be so ignorant.' She sat forward, suddenly enthusiastic. 'Perhaps we should pay him a call. He did after all invite us to one of his meetings.'

'I think that is exactly what we should do,' Elle said. She stood up and straightened her skirts. 'I think, my dear Baroness, that we should go and change into our night visiting clothes. Immediately.'

Half an hour later, the Stanley, the steam-powered automobile that was Lord Greychester's pride and joy, trundled off, buffeted by the strong wind and icy rain. Elle drove and Loisa navigated. This was perhaps not the most efficient system given that the Nightwalker did not know London all that well, but she was an even worse driver so it was the best they could do. At least Loisa could see in the dark, so they managed all right.

The trees waved and shuddered in the wind as they made their way through Green Park and down the Mall.

'Good thing we have the car,' Elle said over the noise of the engine and the storm. 'Horses would have been impossible on a night like this.'

'I think you are right,' Loisa said, as she held on to her top hat to stop it from blowing off. They were both wearing goggles to keep the wind and rain out of their eyes.

'The tavern is below the Savoy Hotel. I have stayed at the Savoy on countless occasions and I never thought to look in on it. Just to the left,' Loisa said.

Elle turned the steering and they trundled down the Strand towards the hotel. Apart from the odd hurrying straggler, the streets were empty. It was strange to see the streets of London so quiet and deserted.

'See if you can find somewhere close by for us to park,' Elle said. Finding parking in the West End was always a veritable nightmare, even at this time of night.

Fortunately, Loisa spotted a folly of plane trees near the Embankment gardens. Elle cast a wary eye over the Stanley as she pulled up underneath them. Curse Marsh for his vanity. The white paintwork and chromed rivets gleamed even in this bad light. Could the man not have chosen a black automobile like a normal person? Elle hoped against hope that the motor would not be too conspicuous and that it would be safe and unharmed when they got back.

'The pub. It's this way.' Loisa dragged Elle by the arm up the little hill behind the Savoy Hotel. They stopped under the flickering street lights outside a door with a heavy brass knocker that looked like the head of a wolf.

'This must be it.' Loisa lifted the knocker and banged on the door six times.

A small peephole opened and someone on the other side studied them.

'The wolf howls not only when the moon is full,' Loisa drawled. 'Jasper told me the password last night,' she explained.

The peephole closed and Elle heard the bolts slide open.

A man dressed in shirtsleeves let them in. His gaze flickered over Elle's leather coat and jodhpurs for a moment, but he said nothing. Elle shook the water off her sleeves and took off her aviator cap and goggles. They had done a remarkable job of keeping her hair dry.

'State your business,' the man grunted.

Surreptitiously, Elle clenched her elbow to her side. Her revolver was sitting safely in its corset holster, ready for action.

'Is Jasper Sidgwick here this evening?' Loisa enquired.

The doorman huffed. 'Downstairs. You'll find him in the cellar. You're late.'

'Thank you.' Loisa gave him one of her alluring smiles, but it seemed to have no effect on the doorman. He did, however, shuffle aside to let them pass.

They climbed a set of narrow stairs that led down to what Elle assumed to be the cellar. Above her, she noted the heavy black beams that made up the floor of the pub above them. The sound of people talking over the noise of the piano filtered down through the boards.

'Sounds like a jolly establishment,' Elle said.

They reached a set of black doors, ornately decorated

with all kinds of esoteric symbols. Inside was the low hum of voices singing a solemn hymn. The sound of the occultists' voices was out of keeping with the jolly celebrations that were going on upstairs.

'Just play along and, for heaven's sake, don't do anything magical that might give us away,' she whispered to Elle.

Loisa lifted the latch and pushed it open. 'Jasper! Are you here?' she called out in her deep musical voice, as they entered the cellar.

Elle gave her a sardonic smile. Attending an occultist meeting was just about the last thing she wanted to do, but if needs must then they certainly would.

Chapter Twenty-one

The singing stopped rather abruptly when they entered the cellar. Elle and Loisa turned to face a congregation of about eight people all sitting in a circle on benches.

Jasper was standing in the middle of the room dressed in rather fetching velvet robes of emerald green. His jovial round face lit up when he saw them. 'Ladies! Welcome to our humble society,' he beamed.

There was a murmur of agreement from the others in the room. The inside of the cellar was lit by a multitude of candles wedged into every crevice and sconce. Large stalactites of wax hung from the walls and candelabra. The cellar looked like it hailed from the days before spark had replaced coal: the fine dust had stained the walls pitch black. Even Elle had to admit that it was the perfect place to hold occult meetings.

'Jasper! Thank you for inviting us,' Loisa cooed.

'Sorry we're late. Terrible weather,' Elle said in an attempt to be polite. She stepped forward and immediately hesitated, balancing her weight on her toes. The tips of her boots were on the edge of a Delphic circle, inlaid entirely in a black and white pattern. She grabbed Loisa's arm and looked at the floor.

'Careful,' Loisa murmured as she steered Elle around the edge with her supernatural strength.

'This is certainly a surprise. You are most welcome,' Jasper said. 'Do sit down. We have just started.' He gestured for them to sit on the benches.

He resumed his position in the centre of the room and the singing began again.

Elle rolled her eyes as she mumbled along in tune to the music, hoping against hope that this would be over quickly, for she could feel time ticking away for Marsh with every beat of her heart.

'All right then, everyone. If you could please join hands, we will begin with our séance,' Jasper said.

Elle and Loisa joined hands with the other eight people in the room.

'We call on the spirits of the departed, asking them to cross the divide between living and dead,' Jasper said, rather dramatically.

'We call on the spirits,' the others murmured.

Elle bit her lip. She had her very own set of ghosts who spoke to her on regular occasions. And judging by their recent persistent silence, she was sure they were none too pleased with her imposing a ban on them. Elle just hoped they wouldn't do something embarrassing or too revealing, but judging by the potency of the séance she was witnessing, Jasper would be lucky if he managed to conjure up the spirit of a dead mouse, let alone a former Oracle.

'Is someone there?' Jasper turned his face to one side as if he was listening for something. 'We ask that the spirit who has come forward, please make itself known to us,' he murmured.

'We ask this,' the others intoned.

There was a brief, breathless moment where it felt as if all the air had been sucked out of the room. All the candles went out and they were plunged into darkness.

More than one of the ladies present let out a little cry of surprise.

'Maintain the circle, please,' Jasper warned. Elle felt her fingers go numb as the woman next to her gripped her hand with fervour.

Elle sighed. Please spirits of the oracle, not now. I really don't want to have to explain myself to these good people, she prayed silently.

'I am getting a name!' Jasper said in the dark. 'Vivienne!'

Elle sat up straight. Vivienne was the name of her late mother. Her mother had been the Oracle before her, but she had died when Elle had been very young.

'Vivienne. Thank you for joining us,' the others murmured.

'She says that her daughter is here. Is there a daughter of a Vivienne present?' Jasper asked.

'Yes,' Elle mumbled, hoping that no one would recognise her voice in the dark.

'What would you like to say to your daughter, Vivienne?' Jasper asked. 'Use me as your vessel to communicate. You are in a circle of safety here.'

Suddenly, Jasper's voice changed. It became higher, more feminine. The voice sounded high and strained, as if the speaker were in distress and fighting to make herself heard. 'My darling, I don't have a lot of time. The others don't know I am here and I cannot fight the banishment placed upon us for very long,' the voice said.

Elle felt a lump rise in her throat. These words were touching that painful part of her childhood she did not readily share with others.

'I want you to know that I am terribly proud of you. And I am so very sorry that I cannot be there to guide you. This path of ours is not easy, but the rewards will be infinite.' Jasper's voice echoed in the darkness.

'What do we need to do to help him, Vivienne?' Loisa said.

Elle poked her friend with the toe of her boot to try and shut her up.

'Look for the Lady in White. She has the answers. He can be saved...' Jasper's voice trailed off.

'Where is she?' Loisa said.

'She is near water. Always near water. Follow the storms. And beware of the shadows. Don't go into the garden alone at night.'

'But where is the garden,' Loisa said again, but the ghost ignored her.

'Eleanor, you need us. You must unbanish us. Please!'

'Mother!' Elle blurted out, but the voice was gone.

The others in the room started muttering and shifting around. Clearly this was a momentous event for them, but Elle had had enough. She let go of Loisa's hand and the hand of the woman next to her and went over to the wall. With deft fingers she felt around in the dark until she found a box of matches. She struck one and set it to the wick of one of the candles. The room suddenly filled with flickering candlelight, obliterating the séance.

Jasper blinked. 'The spirit has left,' he muttered, sounding more than a little disappointed.

'Perhaps it was for the best,' Elle said.

The others stared at Elle in amazement 'But why did you come to this meeting if you did not want to communicate with the dead?' one man asked. Elle did not answer. The last thing she wanted to do right now was to confront the memories of her mother in front of all these strangers. And yet, the aching longing she had lived with for all her life felt somehow less. Her own mother – the one who was Oracle before her – had taken the trouble to reach out across the void to speak to her.

'Jasper, may we have a word? In private please,' Elle said.

Jasper turned to his fellow society members. 'Ladies and gentlemen, the spirit who spoke was most powerful and I fear that she has taken it out of me somewhat. Shall we adjourn until next week when we can compare notes and thoughts on this evening's meeting?'

Others murmured in agreement. 'Drinks upstairs in ten minutes,' one of the men suggested.

'Very well, then. Till next week. I am looking forward to reading everyone's findings on what has been a most exceptional meeting.' He spread his arms and herded everyone out of the cellar with a little more speed than courtesy.

'Well then, ladies. How may I be of assistance?' he said to Elle and Loisa once everyone else had left the cellar. 'Better come with me to the back where we can speak in a little more privacy.'

He gestured to an old velvet curtain that separated

a part of the cellar from the rest. Behind the curtain was what looked like an office and a storeroom. There was a table overflowing with all manner of books and scrolls. On the shelves behind it, boxes of candles and other divination paraphernalia sat where they had been shoved in a somewhat haphazard fashion. Mr Sidgwick was clearly not a meticulous man.

'This is where our little club keeps the things we need for our rituals. Sorry for the mess, we don't normally allow people back here,' Jasper said apologetically. He lifted his robes from his shoulders and bundled them up.

Elle looked at one of the open books on the table. It was a book on alchemical runes and formulae. She shuddered and looked away from the concentric circles. Alchemy was her least favourite subject.

Jasper ran his hand over the patch at the back of his head that was already balding. 'Our society is not devoted to just one discipline. We are scientists and we use this place to study all forms of the occult,' he explained with a touch of pride. 'We also engage in all manner of occult practices. Fortune telling, communicating with the dead, mesmerism. In fact, I am currently postulating the theory that the channelling of power comes via an independent source, a cornerstone, if you like, and I am working on a way to access that power. Just think of how wonderful we could make the world if we could harness both halves of the divide. Just think of all we could achieve if we had access to infinite energy.'

'But isn't that inordinately dangerous? You could throw the whole world into anarchy if you get it wrong.' Elle gave Loisa an anguished look. She was not about to tell Jasper that *she* was the way that all that power could be accessed. 'Knowledge of such things usually comes at a price, Jasper. The question is whether you are prepared to pay that price,' Elle added.

Loisa laughed. 'Nonsense. I think Jasper proved without a doubt that he is most fearless in the face of adversity.'

Jasper blushed. 'It was nothing. I am very pleased to have been able to get so close to the creatures. But tell me, how is the one that you caught?'

'My husband is fine. Resting at home,' Elle said.

'You should bring it to a meeting. I am sure all our members would love to see it up close.'

Elle felt Loisa grip her elbow, warning her not to say anything.

'Jasper, we were wondering if you could help us a little with our experiments?' Loisa said tactfully.

'Of course. All you need do is ask.'

'Do you have anything in your collection of works on the subject of necromancy?'

Jasper thought for a moment before his face lit up. 'Of course! Why didn't I think of that sooner? It makes perfect sense.'

'But necromancers are so very rare. I thought they had all been exterminated,' Loisa said.

'Ah, even you don't know everything, my dear immortal lady,' Jasper said. 'My studies have suggested that necromancy is simply a technique. Any of the magically adept can turn to the dark arts of the dead. It's just a case of learning how.'

'So a Witch or a Warlock or anyone with the Shadow in their blood could be a necromancer?' Elle asked. 'Do they learn their craft like the alchemists do?'

Jasper nodded. 'Little is known about them. I would have thought some sort of apprenticeship would be the way.'

'If I were a necromancer, where would I hide if I came to London?' Elle wondered.

Jasper let out a puff of air as he contemplated the question. 'Impossible to say. I suppose it depends on the necromancer. If they draw their power from the elements, then water would go to water. Fire to fire and so on. Specific Shadow creatures have different predilections for certain environments. Or so the theory goes.' He fussed around the table and pulled out an illustrated chart. It was filled with Cabbalic symbols. 'See here. Mermaids and kelpies like water. Nightwalkers cannot abide daylight, so they favour the night. The various fairies favour whatever plant or stone they were born of. But there are myriad sources of power. The sea, lightning, volcanoes. They could be anywhere.'

'Lightning,' Elle said. She looked at Loisa.

'Actually, I have a book about necromancy. My cousin Aleister briefly explored the darker reaches of power a few years ago when he was at Oxford. He let me borrow some of his books, but I forgot to return them. He is in Paris at the moment, so I'm sure he wouldn't mind if you took a look.'

'That would be extremely helpful,' Elle said.

'Very well.' Jasper looked excited at the prospect. 'Why don't you come round to me tomorrow evening? I shall arrange for some tea and a cold supper and we can discuss the matter in more detail. You have the address?'

'Yes, I will be able to find your rooms again,' Loisa said.

Jasper smiled. 'Splendid. I am entirely at your service,' he said, beaming.

'Thank you, Jasper. We will call shortly after sunset,' Elle said.

As they turned to go, Jasper called to Loisa. 'Um, Baroness, may I have a word in private?' he said.

'I'll see you at the car,' Elle said as she carefully stepped round the Delphic circle.

The Stanley was thankfully untouched when Elle returned to it. She waited outside the motor until Loisa returned. 'What on earth was that all about?' she asked her friend.

Loisa shrugged. 'Jasper has asked if I would consider turning him to the nightside.'

Elle shuddered. 'Why would someone deliberately want that?'

'The power. The allure of immortality. Who can say? I suspect that he has been so helpful because he was looking for an opportunity to ask me.'

'And what will you do?' Elle asked.

Loisa shrugged. 'He is far too young for the burdens that those of us who walk the night must bear. I told him that we should be friends for a few years yet. And if he still wishes to make the transition, then I shall help him.'

'Fair enough. Let's see what he comes up with tomorrow night,' Elle said.

'My thoughts exactly. It takes a long time before one can truly know the depths of someone's character. Turning someone to the nightside is not a decision made lightly.'

Elle sighed as she got into the motor and started up

the engine. 'Loisa, I'm cold and tired. Perhaps we should go home for tonight.'

Loisa did not make any move to get into the car.

'Well, come on, then,' Elle said. 'The weather is not getting any better.'

'You go home and get some rest. I am going to take my leave from you for a little while. Making the journey here was extremely taxing. I have spent far more time in daylight than I should have.'

'Oh Loisa, you should have said something!' Elle said.

The Nightwalker shook her head. 'Your excellent dinners have sustained me, but I need a little bit more than animal blood to build up my strength. So I think I will take a short walk through the West End before I return home.'

'Are you sure? I could wait for you,' Elle said.

Loisa gave her a wicked smile. 'My dear, you forget that I am a very old, very strong Nightwalker. I am quite accustomed to looking after myself. It is the people of London you should be worried about.'

Elle frowned. 'Surely you are not going to grab the first poor fool you find in the street, are you?'

Loisa threw her head back and laughed. 'What do you think I am? No, I know of a lovely little crypt not far from here where people go to make...donations. It's all perfectly legal.'

'At least let me send someone to collect you when you are finished.'

Loisa tutted. 'Don't worry about me. I will see you tomorrow.' And with those words, she slipped off into the night.

Chapter Twenty-two

Clothilde threw her hands in the air and howled in frustration. 'What do you mean he got away?' she stormed.

Emilian hung his head. 'The minders lost him on one of their training walks, mistress.'

'And who told you to let him out? I thought I made it clear that the tall one was special. He was to stay within these walls at all times.' Dark clouds roiled in the sky above Battersea and great purple flashes of lightning crackled between the high towers of the monastery as her temper raged.

'I'm sorry, mistress, but the monks opened the cages for the minders last night. I didn't see that they let him out until he was gone.'

'And whose responsibility is it to supervise these stupid little men?'

Emilian bowed. 'Mine, mistress,' he said.

'So it is your fault and more so for trying to blame your underlings. That's very poor, Emilian. I am deeply disappointed in you.'

'I am sorry, mistress.' He kept his eyes trained on the ground as he spoke, but even now he exuded an air of subversive arrogance that she found deeply annoying. As if she could not see through his feigned subservience.

'Did they even see where he went?' she seethed.

'He was with the group that went out hunting for recruits near the Tower Bridge docks. The minders say they were ambushed. People waiting in the shadows as if they were expected. There was a woman and a Nightwalker. I'm not sure if I believe them, but Vargo says that the women stole him and ran off.'

'How is that possible?' she said. 'Do you honestly think I am that stupid? All my walkers are spellbound. They cannot be separated from the herd unless I will it.'

'I know, mistress. Vargo must have made a mistake.'

'Well, go and find out what really happened!' she shouted.

'Yes, mistress.' Emilian tipped his hat and made to leave, seemingly grateful for the opportunity to escape.

'And Emilian,' she said as he reached the door. 'I want him back undamaged. Whatever it takes. Don't make me regret saving that little sister of yours.'

Emilian turned and glared at Clothilde. His dark eyes blazed with anger. 'You leave my sister alone,' he said through gritted teeth. 'We may work for you and call you mistress, but know this, *La Dame Blanche*, we are no one's slaves.'

'Enough of this insolence, you miserable little cockroach!' Clothilde screeched. With a flick of her wrist, she summoned the power of the storm above her and flung Emilian from her chambers into the hallway. He landed on the hard floor with a satisfying thump. As a final touch, she made the door slam behind him for effect.

She turned and stalked to the large bank of windows behind her. From this room she could see London as it sprawled out before her, shrouded in the purple storm clouds that followed her everywhere she went.

She sighed and rubbed her forehead. That Emilian had given her such a headache. Sometimes the temptation to turn the insolent man and his sister to dust was almost too much to resist. But she needed them for the moment. As a trueborn son of the travelling people, he was immune to her powers and charms and it was most necessary that she had someone she could rely on, but whom she did not affect. Emilian did not know this, but his presence served as a grounding mechanism, much like a lightning rod assisted in a storm. It was very easy to lose touch with reality when immersed in so much power. It was the only reason she kept the brother and sister alive.

Clothilde glared out into the driving rain. Her beautiful Warlock was gone. And it was all due to the utter incompetence of the electromancers in her charge. It was yet again time to mete out some much needed discipline.

One of the electromancers knocked softly on the door.

'What is it?' she snapped.

'It's time for the feeding, mistress,' he whispered. 'You said to call when it was time.'

'I'll be there in a moment.'

The little monk bowed his head and retreated.

'You!' She pointed at the monk.

The little man froze.

'Tell me . . . who was the monk in charge of letting our soldiers out of their cages last night?'

'I–I'm not sure, ma'am,' he muttered.

'Well, can you find out?' she said, her voice suddenly silky with menace.

'I surely can, ma'am.'

'Then do so. And bring him to me.'

'Yes, ma'am.'

Clothilde donned her white outer robes and strode along the gallery to the control room where she could conduct tonight's feeding. As she passed them, electromancers bowed and retreated into the shadows and long narrow passageways that made up the galleries.

The monastery was built in a large rectangle with a chimney at each point. Each chimney reached high up into the sky and was designed to collect the lightning the electromancers needed to make spark. In the middle of the complex was a cavernous glass-covered courtyard, which the electromancers called the spark turbine hall. It was in this hall that the electromancers channelled the static electricity that they fed into the turbines, where it was mixed with the magic they drew from the Shadow. Once combined, the bright blue spark was fed into massive holding tanks. Some was pumped into glass cylinders and tanks to be sent off to power airships and assist all manner of steam-powered machines. The rest was piped along the network into the city where it was used for light, heating and the grinding machines that made the city run.

Clothilde gave a small smile of satisfaction as she climbed the square staircase that led up to the control room. Despite her misgivings, the Consortium could not have chosen a better place to set up a factory. Here she had all she needed to bring their plans to fruition.

But the monastery was so large that it was almost impossible to police on one's own. Especially since she was surrounded by such weakness and incompetence. Grudgingly, she had to admit that the little men did work hard once motivated, and apart from a few newspaper headlines proclaiming shortages, they managed to produce enough spark to stop anyone from noticing what was really going on under their very noses. And she liked that.

Emilian was waiting for her in the control room.

'I thought I sent you on an errand,' she said as she stared out the finely panelled glass windows. Some of them had been opened, allowing sound to reach her from the hall below.

'All done. The culprit took only moments to find,' he answered drily. 'I thought it would be more fun to watch the spectacle up here with you.' He gave her a sarcastic smile which made her ache to slap him.

Below them, a section of the turbine hall had been fenced off with sturdy cattle pens. In these pens, her undead soldiers waited in silence for her to command them. The only sound they made was the ticking of their clockwork hearts which beat in unison with her own. Eight hundred so far. Eight hundred fearless soldiers, incapable of feeling pain. Each one set to obey every command given by the one who commanded them.

A group of electromancers shuffled in through a side gate. One of them stepped forward nervously.

'Are you the one who was in charge of these yesterday?' she said through the speaking tube. The voice conveyance replicator squeaked and whined and a few electromancers flinched.

'Well? Are you?' she said, this time a little more carefully.

'Yes…yes I am, my lady,' the monk said.

'Stay where you are. The rest of you, please go to your designated viewing posts. Vargo, Hutch: let the feeding commence.'

Two of the minders she had employed nodded and signalled for the main doors to be opened. A herd of bewildered goats were ushered into the hall. They were wet and shivering from the cold outside.

The undead shifted. A few grunted as the goats leaped and bumped against each other, bleating as they sensed impending danger.

Vargo and Hutch closed the doors, securing them with the heavy iron crossbar. She watched them climb the spiral stairs to the first floor gallery where the other electromancers had taken their places as they had been commanded. They were all to watch the feedings. This was her way of showing them the magnificence of her creations. It was also a warning for those who disobeyed.

'Everything set?' she asked.

Vargo nodded.

The monk who remained on the ground looked at the goats with a growing sense of horror. 'M–mistress! What about me?' His voice echoed through the hall.

Clothilde ignored him.

'Electromancers! Let this be a lesson to you,' she said through the speaking tube. 'I will not tolerate disobedience in any form. And this is the fate that awaits anyone who disobeys my orders. Is that understood?'

The electromancers stirred. A few muttered and looked on with worried faces.

Clothilde pointed at the guilty monk and in an instant he was floating in the air. The man gasped in surprise as she dropped him; he fell in the middle of the herd of frightened, bleating goats.

'Please. Please don't hurt me. I am sorry for what I have done. I did not mean to let him out. I–I didn't know,' he begged.

Clothilde did not waver. She raised her other hand and made a turning motion – as one would do with a key in a lock.

As one, like the visors of the knights of old but in reverse, the muzzles of all eight hundred undead slipped down from their faces to reveal their open gaping mouths. Some of them were drooling profusely at the smell of goat and man, so close.

Clothilde closed her eyes and drew a globule of power into herself. Then she exhaled and projected her will across the gallery. 'Go, my children. Feed,' she said.

Suddenly, the undead all started moving. Without hesitation, they set upon the terrified goats, tearing great chunks of living flesh and feeding in the gush of blood that ensued. The last that was heard of the poor doomed electromancer was a thin wailing cry as he was overwhelmed by the surging undead.

Clothilde wrinkled her nose at the sight of entrails and death as she watched the feeding frenzy below. 'Soon the only thing left will be a few blood splatters as my soldiers devour everything they can, including bone and skin,' she observed.

Emilian did not answer. He was lounging in one of the tall-backed Queen Anne chairs that adorned the control room. He had thrown a leg over one of the arm rests.

'That was part of the beauty of their design,' Clothilde continued, unperturbed by his silence. 'They will clean up the mess of war by gorging themselves on the enemy, thus negating the need for supply trains. It is indeed the work of genius, don't you think?'

'Some might call it madness,' Emilian said.

'Madness is often the prerequisite for genius, my dear Emilian. With control of the stock markets of the world, the banks and this army, the Consortium will soon be unstoppable,' she said.

'Then the Fates help us all,' Emilian said. He rose and strode out of the control room.

Clothilde smiled. That was a lesson well learned. Emilian would think twice before defying her again.

'Once the feeding is completed, please ensure that all soldiers are safely in their cells. It is time to commence the next batch of Making,' she said through the speaking tube.

Those waiting for her commands sprang into action as they started preparing the enormous machine that took up the other half of the hall for this evening's work.

But even Emilian did not know about her special project. The Warlock...she felt another surge of irritation. When she had done the conversion, she had made him more intelligent, more capable of being civilised. And while he was settling in with his new heart she had painstakingly unstrapped the nodule of power he held compressed inside him. She was very surprised when, even once released, she could not access his power. It was almost as if he was fighting her, refusing to yield to her will. And even though she knew that it would only be a matter of time before he yielded, the challenge of breaking his resistance fascinated her.

And now he was gone. She slammed her fist down on the counter with such force that the corner of one of the glass panes in the windows before her cracked.

She lifted the ornate brass key from around her neck and examined it.

'I don't know where you are, my love, but at some stage you will come back to me. For I have worked it that we will seek each other out before the clock spring inside you winds down. And when we are reunited, we will go away from this place. We will go to a place where we will be together forever.'

Clothilde felt a shiver of anticipation. What sweet magic they would make together one day. In response, purple fingers of lightning crackled in the clouds above the building. Yes, it would be good to have a mate to share things with, she thought. She had been alone for far too long.

Chapter Twenty-three

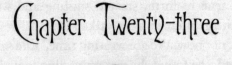

The next evening, Elle and Loisa found themselves in a horse-drawn hansom heading for the suburb of Soho where Jasper lived.

His rooms, as was fashionable for unmarried gentlemen living in London, were just off Denmark Street. This was one of the slightly less salubrious parts of the West End, but a favourite with occultists, bohemians, absinthe drinkers and those other folk who liked to indulge in the various opium dens and other clubs that dotted the place.

'Here is good enough, driver,' Elle said. The cab trundled to a halt in Charing Cross Road, causing a slight traffic jam as they got out.

The driver pulled off before she could tell him to wait for them, leaving them standing on the pavement.

'Well, that was ever so rude,' Elle said.

'Oh, never mind. This is far too early to be awake,' Loisa muttered. She stretched as gracefully as only a Nightwalker could. 'Especially after yesterday's adventure.' Loisa was once again dressed in her black leather trouser outfit and the two of them were drawing more than one surreptitious glance from passers-by. Two ladies dressed in leather coats and trousers was something which drew attention, even from Londoners and even in Soho.

Loisa, true to form, started smiling and winking at some of the gentlemen who walked by.

'Loisa, not now. We are wasting time,' Elle said. As the days passed, she found she was struggling to maintain her patience.

Loisa turned her attention to her. 'My, we are a little grouchy this evening. But never fear. Jasper's lodgings are just up ahead.'

They knocked at the door, which was opened by an ancient lady with a crooked back.

'We are here to see Mr Sidgwick. He is expecting us,' Elle said.

'I'm afraid he's not here,' Jasper's landlady said. 'But do come in. It's not seemly for ladies to stand in the street. You can wait in the front room.' She stood aside to let them into the hall. It was a damp, sweaty-looking place with paint flaking off the casements and greyish patches on the walls.

'Upstairs?' Elle said.

'Second floor. But I'm telling you, Mr Sidgwick is not there.' The landlady was looking visibly distressed.

'Loisa, come,' Elle said as she passed the landlady and strode up the stairs to the second floor. They stopped outside a door that was also in need of a fresh coat of paint.

'Jasper?' Elle rapped on the door. The sound echoed through the dank stairwell, but there was no answer.

'That's odd. He did say that we should come shortly after dark.'

Elle tried the door handle. It turned and the door sprang open. 'Not locked, then.'

Loisa pressed her perfect lips together for a moment. 'Best we proceed with caution. I'll go first,' she said as she entered the rooms.

'Good heavens,' Loisa exclaimed. Jasper's rooms were in a most deplorable state of chaos. The furniture he owned was all upturned. Books, papers and other bits of occult paraphernalia were strewn around, intermingled with discarded bed linen and what appeared to be the complete feather contents of a pillow.

'What a mess! What happened here?' Loisa breathed.

Elle reached inside her coat and drew out her Colt. 'Well, my guess is that Jasper did actually know something, but someone has beaten us to the information.'

Loisa looked at her in alarm. 'Do you think they've taken him, like...Hugh?'

Elle closed her eyes for a moment banishing the image of Hugh from her mind. 'It's possible.'

'I told you he wasn't here.' The landlady had finally managed to shuffle up the stairs. 'The place was like this when I got up this morning. There has been no sight or sound of poor Mr Sidgwick. Do you think we should alert the police?'

Elle shrugged. 'Given past experiences, I doubt they'll do anything about it.'

'Poor Jasper. I was quite looking forward to sharing his turning to the nightside with him when the time was ripe.' Loisa ran her fingers along the edge of the upturned desk. Her fingers were white against the polished mahogany.

'Would you mind giving us a few moments?' Elle asked the landlady.

The landlady looked a bit dubious. 'Well, if you promise not to disturb anything further I suppose it could be all right. I will go and make us a cup of tea,' she said.

'Thank you, we are ever so grateful,' Elle replied.

'Just call if you need anything, my dear,' the landlady said as she shuffled downstairs.

'I wonder whether the book is still here. Most of it looks frightfully boring if you ask me.' Elle started rifling through the papers strewn on the floor.

'Strange.' Loisa pursed her lips. 'I suspect nothing has been taken. Except Jasper. And the overturned furniture in the room suggests that he put up quite a fight.' She picked up one of the overturned chairs and sat down in it.

'Loisa, have a look at the shelves. See if there is anything that might relate to the undead. Some of the books Jasper mentioned might still be there.'

Elle lifted a leather-bound volume up off some papers where it had been discarded, open and face down. She wrinkled her nose in annoyance as she carefully closed the book and eased the binding into place. She hated it when people mistreated books.

'I'm not sure if this is helping,' Loisa said. 'All these tomes look the same to me. See, some are in languages even I can't recognise.'

Elle found a gap in the row of books where a poor abused volume seemed to have been removed. She picked it up to slip it into place, but there was something in the way. She put her hand into the gap and pulled out a manila folder. It had been wedged in between the books on the shelf.

'What is this?' Carefully she opened the folder. 'Press cuttings and the back pages of penny dreadfuls where the hanged and missing are reported,' she muttered. 'How odd.' She leafed through the pages. 'These are all recent. Look.'

Loisa picked up an overturned occasional table and they spread the contents of the folder out on it. Before them, the headlines of newspaper clippings from almost every major London newspaper stood out in bold black letters: SPARK SHORTAGE LOOMS. ELECTROMANCERS IN TALKS WITH AUTHORITIES.

Another read: WETTEST WINTER IN LIVING MEMORY RECORDED. FEAR OF FLOODING.

A further article was the same one Elle had read just days before: TICKING MONSTERS PROWL THE STREETS. PUBLIC ADVISED TO STAY INDOORS.

The rest of the cuttings referred to people disappearing along with various advertisements in the obituary columns for people presumed dead.

'I think he was working on the theory that the problems with the electromancers is somehow linked to the disappearances. But how?'

At the back was a list of names, written in Jasper's scrawl.

Loisa leaned in over her shoulder. 'That's a lot of people, if those are the missing. See. He even has Hugh's name.' She pointed at the list. 'I think dear Jasper was not entirely open with us about his investigations. He knows far more than he let on.'

'It doesn't matter now.' Elle gathered up the clippings and slipped the folder into her holdall. 'I'm willing to bet that whoever took Jasper is behind what happened to Marsh.'

'Well, then,' Loisa said, gathering up her top hat and gloves, 'I suggest that we pay the electromancers a little visit. What do you say?'

ᖇᖇ

Life among the travelling folk is not so bad.

My new mistress has turned out to be a lot kinder than I had feared. Below all the hardness she exudes, there is good in her.

But she keeps me tied to this place with her red silk, even though I am quite content to stay. And all things considered, she does always make sure that I am looked after, for the travelling folk understand the way of fairies. She has even given me my own fern to sit in during the day.

I am starting to enjoy the freedom that the wagons bring. It is far preferable to the stuffiness of my last home. I always dreamed of being a fine lady in a big house with servants, but in the end, all that English pretentiousness did not suit me after all. For no matter where I am or who I pretend to be, French blood will remain in my veins.

My new mistress worries. She spends hours studying the cards laid out on a silk cloth. She peers into the future without really knowing what she sees, for she is no Oracle. It is only when the man with the peacock feather shows up that she relaxes.

He stepped into the wagon, bringing the stink of horses and the street with him.

'Emilian! Boots outside,' my mistress said.

'Sorry.' He kicked his boots off and shoved them out the door.

She went up to him and they embraced. 'What news do you bring, dear brother?'

He sighed and rubbed his eyes as if to rub away a great tiredness from them. 'The same. She is as insane as ever. Would you believe that she actually tried to trick me into making a promise of servitude?'

Florica, for that is the pretty name of my new mistress, tutted with disapproval.

'Have you eaten?' she said.

'No. There is no proper food in that place. The little men live on gruel and dry bread. And her highness lives off her own evil.' He spat into the glowing heart of the stove as if there were an awful taste in his mouth.

'Here, have some stew. Good rabbit. The boys caught some last night. I made it with dried apricots. I saved some for you.' She spooned the stew into a bowl for him and I could smell the hints of clove and parsley that rose up from the pot.

He picked up the spoon and started eating. The flavours must have pressed his hunger, for he cleaned out the bowl, mopping up the last bits with a crust of bread.

'I don't like it, Emilian. We should never have become involved with that woman. The women here say I have the shadow of darkness hanging over me. They make the sign of the eye at me when I go to fetch water.' She sighed. 'Perhaps they are right. I have nightmares about all those lost souls at night.' Her fine brow crinkled as she spoke.

'I wouldn't worry if I were you. You know we had no real choice in the matter. She would have let you die.'

My mistress sighed. 'Don't remind me of that.' Her fingers went to the row of buttons in her dress, slightly to the left. 'So tell me, how is our beloved lady?'

'She's very angry with me. One of the monks let her pet go roaming with the others in the night and someone stole him.' Emilian laughed. 'I mean, who would steal something like that?'

'Perhaps someone who cares about him,' Florica said. 'You forget that those things were all once people with families. Would you not come looking for me if I went missing?'

Emilian put down his spoon and smiled at his sister. 'Of course I would.'

'I suppose you should find out who the man was and then see if you can find his family, his home. That's where I would look,' she said.

'You are the cleverest little sister in the world, did you know that?'

'Why do you say that?' she asked.

'Well, Mistress Evil was so angry that she fed the monk who did it to the creatures. And now I am out looking for whoever stole him so she can get revenge. A loved one or family. Of course, that's exactly who took him. All I need to do is trace his steps home and I will find him again.'

'Oh, Emilian, do be careful,' Florica said.

'Don't worry. I've already got one lead. You don't go around making a spectacle of yourself without attracting someone who will be a witness. And I am paying a pretty penny to find out what her evilness wants to know.'

'Do you really have to do this? Can't she just make another pet?'

He shook his head. 'Apparently this one was very special. One of a kind. But don't worry about it, little sister. It's only for a little while longer. Her army grows stronger each day and soon she will move on.' He smiled at her. 'And when that *happens, we will be rich beyond your wildest dreams. I will buy you a house painted with real gold. And fine dresses made of silk. And then you can languish in your drawing room while servants bring you cake. You will never have to carry heavy buckets of water again.'*

Florica shook her head and laughed, for this was a game the two of them played often. 'I don't want a house painted of gold. It would need too much polishing.'

'I will buy you a wagon of solid silver with four fine white horses.'

'I don't want a wagon of pure silver and fine horses – they eat too much.'

'What do you want then, little sister?'

'All I want is to be happy and free with the whole world to roam.'

Emilian's expression softened. 'You have the true blood of the travelling folk in your veins, little sister. And because of that and no matter what happens, we will always be free.'

'But we are not free as long as that woman has a hold over us. I cannot take much more of this, Emilian. I tell you I cannot.' Her lip trembled.

He put a hand on her shoulder to console her. 'And that is why we must let her evilness succeed. It is the quickest way to be rid of her. I promise you that it won't be very much longer. You'll see.'

And as I listened to them speak, I took note of their wishes. For even bound and held in this place, I still might have a few tricks up my sleeve. And sometimes, for those who are true of heart, wishes can come true.

⍦

Chapter Twenty-four

'Does it ever stop raining in this place?' Loisa scoffed as she lifted her shawl of the finest Spanish mantilla lace over her top hat like a veil to protect her curls from the damp.

Elle strode out into the street to look for a cab but, as was invariably the case when seeking a cab in London, there was never one to be found when needed.

They turned into Charing Cross Road and started walking towards Trafalgar Square.

'I'll try on this side of the road,' Loisa said. 'You take the other.'

'Jellied eels, madam? The best in the West End,' said a coster with a barrow perched on the street corner as Elle passed.

'No, thank you,' she said quickly. She had never been partial to eels boiled in vinegar and suspended in a jelly made from their own cartilage.

'I have oysters too. Freshly caught,' he offered.

'Thank you, but no,' she said. Then she paused and looked at the coster. He was a surly-looking man with a salt-and-pepper beard that did not do much to cover up the scars from whatever painful diseases had marred his life. His eyes were sharp though. This was a man who missed very little.

'Perhaps you might help me with some information,' she said after thinking for a moment.

'Well, I can't say as I know much. I tend to stick to minding me own business, I do.'

'That a fact now?' Elle arched her eyebrows. 'And you work this corner every day?'

'Every day that God gives,' the coster said.

'Hmm. Perhaps I will try some of your eels after all,' Elle said. She opened her holdall and pulled out two pence.

The coster took a moment to examine the money in the light of his lantern before he started spooning eels into a newspaper funnel.

'Down the road, opposite that corner, lives a gentleman. He has sandy hair and wears glasses,' Elle said.

The coster nodded slowly. 'There's many gentlemen with sandy hair round here, madam,' he said.

'He's a fellow who likes books. Involved in all sorts of funny magic business. Comes and goes at all hours. Have you seen him today?'

The coster pursed his lips. 'I may have.'

'Did you see anything unusual happen in Denmark Street today?'

'Perhaps,' the coster said, scratching his ear.

Elle pulled another coin out of her holdall. 'I will give you this shiny new shilling if you tell me what you saw.'

The coster palmed the coin and smiled at her. It seemed that they were now speaking the same language.

'It were them gypsies. The one had a peacock feather in his hat. That's the evil eye, that is. They came here while I was setting up my pitch across the road. Carried him out and loaded him into a carriage as if he were a side of beef. I thought it must have been a gambling debt or something. Didn't think more of it.'

'Do you know where they went?'

The coster rubbed his jaw 'They headed off towards Tottenham Court Road. Could be anywhere by now.'

'Thank you kindly.'

'Much obliged, madam,' the coster said. 'Bless you and have a good evening.'

'I will,' she said. 'But before I go, where would I look if I were out to meet the travelling folk?' she said, trying for just that little bit of extra information.

The coster scratched his head. 'Well, you might want to have a look at the Black Stag pub. It's in the East End, mind. But there are loads of travelling folk in the area and the landlord lets them drink there sometimes. One of the few houses round there who do.'

'The Black Stag,' Elle said. 'Thank you for the tip.'

'Do take care if you go there though. The Black Stag is no place for a fine lady on her own,' the coster said.

'I found one!' Loisa called out from the inside of a steam cab that drew up beside Elle.

Elle smiled at the coster. 'Well then, it's a good thing I am not a fine lady then. Good evening to you, sir.'

She stepped into the cab and sat down next to Loisa.

'Are those eels?' Loisa wrinkled her nose at the fishy vinegary smell that emanated from the newspaper parcel Elle held.

'They are indeed. Horrible-smelling things, aren't they?'

'So what did the man say? I presume you did not puchase those for the purpose of eating them?' Loisa said.

'I know my father is quite fond of these,' she said, stowing the parcel in her holdall. 'I'm sure Mrs Hinges will make them presentable with a few slices of brown bread and butter, but yes I do believe, my dear baroness, that we have ourselves a clue.'

Loisa looked at her with expectation.

'After the monastery, we're going to the pub.'

'Well, this isn't going very well,' Elle said. The cab had dropped them off just outside Battersea Park and at that moment they were standing ankle-deep in cold mud. Water dripped down in big, insulting drops from the branches of the trees above them. One hit her right on that warm spot where ear and neck connect and she shivered.

'Jasper says that this is the mist that draws forth the Tickers,' Loisa remarked, unaffected by the cold. 'But they must go somewhere during the day. Do you think that this place might be it?'

The spark monastery loomed up ahead of them. Its four chimneys were silent and ominous against the gunmetal sky.

'If Jasper's newspaper clippings are anything to go by. I must admit that it does make for a really good place to hide. Spacious and with as much spark as is needed to create these monsters,' Elle said.

Loisa lifted her head and sniffed the air. 'I smell death,' she murmured.

'Oi, what are you two lovelies doing standing out here, eh?' someone said behind them.

Elle and Loisa both turned to face the man who spoke, but they were blinded by the bright beam of a spark lantern that splashed light across the grass and trees. Elle could just make out the outlines of three large men. The one with the light was close and the other two were lurking a few paces behind him.

'The park is closed to the public. But seeing as you are here, why don't you two pretty darlings come over 'ere so we can have a little cuddle? There's a penny in it for each of you if you do,' one of them said.

'That one is mine,' Loisa said softly.

Elle nodded and stepped aside.

Quicker than the eye could see, Loisa leaped into action and grabbed the man. She tilted his head and she sank her fangs into his throat.

Elle shuddered. She had never seen a Nightwalker feed on a person before and it was utterly terrifying. Loisa was every bit the predator that books and legends spoke of.

Suddenly Loisa let out a choking sound. She let go of the man and she fell to the ground gasping and clutching her throat.

'Loisa!' Elle ran over to where she lay curled up on the ground.

'Silver!' Loisa gasped. She doubled over and started vomiting bile as black as peat on to the ground.

Elle held her friend by the shoulders as she retched. 'What do I do?'

'Run. Get away from here,' Loisa choked out between bouts of retching.

The man she had attacked started laughing as he pulled out his handkerchief to wipe his neck. 'That's right, little Nightwalker. Thought you could have a bite of old Tom?' He laughed again. 'You nearly got me once, but not twice my dear. I've been drinking my silver every day with my porridge, just in case we met again, so there's to be no sipping from my neck, all right?' He let out a shrill whistle. 'Vargo. Hutch. It's them two girlies from the docks. I knew they'd be back for more trouble. Let's load them up. The dark one will be dead soon, but I'm sure the mistress won't say no to the other. At the very least, she'll want to know where her Ticker's gone off to. She's not very big, but who knows, the mistress might have a use for her.'

Loisa was on her hands and knees, dry-heaving. Her body arched in spasms every time she retched.

Elle reached inside her coat and pulled out her Colt. 'No amount of silver will stop a bullet to the chest, so don't even think about it,' she said to the two lumbering assailants who were bearing down on her. She cocked the revolver with a satisfying click. 'I have one bullet to the head and one to the heart for each of you, with plenty to spare in case I miss, if you take even one step closer,' she said.

They hesitated. One of the men raised his hands in a gesture of submission.

'Loisa, can you stand?' Elle said.

Loisa groaned and gagged, but she nodded.

'Then on the count of three, I am going to support you so that we can run. All right?'

Loisa nodded again.

'One...two...three!' Elle slipped her arm around Loisa and dragged her up off the ground. The two of them stumbled past the men, Elle keeping her revolver trained on their would-be attackers. The three men had spread out to catch them as if they were locked in some bizarre rugby game where Loisa was the ball. Elle felt her shoulder connect with the soft part of someone's abdomen. The man gasped with surprise and stumbled backwards.

'Get them! Get them!' the one who called himself Tom shouted as Elle and Loisa broke free and ran for cover. Elle skidded and slid under the dark branches of a yew hedge. They landed in the freezing mulch where they lay for several long silent moments, hoping the men would miss them in the dark.

Loisa groaned and retched again. She looked to be in a terrible way.

'They went this way.' She heard the trudge of hobnailed boots on wet leaves just outside their makeshift hiding place and she held Loisa tighter, lest she make another sound that might give them away.

But Elle's attempts were in vain. 'Got ya!' Tom crowed. She felt a huge hand grab her by the collar of her coat in order to drag them out of the hedge. Without thinking, Elle turned and fired at her assailant.

The two shots she fired rang out in quick succession across the silent park.

The man let go of Elle and she heard him drop to the ground. He gave a strange little gurgling grunt, and then he lay perfectly still. A shout went up in the distance as the two others realised their comrade had fallen.

'Loisa, you have to run with me. Just for a little while, all right?' she whispered.

The Nightwalker nodded and Elle dragged her up.

The two remaining henchmen were crouched over their fallen comrade on the other side of the hedge, but they both sat up when Elle and Loisa broke cover.

'No one comes a step closer, do you understand? I don't want any more trouble,' Elle warned. 'Just let us go and nobody else needs to get hurt this evening. Understood?'

The one she thought was called Vargo lifted both hands in a gesture of surrender.

Elle did not wait to see if he meant it. She turned Loisa round and together they stumbled along the pathway and into the street. For once the Fates were looking out for them and to her unending relief, an unsuspecting steam cab pulled up just as they stepped on to the pavement.

'Grosvenor Square. And be as quick as you can about it. This is an emergency,' she told the cab driver.

'Will fresh blood help?' Elle whispered to Loisa as they rattled through the streets. Loisa was so pale that her skin shone with a bluish hue in the half-light of the spark lamps that shone through the cab windows in bursts as they drove past. Black veins spread under her fine skin as the silver made its way through her system.

The Nightwalker nodded. 'It helps us heal,' she mumbled.

Elle sat Loisa up against the seat and wrenched herself out of her damp leather coat.

'Wha— what are you doing?' Loisa mumbled. Her head lolled to the side.

Elle rolled up her sleeve to expose her wrist. 'I am not going to let you die in the back of this cab, Loisa. Not while I can do something about it.' She held her wrist before the Nightwalker's white lips. 'Take some blood from me.'

Loisa shook her head. 'No.'

'This is a matter of life and death. Do it, damn you. Before I lose my nerve and you die.'

Loisa's eyes flew open at the sensation of Elle's pulse against her lips.

'Go on! What are you waiting for?'

Elle gritted her teeth and closed her eyes as she felt the sharp jab of fang pierce her skin.

Loisa started making strange little slurping sounds that chilled Elle to the bone, but she held herself resolute. They both knew that without blood her friend would die.

Seconds ticked by as they sat, huddled together in the dark. Elle felt herself grow woozy and she gently touched Loisa's cheek with her free hand. The Nightwalker stopped feeding and fell back against the seat. Without missing a beat, Elle quickly wrapped her handkerchief around her wrist, sealing off the puncture wound that marked her arm.

'We are now blood sisters. Forevermore,' Loisa mumbled. She closed her eyes with a little sigh.

Elle watched her for a few anxious moments. The black under Loisa's skin looked like it was slowly receding. She would probably need more nourishment before she was well, but hopefully she would make it.

And so, for the second time in three nights, Elle found herself dragging an injured loved one up the stairs of Greychester House while the doctor was summoned. But at least this time there was hope. They had found the lair of the necromancer.

Chapter Twenty-five

A large man in a bowler hat stepped off the train at Paddington Station. He had no luggage, save for a brown leather Gladstone bag which he carried with him always.

Patrice Chevalier had come to London.

Outside the station he paused and sniffed the air. It had stopped raining, but the air was thick with freezing fog. It was the kind of damp that soaked into the lungs, filling them with the miasmic pneumonia that could spell death.

Unperturbed by the damp, he held up his arm and hailed a cab. 'Soho, if you please,' he said in heavily accented English.

'Walk on!' said the cabbie as the hackney lurched forward. Patrice studied the clockwork taximeter which whirred and ticked as the fare mounted up. London was such an insanely expensive city. He hated coming here.

Outside Dean Street he bade the cab driver to wait for him. His business here would be quick, he was sure.

Upstairs, Police Commissioner Willoughby was at lunch. He was slicing into the hunk of rare roast beef that sat in a reddish pool in the middle of his plate.

'Police Commissioner...no don't get up,' Patrice said smoothly as the startled man recognised him. 'Do you mind if I sit?'

'Of course,' Willoughby stuttered. He put down his knife and fork and wiped his face. 'I am so sorry, Mr Chevalier. I was not expecting you.'

'I like to drop in on my contacts unannounced. It keeps them on their toes.' He pulled out one of his little black cigarillos and lit it, blowing a fine plume of scented smoke into the air. 'It has been a while, though. How are things?'

'I am glad you stopped by.' The commissioner beamed, regaining his composure. 'How are your clients? I trust they are well?'

Patrice gave him a sly smile. 'I have various clients, Commissioner. Some are better than others.' Of course, the commissioner was referring to the Council of Warlocks. Patrice had kept him on their payroll for some time – even while he was working with Marsh. Sometimes it paid to have a few secret resources.

The commissioner pushed his plate aside. 'Well, I think I might have some excellent news for them. You know our little problem...the one with the red hair?'

'Yes?' Patrice said slowly.

'I think I might have dispensed with the obstacle. Let's just say that I had an important task for the good viscount and it has taken him away from home. The way is open for your clients to take what is theirs.'

'Is that so?' Patrice said. He did his best to keep his expression impassive, but Willoughby was right, this was excellent news.

'It is indeed.'

'Do I want to know how you achieved this most interesting state of affairs?'

'It's up to you. If you don't ask, I won't tell. But let's just say he's not coming back.'

'I shall have to pay the lady a visit. Payment will be forthcoming once I have confirmation that your plan has actually worked.'

The commissioner grinned with glee. 'I had the lady in my office just a few days ago. I had her in readiness to deliver to you, all trussed up like the pretty little goose she is, but her dastardly uncle intervened and so I had no choice but to let her go.'

Patrice let out a chuckle. 'I'd hardly call Eleanor a pretty goose. She is most extraordinarily talented when it comes to escaping capture, but you did your best, sir, and I will not hold it against you.' He picked up his bowler hat and stood. 'I had better be off then. I am pleased with your news.'

The commissioner nodded and picked up his knife and fork. He stabbed into his cooling beef even as Patrice turned to go.

'Battersea Monastery,' Patrice said as soon as he was seated back in the cab.

'Are you sure?' the driver said. 'It's closed to the public. Lots of rumours of trouble in the area, so it's best avoided, sir.'

Patrice inclined his head. 'I have an appointment. Now take me there before I find another cab. And don't think I'll pay for the trip here, either.' Patrice was not interested in debating this with a mere driver so he balled his fist and stared at the man with the promise of violence clear in his eyes.

The cabbie did not quibble, but drove off at top speed.

As they made their way through the congested streets, Patrice was pleased to note that London had not changed much since he last visited. Apart from the extension of the rail system, it was still the same cold, damp, over-crowded place.

They slowed to allow a spark-tram to pass. A little newspaper boy ran up next to the carriage and thrust a newspaper at the window. It read SPARK SHORTAGES PLUNGE CITY INTO CRISIS in big bold letters.

Patrice smiled to himself. This place had not even begun to know what the word crisis meant. It was going to be so satisfying to see these smug people running from the terror that he, Patrice Chevalier, or Sir Patrice Abercrombie as he was known in the northern parts of the country, had brought about. Yes, it would be satisfying indeed. But first he had to go and see what his newest clients were up to. The Consortium paid well and he was curious to see the work they had told him about. With their money and influence, they were so much more powerful than the Council. Eleanor would have to wait until later. If Marsh was really gone, then a few hours would not matter. He would pick her up on his way back. The thought of her surprise at seeing him again made him smile. Yes, it would be sweet to deliver the Oracle to the Council on his return journey. This little trip to London was proving to be most profitable indeed.

The driver refused to drive into the grounds, but instead dropped him off outside the park. This meant he had to walk the last part – a task he did not relish with his bad leg. In fact, his bad leg was something he preferred not to think about at all, if he could help it. The knowledge that he was only half a man, existing partly in the Realm of Light and partly in the Realm of Shadow was a bitter topic indeed.

Outside the heavy oak doors he paused to knock with his walking cane.

In answer, a tiding of magpies rose up from the rooftops. 'Here! Here! Here!' they crowed as they circled the two lightning collector chimneys high up in the air above him.

The door opened with a low creak to reveal a monk dressed in the grey robes that the electromancers wore.

'Good afternoon, monsieur. We have been expecting you,' the monk said. He stepped aside to allow Patrice access.

Patrice nodded at the monk and stepped inside.

'Please follow me,' the monk said.

Patrice suppressed a shiver as they walked. He did not think it possible, but the inside of the monastery was even damper and colder than it was outside.

He wiggled his knee to allay the aching tingle that ran up and down the bottom half of his body.

'Everything all right, sir?' the monk asked.

'Fine. It's an old injury that plays up when the weather is bad,' Patrice said.

He was led down into a long corridor that took them through one of the refectories and on to the control room.

Patrice felt a chill pass over his shoulders. This was a strange place and it made his skin crawl. But he was not a man given to fancy or squeamishness and so he walked on as if he were on a gentle afternoon promenade on the shores of the Mediterranean.

The lady he came to see was waiting for him on the mezzanine that overlooked the turbine hall.

Patrice fought the surge of fear and desire that coursed through him as soon as he laid eyes on her. He had been warned about *La Dame Blanche*, but no number of warnings could prepare him for the physical impact she had on him – on all men, if the legends were to be believed. The harlot.

'Madame,' he said, nodding politely.

'Monsieur Chevalier. I am so pleased you have arrived,' she said with a gracious smile.

'I see you have been busy.' He motioned to the massive machine and the cattle pens that took up large parts of the turbine hall.

'I have indeed. We have managed to produce almost a thousand of them now. They are all in cells on that side of the building.'

Patrice felt himself fill with glee. A thousand unstoppable, infallible soldiers who were nothing but utterly obedient was almost enough to overrun London.

'I will take you to see them a little later. The insertion process is working very well and they are simply splendid specimens.'

'Quite so, madame. What better soldier is there than one who does not fear anything and who cannot be killed?'

'Please, call me Clothilde. Would you take a coffee?' she said.

'I might. But don't you have anything stronger?'

She laughed. 'Of course. One needs it in this cold damp place.' Clothilde snapped her fingers and a monk appeared with a tray.

'Absinthe, if you have some,' Patrice said. 'And don't let the fairy out. I like to hear them scream when I light my drink. They are such bothersome creatures, are they not?'

'Indeed. They can be,' the lady said with a tight little smile.

Patrice sat down in one of the overstuffed chairs. 'I have brought the new prototype as requested.' He opened his portmanteau and pulled out a glass case. Inside was a shiny clockwork device, the size of a human heart. It was made entirely of silver.

'Oh, isn't it lovely? So he has perfected the perpetual motion mechanism. These silver hearts will require no winding, they will simply keep running, yes?'

'That's what they claim,' Patrice said.

Clothilde smiled. 'The Clockmaker is indeed a master of his craft,' she said as she took the case from Patrice.

'I gather that you have enough silver to replicate this for the second project?'

'Yes. My men have been hard at work liberating silverware from donors who can afford to part with some of their wealth.'

'You mean they have been robbing houses?' Patrice said.

Clothilde shrugged. 'If you want to be vulgar about it, I suppose you could call it that.'

'What about the next stage of the project?' Patrice asked.

Clothilde looked up. 'Ah, Emilian. You have brought the drinks. This is Monsieur Chevalier, our honoured guest.'

Patrice looked round to see a man with dark hair and eyes carrying a tray.

'Bonjour, monsieur.' Emilian bowed and set about pouring their refreshments.

'We aim to capture the first Nightwalkers for fitting with the devices within the next few days. I believe they would make a splendid addition to our armies,' Clothilde said, continuing the conversation.

'The chairman will be pleased,' Patrice said.

Clothilde smiled sweetly. 'If the chairman is pleased, then I am pleased.'

Emilian snorted as he set the fine absinthe glass with the spoon resting over the rim before Patrice.

'I'm sorry, did you say something?' Patrice said.

'Ask her about her special project. The one she's keeping a secret,' he said.

Patrice looked at Clothilde who was glaring at Emilian with such venom that it made Patrice break out in goose bumps.

Clothilde gave a shrill little laugh that belied her composure. 'Emilian is so impudent. He really should be whipped for being so cheeky,' she said sweetly.

Emilian just shrugged, seemingly unimpressed by the fury of his mistress.

'Special project?' Patrice said.

'Oh, it's nothing really. They brought in a most interesting find about a week ago. A man unlike any other. I thought him to be the perfect candidate for some of my advanced tests. I was going to speak to you about the matter when you got here as I know that you are a man who gets things done.' She walked over to him and laid her hand on his arm. 'And I was hoping we might be able to help one another. Off the books, as it were.' She gave him one of her most alluring smiles.

Patrice felt a gentle shiver run through his body that led to a most inconvenient stirring in his loins. It had been the first such stirring Patrice had felt since his accident and he found this to be deeply disturbing in the circumstances.

'Ah, now that is a completely different situation,' he said without showing his discomfort. He took a sip of the mixed absinthe Emilian had placed before him. Somewhere, a fairy screamed softly.

'So where is he?' Patrice said.

Clothilde looked slightly embarrassed. 'This is where we ran into a slight problem. We fitted him with one of the special devices the Clockmaker sent, but one of these incompetent little monks let him out for the night with the others. And now he is gone.'

'Gone?' said Patrice.

'Someone stole him.'

'Someone stole him,' he echoed. 'And there is no way you can get him back?'

'We are working on it, but so far we have not been successful.'

'Why is that?'

'We haven't managed to locate him yet.' Clothilde toyed with the brass key she wore on a chain around her neck. 'We almost caught the thieves but they shot one of my men. Who would have thought it? My men tell me that it was a puny little woman with red hair and her even tinier Nightwalker friend that caused so much trouble.'

'Can't you just catch another specimen and proceed with that?'

She shook her head. 'It is unlikely that we will ever find one as good. I was most surprised when I examined him. A most unusual set of circumstances. Can you imagine my surprise when I started probing him, only to find out that he was a Warlock? And not only that, but he also seemed to have bound his own powers within himself?'

Patrice froze, his drink halfway between the table and his lips.

'I unbound the man's powers and tied them to me of course, but even in his reduced state, he fought me.' She gave Patrice another smile. 'Which is why I wanted to speak to you. Just think of all the power one could channel through a Warlock. There is so much one could do with such an individual.'

Patrice stared at her, but said nothing. Slowly he set his glass down.

'And besides, you are the kind of man who believes in keeping one's options open, are you not? I believe in doing so too.'

'Your men are sure the thief was a woman with red hair and a gun?' he said slowly.

'That's what they tell me. And they say she was dressed in trousers. Who would have thought it?'

Patrice rose from his seat. In two strides he walked over and struck Clothilde in the face. The impact of the blow sent her flying to the floor.

Emilian looked up in surprise at the suddenness of the attack.

'You stupid woman,' Patrice bellowed. Spittle flew from his mouth as he spoke.

Clothilde stood up and wiped a thin trickle of blood from her face, too shocked to say anything.

'Do you even know what you have done?' Patrice shouted. He loomed over her again, fist at the ready. 'Tell me, do you?'

She shook her head.

Patrice sat down heavily on the bench and loosened his tie. '*Merde*. How on earth did you manage to capture the Viscount Greychester?'

'Viscount?' she said.

'Hugh Marsh, Lord Greychester. Master Warlock. Former member of the Council of Warlocks. Special envoy to the Ministry of Intelligence. And to top it all off, husband to the current serving Oracle.'

'The Oracle?' Clothilde's eyes widened in surprise. 'The Oracle is in London?'

'Yes, the Oracle. And I happen to know for a fact that she is little, has red hair, carries a gun and wears trousers. That is her husband you took and she will stop at nothing to get him back.' Patrice rubbed the back of his head and started laughing. 'Oh, this is just perfect. And the best part is that you still don't have the faintest idea what you have done.'

Clothilde had grown deathly pale. The only colour in her face was the angry red welt where Patrice had struck her.

'What are you talking about?' she said.

'Never mind that now. You were very lucky that you called me and not the chairman with this news.'

'So what do we do?' she said.

'That is my question exactly. While we are at it, why are there spark shortages across the city? I thought your orders were to remain imperceptible and to ensure that none of our preparations draw anyone's attention.'

'We have been busy. The monks are lazy. After a long night of processing soldiers, they refuse to work the next day. It has been all I could do to get them to do as much as they have.' Clothilde rubbed her brow. 'In fact, I have executed so many already that I can hardly afford to lose any more. And yet, it has only made a limited impact on the stupid little brutes.'

Patrice shook his head. 'Well, madame, in a very short time you have brought the city of London to the brink of chaos. You are very lucky that the Consortium has influential contacts within Scotland Yard who have been able to quash most of the questions that have been raised as a result of your activities.'

'I have done exactly as the Consortium ordered,' Clothilde said, with no small amount of indignation.

Patrice shook his head. 'Added to that, you have provoked the wrath of the most powerful Oracle of our age by stealing her husband. I would say that you have done an extremely poor job. And I shall have to make mention of this in my report.'

'Surely she cannot be all that?' Clothilde said, looking uneasy.

'Oh yes she can!' Patrice shook his head and lifted his trouser to reveal a leg. It was a very unpleasant sight.

Part of the limb was black as night and translucent, as if it was in a completely different plane of existence. The skin around the affected area was covered in an array of terrible bruises that ranged from yellowy-green to the blackest of purples.

Clothilde gasped when she saw it.

'Yes, gasp and feel horrified, my lady. For this is what that little redhead in trousers, as you call her, did to me. She is going to crush *you* until you are nothing more than a little pile of meaningless dust, you stupid, stupid woman.'

Clothilde sank into a chair. She stared at Patrice for long moments before she spoke. 'There must be a way we can salvage this situation.'

'There had better be. Because I am not leaving London until you have fixed this mess.'

She turned and gave him a radiant smile. 'I think I have a plan. One that will resolve all of our obstacles in one brilliant stroke. But first I need to think about the details.'

A gong sounded somewhere deep inside the monastery, signalling nightfall.

Clothilde closed her eyes and moved her hands in a swirling motion. Patrice felt an icy draft in the back of his neck and then great big clouds of fog started swirling upwards and out of the chimneys above them.

She opened her eyes and stood. 'The fog is set and it is time to loose the hunters. Every night they bring more and more candidates. We process them as fast as the machine can produce chest devices and muzzles. By day, it stamps out the spare parts and by night it implants them into the new recruits. It is quite a remarkable thing.' She gestured out of the control room window at the machine in the turbine hall. 'Once we have built the chairman's army, I intend to diversify. Just think of the legions of servants, drivers and workers we could create. They would require minimum food and lodgings and would be capable of doing three times the work that a living worker could do. We are sitting on a veritable goldmine of opportunity.'

Patrice frowned. He wasn't sure that he wanted to adapt the machine to diversify. But then again, if there was a chance that money could be made...

'The automaton market has never quite taken off as everyone had hoped. The machines are too unreliable and expensive to maintain. But with these organic automatons, we could be on to something,' he said.

'My thoughts exactly,' Clothilde said. 'But let's go and watch as the monks set the hunters free.' Below them, a group of undead soldiers were being marched out into the pens. Some of them were shackled.

'Those ones are the most aggressive. We liberated them from a prison. They are the best ones for the task of finding more recruits. They run well as a pack and we can send them out completely unsupervised, so effective the training has been.'

'Fascinating,' Patrice said. He heard a small sound to his left. Before he could react, a large hand grabbed him by the neck and pushed him to the floor. A pair of cold shackles clicked around his wrists with alarming finality.

'What is the meaning of this?' he shouted. 'Release me, immediately!'

'Thank you, Emilian, well done. You may have bought a few more days of life for yourself.' Clothilde laughed and pressed her fingers to her décolletage in amusement. 'Oh, Mr Chevalier. Can I call you Patrice? Did you honestly think you could walk in here, assault and intimidate me, and I would meekly sit back and endure it?'

'You don't know who you are dealing with. Now let me go immediately!'

She smiled. 'I am dealing with a former airfield clerk who, by virtue of a series of unfortunate events, managed to acquire a lot of money and a dip in the black vortex. And while it is most unfortunate that my servant here let the cat out of the bag, as it were, I also know that you arrived in London alone and that despite all your bravado and brutish behaviour, you really cannot do anything else but shout.'

'Release me immediately!' he screamed.

Clothilde patted him affectionately. 'All in good time, my dear.'

She turned to the two undead guards who had appeared at the door. 'Take him to my laboratory. And make sure he is locked up securely. I don't want this slimy peasant escaping.'

'What are you doing?' Patrice said. He was starting to get extremely worried.

'I am working on that solution you so violently demanded a moment ago. I must say that these brass muzzles are truly excellent at silencing people who ask awkward questions. Granted, you are not nearly as desirable as my Warlock was, but with one foot firmly within the Shadow Realm, I suspect that you would nonetheless be useful to me.'

'You can't do that! I am your boss!' he shouted.

'Oh yes, I can,' she said. 'And now that you have given me this information, I think I just did.'

'Wait! Let me go,' Patrice said, as the two guards groaned and hoisted him up. 'You cannot do this! The Consortium will ask questions. Let me go!' But no one listened and all he could hear were the sinister sounds of *La Dame Blanche* laughing.

Chapter Twenty-six

'Do you think she will be all right?' Elle asked Dr Miller. They were both staring at Loisa as she lay in her coffin in the guest room. The black lines under her skin had faded, but she was still asleep.

'Well, my lady, I have to be completely honest when I say that I am not exactly a specialist when it comes to Nightwalker physiology.' Doctor Miller rubbed his chin as he contemplated the matter. 'But, if you ask me, I would say that she must have expelled most of the toxin in the park. She has fed and she seems to be resting comfortably. She is now in the hands of Mother Nature because there is nothing more I can do for the lady.'

Elle nodded gravely. 'Please take a look at my husband while you are here. I think I have noticed a little bit of an improvement in him,' she said hopefully.

The doctor looked at her with much sympathy in his eyes. 'You certainly have had your fair share of run-ins with tragedy, my lady. I am truly sorry for your loss.'

'You don't know the half of it, doctor. But my husband is not dead yet and I refuse to give up hope, so please let us go downstairs.'

Marsh was trussed up before the fire in the drawing room. It was the turn of the professor and Mrs Hinges to watch him. The two of them were engaged in a most animated card game. An outraged Caruthers hovered in the background. The sight of the housekeeper playing cards in the drawing room with the family was almost more than the poor man could take.

'How is he?' Elle rested her hand on Marsh's forehead.

'Much the same, my lady,' Caruthers said solemnly.

'Ah, Elle. How is the baroness?' the professor said, looking up from his cards.

'Good evening, Papa. All we can do is wait and see,' Elle said. 'But Loisa is strong and I have every confidence that she will recover.'

'I have more splendid news!' the professor said. 'Come and sit here with us while the doctor does his examination.'

Elle took a seat next to Mrs Hinges.

The professor's eyes twinkled. 'I think I have discovered how that device in Hugh's chest works.' He pulled out a set of drawings he had shoved under the seat of his chair. 'Look.' He handed Elle the plans.

She spread them open on the card table. They were a complicated set of diagrams and mathematical calculations, written in her father's neat hand. Elle's brow furrowed as she studied the diagrams.

'My theory is, that device is powered by some sort of agent.'

'Spark?' Elle said.

'I don't think spark is enough, although it does seem

to play an integral part in the process. I suspect it's something elemental. Possibly mineral.'

'That makes sense,' Elle said, still poring over the drawings.

'I also believe that the real heart is connected to this element somehow. If we build this machine and we find the real heart, I do believe that with reverse-suction vacuum thaumaturgy and a healthy blast of spark to get it beating again, we could remove the device and reverse the effects.'

Elle looked up from the plans. 'And what about Hugh? Will he emerge from this once it is over?'

The professor sighed. 'Ellie, my dear, there is no way of telling what the long-term effects of this operation will be.'

Elle nodded slowly.

'What do you think, Doctor Miller?'

The doctor looked up from listening to Marsh's chest with his stethoscope. 'It would certainly be worth a try. There are many new rehabilitation techniques we could try afterwards, but more than that I cannot promise, my lady.'

Elle pressed her lips together. 'When can you start building it?' she said to the professor.

The professor gave Mrs Hinges a conspiratorial smile.

'You didn't think we sat here idly while you did all the rescue work, did you?' Mrs Hinges said.

'I never thought about it, to be honest,' Elle said.

'My dear, your father has already started work on the mechanics.'

'Good,' Elle said.

'And I have also taken the liberty to make some of my own enquiries. Let it not be said that Mathilda Hinges sat by idly when something could be done.'

'Oh, Mrs Hinges.' Elle hugged the older woman, deeply touched by her determination.

'There, there my dear. It is all going to be all right.'

The doctor gave a polite cough.

'Yes, doctor?'

'My examination is complete. While I don't want to get your hopes up, I do believe that being in his home environment has brought about a slight improvement. It's just—'

They all looked at the doctor.

'Well, I just wish there were some way we could slow down the ticking. I've noticed that the warmth of the fire and any excitement seem to hasten the process. Perhaps you should keep him somewhere cooler.' The doctor shrugged.

'Thank you, doctor.' Elle rose and called Caruthers who appeared in order to see their guest out. 'Good evening, doctor. Thank you for coming to see us,' she said.

'Not at all, my lady.' He smiled at her warmly before taking his leave.

As soon as the doctor was gone, Elle said, 'Well, Papa, Mrs Hinges, I will bid you a fond good evening.'

'Now, Eleanor, I don't want you going off into the night by yourself. Not without Loisa to help you,' the professor said. 'You've had an extraordinarily lucky escape so far.'

'I suppose walking up to the monastery without a proper strategy was a little foolish,' Elle admitted.

'A *little* foolish?' Mrs Hinges huffed.

Elle nodded slowly. She still wasn't quite sure she had absorbed the events of the previous evening. She had acted on instinct and it had been a matter of life and death, but images and sounds of his lifeless body dropping to the ground had haunted her all day. She wondered if the man was still alive.

Mrs Hinges laid down her cards and stifled a yawn. 'I think that's quite enough fun and games for me. I had better get myself off to bed. There will be much to do tomorrow.'

'Goodnight, my dear Mrs Hinges. Thank you as always for your charming company.' The professor winked at her and bit down on the stem of his pipe.

To Elle's surprise, Mrs Hinges blushed slightly. 'Always a pleasure, professor,' she managed to say.

Elle paused to stare at Marsh. He seemed to be asleep, trussed up in his heavy canvas straightjacket with the leather straps and buckles. She rested a hand on his pale forehead. He gave a soft grunt, which Elle hoped was an acknowledgement of her presence, but that was all.

Elle swallowed down the lump of sadness that was constantly in her throat these days. This had been her fault. She should never have taken that charter to Singapore.

The professor rose from his seat and came to stand next to Elle. 'We will find a way to save him, my dear. I promise you that.'

'Thank you, Papa,' Elle said. She wondered briefly whether she should tell him about her brief encounter with the spirit who claimed to be her mother. That too had been a most upsetting incident and one she hadn't really given herself much time to think about. In the end she decided against it. There were enough upsetting things going on around them as it was. Reigniting her father's grief would not be helpful at all.

But the spirit had told her to seek out the travelling folk. And the voices of the Oracle might sometimes be inscrutable, but they were rarely wrong. The man with the peacock feather in his hat was the key to gaining entrance to the monastery. Of this she was sure.

On impulse she kissed her father. 'Goodnight, Papa. I will see you in the morning.'

'Goodnight, my dear,' the professor said, but she could tell that his mind was already elsewhere, deep in problem-solving thought, which was just as well, for there was much to do before morning.

The Black Stag public house was a dingy old place with a narrow entrance that leaned to one side. Gelatinous yellow-grey light glimmered through the windowpanes, which were sorely in need of a clean.

Within, the pub was as grubby as without. Dirty sawdust crunched under her boots when she walked inside. A few grim-looking patrons looked up from their ale and gin.

Good heavens, this is a sorry place, Elle thought.

'Ladies' saloon on the other side,' the landlord barked. He was pushing a sour-smelling mop through what looked like a puddle of blood and glass.

'I'm sorry, but perhaps—' Elle began.

'I said: ladies' saloon on the other side. Now get out before I throw you out!' he shouted.

Elle put up her hands in a conciliatory gesture and slowly retreated out the door. She stood outside in a moment of indecision. The eel-coster had been right. This was not a friendly place, but she had to find out if anyone knew something or had seen something.

She needed to find someone who could help her find a way into the monastery.

She squared her shoulders and walked into the saloon entrance, which was really nothing more than a second entrance that led to the other side of the bar counter.

This side of the pub was as dingy as the other, except here a few bare-shouldered women clung to counters and doorways.

Elle walked up to the counter. As she did, she felt a familiar shimmer of magic wash over her. She looked up at the ceiling and spotted the flicker of yellow light above. Gin fairies lived here.

'What will it be?' The landlord had stepped behind the counter and was eyeing her suspiciously.

'Pint of London Pride and a bowl of sugar, please,' Elle said.

He snorted knowingly as he pulled her a greasy pint.

Elle met his gaze. Let him think she was a gin whore if he wanted. She did not have the time, energy or inclination to rectify his assumptions.

The landlord plonked the pint and a bowl of brownish sugar lumps in front of her.

'Say, does anyone know how to speak to those fairies?' Elle asked as she handed the man payment for her drink.

'That'd be Georgie over there,' he said, pointing to a woman who was sitting on her own at a table.

Elle took her glass and the sugar cubes and walked over to the woman. 'Excuse me, but are you Georgie?'

The woman glanced up and nodded.

Elle noted how thin and tired the poor girl looked. There were deep purple hollows under her eyes that spoke of a life hard-lived.

'What do you want?' she said in a voice roughened by hard living and tobacco.

'The landlord tells me that you know how to speak to fairies.'

'I might.' Her voice softened into a lilt, which sounded as if its origins were in Ireland.

'Do you think you could ask them a few questions for me?'

Georgie nodded and extended her hand, palm up. 'Five pence, for your fortune told.'

Elle sighed inwardly and pulled the money out of her pocket. Five pence was ludicrously expensive for fortune telling, but she put the coins into the woman's hand.

Georgie glanced up and clicked her fingers.

Little yellow lights dropped down from the ceiling and morphed into fairies before her. There were three of them. Up close they were strangely ugly and beautiful at the same time. They all had grey hair and large dark eyes with queerly long lashes. They reminded her very much of Adele, Elle thought, with a pang of guilt. She had not even started looking for the absinthe fairy with all that was going on.

'I don't need my fortune told, I just need to know if they've seen someone,' she said, as she placed the sugar cubes on the already sticky table.

Georgie stared at the fairies and nodded briefly. 'They thank you for the sugar and they say that you are touched by the magic of the Fey. They say they will speak to you because of this.'

'Thank you,' Elle said, relieved that she had passed the first test. Fairies had a way of making people feel so inferior. Fortunately there was nothing that fairies loved more than sugar. It was the great negotiating tool.

'I am looking for a man. They tell me he wears a peacock feather in his hat. I am also looking for *this* man.' Elle pulled the photograph of Marsh she had taken from the house and laid it on the table. 'He may have come here sometime in the last week or so.'

The fairies started chattering amongst themselves. Every so often one of them would look up from their huddle, stare at Elle for a moment and then re-join the conversation.

'What are they saying?' Elle whispered to Georgie after a few moments.

'Don't know. They are whispering. I think they are deciding whether or not to talk to you. You seem to have some sort of a mark on you, miss.'

Elle took a deep breath and waited.

After a good few minutes one of the fairies turned to Georgie and spoke.

'They say that the man was here. He was followed by one of the Fey. One of the wormwood clan, far from home and not welcome in this place.'

Elle felt a surge of excitement. 'Was the fairy French? Where did they go?'

'She was from the absinthe,' Georgie said after a short

conference with the fairy. 'The man was here and then he left. He followed the peacock feather. That's all they seem to know.'

'Where can I find the man with the peacock feather in his hat?'

The fairies shrugged.

Elle felt her hopes fade. 'Did they see what direction they went?'

'No. Fairies don't care about things like that,' Georgie said.

'Does the man with the peacock feather come here often? Do you know his name or where to find him?'

Georgie's shoulders tensed slightly at her question and she briefly joined the conversation. The leader of the fairies folded her arms and lifted her nose in the air with disdain. Georgie shrugged and all three of them blinked into the light, scooped up the sugar and dashed back up into the rafters.

'What is happening now?' Elle asked.

'That's all they have to say on the subject.' Georgie shrugged. Then she looked Elle in the eye. 'The man you are looking for comes here from time to time. But you are better off staying well away from him. He brings bad luck wherever he goes.' She grabbed Elle's arm. 'Go home, fine lady. This is no place for you.'

Elle gritted her teeth and moved out of the woman's grip. 'Not before I'm told where this man went,' she said, pointing to the photograph.

Georgie sighed. 'If he was taken by the man you seek, then he is lost to the world.' Georgie narrowed her eyes. 'The fairies told me one more thing. They told me that you should be wary of making wagers with crafty old men like Jack. He will come to collect his debts and there will be much weeping when he does. Beware and find a way to undo the contract or you will be the one who weeps!'

Elle felt a cold shiver run over her skin and suddenly the air was full of the whispers of fairies.

Georgie leaned forward even further. 'There are wagons by the river. They like to camp under the bridges this time of year. Go and ask if anyone knows the man with the peacock feather. I believe his name is Emilian. They may help you. They may not. But it's dangerous, so be careful!' Georgie whispered fiercely. 'Now go! I can tell you no more.'

'Thank you,' Elle said with no small measure of gratitude. She turned and walked out of the pub, leaving her untouched pint on the table.

Chapter Twenty-seven

———❖———

Outside the pub, Elle stopped in the pool of light of a street lamp. She rested her forearm against the cold iron and took a few deep breaths to calm herself. The freezing air stung her nostrils and made her lungs ache, but it was better than the claustrophobia of the Black Stag.

Around her, people went about their nightly business. Tired men were trudging home from work. A few determined costers were still about, trying to sell their wares. Here and there a barrow gave off wisps of steam as dinners wrapped in paper were sold to passers-by. It was a typical evening, but Elle could feel eyes on her. As is the case in almost any city in the world, the locals can always tell if you don't belong. And this part of London was as foreign as any strange city Elle had been in. Those gin fairies were right. She did not belong here.

But this was no time to show weakness. She straightened up. She was being a complete ninny. She had to see this through. Marsh would do the same for her.

Suddenly a little yellow light appeared in front of her face. Elle stepped away from the iron street lamp and, as the influence of the iron lessened, one of the gin fairies materialised. It hovered before her, slowly blinking at her.

'I'm sorry if I offended you earlier,' Elle said.

The fairy shook its head and shrugged. Elle peered a little more closely at the fairy. Its hair was shorter and its wings oddly more muscular than she had observed on Adele. With a small burst of surprise, Elle realised that the fairy was male, which was odd, because she had never thought about male fairies before. It was usually only the female of the species that ended up in the tragic life of magical prostitution that can only be found at the bottom of a bottle.

The fairy pointed into the darkness and made a gesture with his hands that looked a bit like an hourglass. He put his hand on his hip in an effeminate gesture and closed his eyes.

'A girl?' Elle asked, slightly amused.

The fairy seemed to be concentrating. His face scrunched up with the effort and slowly his yellow light changed to flickering green. He held the pose for a moment before the effort almost made him drop from mid-air.

Elle held out her palm to stop him from falling as he righted himself.

'Absinthe? Is that it?' The fairy nodded.

'Did you see an absinthe fairy?'

The fairy nodded again and pointed in the same direction again.

Elle bit her lip. There were quite possibly hundreds of absinthe fairies in London, but it was worth a try.

'Why are you telling me this? Is this a trick?' Gin fairies were terrible creatures, worse than absinthe fairies, so it was wise not to be too trusting.

The fairy hugged himself.

'You took a fancy to her and you want me to bring her back here. Is that it?'

The fairy nodded. Then he looked up as if he had heard a noise.

'Where is she?' Elle said.

The fairy looked a bit agitated and pointed at the same dark alley. Then his light blinked out and he disappeared.

'Wait! Hang on a moment,' Elle said. But there was only silence around her now. The gin fairy was gone.

She sighed and unclipped the little spark light projector she had brought with her. The answers she sought, whether good or bad, were somewhere down that dark, mucky alley.

The alley led into a winding maze of passageways between the haphazard buildings. One lane fed off on to another with no rhyme or reason to them. The only landmark was the distinctive smell of mud and sewers that came off the Thames. Its putrid odour wafted towards her on the night air.

Her light cast an eerie blue beam over the clapboard buildings that rose up around her. Above her, despite the lateness of the hour, hollow-eyed children watched from plank walkways that spanned between the buildings. Grey rags of laundry that no one had bothered to pull in from the night damp flapped forlornly in the chilly air as if they had resigned themselves to the fact that they would never be dry.

Elle's breath steamed as she walked along and the sound of her boots echoed against the wooden planks that were laid out for people to walk on.

The buildings thinned a little as the graceful arch of one of London's many bridges rose up.

The girl in the pub had told her that the travelling folk favoured bridges to camp under when the weather turned cold. And so Elle made her way towards the bridge. She turned a corner and a piece of derelict land opened up before her. Elle felt her spirits rise, because, in the shadow, she saw the flicker of yellow light from a wagon.

As she approached, fine images of flowers and animals became visible in the light of her lamp and even in the blue light from her spark projector, Elle could see that the wagon was beautifully painted in bright hues of yellow, red, blue and green.

As she approached, she felt the soft shimmer of the Shadow ripple over her skin. It made the hairs on her arms prickle, warning her to proceed with caution. She slid her stiletto out ready in case she needed it for close combat.

She turned off her lamp and slowly made her way up to the wagon with its ornately curved stepladder.

Everything was silent. The curtains were drawn and apart from the single yellow light on the porch there was no sign of life.

Elle waited in silence as long moments ticked by. No one moved. Carefully she balanced the tip of her boot on the centre of one of the large spokes of the wheel beside her and hoisted herself up, for the windows were too high for her to peer through from the ground. Inside, she could just make out the fuzzy shapes of furniture, but nothing more.

'Don't move.' A woman's soft voice came from behind her.

Elle heard the fine shuck of metal on metal that could only be the sound of a shotgun gun being cocked and did as she was told. Slowly, she jumped off the wheel, raised her free hand in the air and turned to face the double barrels pointed at her.

'Drop it,' the woman holding the gun said.

Elle let go of the stiletto and it fell, blade first, to the ground.

'A blade in the ground is powerful magic,' the woman said. Without taking her eyes off Elle, the woman retrieved the blade and slipped it into one of the pockets of her ample skirts.

'I don't want any trouble. I am only looking for a little information,' Elle said. 'I am looking for a man named Emilian.'

The woman's face was hard to make out in the dark, but Elle noticed the barrel dip ever so slightly in hesitation. There were a few other wagons within running distance, but she had no guarantee that she would meet friendly faces.

'Inside,' the woman said as she gestured towards the steps.

With the shotgun at her back, Elle climbed the steps and stepped through the door.

The inside of the caravan smelled like cinnamon and incense. A small cast-iron stove glowed warmly at one end of what was a surprisingly spacious interior.

'Sit.' The woman gestured to one of the little benches. Elle did not argue.

The woman moved with easy grace and sat down opposite Elle. In the soft light Elle could see that she was very young and rather pretty. Her light brown hair escaped in ringlets from under the scarf that held it in place and her nose was dusted with a fine pattern of pretty freckles. This was definitely not one of the crones that nannies told stories of, to frighten children to bed.

The girl said nothing but stared at her with eyes that were as hard and dark as a magpie's.

It was then that Elle noticed the sound of frantic buzzing. She felt the shimmer of the Shadow Realm pass over again. Something very strange was afoot in this caravan.

The girl stamped her foot on the floorboard and the buzzing ceased, but only for a few moments before starting up again.

'My name is Elle,' Elle said in an attempt to start the conversation.

'Why are you sneaking around my home in the dark, lady?' the girl said.

'I'm sorry. I meant no offence. I should have knocked on the door,' Elle said, suddenly embarrassed for being so rude.

'That's an apology, not a reason,' the woman said.

'I am looking for information and I was told that you might be able to help.'

The girl eyed her suspiciously. 'Who told you that?'

'Someone at the Black Stag.'

'Did they now? I trust no one at the Black Stag. And neither should you.' The girl stomped her foot again to make a renewed buzzing stop. The motion made the shotgun that was resting on her lap tilt dangerously in Elle's direction.

'I'm not going to argue with you on that count. The Black Stag is certainly not one of the better establishments in the city. But they did send me in your direction.'

'And why did they do that?' the girl asked.

'I am looking for someone. They say there is a man here who might have seen him. Emilian is his name.'

The girl's expression softened ever so slightly and Elle lowered her hands that she had been keeping in the air.

'Where I can see them,' the girl said motioning with the shotgun.

Elle raised her hands again. 'I am looking for a missing person. The last person who saw him was a man named Emilian. I only want to ask this Emilian about it.'

The girl said nothing.

'I have a portrait of the person who is missing. It's in my coat pocket. May I show you?'

The girl nodded once. 'I will shoot if you try anything,' she said in a matter-of-fact way that suggested she meant it.

Carefully, Elle reached into her coat and drew out the photograph of Marsh. It was her favourite, because unlike in most photographic portraits, Marsh had smiled when the shutter was opened. The corners of the portrait were slightly curled from travelling in her pocket. She laid it out on the table between them, smoothing the edges gently with her fingers.

The girl lifted the photograph up and stared at it for a few moments. Her only reaction was a tiny furrow in her brow that disappeared almost as quickly as it appeared.

Then she dropped the photograph on to the table and shrugged.

'They say Emilian is a man who wears a peacock feather in his hat. They say he knows about the missing people. And the ticking hearts.'

The girl's gaze shot up and her face grew fierce. 'I know nothing of this man. Never seen that one either.' She gestured at the photograph. 'Who tells you these things?'

Elle took a long, slow breath. 'As I said, the little people at the Black Stag told me.'

At that, the girl grew angry and raised the shotgun at Elle. 'It's time for you to go.'

Elle picked up the photograph and slipped it into her coat pocket. She wasn't going to get anything more out of the girl, that much was clear. With a heavy heart, she rose carefully from the bench. 'Look, the man in the photograph is my husband. He went out a few nights ago and disappeared. He came back to me…different to the person he was when he left. Time is running out and I am beside myself with worry. If you have any information – even the slightest clue that might help save him – then I would be eternally grateful. Please. I am begging you.'

The girl hesitated for a moment, but the buzzing sound had started up again and had increased in intensity until it was now almost a frantic whine. Elle watched her last hope disappear as the girl's face hardened. With the barrel of the shotgun she gestured for Elle to stand.

'I thank you for your time. And please accept my apologies again for barging into your home—'

Elle did not finish her sentence, because in a flash of light an absinthe fairy burst out of the woodwork. She darted to and fro in movements that were most unfairylike and it took Elle a moment to realise that the fairy was tethered to the wagon with a strand of bright red silk.

'Adele!' Elle exclaimed as she recognised her friend.

The fairy stopped struggling and hovered before her in a gesture that seemed to say, 'Finally!'

'You know one another?' the girl said, looking at Elle and the fairy in turn.

'Yes, this fairy is my friend. What have you done with her? I demand that you release her at once!' She looked at Adele. 'Oh my little friend, I'm so pleased to see you. We thought we had lost you for good.'

Adele did a little twirl but the strand of silk stopped her short and she fell back to the ground.

'She stays with me now,' the girl said.

'No, she does not. Not if you are going to tie her to the wagon like that. Adele is a free agent. She is a person and you have no right to hold her here against her will. What did you say your name was?'

'Florica,' the girl said, looking flustered.

Elle sat back down on the bench. 'Well, Florica, we don't know one another very well, but you now appear to have Adele and my blade. And the fairy had instructions to stay close to my husband, so if she is here it means that he was too.' Elle folded her arms. 'So I think you had better put the kettle on, because I am not leaving this wagon until you and I have had a little chat.'

Florica stared at Elle, slightly nonplussed, but Adele rose up and hovered before her. Elle wasn't sure but it looked like they were having a conversation. Adele was gesticulating wildly with her arms and wings.

Florica blanched and looked over at Elle.

The fairy nodded in an I-told-you-so gesture.

Florica sighed as if she was very tired. With great care, she breached the shotgun and placed it on the table, within reach. Then she pulled the stiletto out of her pocket and laid it out on the table next to the gun.

'Very well. This Fey tells me who you are, my lady.' She bowed her head in reverence. 'You must forgive me, but I did not know that you were the Oracle. My people live on the fringes of the Shadow and we do not meddle in matters of high power. But if this Fey is right, then I must listen.'

Elle opened and closed her mouth in surprise. She had no idea the word 'Oracle' meant so much.

Adele gestured for her to do something.

'Er, yes. I am Pythia. And I would that we speak of these matters,' Elle said, trying to sound as official as she could.

Florica bowed her head. 'The Fey says you can be trusted and that you have the power of the Shadow within you. And so I shall comply, for my people have followed Pythia for more centuries than anyone can count.'

'Thank you,' Elle said as she leaned back on the bench. 'But I am only here as a concerned wife, looking for her husband.'

Florica folded her hands in her lap and her face softened. 'Only someone as powerful as the Oracle could stop her evilness.'

'Her evilness?' Elle frowned.

'*La Dame Blanche*, the Lady in White.' Florica sighed. 'It is a difficult situation.' She opened the laces of her dress to reveal a small brass plate embedded in her skin, just above her heart. 'She let me keep my heart, but one misstep by either Emilian or myself and I am dead. She has the power to stop my heart in an instant.'

Elle recognised the metalwork and her mouth went dry in alarm. She didn't know exactly what Florica meant by 'Lady in White', but the ominous way the girl said the words was enough to tell her that this was the answer she had come for.

Florica rubbed her forehead. 'So we do her bidding. Emilian goes to her every day and I help with the . . . recruitment. She has commanded us to do so many awful things, but there is nothing we can do to resist her.' Her eyes grew intense. 'But she must be stopped, of that I grow more sure every day.'

Elle leaned forward. 'If there is anything I can do to help, I will.'

Florica nodded. 'It is for that reason that I shall help you.' She pressed her lips together. 'But only if you agree that neither Emilian or myself are ever to be mentioned, for we shall surely be put to death if it is ever known that I spoke to you.'

'Your secret will be safe with me,' Elle said. 'I give you my word as the Oracle. I will do everything in my power to stop whoever is behind this.'

'I shall make us some tea,' Florica said.

'That would be lovely,' Elle said, feeling her hopes rise.

And so Adele settled on the edge of the table, legs crossed at the ankles as Florica filled up the copper kettle that hung from a hook by the stove.

Chapter Twenty-eight

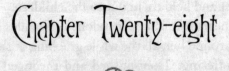

About an hour later, Elle cursed under her breath as she took yet another wrong turn that brought her to yet another blind alley. She turned back and started trudging the way she had come. The walk back from Florica's wagon was turning out to be rather trying. It was late and she was cold, tired and desperately annoyed.

The houses and buildings in this area of London were slapped together in such a haphazard way that they formed an almost impenetrable maze. She rounded another corner and her spirits rose as she spotted cobbles that signalled the fact that she had found a main road.

She walked on and was even happier when, to her amazement, she spotted Neville waiting by the motor which was parked under a streetlight.

At that moment, he was hard at work defending the car from a clutch of dirty children led by a stray gin fairy. They were hovering around him, each looking to distract Neville so another could try to steal something. Neville was brandishing a large black umbrella and threatening to thump anyone who stepped too close. The fairy keened with delight as it hovered above

Neville's head, attempting to knock his bowler hat off his head.

'Hey, over here!' Elle fished a handful of pennies from her pocket and held them out to the children.

In a heartbeat they abandoned Neville and were flocking around her, all the while grabbing at the pennies she was offering. They pushed and thronged until the money fell to the cobbles and little hands and bodies darted for them.

'Neville! My goodness, you are a sight for sore eyes,' Elle said, barely escaping the scuffle of children and fairy that had erupted around her.

'Thank heavens you are safe, my lady,' Neville said. He opened the front passenger door for her.

Elle climbed into the car, grateful for the reassuring feel of the leather seat against her back. 'Oh Neville, I have no idea how you found me, but thank goodness you came. Let's go home,' she said.

Neville did not wait to be asked a second time. He revved up the engine, which had been softly puttering in the background. They were in motion and barrelling down the road almost instantly, leaving the rank squalor behind them.

'The baroness said you might be here so I took a chance to try to find you,' he said after a mile or so when they had slowed down a little.

'Is Loisa awake?'

'She woke briefly this evening after you left, but she is still resting. The doctor checked in on her again on his way home, and he says she is much improved, but still in danger.'

'And how is *he*?' She leaned forward to speak.

'Same as before, my lady. The doctor says he thinks the ticking is still increasing, it grieves me to say.' Neville's profile was grave as he drove.

Elle closed her eyes and rested her head against the seat. Despite her initial willingness to help, it had taken two cups of tea, a generous glug of cheap whisky and the tender of Elle's stiletto as payment for the information before Florica had finally talked. And talked she had.

Adele, as it turned out, was rather taken with living with the travelling folk, despite her dramatic entrance earlier that evening.

In the end the three of them had agreed a compromise: the fairy was to stay with Florica for the moment, mostly because the charm that bound her to the wagon was too complicated to undo quickly. Elle had promised to return and, as a token of trust, Florica had given her a brass button off her coat. With it Elle would always be able to find the wagon. Florica had also given her a potion that was said to cure Nightwalkers who accidentally ingested silver. And so Elle had parted on good terms with Florica and with the promise to return once her quest to save Marsh was over.

And that was a most excellent result. Because now she had a plan.

The sky had turned to murky grey by the time they pulled up to Greychester House.

Elle took off her coat as she strode across the black and white squares of the hallway floor and up the stairs.

Loisa was still in bed, fast asleep and pale as moonlight.

'Loisa, I have found help,' Elle said. 'She gave me this potion for you to take.'

Loisa did not answer and without hesitating, Elle pulled the stopper from the bottle and dripped the amber liquid into Loisa's mouth.

Loisa almost choked, but she managed to swallow the medicine without waking up.

Elle sat beside Loisa for a little while and as she watched, it seemed as if the black tracks that still spidered under her skin were fading slightly.

'Rest now, dear friend. I will be in to check on you a little later.'

Elle said a quiet prayer to anyone who might be listening that Loisa would be all right, before she turned and left Loisa's room to see her next patient.

In the library, Marsh's cot was empty and her heart leaped into her throat.

'We've put him in the cold larder,' Mrs Hinges said behind her.

Elle spun round. 'Mrs Hinges! You startled me. What are you doing up so early?'

'I'm sorry, my dear. I didn't mean to do that.' She smiled at Elle. 'This house now runs at all hours with the baroness and his lordship being so ill. Mr Caruthers and I are manning the fort in shifts in order to keep an eye on things.'

Elle hugged her. 'Oh, Mrs Hinges, I'm so sorry about that. You must be exhausted. All this is my fault. All I seem to do is bring misery and destruction upon everyone unfortunate to cross paths with me.'

'Oh, what utter nonsense! I will not stand here and

listen to you spout such silliness.' The older woman patted her reassuringly. 'But we haven't any time for feeling sorry for ourselves right now.' She stepped back from Elle and stared at her with concern. 'How about a nice hot cup of tea? You look like you are chilled to the bone. And we can check in on his lordship while we are at it as well.'

Elle smiled. After two cups of Florica's brew, tea was the last thing she fancied, but a talk with Mrs Hinges would certainly help, so she followed the older woman downstairs.

In the kitchen Elle stood on tiptoes and peered through the little glass window of the door of the cold larder.

A row of large blocks of ice had been placed around the stone floor in order to keep everything inside the room cold. The room was completely empty except for Marsh. He sat perfectly still in the bath chair, trussed up in his muzzle and canvas jacket. At that moment he was looking up at the ceiling as if he was listening for a sound that wouldn't come.

Elle tapped against the glass with her wedding band. He turned his head ever so slightly at the sound and she felt her heart contract at the sight of him.

'The cold seems to slow him down a little. Doctor thinks that the less he moves about, the slower that thing in his chest will wind down. And don't worry, dear, I made sure they put an extra cardigan on him before they strapped that canvas on. I couldn't let the poor man suffer,' Mrs Hinges said. 'I'm also rather grateful the butcher hasn't been for this week's delivery or we would have had a real problem on our hands. The smell of raw meat sends him into a right bother.'

Elle smiled at her. 'Thank you for doing all this.'

Mrs Hinges patted her on the arm. 'Never you mind. Let's go and have that cup of tea and you can tell me all about what you've been up to tonight.'

Elle shook her head and gripped the older woman's hand. 'There is no time to waste, Mrs Hinges. Every moment we sit here is a moment wasted. I must go to my room now. Please see that I am not disturbed for the next few hours.'

The house was very quiet as she made her way up to her room. All the curtains were drawn.

Elle felt bone tired as she undid her hair and brushed it. Her whole body ached from physical exhaustion and lack of sleep. She wanted nothing more than to curl up in bed, coddled in the warm lusciousness of deep, dreamless sleep. But she could not rest. Not yet.

She retied her hair in a braid that fell down her back and slipped on her linen robes. She was ready to go to the Realm of Shadow. There were a few people she needed to see before she could rest.

Inside her secret chamber, she did not even bother to light the candles. She stepped into the circle and closed her eyes, willing herself to the place where she wanted to be.

Travel to the other side was becoming easier and within moments she felt the rush of energy that filled her senses as she slipped through the barrier.

*

Finding the dark woods took almost no time at all once she had crossed over. The bare branches of the trees stretched up to a sky that was the colour of watered milk.

No matter what the time, it never seemed to grow completely dark here, almost as if the sky was afraid to surrender this place to the shadows.

The ever-present dip-dibs watched her with large eyes. They chattered their sharp little teeth at her as she passed them by. And above her, the magpies kept silent watch from the gallery of boughs, peering down at her with eyes like shiny black beads.

Elle walked until she found the largest tree she could. The elm stood in silence as if it had been waiting there for her.

She looked up into its branches and shouted, 'Jack!'

'Here! Here!' the magpies above her said, but otherwise there was nothing but silence. Even the bloodthirsty dip-dibs held their breaths.

'Jack!' she called again. Her voice echoed a few times in the silence before it too was swallowed up by the woods.

Elle took another deep breath and shouted one last time, 'Jack!'

The magpies took to the sky, circling in a flurry of squawks and black and white feathers.

'All right, all right. Here I am. No need to be so impatient.' Jack hobbled out from behind the tree. He opened his cloak and peered at her in the light of his lantern. 'Oh, it's you,' he said. 'Any news on my holiday?'

'Hello, Jack. I've come to ask you a favour,' Elle said, getting to the point.

'Favours, favours. Everyone always wants a favour,' Jack muttered. He leaned over and rested his lantern on a tree root. 'No one spares a thought for Old Jack. Not a single thought, I tell you.'

'I need you to tell me how one stops a Lady in White.'

Jack gave her a wily look. '*La Dame Blanche*? Sounds like you have got yourself into a spot of trouble, young lady. Those elemental witches hold grudges for more years than you have to live.'

'But how does one stop one? And I need to make her undo something she's done.'

'Ah, an undoing.' Jack leaned forward with an air of amusement. 'Even more tricky because it requires reversing the intent of the doer.'

'There must be a way. There always is.'

Jack smiled and looked up into the branches above him. 'So impatient. Always want the answers immediately, don't you?'

'Jack, please. I don't have a lot of time. I wouldn't be asking if it wasn't an emergency.'

Jack looked at her for a few long moments. 'Tell me first, what are you going to do for Old Jack? What news do you bring about my holiday?'

'News! News!' the magpies squawked.

'I haven't had a chance to discuss the matter with anyone yet.'

He shook his head. 'There is nothing to discuss. All I need is for you to say yes. It's a very simple matter.'

Elle was starting to wonder whether coming here had been a good idea. She had been warned about Jack. But right now, she didn't have the time and there was no one else she could ask. 'I think a short visit would be fine as long as you promise not to harm anyone.'

Jack narrowed his eyes. 'This is a trick. You know I cannot promise that. What control do I have over the universe? What if I step on an ant or accidentally squash a worm while I'm there? I would be punished by bursting into flames and that, my dear, is most unfair.'

'Jack, I don't make the rules. I am bound to obey the Council just as much as you are.'

'The Council of Warlocks. Now there is a fine institution if I've ever seen one. Not a fan of them, I gather.'

'Not really, no,' Elle had to admit.

'But back to my holiday. Do you think I would be harming something if I ate anything? You know I am very fond of a bit of fried bacon with butter on bread in the morning. Would I be harming the pig if I did that?'

'I don't know, I never thought about it like that,' Elle admitted.

'You see, it's a very old and very stupid rule.'

She sighed. 'Very well, but as long as you promise not to harm anyone on purpose.'

Jack grinned at her and held out his hand. 'I accept. The bargain is struck.'

Elle took his hand, and immediately she felt a cold ripple of magic spill over her arm and run all the way up to her shoulders. She shivered and let go of Jack's knobbly old fingers.

'Deal! Deal! Deal!' the magpies squawked as they flew off into the darkness of the forest.

'Now, tell me about the lady and how I make her undo something.'

Jack shook his head. 'That was payment for the last favour. When I let you out of the forest. This one costs different.'

Elle closed her eyes in exasperation. 'My patience is wearing thin, Jack. You are being tricksy and I don't have time for that, I'm afraid. How do I even know that you are telling the truth? You could be pretending that you know when you don't.'

Jack looked indignant. 'Do you know who I am? Do you even comprehend who you are speaking to?'

'It is I who must ask you that question.' Elle felt herself grow angry. She was not going to allow this twisted creature to trick her again.

Jack stared at her for a long moment. 'It seems, little Oracle, that you and I have reached an impasse. How can there be a bargain when both parties carry tricks up their sleeves?'

'I have told you why I am here and what I want. Now it is time for you to do the same. Or else I will revoke my permission and you shall have no entry into the Realm of Light. Ever.'

Jack looked alarmed. 'You cannot do that. A bargain struck is a bargain binding. *Pacta servanda sunt.* Pacts must be served.'

'Not if the bargain was struck through trickery. Now tell me straight what it is that you want. I do not have time for this.'

Jack was silent as he thought the matter over. 'I want you to take me through the barrier when I come. Will you do that?'

Elle thought about it for a moment. She had no idea

why Jack would want something so specific. It had to be important, but she could not think why.

She watched a little black spider drop down from the branches above them on its silken thread, only to quickly climb back up it again.

'If you let me through the barrier, then you would know where I was,' Jack said.

Jack had a point. And knowing what Jack was up to was certainly better than leaving him to his own devices.

Oh voices, what should I do? she thought. But there was nothing but silence. Elle suddenly regretted banishing her allies, with all her heart.

Elle sighed. She would have to make the decision on her own. And right now Marsh was her only concern.

'Done,' she said. She could worry about Jack later when the time came.

Jack gave her another crooked-toothed grin and rubbed his hands together. 'That is splendid, my dear. Splendid indeed.'

'Now tell me about the Lady.'

'All right, all right, I am getting to that,' Jack said. He scratched his wispy beard. 'The Ladies in White are difficult creatures. Wilful, stubborn. And they hold grudges like no one else in the two realms. Oh, I remember a little dalliance with one when I wore a younger man's beard.'

Elle pulled a face. 'That's not much help. How do I stop one?'

Jack shrugged. 'That depends on the situation. As far as I know there are only two ways to stop her. You must either make her want to change her mind. Or, if she won't, then the only other way is to change her mind for her. You know what I mean?'

'Not really, if I'm honest,' Elle said.

Jack looked at her with his sharp little eyes. 'Oh, don't be so slow. You have to *kill* her.'

Elle shuddered. The image of the man in the park was still vivid in her mind. 'More blood on my hands,' she murmured.

Jack tutted. 'I heard rumours that the new Oracle was a little behind on her training, but really, this is too much.'

Elle glared at him. 'My training is just fine, I'll have you know, sir.'

Jack held a hand up to placate her. 'Easy now, I meant no offence. I'm sure you are well aware that you are one of the few forces in existence that can stop almost anyone from the Shadow with your power. You *are* the Shadow, my dear, and so you control the energy that flows within all of us.' Jack nodded slowly. 'I suspect that there are some here who would see me lynched for letting the secret out, but we are all yours to command, my Queen.'

Elle blinked. She was queen of the Realm of Shadow? This was certainly news to her.

Jack chuckled and gestured towards her hand. 'Also, that bit of silk around your finger might come in handy. That would tie her up in knots in no time.'

'But if I unwound the ring, would it not sever the bond?'

'It might. But I thought you wanted to stop the Lady no matter what the cost?'

'I do.'

'"At all costs" is sometimes very expensive, you know.'

Elle thought about this. Jack was not being particularly helpful and she was wasting time. 'Jack, I thank you for your time.' She drew up her cloak and rose.

'Right, so it's settled then,' Jack said. 'Just give me a moment to gather a few things.'

'What? You want to come with me now?' Elle said.

Jack shrugged. 'Now is as good a time as any, don't you think? I hear the Orient is lovely this time of year.'

'I have no idea.' She had not bargained on him wanting to go immediately.

'Stay where you are, let me just get my things. I won't be a moment,' Jack said as he disappeared behind the tree. Elle watched his lantern flutter and flicker on the ground where he left it.

This sudden turn of events was most inconvenient. She did not trust Jack one little bit and the last thing she needed right now was to be playing governess to an old fairy.

'I'm sorry, Jack, but I'll have to come back for you another time,' she whispered as she snuffed out the light of the lantern. Then Elle turned and ran for the barrier as fast as she could.

As she ran, she heard a strange howling noise behind her. It was the sound of pain that ran deeper than any mortal could withstand, paired with utter and desolate disappointment. The sound was so awful it set her teeth on edge.

'Run! Run!' The magpies appeared overhead, squawking loudly.

The dip-dibs screeched as she flew past them.

'Rrrrrrun!' the magpies said.

As soon as Elle cleared the trees, the world sped up to a pace that made her nauseous. And just when she thought she could not stand moving any more, she felt the barrier before her. She closed her eyes and dove headlong through it. The moment of weightlessness, as if she were underwater, passed in an instant and then she landed on the cold, hard floor of her secret chamber.

She stood up, shivering. All her limbs were damp and cold as if she had been lying outside in the rain. She stumbled out of her secret chamber and closed the door firmly behind her. Grateful for the safety of her own room, Elle crawled to the bed and slipped in between the covers. She lay there shivering and thinking for a very long time. She had many plans to make before nightfall.

Chapter Twenty-nine

Elle found Loisa and the professor in the dining room that evening when she came downstairs.

'Loisa! You are up,' Elle said.

Loisa still had half moons the colour of bruised damsons under her eyes, but she was alert and seemed much better. 'Thank you for the potion, it has worked absolute wonders,' she said.

'That was a rather close call you had, Ellie, my dear. Loisa was just telling me all about your little adventure in the park.' The professor rose from the table. 'Blasted business, shooting a man, isn't it?'

Elle did not meet her father's gaze. 'I'm sorry I'm late. I overslept a little,' she said avoiding the subject.

'You look like you needed it, darling.' Loisa took a sip from the ruby-coloured liquid in her goblet. 'But in answer to your question, Professor, Elle is a deft hand with that revolver and we were lucky we managed to get away when we did. A few moments later and it would have been too late. Even for someone as skilled as me. I owe her my life.'

Caruthers started serving the meal, which was a

strange mix of dinner and breakfast dishes. Elle helped herself to some kedgeree. 'How is he?' she said.

There was an awkward silence as her question hung in the air.

'Ticking along as ever, my dear,' the professor said softly.

'I know this might not be the best topic for the table, but as we are all here, we might as well talk,' Elle said.

No one objected.

'How is work on the device coming along, Papa?' Elle continued.

'Very well, actually. I tested it out on a pig carcass that Neville picked up from Smithfield for me. You know, even though I hated every moment of it, the time spent with those alchemists was most illuminating. I actually ended up learning quite a lot from them in the end,' the professor said.

'But what about the device, Papa?'

'Oh that. The device made the transference of the organs still attached to the pig without a problem. I can't say the same about the mantle clock in my room though. I hope you don't mind.'

'As long as you can make that machine work, you may use anything you can find in this house, Papa.'

'I take it that you have been up to something while the rest of us were in repose,' Loisa said.

'Actually, I went to the Shadow side before bed this morning. I went to find a very recent acquaintance of mine,' Elle said.

Loisa gave her a look. 'I think you had better tell us about it.'

*

'That was a very risky thing to do. Dealing with the old Fey is always tricky business and there are always consequences,' Loisa said, when Elle had finished relating her story.

'Desperate times, Loisa,' Elle said.

Loisa patted her bee-stung lips delicately with the starched table linen. 'At least we know what we are dealing with now.'

'I will handle Jack if he shows up,' Elle said.

'A real Lady in White,' Loisa mused. 'They are very rare creatures, you know. Elemental witches. And judging by the splendid weather we are experiencing at the moment, I'd say her element is storms.'

'So that's the explanation,' the professor said. 'I knew there was something behind all this rain.'

'Exactly my thought,' Loisa replied. 'And what better place for an elemental who specialises in the use of thunder and lightning...'

'...than a spark monastery.' Elle finished Loisa's sentence for her.

'What we need to do is plan the offensive,' the professor said.

Elle looked at him in surprise.

'You didn't think I was going to let you go in there all by yourself, now, did you?'

'I am coming too,' Mrs Hinges said from the door. 'There is no way I am going to allow that thundering valkyrie to get away with what she has done to his lordship.' She shook her head. 'Not in a million years.'

'And neither will I,' said Caruthers, not to be outdone by Mrs Hinges.

'I'm coming too,' said Neville. Clearly they had all been listening from just outside the dining-room doors.

'That's wonderful, but I cannot allow you to place yourselves in harm's way,' Elle said. 'I caused this problem and I need to solve it on my own.'

'Oh, here we go with the it's-all-my-fault nonsense again. I knew she was going to say that, didn't I?' Mrs Hinges said. 'No, my dear, this calls for teamwork. United we stand and divided we fall.'

'Hear, hear!' said the professor. 'Caruthers, see if you can find us a bit of that nice sherry in the study. I say we all retire to the drawing room to toast this endeavour.'

'Splendid idea,' Loisa chimed in.

Caruthers wandered off looking somewhat scandalised at the thought of servants and members of the family drinking together, but by the time they were all assembled in the drawing room he had found the sherry glasses.

'I have been formulating a battle plan,' the professor said as soon as the sherries were poured. 'Neville, bring in the drawing board!'

Elle turned around in surprise as Neville wheeled in a wooden drawing board, the kind the professor used for presenting lectures. Pinned to it was a big sheet of paper with a number of diagrams and formulae.

The professor pulled his telescopic lecture cane with the brass tip from his pocket and opened it up with a flourish.

'Right. If everyone could please be seated where they can see the plans, I will begin,' he said in his best lecture voice. 'Ladies and gentlemen,' he said when everyone had settled down, 'before you I have a floor plan of the monastery. Here is what I suggest we do.' And with that, the professor launched into a detailed account of his proposed strategy.

Elle listened to the professor outline his plan with a growing sense of enthusiasm. It might just work.

'Very well then, if everyone is agreed and sure they know what to do, then I suggest we set about completing our preparations. We move tomorrow night.'

'Yes, sir!' Neville and Caruthers said in unison.

Mrs Hinges nodded slowly as she thought matters over. Elle could see that the housekeeper was working on a few embellishments of her own, but she was wise enough not to get into a debate with the professor about them.

Loisa just sat in silence with that secret little smile of hers on her face and Elle wished she could tell what the Nightwalker was thinking.

'Neville, would you mind driving me into the West End this evening?' Loisa asked.

'No problem, Baroness. Just let me know when you wish to go,' Neville said.

Loisa gave Elle an apologetic look. 'I still do not have my full strength back quite yet. I need to go out.'

'Think nothing of it, dear Loisa. Just please be careful.'

'Of course, my dear,' Loisa said. 'I always am.'

'Then we are all set,' Elle said. 'We will convene here in the dining room tomorrow evening.'

After the meeting dispersed, Elle wandered into the kitchen. She walked over to the meat room and stared through the windows. Marsh was still in the position she had seen him earlier. He sat completely still with his head bowed forward as if he were extremely weary. His hair had flopped forward on to his brow.

Elle wanted to pull the door open and hold him in her arms, but she knew she could not. Any agitation would simply make the clock in his chest tick faster.

'We will fix this, my darling,' she whispered. Her warm breath fogged up the glass that separated them and then, just as quickly, it was gone.

Marsh did not respond.

Elle closed her eyes and turned away from the window. As she did, she prayed that their plan would work and that tomorrow evening would not be too late.

Chapter Thirty

Clothilde stood very still in front of the magneto generator in her laboratory. Somehow, even though they could not see her, she felt she had to stand when she was speaking to her employers.

'You are sure you linked this connection to the telephony line securely?' The chairman's voice crackled and echoed through the brass speaker horn which stood to the side of the cabinet.

'Our cable is spliced into the transcontinental line, bypassing all the exchanges. I had the electromancers attend to the matter,' Clothilde said. There was a brief pause as her voice carried down the line, for she was speaking long-distance.

'Nonetheless, we will keep this communication short. There is never any way of telling who might be listening in,' the chairman said. Another whizz and crackle on the line ensued. 'We are all assembled. You may report,' he added.

'All is going according to plan. I now have a thousand made and ready for shipment.'

'Very good,' said the chairman. 'And the quality?'

'The best I could find. Very strong and durable.'

'And your visitor? We are surprised that he has not made contact with us.'

'He is not here at the moment. He said that he had some other business to attend to. He left us the day after he arrived, but he said he would be back soon. Apart from that, I do not know what he is up to.' As she spoke, Clothilde stared at the glass tank that had been erected in the corner of her laboratory. Inside the blue spark-infused liquid, Patrice floated silently. A grotesque array of wires and springs sprouted from the cauterised hole in his chest. He was awaiting the insertion procedure, but somehow Clothilde had not quite got round to completing the process. The solution he was suspended in would preserve him indefinitely, and his heart floated in one of the jars of the shelf, neatly lined up and numbered, so there was no rush.

She stroked the side of her face. It was still slightly tender from where he had struck her. It would do the odious man some good to marinate for a while, she thought with a warm pang of satisfaction.

'I am sure we will hear from the good monsieur before long.' The chairman interrupted her thoughts. 'In the meantime, I will arrange for transport of the first shipment by dirigible. Choose a hundred of the best specimens and have them ready for collection. The Emperor is willing to allow us to deploy a small batch in the East as a demonstration. He wishes to see how they perform before completing his purchase negotiations.'

'When shall I expect the flight?'

'Tomorrow evening.'

'I will see that they are ready,' Clothilde said.

'Then we are pleased. You have done excellent work so far, Miss de Blanc. Very good work indeed.'

'Thank you, sir.' Clothilde inclined her head even though she knew they could not see her.

With another crackle and a hiss, the connection was terminated.

'You know that it's illegal to have one of those without a licence,' Emilian said behind her.

Clothilde swung round. He was sitting in a chair eating an apple that he was slicing with a rather large and dangerous-looking knife.

'How dare you listen to my private conversations?' she blazed.

'Oh, don't be so touchy, lady. You called for me, remember?'

'Yes, of course.' Clothilde frowned. Maintaining control over the soldiers was becoming more and more taxing and she was so tired some days that she found herself forgetting things. And making mistakes – mistakes she could ill afford.

'Well, you heard the man. We need to round up a hundred and have them ready for shipment.'

'Shouldn't be a problem.' Emilian put a slice of apple into his mouth. 'I was thinking that batch of prisoners we stole would do nicely. They are the most bloodthirsty. If they want to do a proper demonstration, those ones should put up the best show.'

Clothilde nodded. 'Yes, I think you might be right. Those would be good specimens to send.'

'What are you going to do with Fatty over there?' Emilian pointed to the tank.

Clothilde's eyes blazed. 'Don't think I have forgiven you for that little faux pas, Emilian. You should be the one floating in that tank at the moment. How dare you speak out of turn like that?'

Emilian met her gaze steadily and smirked. 'I thought the man needed to know that you were running your own little business on the side.'

'Such insolence,' Clothilde grumbled. Emilian's message was clear, though. He was not going to allow her to treat him as she treated the electromancers. She would have to put up with him for now. But when the time came, sending him into the machine would be so much sweeter.

'So what about Fatty?' he said, pointing the knife at the tank.

'Not that this is any of your business, but he is touched by the Shadow side and so is an interesting subject for research. Once the insertion of the heart device is completed, he will be part of my personal guard. So I would be more careful if I were you.'

Emilian held up the hand holding the knife, palm out but with the blade between his fingers. 'Understood, dear mistress.' He went back to slicing his apple. 'What do you want me to do with the other special ones? The little lordling and the table-rapping fop you had Vargo pick up from Soho?' Emilian placed the square apple core on the little ledge beside him and carefully wiped his knife clean. 'The fop keeps wailing and whining about wanting to get out of here. Can't you sort him out for us?'

'He can wait, for the moment. We have other, more important business to attend to.' Clothilde thought for a moment. 'Actually, I think we should send the young lord along with the prisoners. They will need a pack leader to herd them and he could do with a little training.'

Emilian nodded. 'All righty then, I shall do as you command.' He made a little bow, which had nothing to do with respect or subservience.

'Thank you. You are dismissed,' Clothilde said.

'Oh yes, before I go.' Emilian rose from his chair. 'In case you were wondering, Tom is dead. He died this morning from the gunshot wound to his stomach.'

'I trust that the search for a replacement is underway?' she said, without batting an eyelid.

'Yes, we are looking.'

'Any news on the whereabouts of the woman who shot him?'

Emilian hesitated.

'Speak!' Clothilde barked.

'Vargo says the Nightwalker got a nasty mouthful of silver when she sank her teeth into Tom.' He paused for effect. 'We don't think she should be long for this world.'

'And the other, the one with the red hair?'

'We don't know.'

Clothilde went very silent. Was this the same woman who chased her in the opera house? The one who sensed her using Shadow magic was the Oracle herself? It was too much of a coincidence for it not to be.

'Also, Georgie from the Stag said that the Warlock's wife came looking for him last night.'

'No!' Clothilde shouted. She could tell that Emilian was not being entirely forthright in his reporting. Lightning crackled and struck the conductor chimney high above them.

'Did she find your sister?'

Emilian shook his head. 'She did not. Besides, even if she did, Florica would not betray you.'

'I very much hope for both your sakes that this is true, Emilian. You and your sister have tried my patience for the longest of time with your insolence. Don't make me regret my decision to hire you more than I already do.'

Emilian stepped back a few paces at the sight of her wrath. 'Just the messenger, remember. I'll go see to your hundred.' He turned on his heel and made his way out of the room, ostensibly ignoring her anger, but she saw a little shadow of worry pass over his face and this pleased her immensely.

Once Emilian was gone, Clothilde sank into a chair and rested her head in her hands. Patrice had been right. There was a powerful Oracle hunting her now. And if she knew anything about the world it was this: neither the seven hells nor the darkest recesses of the Shadow hath as much fury as an Oracle scorned.

She looked up at the tank. Patrice still floated motionlessly before her. It was time to take some precautions.

She turned to the long gallery of glass jars that were lined up on shelves along one side of the room. Each jar was filled with the same liquid as the solution in the tank. Each jar was connected to a network of copper tubes and cables that fed the spark current into them.

She liked seeing the hearts beat gently in unison with one another. Watching them brought her a rare sense of tranquillity, but she had no time for heart-gazing right now.

She walked along the gallery until she came to a specific heart. 'It seems, Monsieur Chevalier, that today might just be your lucky day. For I need you alive and with all your faculties at your disposal more than I had initially realised.'

Carefully she lifted the jar off the shelf and carried it over to her operating table. There was work to do.

Chapter Thirty-one

Patrice gasped like a goldfish out of water as the world came into focus. It took him several moments to work out that the metal beams before his eyes were roof trusses.

He groaned and tried to sit up, but a terrible pain shot through his chest.

'Be still or you will reopen the wounds,' a woman's voice said with measured calmness.

'You!' Patrice croaked as the sight of Clothilde swam into view. 'What have you done to me, you harlot of Shadow?'

'Now, is that really necessary?' she said.

Patrice ran his hand over the thick padded bandages that were strapped tightly around his torso. 'What is this?' he mumbled. 'Why can't I feel my legs?'

'The wound has been sealed up, and I have taken the liberty of numbing your body from the waist down so you won't accidentally hurt yourself by trying to run away too soon. You should be able to move in a few hours – as soon as your insides settle.' She was busy with her equipment and packing things away on the shelves and in cupboards.

'My heart,' Patrice said. 'You cut out my heart!' Patrice felt a fresh wave of horror and outrage wash over him, temporarily numbing the pain.

'I must thank you for that. It was a most useful experiment with surprising results. I have, for the most part, managed to reverse the effects of the organ removal. Apart from a scar on your chest, I expect you will fully recover.'

'Why?' he said. This woman baffled him utterly.

'When the charming Emilian blurted out my secret, I needed to make sure that you would keep your mouth shut. With the Warlock missing, I thought you might make a passable replacement.'

'Then why bring me back?' Even in his current state, Patrice was a pragmatist. Nothing in this world came without its price.

'It appears you are more useful to me fully alive than undead. So here you are.'

'It's the Oracle,' he said. Of course it would be.

Clothilde's expression remained impassive.

'She's hunting you and you need me to tell you how to stop her.' Patrice started laughing at the irony, but the laugh ended up in a painful cough.

'A bit of advice would be gladly received,' Clothilde said, with a feigned air of nonchalance.

Patrice started chuckling again, this time with a little more caution. 'What makes you think I would be inclined to help you?'

'I had a little look at your legs while you were unconscious,' she said sweetly.

Patrice tensed. He hated the hideous half-shadow mess

the lower half of his body had become. The anguish and embarrassment of being only half a man – a man who was absolutely no use to any woman – burned and . . . he looked away.

'That's quite an injury you have there. I could not neutralise it completely, but I did manage to turn it to your advantage.'

'What do you mean?' he said.

'Only if you tell me how to stop the Oracle.'

Patrice started laughing again. 'Oh, you poor simple creature. It was the Oracle who did this to me.' He tried to wiggle his feet, but they were completely numb. 'Unless you kill her, there is no stopping her.' He coughed. 'A hapless monstrosity like yourself does not stand a chance. All she'll do is make you obliterate yourself with your own power.'

'But she can be killed?' Clothilde's voice held some hope.

'Oh yes, she's just a mortal girl. But I wish you much luck with that. If I know Eleanor Chance – and I do – she'll not submit to death without putting up one serious fight.'

'I wouldn't be laughing this much if I were you,' Clothilde said. 'You have a powerful *meticule* at work within you. It needs time to settle or you will die.'

Patrice turned his head towards her. 'I laugh, *madame*, because I am already a dead man. And so are you.'

'What do you mean?' Her voice rose to an eardrum-splitting pitch. 'Tell me!'

'If you don't kill her, she is going to murder you. You took her husband away from her and that is not going to sit well with the lady.' Patrice wiggled his shoulders as if he were trying to get more comfortable on the wooden table that held him. 'And if you kill her,' he started laughing again, 'the men who will come after you for killing their Oracle are far worse than she could ever be when it comes to extracting vengeance. You will die slowly, chained up in darkness while they sap every bit of Shadow magic out of you. Drop by drop. And no one will hear you scream.'

'I don't believe you,' Clothilde said.

Patrice turned his head away. 'You don't have to.'

'What shall I do?' Clothilde said. She stood before the rows of jars before her. 'All my work…it will all be in vain,' she murmured.

Patrice did not answer. He felt too tired to bother. Strange waves of nausea, alternated with sensations of giddiness, vibrated through him.

She swivelled round and walked over to him. 'Perhaps there is a way,' she said.

'Let me alone,' he mumbled.

'Join forces with me. Together we can destroy them,' she said. Her voice assumed a seductive tone, but to Patrice it sounded hollow and false.

Patrice smiled at her. 'You may do whatever you want, my dear. I am going to lie here and watch this little performance unfold. At least I will die entertained.'

'No!' she said. 'You have to help me! I demand that you tell me what I want to know or else I will end your life right here and now.'

Patrice turned his face away and grunted. Enough was enough. He had been pandering to this crazy witch for long enough and his patience was at an end. He gathered what little strength he had and reached up to grab her. Suddenly, a strange sensation of power flooded through him and his large hand closed around her delicate throat without any difficulty. He dragged her face close to his.

Her eyes widened with surprise and she let out a noise in the back of her throat.

'What have you done to me?' he said through gritted teeth.

'Set the power trapped within you loose … was a chance you might become a Warlock … it's working,' she choked.

Patrice let go of her and stared at his hand in surprise. It looked exactly as it had before.

Clothilde had stumbled to the ground where she was coughing violently and gasping for air.

'Explain!' he barked.

'Instead of allowing the Shadow to simply eat away at you as it has done so far, I reworked it so you would be able to harness it. It's not the same type of power that the Warlocks use, but it works on the same principles. In time, as you adapt, your body should become your own again.'

Patrice stared at her in wonderment. If what she was telling him was true, he would have real power. And he would be whole again.

'I thought we might be good together,' she whispered.

Patrice started laughing again, but this time he tapped into the delicious darkness that swirled within him. His voice rose and filled the laboratory. 'Now I am too powerful. You cannot kill me. And the puny tricks you use on men are but an insignificant crumb by comparison. Behold the monster you have created!'

She did not answer him, but her look told him that he was right.

She rose and turned to the door. 'I have neither the time nor the inclination to argue with you, *monsieur*. You have your heart back and I have done what I can to heal you, so the debt has been repaid.' He could see that she was scrabbling to regain her composure.

'*Madame*,' he said as she reached the door.

She turned and for a moment her face showed such a sad loneliness that it made him bite back the nasty comment he was about to throw at her. 'Here is a little advice that you can have for free...Don't poke anything that looks like a nest unless you are absolutely sure it's not full of hornets,' he said instead. Great waves of dizziness were making the world tilt around him.

'I fear it may be too late for that,' she said. 'Rest now. You will be ready to move very soon.'

Those were the last words he remembered the Lady in White say before the world went black around him again.

Chapter Thirty-two

'Is everybody ready?' Elle looked over her shoulder at the motley crew of people who made up the Greychester household. They were all assembled in the entrance hall, dressed to kill and ready to set out on what was, quite frankly, an insane plan.

The professor donned his pith helmet and ran his fingers over his moustache, which he had waxed especially for the occasion. 'Huzzah!' he said, using an expression from his military days.

Dr Miller stood beside him, dressed in his white coat and holding his medical bag at the ready. He donned his bowler hat. 'Ready, my lady,' he coughed politely in answer. He had agreed to be on hand, in case of any injuries.

Neville and Caruthers were also both suited and booted. Neville had his trusty cricket bat by his side and Caruthers had, with permission of course, taken one of the cavalry swords from the library. It gleamed, finely polished and sharpened, at his side.

The Stanley motor had been parked outside the front door, waiting for their departure.

Elle turned to Mrs Hinges. 'You are sure you will be all right manning the fort here while we are gone?'

Mrs Hinges waved Elle off. 'Of course I will be fine. Never you mind me.'

'Where is Loisa?' Elle looked around, but the Nightwalker was nowhere to be seen. 'Has anyone seen Loisa?'

Just then, a black steam cab pulled up to the door. Loisa was in the driving seat and by the way she was swinging the steering this way and that, it was apparent that she was not completely *au fait* with the driving of the vehicle. She skidded to a halt, just inches away from the bumper of the Stanley and let the engine stall. The cab backfired with a blast of steam that rocked its suspension.

Quite unperturbed by her terrible driving, Loisa waved at them and hopped off the top of the cab. In one graceful motion she was beside Elle at the front door.

'Loisa, what on earth—?' Elle said, taking in the Nightwalker's elegant little black goggles and a black-and-white striped scarf.

'I thought we might need more transport for this evening, so I picked up this little darling in town. Do you like it?'

'That's very generous of you, but a cab?' Elle said, still somewhat surprised.

'Actually, I can't believe it has taken me so long to make the switch to steam. Horses have always been afraid of my kind. And you have to feed them and stable them. And then when you drive through the mountains, wolves try to eat them, leaving you stranded in the snow. Always such a bother.' She shrugged. 'But I suppose I am old and very set in my ways.'

'Where on earth did you manage to buy a London cab at this hour?' Elle said.

Loisa shrugged in her typical non-committal way. 'Let's just say that the previous owner and I negotiated an excellent exchange.'

Elle thought better of enquiring any further. What she did not know, she did not have to lie to the police about later. Instead, she hugged her friend warmly. 'Loisa, I don't know what I would do without you.'

Loisa just patted Elle's cheek. 'Let's not get too sentimental quite yet, my dear. We still have a way to go before this awful nightmare is over.'

'Quite right,' Elle said, composing herself. 'Caruthers, let's load his lordship into the cab. I think he might stand less of a chance of falling out in there.' Elle started directing everyone about. 'Neville, I think you are a better driver than Loisa.' She glanced at her friend apologetically. 'So I think you should take the cab with the doctor. I will take the Stanley with Caruthers and my father.'

'Yes, my lady.' Neville and Caruthers disappeared back into the house to fetch Marsh.

Elle stood by with her heart in her mouth as she watched them wheel Marsh down the makeshift ramp of planks placed over the stairs to the cab. The bath chair wobbled dangerously and the professor had to step in and grab hold of one side to stop it from toppling down the stairs, but they finally made it.

Marsh was trussed up from head to toe in strong canvas that had been buckled down with leather straps.

He groaned mournfully and moved his muzzled head from side to side as they secured him in his seat of the cab.

Elle put a reassuring hand on his forehead. 'Shh, my love, it's nearly over. We're going to fix this, I promise,' she said softly. Her voice seemed to calm him enough to allow Dr Miller and one of the maids to get into the cab with him.

'Wait! Before we go!' The professor ran back up the steps and into the house.

Oh, what is it now? Elle wondered, growing impatient.

The professor appeared a few moments later, with a leather carrying case.

'It's the spark blaster. I've been tinkering about with it since Constantinople.' He opened the case to reveal what looked like an old-fashioned blunderbuss with a glass bottle attached to the top. 'You'll get about four clear blasts out of this reservoir,' he said.

'Thank you, Papa,' Elle said. She hugged him and kissed his cheek.

'Now, you all remember the plan or do I need to repeat it?' the professor said.

'I think we are all fully briefed,' Elle said. 'If everybody is ready, let's be on our way. Time is wasting.'

Elle felt a rush of affection as everyone hurried to take their positions. She would have to remember to tell Marsh all about this later.

As she climbed into the driving seat of the Stanley, Elle gave a little smile. The professor might have planned this expedition right down to the smallest detail, but she still had a few trump cards to play. As a precaution, she had sent an urgent telegram to Ducky up in Farnborough where he was seeing to the repairs to the *Phoenix*.

To her relief, he had telephoned her long-distance that afternoon to tell her that he was about to leave and that he would meet them at the monastery. It did not hurt to have a contingency plan, in case things went wrong. And an air evacuation was the quickest, safest plan she could think of. She was not going to allow any of the people she loved to be hurt, she vowed.

Elle took a deep breath to calm herself and released the brakes of the car. 'Let's go and find my husband's heart,' she said to her passengers.

The full moon fought with the craggy clouds as the Greychester convoy pulled into Battersea Park. Elle had not noticed it the last time she had been here, but the normally well-tended hedges looked shabby, as if someone had forgotten to prune them in a while. This was very odd, because the electromancers were known for their fastidious care of plants and gardens.

'Let's stop here, so they won't see the cars.' Elle motioned for Neville to pull up behind an overgrown coppice of trees. The cab shuddered to a halt next to the Stanley.

'There she blows,' the professor murmured.

The monastery rose up before them with its four imposing spark collection towers. The building looked like a gargantuan dreadnought, armed and ready for battle.

Elle got out of the Stanley and strode over to the cab. 'Neville, I think you should keep the spark blaster with you. Stay here with Marsh until we give the signal. And don't let anyone near him,' Elle said.

'I won't, my lady. The professor had me practise with this thing to test it the other day. Rest assured, no one will come near us, not if I have anything to say in the matter.' He slipped the leather strap attached to the blaster over his shoulder. The blue spark glowed in the glass canister and cast an eerie light over Neville's face. Elle realised, to her sudden embarrassment, that despite the fact that Neville was prepared to die in service, she did not know his Christian name.

She turned and faced him. 'Say, Mr Neville. If you don't mind me asking, what is your first name?'

Even in the half-light Elle noticed Neville colour. 'It's Giles, my lady. Giles Neville.'

'Well, Giles Neville, if I do not return from this errand, please take care of my husband as long as you can. It has been an honour knowing you, sir.' Elle found that she had to swallow down a lump that had suddenly formed in her throat.

'And you, my lady,' he said with a gracious bow.

Elle turned to Loisa who was waiting by her side. 'Ready?'

'More than ready.' Loisa smiled at her and in the faint moonlight Elle caught a glimpse of fang.

She led the way through the park towards the monastery. Behind them, Dr Miller and the professor made hardly a sound. Everything was deathly quiet. Not even the crickets chirped in the shrubs and bushes around them. It was as if the world was holding its breath, waiting for something to happen.

Chapter Thirty-three

The doors of Battersea Monastery were not locked when Elle and Loisa tried them. The heavy oak panels embellished with brass creaked open, sending a groaning echo deep into the building. Above them, in the eaves, Elle spotted five magpies. They sat perched high up, their beady eyes turned towards her. The sight of these birds – the very embodiment of Shadow and Light – made the hair on Elle's arms prickle with apprehension.

'They are waiting for us,' Loisa said under her breath, looking up at the magpies.

Elle pulled her Colt out of its holster and cocked it. 'Let them send out the welcoming party then. I very much look forward to meeting these villains,' she said.

'I don't like this. It's too quiet,' the professor murmured behind her.

'Quiet, maybe. But we are not alone.' Loisa pointed off into the shadows.

A row of undead dressed in strange-looking metal armour stood perfectly still in the shadows of the turbine hall as if they were awaiting a command. Each one was wearing a brass muzzle just like the one fitted to Marsh. Not one moved as they passed.

'Outnumbered, many to one,' Loisa murmured.

'We don't have a lot of time,' Elle said. 'We need to divide into groups.'

'Agreed,' Loisa said.

Elle turned to the professor and the doctor. 'Papa, Loisa and I are going to draw these undead away. You and Dr Miller stay out of sight and keep to the shadows. Find the heart. That's the most important thing. The rest we can deal with later.'

'Whoever runs this place must have some sort of workroom or laboratory. We'll try there,' the professor whispered. The professor and the doctor were walking very close to one another as they slipped away.

'Just look at that thing.' Elle glanced up at the enormous machine with its metal and copper tubes that reached all the way up to the glass-covered roof. The configuration of the machine looked very much like the organ pipes of some terrible cathedral organ.

'What do you think?' Loisa whispered.

'Those are innocent people underneath those muzzles. I am not sure I want to kill any of them,' Elle said.

None of the undead had moved even a hair since they walked into the massive hall.

'Never mind the undead. There are two of us and one of her. If we take out the head, the rest of the body will be powerless,' Elle said.

'Then let's go find the head of this monster,' said Loisa.

Elle stepped into the middle of the hall and looked up at the glass-fronted mezzanine level that looked like some sort of control room. It sat on the first floor before her.

'*La Dame Blanche*! We know that you are in here somewhere and that you can see us. I demand that you show yourself immediately!' she called out. Her voice echoed in the silence. A few of the undead rustled slightly as if an invisible wind had moved them.

'I said, show yourself, you coward!' Elle shouted.

There was a soft ripple of light and a white apparition stepped forth on the balcony before them.

'Lady Greychester and the baroness, I presume?' The woman's voice echoed through the hall. She spoke in a soft French accent. It was definitely the woman she had encountered at the opera house, Elle realised.

'You presume too much, err . . . what did you say your name was?'

The woman smiled. 'I didn't. But you may call me Clothilde, for it is the name I favour in this realm.'

'I want my husband's heart back. You have exactly one minute to produce it,' Elle said, cutting to the chase.

Clothilde laughed. It was a high-pitched sound that tinkled through the open space. 'Now it is you who presume too much. What makes you think I would do that?'

'I have no time for silly games,' Elle warned.

'Neither do I.' Clothilde's expression hardened. She raised her arms and clapped twice. The undead beside Elle and Loisa drew to attention. 'What exactly will you do if I don't comply?' She smiled at Elle. 'It seems to me, my dear Lady Greychester, that I have the upper hand here.' She motioned with her hand and the undead responded, raising the long knives they carried. 'And you have nothing.'

'Run for it. I will keep them back,' Loisa whispered, indicating the stairs that led to the mezzanine level.

Elle inclined her head ever so slightly in agreement.

'Go,' Loisa said.

Elle took off towards the stairs as fast as she could run. Loisa was close behind her, matching her pace.

'I'll hold these off as long as I can. But you must hurry!' Loisa said as she stopped halfway up the stairs. She turned to face the undead who were closing in on the staircase in menacing silence.

Elle took the remainder of the stairs two at a time. Glancing over her shoulder, she glimpsed Loisa take a stand, fangs bared.

In the last few steps before she bounded into the control room, she raised her Colt in their direction. 'Don't move or I'll blow your head off,' she said as she pointed the gun at Clothilde. 'Now alter your will so I can put my husband's heart back where it belongs. Let him go. I am not going to ask you again.'

Downstairs, Elle could hear Loisa making most vicious fighting noises punctuated by the groans and dull thud of undead tumbling down the stairs and hitting the floor below.

Clothilde laughed. 'Do you honestly think that silly thing could hurt me?' She waved a hand and Elle felt a sharp tug of power as the Colt was wrenched from her grasp. The revolver fell to the floor, discharging a bullet with deafening force. The glass panes to one side of the mezzanine shattered in a million pieces.

Elle felt tendrils of power snake around her arms and legs, restraining her as she made to retrieve the gun.

Clothilde's hold on Elle tightened painfully as she was lifted into the air.

'Ah, always so stubborn, you oracles,' Clothilde said. 'I am looking forward to killing you.' She paused to sneer at Elle.

'I'd like to see you try!' Elle said, struggling against the power that held her.

'See, you can do nothing against me, you frivolous little fool. And now I am going to do to you what I did to your husband.'

'Over my dead body,' Elle growled.

'*Exactement*!' Clothilde said. 'Your silly little heart is going to end up in a jar in my laboratory right next to his – where you can be separated by fluids and glass for eternity. But before we proceed, you are going to tell me where he is. You see, I am quite taken with your husband. Such a handsome man.' The tendrils of power which held Elle aloft moved to give her a little shake. 'He is mine now, do you understand?'

'Oh no he is not,' Elle said.

Clothilde laughed. 'A woman like you does not deserve a man like that.' She tightened her grip on Elle's throat. 'Now tell me where he is, or I will kill you and that ridiculous little Nightwalker who came here with you.'

Elle turned her head to see Loisa tossed on the stone floor by two surly undead. Loisa's face was covered in blood and she was breathing heavily.

'Thank you, boys,' Clothilde said to the undead barring the entranceway. 'Now I have both of you in my grasp.' Elle felt the tendrils of power move as Clothilde also grabbed hold of Loisa. The Nightwalker put her hands to her throat gasping. She looked up at Elle from under her beautiful curls and shook her head to signal defeat. Loisa had fought bravely, but they were hopelessly outnumbered.

'Wait!' Elle said.

Clothilde paused and looked at Elle.

'He is here, close by. If you let us go I will tell you where he is.'

'Elle, no!' Loisa said.

Elle felt the tendrils loosen and she fell to the ground. 'I'm listening,' Clothilde said.

Elle stood up and dusted herself off. She kept her face impassive. Jack had said that the Shadow was hers to command. She closed her eyes and focused on the energy that was swirling around her. In that moment, Shadow and Light seemed to merge into one. It was as if she could see the two dimensions at the same time. She felt the dark fog rise. It was the same fog she had seen in the Shadow Realm before. The blurry double vision caused by looking into both dimensions was nauseating and extremely disconcerting, but she gritted her teeth and grabbed hold of the fog that could only be Clothilde's power.

'I am Pythia!' she said in her strange booming Oracle voice. 'You will heed my command, Shadow creature!'

Clothilde gasped as Elle tried to grab her, but she managed to slip through Elle's fingers.

'So you do know a trick or two?' she said. 'But your grasp of your power is rather clumsy. Ineffectual, despite all the booming commands.'

'Unwill my husband's heart. I command you!' Elle said, as she tightened her grip on Clothilde's power.

Elle noticed the witch flinch slightly.

'Very well then,' Clothilde said sweetly. 'But we will have to go to my laboratory. I cannot do it from here.'

'Take us there, then,' Elle said.

'First you must let me go.'

'I will not,' Elle boomed. 'You shall harm none in the Realm of Light.'

'Oh, and who is going to stop me? You?' Clothilde laughed.

Elle did not answer.

Clothilde stopped laughing. 'Then we will simply stand here staring at one another until you loosen that incredibly clumsy grip you have on my power,' Clothilde said. 'By the looks of things, that won't take too long.' She flicked her wrist and Elle felt her grip on the woman slip again. She hated to admit it, but she did not think she could hold on to the other woman for much longer.

'I will let you go for now. But know that I will not hesitate to take action if you try to trick us,' Elle said with as much bravado as she could muster as she released Clothilde.

'Oh, I don't doubt that,' Clothilde said, shaking herself free of Elle's control. 'In fact, I'm always extremely happy to show people my work. There are so few who truly appreciate the intricacy of it.' She sashayed towards the door and the undead parted to allow her to pass. 'This way, if you please.' She motioned for them to stand. 'I believe the two gentlemen in your company are already waiting for us there.'

Loisa gave Elle a look, warning her to keep silent and follow the Lady.

The narrow halls and winding staircases of the spark

monastery were all dark as they passed through them. The only light was that which seemed to radiate from Clothilde herself.

'Where are the monks?' Elle asked.

'Oh, here and there,' Clothilde said non-committally.

'But the city needs them to make spark. Without the electromancers we have no means to drive our machines.'

Clothilde smiled at her. 'Most inconvenient, isn't it? That the Realm of Light has to rely on the electromancers so. It is an irony not lost on many of us who dwell on the other side.'

They had reached another set of doors, which Clothilde pushed open. 'Inside!' She stood aside so the undead could shove Elle and Loisa through the entrance. Elle stumbled into the room.

'In the cage!' Clothilde commanded as she opened the gate of what looked to be a large metal construction of bars that made up a cell. The professor and the doctor were both inside.

'Papa, doctor, are you hurt?' Elle said as soon as they were shoved inside.

'We're fine,' the professor whispered. He gave Elle a little wink. 'We have a plan.'

Loisa rolled her eyes and set about cleaning her face with the fine silk handkerchief she had produced from one of her pockets.

'Behold, my laboratory!' Clothilde swept her arms through the air and the row of spark lights that hung from the roof lit up in sequence.

Elle and Loisa stared, open-mouthed. Clothilde's laboratory was huge. It was a long, narrow room that spanned almost the entire length of the building. The roof was a network of wood and metal beams. From them, an array of tubes and pipes led down into vast rows of glass jars lined up neatly on shelves that lined one wall. The glass jars, which were, in turn, all interconnected by various copper and rubber tubes, glowed with an eerie blue light.

All the tubes led into a console of dials and gauges that seemed to regulate the flow of whatever was in the pipes.

'My goodness, that is quite something,' was all Elle could say. There was enough spark in the laboratory to power a hundred airships for a very long time.

'Necromancy,' Loisa whispered. 'I can smell it.'

'Welcome to my chamber of hearts. I'm so pleased you like it,' Clothilde said as she gestured at the rows of jars.

Elle repressed a surge of revulsion as she looked closer at the jars on the shelves. A lot of them were empty, but many were not, and their gory contents made bitter bile rise up into the back of her throat.

'*Mon Dieu*,' Loisa said as her gaze followed Elle's around the room.

Inside each jar, suspended in the blue glowing liquid, was what appeared to be a pulsating human heart. And they all seemed to be beating in unison.

'There must be thousands of jars,' the professor said.

'There are,' Clothilde said. 'But sadly we are not quite up to full capacity just yet. But we are making progress.'

'Why are you doing all this?' Elle said.

Clothilde laughed. 'Oh, don't be so stupid.'

'I need to know.' Elle steadily met her gaze, challenging Clothilde to continue.

'If you insist, we are building an army of soldiers that feel no fear or pain. An army that requires no supplies. One made up of soldiers who can fight night and day and who obey every command fearlessly and without question. And whoever commands this super army will rule the world.'

'But this is madness,' Elle said as Clothilde's words sank in.

'Only for those who are on the receiving side,' Clothilde said. 'And with my unlimited spark production upstairs, soon no one will be able to stop me.'

'Who are your masters?' Elle said, grabbing on to the only piece of information that made any sense to her.

'The Consortium. That is all you need to know. That and the fact that they have a most skilled clockmaker in their ranks. He is the one who designed the beautiful mechanical hearts.'

'The Clockmaker?' Elle felt a cold shiver of apprehension move through her.

'But we digress. Would you like to see your husband's heart now?' She ran her pale hand along the row of jars. Elle noticed that each jar had a number on a little brass tag attached to a tie around the top.

Clothilde stopped in front of one of the rows and studied the tags. 'Ah, here he is. Number 493.' She peered at the heart, which was a strange shade of purple in the blue light. To Elle's dismay, she noticed that Marsh's heart beat ever so slightly quicker when Clothilde rested her hand against the glass.

'You mean to bring war and destruction to this world,' Loisa said. 'We cannot allow it.'

Clothilde arched one of her finely curved eyebrows at Loisa. 'Oh, and your kind has not preyed on the living for centuries? You may dress and act civilised, but for more centuries than anyone cares to remember, your kind treated the Realm of Light as nothing more than a feeding ground. I would be slow to criticise if I were you, Nightwalker.'

Loisa hissed and bared her fangs.

Clothilde just laughed. 'Don't forget that you are still within my power. One flick of my wrist and your head rolls over the floor.'

'I would like to see you try,' Loisa growled.

'Ah, she shows her true nature,' Clothilde said. 'You are lucky that I need you alive for the experiments I am planning. Having Nightwalkers in the ranks is going to be an exciting addition to the armies. But we can have a little duel of wills before we proceed, if that would make you happy.'

Loisa sprang towards the bars of the cage with such force that the entire structure wobbled.

Clothilde turned away from her to the elaborately fitted-out operating table that took pride of place in the centre of the laboratory, as if Loisa's anger was insignificant.

Suddenly, they heard a loud thump, like metal hitting stone. Clothilde's expression froze as she was suddenly engulfed in a shroud of blue spark. Before anyone could say anything, she sank to her knees and vaporised before their very eyes.

'What on earth?' Elle said as Neville stepped forward holding the spark-blaster at the ready.

'Ah, Neville, old chap,' the professor said. 'Right on time. That was a jolly good shot. Would have been a six if you were on the Oval.'

Neville grinned from ear to ear at the compliment.

'Look out!' Loisa said, for the four undead soldiers grunted and came at Neville in a sudden rush. Neville blasted them with the spark blaster, which knocked them to the floor.

'Stand back!' Loisa shouted. She kicked the door of the cage with such force that the lock cracked and the door sprang open.

'That wasn't much of a difficulty then,' the professor said, glancing at the lock.

'Clearly not,' Elle said drily. 'Neither was the Lady in White, by the looks of things. Let's herd those guards into the cage. Quickly. I'll see if I can find something to secure the gate.'

'Shall I bring his lordship in now?' Neville asked as soon as they had secured the gate with an old chain and a padlock they had found in one of the cupboards.

'Without delay, my dear man. Without delay,' the doctor said.

Neville whistled and Caruthers appeared at the door with Marsh. They had loosed his feet from the canvas and somehow he had managed to walk Marsh there. Marsh moaned as soon as he saw the other undead. It was a terrible sound that emanated from the back of his throat.

'Neville, you stay and guard the entrance while my

father and the doctor get to work. Vanquishing *Madame Blanche* seemed a little bit too easy to be believed. No offence meant, of course,' Elle said.

'None taken, my lady,' Neville said. 'But this thing seems to work really well on those undead.' He shifted the spark blaster to a more comfortable position. 'Well, see if you can refill the canister. Heavens knows, there is enough spark around here for that.'

'I don't trust the silence either,' Loisa said. 'We had better make sure she is really dead.'

'Lead the way, Loisa,' Elle said. She picked up a spanner the length of her arm off one of the shelves and lifted it over her shoulder. 'Besides, the evil old hag stole my Colt too. And I want it back along with my husband and my life before we go home this evening.'

Chapter Thirty-four

'How many did you fight while you were on the stairs, Loisa?' Elle asked as they crept along the narrow passageway that led back to the main hall.

'Oh, I think about a dozen or so. The problem is that they won't stay down. You have to break their legs so they can't come after you.' She made a face. 'Also they taste really awful if you bite them.'

'Let's hope I never have to sample them,' Elle said, grateful for the fact that she was not a Nightwalker.

The soft sound of rustling caught their attention.

'What was that?' Elle whispered.

Up ahead of them in the passageway something was shuffling around in the dark.

Quietly as they could, Elle and Loisa crept up to the doorway to see what it was.

'Who's there?' Elle switched on her spark lamp and a beam of light revealed a small man in a grey robe.

'P–please don't hurt me,' he muttered, lifting his hands before his face to ward off the blinding light of the lamp.

'An electromancer!' Loisa said.

'Where are the rest of your brothers?' Elle asked.

'We're hiding in the tunnels below the building. She hasn't found those yet,' he said.

'We've come to liberate you,' said Elle.

The electromancer's face lit up but fell again. 'You won't get past the Lady. And if she gets angry, you end up being food for the troops.'

Elle shuddered at the mental image of Marsh gorging on fresh liver, but pushed the thought firmly from her mind. 'The Lady is gone for the moment, so I would suggest you get your people out of here as quickly as you can,' Elle said, 'in case there is more trouble.'

The little man nodded and gripped her hand. 'Thank you ever so much!' He opened a small hatch in the floor and disappeared into it.

'That solves one of the mysteries,' Loisa said.

'Indeed it does,' said Elle. 'I think those are the stairs to the control room up ahead.' The control room seemed as good a place as any to look, she thought as they walked along. Around them, the building echoed and creaked eerily like a giant ghost ship.

Elle had not been wrong, for a sudden screeching, wailing noise met them halfway up the stairs.

'Head for open ground!' Loisa said to Elle, and they turned and ran down the stairs.

A white cloud of mist boiled out of the stairwell behind them as they burst into the turbine hall. Great flashes of lightning flashed in the sky above them.

'I cannot be vanquished with spark, you stupid fools. I am the very element that spark is made of!' Clothilde rose up before them in a vast cloud of roiling mist that gradually diminished, leaving the elemental standing before them. 'I was foolish to show you mercy before, but not this time.' She was seething with anger.

'I bet you she's cross because you maimed some of her soldiers,' Elle said to Loisa.

'Livid, it seems,' Loisa replied.

'Those soldiers were part of a shipment that you have now ruined!' Clothilde said. 'The time for playing games is over. You must die without delay.' She lifted her arms and rose up above them, ready to strike a deathblow.

At that moment, bright searchlights flooded through the glass roof of the turbine hall. Elle looked up and her eyes widened with surprise. Above her, the hull of a giant airship loomed from the darkness. It was hovering so low that its bottom almost touched the glass panes of the roof.

Clothilde blinked as if she had just woken up from a trance. Ignoring Elle and Loisa, she smiled sweetly as she took in the sight of the ship above them. 'Such brilliant timing! They are here. Vargo, start preparing the soldiers to embark! Find whoever you can to make up the hundred. Do not leave the Consortium waiting. I will see to these – these vermin,' she said, motioning towards Elle.

Vargo and two other men appeared from the doorway to the stairwell behind Clothilde. They were the same men from the park, Elle realised with a shudder.

'I said move!' Clothilde bellowed.

'Yes, mistress.' Vargo stared at Clothilde as if she had gone completely mad, which was, it seemed, a conclusion that did not require a huge amount of deductive reasoning. But he shrugged and strode off into the distance.

'Where are you taking those people?' Elle demanded.

'They are a special order for the Emperor of Japan. He

will be very pleased with his consignment,' Clothilde said rather smugly.

'She really loves the sound of her own voice, doesn't she?' Elle said out the side of her mouth to Loisa.

Loisa snickered in reply.

'I will not abide such insolence. Neither you, nor anyone else is going to stop me,' Clothilde said.

Elle shook her head. 'Did you know, your voice is becoming shriller by the moment? You are liable to start shattering glass soon if you don't watch out.'

'Don't you shake your head at me, *Oracle!*' Her voice had become like nails dragging on a chalkboard and, despite their best efforts to ignore it, Elle and Loisa both flinched.

At that very moment, there was a terrible rumble and a crash. The dirigible hull above them shifted sideways and tapped the panes. Large cracks appeared in the glass and spread across the roof like spider webs. There was one loud crack and then the air filled with sounds of shattering glass. Deadly shards started falling to the ground.

Clothilde screamed as a shard of glass sliced into her shoulder. Great bolts of lightning flashed and started hitting the ground all around them.

'Loisa run! Get out!' Elle covered her face with her hands and made for the door. The bits of glass slashed at her, cutting through the hide of her sturdy leather coat. She felt the skin of her arms and scalp slice a few times before Loisa grabbed her by the scruff of her neck and shoved her through the open doors.

Outside the monastery, Elle skidded to a halt. Before them a state of utter chaos reigned.

The undead were running about lashing out at anything and everything. Around them groups of people, armed with a startling array of home-made armour and weapons that ranged from frying pans to sheets of corrugated iron, were trying to round up the herds of undead. It looked more like a giant game of tag at a village fete than a battle to the death.

'Where did all these people come from?' Elle looked at Loisa in amazement.

Loisa shrugged, but before she could say anything, she was interrupted by someone shouting and running towards them at full speed.

It was Jasper. He was covered in grime and his clothes were tattered, but he was alive and, at that moment, he was waving his arms frantically while shouting, 'Take cover!'

The sound of wood splitting and the groan of distressed metal rose up from the general pandemonium around them. It was a terrible sound that Elle had heard only once before – it was the sound of an airship dying.

Elle spun round in the direction of the noise and stared, transfixed with terror. Two dirigibles, locked together like beasts at each other's throats, were hovering just above the roof of the monastery. The tether ropes of the bigger ship had become entangled in the roof beams. As if suspended in water, the two vessels slowly tilted sideways and crashed to the ground, taking most of the monastery roof with them. The patch of land that was immediately to the east side of the monastery was suddenly filled with billowing canvas and the impact of the crash made the ground shudder.

Splinters of wood, the size of a man's forearm, along with other debris flew through the helium-laced air, piercing everything in their path.

'Get down!' Elle shouted, but her voice was drowned out by the general din of the crash.

A few people, undead and living, were knocked to the ground by bits of flying plank and Elle watched in horror as one of the undead was skewered and pinned to the ground by a piece of metal. He continued to move, his arms and legs flailing pitifully.

'Look out!' Loisa cried. Her voice was comically high from the helium in the air. A large chunk of metal came hurtling towards Elle. She grabbed on to Loisa and they sidestepped the missile which jolted to a stop just beside them. Elle peered at the hunk of metal in amazement. It was the head of a fierce-looking bird.

'Oh my goodness, that's the *Phoenix*. Ducky!' They both turned to the mangled wreckage in horror and dismay.

As they watched the settling mass of wrecked ship, a few planks shot in the opposite direction, as if someone had kicked them away from the inside. From the wreckage, two men stumbled. One was half dragging the other in a fireman's hold.

'This way! Over here!' Elle called to them. To her amazement, she realised that it was Captain Dashwood, carrying Ducky.

With much care, Dashwood lay Ducky down on the ground. 'There you are, old fella,' he said. 'He got hit by a falling beam. Knocked him out cold,' he said.

Ducky groaned and opened his eyes.

Elle crouched beside him and rested her hand on his

forehead. 'Ducky? Can you hear me?' she said.

He gave her a lopsided smile. 'Sorry about the ship, Bells. Made a bit of a mess of the landing.'

'Oh, Ducky,' Elle said with a sob of relief.

'He'll be fine,' Dashwood said.

'How did you get here?' Elle blurted.

'Ducky asked me to co-pilot for him. The *Phoenix* needs two pilots, remember?' He looked at her. 'And you, lady, owe me a ship.'

'Rally! Rally! Come on, ladies, secure those stragglers!' someone shouted through a loudspeaker behind them. 'Left flank! Suffragette unit! Send in the medics and get someone to look for survivors on those ships!'

Elle put her hand before her mouth in amazement as the group turned their attention to the spectacle that was playing out before them. Loisa's cab, which at that moment was being driven forward ever so slowly by a rather flustered-looking Caruthers, came into view. On top of the cab, Mrs Hinges stood with a loudspeaker before her face. She was directing the crowd of people before her like an army general.

'To the left. To the left! They are escaping!' Mrs Hinges waved her arms directing the troops.

'Jasper!' Loisa said, catching Mr Sidgwick by the lapel as he raced by. 'How on earth did you get here?'

'They jumped me in my rooms, and the next thing I knew I was in a cell, ready for processing into one of those things. But something must have gone wrong, because they never got round to me. Good evening.' He rubbed the little thinning patch on the back of his head and nodded at Dashwood. 'The monks were whispering about someone who had come to save them and I thought to myself that it had to be you two. So I lifted a key off one of the minders and opened the cells.'

'Bravo, Jasper!' Loisa said. Jasper beamed back at her.

Someone had switched on the monastery's outside lights and they shone across the open space with blinding intensity. Elle peered through the spark-light-illuminated half-dark. People from all walks of life loomed out of the dark. Some were servants, dressed in uniform – as if they had abandoned dinner to come here. Others were wearing green and purple sashes over their dresses.

A woman ran up to them. 'Elle! Thank goodness you made it out of the building.' It was Christabel Pankhurst; she had a streak of mud on her cheek.

'What on earth are *you* doing here?' Elle asked, forgetting her manners in her amazement.

Christabel winked at her. 'Mrs Hinges told the lady's maid of one of the Mandevilles, who in turn told their mistress, who told me. You didn't think we'd let you try to save London all by yourself, did you?'

'I suppose not,' Elle said.

Christabel smiled. 'The Mandevilles are manning the medic and refreshment station which has been set up in the park.'

Mrs Hinges made Caruthers sound the cab horn through her loudspeaker, signalling to the troops to change manoeuvres.

'The electromancers! The electromancers are revolting! Join us, brothers!' someone shouted.

Sure enough, the little monks started pouring from the building. They were linking arms in a line that effectively flanked the undead, herding them into a group and preventing them from re-entering the monastery.

'About my ship,' Dashwood said.

'Christabel,' Elle said, ignoring the captain, 'this is Captain Logan Dashwood. He is most interested in the ladies' cause and would like to join in the fight for the vote. He told me just the other day that he would love to discuss the issues in detail. Perhaps you could take him under your wing, as it were.'

'How do you do?' Christabel said, as she took in the handsome captain. She ran her hands over her hair to make sure her fashionable Gibson girl knot was still in place.

Dashwood blanched and gave Elle a horrified look. Ducky started laughing.

'Let's get this wounded fellow to the medic tent. He looks as if he could do with a bit of a patch-up,' said Christabel. 'I see my squadron of ladies is faltering without me and we need to round up as many of these Tickers as we can so they can be restored to health. There is no time to waste. I'm sure we can have a lovely long talk about all this later. Come along then. Chop chop,' she ordered the captain. Between them, they lifted Ducky and headed off towards the park.

The last Elle saw of Dashwood was his pleading look for help, as Christabel led him into the squadron of Suffragettes.

'We need more light!' Mrs Hinges bellowed.

To her left, Elle caught sight of flashes of yellow that were almost as bright as sunlight.

At least a dozen fairies of various descriptions were

blasting shafts of their light into the undead, illuminating the whole area. From the corner of her eye, Elle could have sworn she saw a flash of green light, which could only have been Adele, but she wasn't sure and there was no time to check. Clearly the travelling folk and the patrons from the Black Stag had also decided to join in the fight. Elle caught a glimpse of Emilian's peacock feather bobbing through the crowd as he sprinted towards the fairies.

The undead seemed utterly disorientated by all the activity and started huddling together in a big herd in the middle of the open ground in front of the monastery.

'Is anyone we know *not* here tonight?' Elle asked Loisa.

'We had better go and see how your father is faring,' Loisa said. 'Hopefully that breaking glass has killed the witch once and for all.'

'Let's hope we are so lucky,' Elle said. She looked back at the wreckage and bit her lip. About half a dozen Suffragettes were sifting through the rubble, looking for the other pilot.

'There is nothing you can do for him now,' said Loisa, who could see better in the dark.

'As always, you are the voice of reason, Loisa,' Elle said, feeling suddenly utterly exhausted. 'Let's go and collect Hugh. I want to go home.'

Chapter Thirty-five

Patrice stood in the shadows under a tree on the opposite bank of the Thames. He watched the dirigibles plunge to the ground and shook his head. What a debacle.

He bunched his fists at his sides. Once again the Oracle had ruined his plans beyond the point of redemption.

There was one consolation, though. At least this time, he could blame it on *La Dame Blanche* when it came to reporting to the Consortium. The Consortium, Patrice chuckled. These men, the captains of industry, rulers of the world's stock markets – how utterly foolish of them to place such an important project in the hands of a mere woman.

But it mattered not, because for once, he, Patrice Chevalier, had come up trumps.

He closed his eyes and felt the surge of dark magic flow through him. This new energy that he felt deep within him was more powerful than anything he had ever imagined. No wonder Marsh had always been so smug.

He chuckled lightly, but this time the wound in his chest did not hurt. He had sent a little bit of his own magic to the area and he seemed to be healed up entirely. This filled him with much excitement, for he was one of the few people in this world who knew the true secrets of the

Council of Warlocks. For years they had been nothing but an impotent group of posers, pretending that the power they had once yielded still existed. They were nothing but a bunch of stage magicians putting on a show.

All that was about to change.

A smart black car rumbled up the road and came to a halt before him.

'Evenin', sir,' the driver said.

'Ah, Mr Chunk. I am so very pleased you found me.'

'Not at all, sir. Always a pleasure to be of assistance,' Mr Chunk said. He hopped out from behind the driver's seat and opened the door for Patrice.

Patrice settled into the back seat with a sigh.

'Where to, sir?'

'Hmm. King's Cross station. I think I might go up north to have a look at my factories there while I'm here.'

'Very well, sir,' Mr Chunk said as he took his place behind the wheel.

Patrice sat forward. 'Actually, we might stop off at Madame Colette's first. It's on the way to the station, is it not?'

'It most certainly is, sir.' Mr Chunk gave a small chuckle of amusement.

'Yes, I suddenly find myself in possession of a raging appetite. And they do serve a splendid plate of roast beef there too,' Patrice mused. It was true. He suddenly felt better than he had in a very long time. He sat back and lit one of the little black cigars he loved so much. He felt the smoke fill his lungs and he breathed out with a deep sense of satisfaction as he contemplated the current state of affairs.

Hugh Marsh had been turned into one of Clothilde's undead creatures. It was unlikely he would survive the ordeal. And that meant that Eleanor was alone. Yes, the Oracle was all by herself and unprotected. Stubborn and immature, she was ripe for the plucking.

A slow smile spread across Patrice's face. Just think of what he would be able to achieve if he could use her to channel and amplify his newfound power. The thought sent shivers of pleasurable anticipation through him.

But he would have to plan it carefully. He could not risk anything going wrong. He would take his time before making the next move.

'Mr Chunk. I have changed my mind. Could you please see if you can book an air ticket for me while I am at Colette's?'

'Very well, sir. First class?'

'If you can,' said Patrice. 'But speed is more important than comfort in these circumstances. I need to go to Venice without delay.'

'Council of Warlocks, sir?'

'Indeed.'

'No need to say any more, sir,' Mr Chunk said as he negotiated the London traffic.

Patrice sat back in the comfort of his seat as he watched London rush past him. It had stopped raining and the whole city was shimmering and icy-wet under the bright light of the moon. The sight of it was extraordinarily pretty after the fog and ice.

Yes, things went very well for him this time. Now it was time to seize the day.

Chapter Thirty-six

The monastery felt eerily empty after the deafening crash of the dirigibles outside. The gaping hole in the glass roof caused freezing cold air to fill the building. Elle shivered as they crept along the narrow corridors.

'Stay close,' Loisa whispered. 'I still don't trust this place.'

'Neither do I,' Elle said.

Outside, thunder rumbled ominously. Elle and Loisa looked at one another. 'I suppose she is not dead after all,' Elle said as they reached the laboratory.

'Dr Miller? Papa? Are you in there?' Elle called.

'Down here,' the faint answer came.

Elle rushed down the stairs and into the laboratory. 'How are things going?' Elle said. Her voice echoed through the room, loudly.

'Shh!' the professor said. 'We are at a very delicate stage of the procedure.'

Marsh was laid out on a long operating table before her. His handsome face was as pale and still as a wax death mask. Rubber and brass tubes protruded from his chest. The tubes were connected to a large machine that groaned and belched air into him at regular intervals.

Elle bit her lip at the awfulness of the scene before her. Seeing him like this was almost too much to bear.

'Right, doctor, are you ready?' the professor said, seemingly unfazed by the bizarre situation they found themselves in.

'Wait!' Elle interrupted. 'Are you sure you have the correct heart?'

The professor sighed. 'Yes, my dear. It was the one marked with the same number as that marked on his arm. The one that woman picked out. Now let us get on with it. We really don't have a lot of time.'

'Doctor, on the count of three,' the professor instructed, resuming the procedure.

Dr Miller pulled back his shirtsleeves and reached into the glass jar before him. Carefully, he wrapped his hands around the heart suspended within the illuminated blue liquid. It was so strangely intimate an act, that it made Elle gasp.

'Better look away now,' Loisa said.

'No, I need to see,' Elle said, bracing herself.

'One . . . two . . . three!' The professor flipped up the connector switch and a series of valves started moving vigorously inside the professor's device, which he had installed on to the side of the table.

'Extracting the clockwork now!' In one swift move, the professor lifted the clockwork heart out. The little device whirred and spat globules of dark blood all over the white aprons the professor and the doctor were wearing.

Marsh jerked violently, but remained restrained by the fabric bindings that held him to the table.

'Now, doctor. When you are ready,' the professor said.

Dr Miller nodded and lifted the heart from the liquid. Every so gently, he eased it back into Marsh.

'Insertion complete,' he said, lifting his hands out of the way.

'Reattachment sequence commencing.' The professor flicked another switch and the machine started humming. The probes cut, then sealed up tissue and muscle.

'Apply spark,' the doctor said.

A squiggle of smoke rose up as they sent a little current of spark through Marsh.

'Now, the rest of this is up to you, Hugh. *Will* your heart to start beating,' the professor murmured.

Everyone stood very still as they watched for the needle of the beat measurement gauge to move.

Elle was too frightened to breathe. And then, in the space it took for a miracle to occur, the needle lifted.

. . . Thump-thump . . . thump-thump.

Marsh's heart had started beating with the slow, steady rhythm that promised that all would be well.

'Oh, thank goodness,' Elle gasped. She wanted to jump up and scream, but she forced herself to stay calm. She glanced over to Loisa. The Nightwalker was smiling from ear to ear.

'Let's close that chest wound,' the doctor said. 'Hold that side, professor.' He started removing the tubes, all the while stitching up the hideous gaping hole in Marsh's chest.

'Not so fast,' a voice said behind them.

Elle and Loisa swung round.

La Dame Blanche was standing behind them on the stairs. She was panting and her white robes were stained with dark blood that oozed from the wound in her shoulder.

'Oh, not you again,' Elle said.

'Surrender!' Loisa said. 'Your airship has crashed and your army is defeated. There is nothing more here for you.'

'*Au contraire*,' she said, shaking her head. 'The Warlock is *mine*!'

'He is certainly not!' Elle said.

Before Elle could do anything, Loisa hissed and lunged at the Lady. They fell to the ground, growling and scratching at one another.

As quickly as she could, Elle ran to the metal cage and undid the chain that held the door shut. Clothilde and Loisa were still rolling around on the floor. Every now and then Loisa gave a squeal of pain.

Elle stepped around them. 'Loisa! Quick. Now!' she shouted.

Loisa pushed Clothilde aside and rolled out of the way. In that moment Elle grabbed Clothilde by her long white hair and shoved her into the cage with the undead, before slamming the door shut.

'Not so much fun being in a metal cage, is it?' Loisa said. She was kneeling on the ground, panting.

'Loisa, are you all right?' Elle said.

She nodded and rubbed her throat. 'I am much better now, actually.' She stood up and straightened her clothes.

'He's waking up,' the doctor said.

'Loisa, hold this door for me, please,' Elle said. She ran up to the table where the doctor and the professor were undoing the bindings that held Marsh.

Marsh groaned and opened his eyes.

'Oh, my darling,' Elle whispered.

His eyes, no longer milky white, focused on her and, for the briefest moment, she and Marsh connected.

'He's very weak and he needs time to recover—' the doctor started saying, but he was interrupted by Clothilde laughing.

'Very good work, doctor, but you have no knowledge of this procedure and, without my will, he is not going to survive,' she said.

'Take cover!' Loisa shouted in the split second before the cage exploded.

Clothilde rose up from the rubble in a whirl of white hair and tattered darkness. A terrible halo of blue lightning crackled around her as she hovered over them.

She lifted one bone-white arm and pointed at Marsh.

By flesh and heart and skin and bone
The Warlock will be cursed to wander the borderlands
alone.
By the four corners of this world and the next,
May he live yet may his heart not beat in his chest.
Ever searching, never to rest.
I call upon the spectres of fear and doubt
To cast all resolve and courage out.
May they curse those they may,
And let misfortune guide them, until the end of days.

Clothilde waved her arms and an inky swirl of cloud boiled above them. Hard, icy rain started pelting down, stinging exposed skin where it hit.

'I cast this curse three times over!' she screeched and pointed at them.

Elle held on to Marsh, trying to shield him from the harm with her body, bracing herself for what was to come. There was nothing else she could do as the bright blue bolt of energy hit them.

Clothilde started laughing again. 'The Warlock is no longer your husband. He is mine. We will retreat to the Realm of Shadow for evermore.' She was breathing heavily as she reached up into the air before her, as if she were going to open a set of curtains. Elle felt the barrier between Shadow and Light rip and she gasped.

'I thank you, Oracle, for your life force. It makes opening the void so much easier,' Clothilde said.

But before she could do anything more, a rush of air filled the room, pushing the rain and clouds out of the way. Elle caught the dank odour of rotting plants and forest floor as white light poured through the opening that Clothilde had created.

To everyone's astonishment, Old Jack stepped through the barrier, carrying his lantern and a bundle slung over his shoulder. Without batting an eyelid, he shoved Clothilde out of the way and she fell to her knees.

'What are you waiting for? Stop her, little Oracle,' Jack said. 'Use the silk around your finger. It's the only way. Do it now, before it's too late.'

Elle closed her eyes. She slipped her fingers round her

wedding band, feeling for the invisible strand that bound her to Marsh.

'I'm sorry, my love,' she whispered and then, using all of her strength, she pulled at the filament to release it. She felt a sharp agonising pain in her chest, tearing at her insides.

As she felt the final strands of the bond between them split and fall away Marsh let out an inhuman wail beside her.

'I love you. I will always love you,' Elle said. Then, with resolve she did not know she possessed, Elle pulled at the strand. It came away into her hands, thick and strong like a hangman's noose.

Before Clothilde could react, Elle rose up and faced her. The raw energy that poured through the rent was splashing through her. It felt as if she was standing under a waterfall that gushed and swirled around her, filling her with exquisite power.

When she found her voice, it projected with such impact that it echoed through the entire building.

'I am Pythia. I am the Oracle. Hear me!' Elle's voice boomed.

Clothilde looked up at her and her face filled with fear.

'White Lady ... you have broken the laws of the two realms. You have interfered with the natural order of things. How dare you show your face before me?'

Clothilde stood. She was still shaking, but her face had grown hard with resolve. 'I dare and I will. Do not think you can frighten me, madam. I am far older and more powerful than you are.'

'You will heed me!' Elle said. 'Undo this curse and

restore this man to his former self. This I command as the One who holds Shadow and Light together!'

'Never!' Clothilde spat. 'I do not care what you do to me, but the Warlock will be mine!' With that she screeched and launched herself at Elle, clawing at her.

The two of them fell on the floor in a cascade of Light and Shadow. They rolled around until they hit the wall on the other side. Clothilde rose up. She was holding Elle by the throat, pinning her to the wall.

'Now you will die, Oracle. And with this opening in the void, all Shadow creatures will be free,' Clothilde hissed.

Elle gasped as the last of the air was squeezed from her lungs. Clothilde's white bony fingers were digging into the flesh of her throat, choking her. Darkness loomed on the periphery of her vision where Death waited.

'No…you…will…not…' Elle managed to say. Then, raising her arms, she looped the glowing rope in her hands around the Lady's neck. She held both ends and pulled as hard as she could. Her mind went blank. This was a fight to the death.

The Lady's sea-green eyes widened with surprise as the rope seared through her hair and into her white skin. She made a horrible gurgling sound.

Purple electricity cracked over Elle's forearms, singeing her skin, but she did not care. All she could think about was ridding the world of this evil woman once and for all. Elle gritted her teeth and held on to the rope for dear life.

Clothilde wailed and shrieked like a banshee as each woman fought the other's hold. Then, quite suddenly, the rope sliced cleanly through Clothilde's neck. There was a massive blast of white light that blinded everyone.

Everything went silent. *La Dame Blanche* was no more.

Elle fell to the ground, singed and wide-eyed.

'Is it over? Is she really dead this time?' Loisa sat up and looked about.

Elle did not answer, but around them small tatters of the Lady's robes drifted down like soft little feathers.

Marsh grunted and crawled away into the shadows.

'Hugh!' Elle croaked and made to follow him, but he hissed at her.

She held back, extending her hand towards him.

He grunted again and shuffled forward, pulling himself up to his full height as he stepped into the shaft of moonlight that fell through the huge windows. The storm clouds had vanished from the sky.

Outside, the soft sounds of the Battle of Battersea reached them. From the whoops of joy, it sounded like the right side had won, but somehow everything, including the victory, felt hollow and distant.

Elle felt her heart constrict with fear and doubt as she beheld the effects of the Lady in White's curse.

Marsh's heart may have been back inside his chest, but the man was gone. All the vibrancy and vitality that had been such a quintessential part of him was washed out of his face. He stood perfectly silent, hunched up in his tattered carriage cloak. It was as if every part of him that had belonged to the Realm of Light was gone. Only remnants of Shadow remained in the wraith that stood before her.

'Please, let's go home, my love,' she whispered. 'We will find a way to fix this.'

He stared at her with a dark fierceness that made her blood run cold. 'I . . . cannot,' he said. His voice was nothing more than a hoarse rasp that sounded like it came from very far away.

'He is not your husband any more, little Oracle,' Jack said softly behind her. He looked slightly contrite as he rubbed the front of his cloak which was none too clean. 'I hate to mention it at a time like this but now you owe me a third favour. Looks like I got here just in time. You should never have left me behind like you did,' he admonished.

Elle ignored the old Fey. She reached out to take Marsh into her arms, but he stepped back, with his arms out to stop her.

'Must go to the Shadow . . . Better . . . Safer for you.' His voice came to her, soft and haunting, like the whisper of wind through conifers.

'Do not go any closer. He must go to the Shadow before it's too late and this portal closes. Wraiths do not survive for long in the Light,' Jack warned.

'Come with me. We can break this curse. Together we can do this.' Huge tears started running down her cheeks, unbidden.

'Don't be sad.' Marsh's eyes softened. 'Better I go . . . be free and forget me . . . better that way.'

'He is right. If he is truly a wraith, he will drain your life force away,' Loisa said.

'There will be nothing left of either of you before long,' Jack said. 'Come along then, sir, before it's too late. Wouldn't want to miss the gap.' He motioned towards the glowing rent in the barrier from which he had just stepped. 'Tell them Old Jack sent you. They will take care of you if you do.'

Marsh looked at Jack and nodded.

'No! Don't leave me, please.' Elle was weeping so profusely now that she felt as if her lungs would burst.

Marsh turned to look at her. A strange look of compassion crossed his face. 'It calls and I must go.' As he turned, his face filled with colour. For a sliver of a second he was human and he smiled at her. Then he turned, stepped through the rent and disappeared.

'No!' Elle fell to her knees and buried her face in her hands. Her tears were mixing with the soot on her skin, dripping large black drops of sorrow on to her clothes.

'The black tears of a grieving widow. You should hang on to those. They are very valuable. Very rare too. Pure sorrow,' Jack mumbled as he picked up his bundle.

Everyone else ignored him. They were all too shocked to say anything.

'Very well, if there is nothing else, I will be on my way then,' he said as he hitched up his bundle. 'Three times, little Oracle. You and me will meet again when the time is right.' With those words, he slung his bundle over his shoulder and walked off into the night.

The Clockmaker sits up in his bed, grasping his nightshirt. Something is amiss. Even here, in his safe, warm little apartment in Zurich it feels like an invisible hand is pressing into him, constricting his chest.

'What waits in the darkness?' he whispers. He shrugs his shoulders in disbelief at his own fear and makes to slip back under the comforting warmth of soft linens and goose down. The Clockmaker does not believe in ghosts or strange creatures that go bump in the night, for he is an artist and a scientist. He puts his faith in the things that can be proven. He believes in the power of money. The power of the Consortium he has created. All those financiers and businessmen, who click and tick together to make the world turn. It is his greatest achievement.

He does not see the wraith who waits silently in the dark. He does not even see the fine garotte the wraith holds in his hand. The wraith is ready to perform his unspeakable task without delay.

By then it is too late and the Clockmaker's eyes widen in surprise for only an instant as the filament winds round his neck. The Clockmaker has time to make only half a choking sound before death takes him.

A single drop of ruby-red blood drops to the front of

his pristine nightshirt, exactly in the place where his heart no longer beats, before his body falls forward, lifeless.

The wraith does not flinch at the sight of the blood. Calmly he gathers up the lasso around his left hand. It is pure white and wound from the purest strand of silk, such as can only be woven by a wyrd-weaver. The end is a little frayed, as if it had been ripped apart by some great force, but this does not matter. As he twists the filament, it shortens and slips around the fourth finger of his left hand where a ring once sat. But the wraith does not stop to remember such things, for they are now firmly in the past. All that remains for him is the burning desire for revenge. It burns within him, white and hot, like a forge, sustaining the empty husk that once held a beating heart.

With a whisper that reminds him of summer meadows and of grass, the wraith slips from the room into the night.

Even in this darkness, he only has a little time before he must return to the Shadow. And he has much work to do.

❧

Chapter Thirty-seven

The days that followed what the newspapers were calling 'The Battle of Battersea Park' would always be shrouded in a haze for Elle.

Gentle hands conveyed her to the car. At some point, she was lifted out of the seat and put to bed. Doctor Miller's face swam in and out of her vision as he administered sedatives and sleeping potions, and applied bandages. But none of these ministrations did anything to ease the shock or numb the pain. Marsh was gone.

She drifted through flurries of days that wisped past. She looked on with cool detachment as if she were a stranger, observing her life from a distance.

Each new day was punctuated by a fresh headline that appeared on the silver tray next to her bed. The same tray that was later removed untouched.

The headlines told their own story: PLOT TO INVADE BRITAIN FOILED, one read.

MRS MATHILDA HINGES, NATIONAL HEROINE, TO BE HONOURED BY THE KING, said another. It had a picture of Mrs Hinges beside it. ELECTROMANCERS OPEN REHABILITATION HOSPITAL ON BANKS OF THE THAMES, one said later.

And later still: ASTONISHING ADVANCEMENTS IN HEART SURGERY PIONEERED.

Then: POLICE COMMISSIONER DISMISSED AMID ALLEGATIONS OF CORRUPTION.

It had been discovered that Commissioner Willoughby had been doing favours for various organisations. The prime minister was said to be outraged and was proposing widespread police reform.

And even later: STRANGE KILLINGS IN EUROPE. ANOTHER RIPPER ON THE LOOSE.

A funeral was held and Elle stood silently and alone in a scratchy black dress next to the empty coffin as it was sealed up inside the Greychester mausoleum. She weathered the countless pats and caresses of affection and sympathy in the same way a tree weathers a summer storm. Stoic and unattached, she stared blankly before her, until all conversation ran out and the world retreated to its own business.

Ducky had escaped the crash with nothing more than a few bruises and a broken collarbone. He had hugged Elle at the funeral and promised her that he would look after the charters till she felt better. The pilot of the other ship had not been so lucky. Elle never found out his name, but somehow she thought him to be the lucky one, for her life stretched out before her like a vast bone-bleached plain.

Marsh was gone.

Loisa and Jasper became the best of friends. After a suitable amount of time, they departed in Loisa's new steam cab, now modified to accommodate two travelling coffins and emblazoned with her red family crest. Jasper had passed Loisa's test and had joined her in the world of the night as a companion, and was completing the training and rituals all young Nightwalkers must learn.

Following the great battle, the professor finally confessed his feelings and proposed to Mrs Hinges, or Dame Mathilda Hinges, as she was henceforth known. Eventually they too departed for Oxford to prepare for a small wedding to be held at the local registry office. Elle had held the cream invitation card for a long time before she fed it into the fire. She watched the copperplate script, which advised rather formally that tea and cakes baked by the bride herself would be served afterwards, blister and disintegrate in the flames.

Adele had chosen to stay with Florica. She had made it known that fairies did not fare well in places that were infused with the kind of sorrow that dwelled within the walls of Greychester House. The travelling folk were always on the move, so it was not long until she disappeared entirely. All that Elle had to remember the fairy by was the small brass button that Florica had given her. It sat in a small ornamental porcelain bowl in the centre of Elle's dresser.

Elle took to sleeping in her secret chamber, curled up in a ball around a red velvet pillow. She clung to it like it was a life raft. Every night, she prowled the Shadow Realm. Her portal to the Shadow Realm became so well used that small shadow creatures now waited for her to emerge in the hope that they could slip through into the Light without anyone noticing. She did not pay them any heed, even when one of the maids shrieked and swatted at a dip-dib who skittered across the marble floors and vanished into the dark night. On and on Elle wandered through the Realm of Shadow. Always searching. Always hoping to find him, but he was never there. She became pale and thin with dark hollows under her eyes, which revealed her unspoken sorrow. But nothing she did helped. Marsh was gone.

One morning, Elle woke and stumbled out of her lightless chamber to find that bright shafts of sunlight were shining into her room. She walked up to the panes and looked out into the street below. Everything seemed hazy and brown, a bit like the sepia of a badly developed photograph, and it took her a moment to work out that the windowpanes were filthy. She walked over to the newspaper which was resting on the tray that had been left out for her as it was still every morning.

It was the fifteenth of May, 1904. Her twenty-fifth birthday.

Three months had passed without her even noticing. And still, he was gone.

She pulled on her dressing robe, hiding the pink scars that now marked her forearms. The scars were a painful reminder of the fateful night when her life had effectively ended.

On a whim, she decided to see who else was about. She pulled on a pair of satin slippers and padded down the hallway.

The house around her felt empty and hollow. Sheets covered all the mirrors and all the curtains were drawn. This was a house of mourning.

In the drawing room, no fire had been lit. Elle shivered at the sight of the abandoned bath chair which was back beside the fire.

She turned and walked through to the breakfast room. It was chilly in here, despite the brightness outside. She noticed that the plants in the conservatory had wilted and turned brown. Only a few brave ferns still clung to life in their dried-out pots.

Edie came by, carrying a bucket, and stopped in her tracks. 'My lady!' she blurted and immediately averted her eyes.

'Edie, is that you?' Elle croaked. Her voice still felt rough and husky after all this time.

'My lady,' Edie said again.

'Where is everybody?'

'Well, ma'am, Neville has moved on. The professor did his best to give him a good reference, so he's decided to join the army. The last we heard they were sending him to the Balkans to see if the trouble brewing there could be sorted out. And for the rest, well, it's just me and Mr Caruthers left now. We do the best we can, but this is a big house to care for.' She looked away, slightly embarrassed at the admission.

Elle sat down on one of the chairs and rubbed her face. Her skin felt greasy and her eyes scratchy. She realised to her dismay that she could not remember the last time she had brushed her teeth.

'Would you like me to fetch you something, my lady?'

Edie said, shifting from one foot to the other, clearly becoming more and more distressed at the sight of Elle, half-dressed and wild-haired, wandering through the house like a lost soul.

This somehow jolted Elle out of her reverie. She focused on Edie who was still holding the bucket.

'You know what, I think you can,' Elle said. 'Bring me some fresh towels. I would like to take a nice hot bath. And afterwards, I shall have some breakfast. Perhaps a cup of tea and some fried eggs.'

She had eaten fried eggs on that first breakfast she shared with Marsh on the day after their escape from Paris. She had had such a fight with Mrs Hinges about setting the table with the best linen. But somehow the memory of it gave her comfort.

'Yes, my lady,' Edie said and rushed off to tend to the task at hand.

Elle walked up to the windows of the breakfast room and dragged the floral print curtains open. A puff of dust rose up off them and drifted on to her shoulders, but she hardly noticed, for the sun shone through the windows on to the carpet in glorious bright shafts.

Elle stared up at the sky. It was the perfect blue of late spring and, judging by the speed of the giant white clouds that crept across it, with only a little headwind.

She took a deep, cleansing breath.

Today was a new day. Her life was beginning again. And the weather looked like it might be perfect for flying.

Acknowledgements

In many ways, a second novel is harder to write than a first. The playing field changes, the demands on the author are different and with this new world comes a new set of challenges.

I can say without hesitation that *A Clockwork Heart* would never have reached fruition in time if it had not been for the magnificent team of people assembled behind me. Writing might be the most solitary of occupations, but bringing novels into the world is very much a team effort.

So to Michael and Tricia, thank you again for everything.

To the lovely Emily Yau. Thank you so much for your patience and your dedication. Your eye for detail is amazing. To Hannah Robinson who looks after all the millions of tiny dots that make up the rather frantic pointillist world of a writer. I don't know how I ever managed without you.

To Joe Scalora and Sarah Peed who look after me in America, and who stay with me in spirit on that side of the world.

Also, a very special word of thanks to Justine Taylor for the copy edits, and Olivia Wood and Margaret Gilbey for the proofreading. Without you, the whole world would find out that I mostly never know what day of the week it is.

And last but not least, a special mention for Oliver Munson and Melis Dagoglu. Thank you for the support and feedback and for knowing just what to say when the clouds roll in.

I have asked Mrs Hinges to bake strawberry tarts for all of you, but even such sublime confections don't adequately express my gratitude.

The story continues...

Read on for a sneak peek at the next book in
The Chronicles of Light and Shadow series:

SKY PIRATES

Available from Del Rey

DEL REY

Chapter One

Khartoum, 29 October 1905

Eleanor tightened her cotton keffiyeh round her face and squinted through the shimmering haze of the afternoon. Before her, the mud-baked flats of the North Sudan spread out as far as the eye could see. They shimmered in the heat, shades of cinnamon, flint and ochre.

Her camel grunted and stepped sideways, instantly disrupting the caravan of beasts as it wound its way along the dusty track.

'Whoa,' Elle said. She leaned forward and, using her long riding cane, patted his sand-coloured neck to reassure him. In response, he turned his head and tried to bite her foot, leaving a trail of foul greenish snot over the leather of her polished boots.

'Oh you are a beast!' Elle said as she shook her foot and crossed her ankles in the place behind the camel's neck. Even though they had set her stirrups to suit a Western lady, she preferred to ride Bedouin-style as her guides did.

Behind her one of the guides laughed behind his keffiyeh. 'That one, we call him Hamsa. It means "lion of the desert".'

'Well he's going to be camel stew of the desert if he doesn't behave,' Elle retorted.

In reply, Hamsa grunted and farted loudly, although he did step into line with the other camels.

The Bedouin guide dropped the fabric from his leathery face and smiled, revealing two rows of white teeth.

'He likes you because you have the fire that burns inside. Not many women can ride the ships of the desert.'

Elle smiled back. 'Yes, I am quite proficient at piloting ships – only not so much the ones that bite. But say, how much farther do you think we need to travel?' The silence and the vastness of this place made her uneasy. Out here there was nowhere to hide.

'Not too much more. We will be at the place soon. From there you can see for days,' her guide replied as he turned his attention back to the invisible path they were following.

They were about half an hour's ride from the fort, which was near Wad Rawah to the south of the city of Khartoum. And it was here, off-the-beaten track in the depths of Sudan that her ship the *Water Lily* was moored, ready to fly a shipment of Nubian artefacts to the British Museum.

When the archaeological expedition that had chartered the *Water Lily* had not returned on schedule, Lieutenant Crosby had ordered a search party of guides to be sent out. It was not unusual for people to run into trouble or lose their way in these parts.

The opportunity to explore this secret gem had been

too strong to resist. So Elle had volunteered to join them. The lieutenant had objected. Elle had argued with him. Vigorously. To this day she had rarely lost an argument – and anyone who had ever tried to disagree with Lady Greychester once she had made up her mind soon learned that resistance was futile. Eventually Crosby had relented, but with much reluctance.

That was before Elle had discovered the quirks of travelling by camel.

'They should have been here by now.' Elle peered out into the distance. Before her the landscape was barren. The sight of it made a lump well up in her throat. Being out here in the vastness of the Sudan was far from a distraction from her inner woe. The emptiness of her surroundings perfectly matched the emptiness she felt in her heart – she felt desolate and alone.

Sensing her inattention, Hamsa lurched forward to bite a lonely tuft of grass, which was poking out from beside a rock. Elle had to grab hold of the saddle to stop herself from being flung over the camel's head and on to the ground.

Elle tried to bring her mount back under control but in her struggle with the camel, her sleeves had ridden up to reveal a series of delicate pink scars that snaked over her hands and up her forearms. She adjusted the fabric of her shirt quickly. Even though the burns had healed up well and were barely noticeable, she did not like to look at the marks. They were a painful reminder of things she preferred not to think about.

Eighteen months had passed since that freezing night in February. The night she had lost her husband and her heart. She shivered at the thought despite the desert heat. Had it been that long already?

The Bedouin shaded his eyes and pulled out a brass spyglass and slipped it open. He studied the horizon for a few long moments. Then he let out a shrill whistle. The other guides started chattering and gesturing animatedly.

'What's the matter?' Elle said as she followed the line her guide was pointing out.

In the distance, two fine plumes of dust appeared. Someone was coming.

The Bedouin turned to Elle. 'You are lucky he is a racing camel,' he said cryptically.

Elle squinted at him. 'And why is that?'

The Bedouin shook his head. 'Because now we must run.'

Elle scanned the dust plume. The familiar glint of sun reflecting off gunmetal caught her eye.

'Bandits!' she breathed.

As if in answer, the distinctive crack of gunfire rose up from one of the plumes of dust in the distance.

Hamsa bellowed and soon all the other camels joined in. They could smell trouble and by the looks of it, it was heading directly for them.

'There are too many. We cannot face them with so few guns. We must go back to the fort for reinforcements!' her Bedouin guide said as he gave the signal to retreat.

'Hold up a moment. Shouldn't we stay and lend them assistance?' Elle said.

Her guide shook his head emphatically. 'You do not know these bandits. They are of the most bloodthirsty and cruel kind. We have orders to make sure we turn back if there is any sign of trouble. Lieutenant's orders,' he added for good measure.

With surprising speed, the small caravan wheeled about and took off in the opposite direction, leaving Elle and Hamsa behind in the settling dust.

Elle did not really need much more persuasion. She had heard terrible stories of violence and cruelty that befell those hapless travellers who chanced upon desert bandits. Her guide's decision to run was not entirely without merit.

'Hold up, wait for me!' she called out, but her companions had no intention of hanging about. That much was clear from the way they were all urging their camels ahead.

Rather clumsily, she led Hamsa round and started following the guides, who were already in the distance. Fortunately her camel needed little persuasion and soon they were kicking up a fair old dust plume of their own. Elle coughed and pulled her goggles over her eyes.

'Hup hup, Hamsa.' Elle nudged the camel with her cane and the beast accelerated, his long legs making short work of the distance between her and the rest of the search party. Soon she was bringing up the rear guard of their caravan.

Slowly the minutes ticked by with only the sound of camels moving and the jingles of riding tack as they bounced along to break the grim silence. Every time she looked behind her, the dust plume was bigger.

'They are gaining on us,' she called out to her guide. He said nothing, but nudged his camel to go faster.

Elle almost let out a sob of relief when the fort came

into view. It was one of the few safe outposts within a two-hundred-mile radius of the city of Khartoum.

The fort was a shabby mud-brick building that melded into the landscape so seamlessly that the only way one could spot it was by the scraggly palm trees growing around it.

They rounded a shallow rocky outcrop. They reached a wide but shallow wadi that ran downhill from the fort. 'Almost there,' Elle said.

More shots rang out in the distance. Elle glanced over her shoulder to see what was happening. The dust plumes were much bigger now – a smaller one in front with a bigger one gaining from behind. They were not the only ones under attack, it seemed.

At the sight of the smaller plume Elle was suddenly seized with an attack of guilt and obligation in equal doses. Instead of providing assistance to people in need as she had volunteered to do, here they were running for their lives. The thought of abandoning someone to the mercy of cruel desert brigands seemed rather poor form, so Elle reined her camel in. Hamsa skidded to a halt with a snort and a puff. His sides were heaving from the effort.

Elle lifted her goggles off and rested them on top of her head, which helped to keep the loose tendrils of her hair out of her face. She drew out her optic binocuscope. Carefully she turned the little dials until the dust plumes came into focus.

'Dr Bell,' Elle breathed. From her vantage point, she was almost absolutely sure it was the archaeologist she had been chartered to collect. She could just make out the curve of a white pith helmet bobbing up and down the smaller group in front.

'Good boy,' Elle said as Hamsa stepped about, somewhat unsure as to whether he should stay or run. Camels – unlike horses, Elle had come to realise – tended to do as they pleased. Hamsa snorted and gave her a knowing look, as if he had just read her thoughts. He grunted and extended his lips, revealing a startling clump of gnarled, brown teeth. It was almost as if he was imploring her to turn back to the safety of the fort.

'Yes, you and me both, my smelly friend,' she said to the beast. 'But we cannot leave the poor doctor out there. It simply will not do.'

She stowed her looking glass and unclipped the leather strap which held her Colt 1878 Frontier revolver. The holster was cleverly attached to the side of the leather corset she wore over her shirt ready for a quick draw, if needed.

In a practised motion, she also reached for the Lee Enfield rifle that was resting in the saddle holster. The rifle was a beautiful thing, brand new and burnished. Lieutenant Crosby had insisted she be issued a weapon before leaving the fort. Which was fine with her as she rarely ventured out without being suitably armed these days; a girl in her position could not be too careful. Sometimes the company she kept in the course of her business was not always gentle.

She opened the rifle to make sure it was loaded and slid the bolt into place. It made the satisfying sound of well-machined metal upon metal. Satisfied, Elle rested it in her lap. She was ready.

The Bedouin whistled behind her from a slightly safer distance, urging her to follow him.

'Take cover!' she shouted.

There would be no help from her guides in this fight. She was going to have to take this stand on her own until help arrived. Courage be damned.

She lifted the rifle, wrapping the strap around her elbow so the butt sat firmly in the hollow where her upper arm met with her shoulder. She was a passably good shot, but the Enfield was new and she had not had time to set it properly before she left the fort. She would save her pistol for close range, if it came to that.

'Steady on, Hamsa. Good boy,' she said in a low voice as she lifted the rifle. The dust cloud was now about five hundred yards away by her estimation, but bullets travelled far in the vastness of the Sudanese plains. However, at this range it was unlikely that she would be able to hit anything with any measure of accuracy. All she could hope for was that cover fire from the fort would be enough to win some time for the doctor. Carefully she exhaled and squeezed the trigger, aiming for the middle of the bigger dust cloud.

The first shot startled her camel for a moment, but he seemed to have been trained to deal with the sound of gunfire. She was rather amazed to see that her aim was true; she could see a camel stumble and a man roll out of the dust on to the ground, where he now lay motionless.

The Bedouin cheered, but Elle pressed her lips together. That was an extraordinarily lucky shot, but there was no pleasure to be found in the shooting of a beast or a man.

Gritting her teeth, she took aim again and fired. Her shot missed, but it did send a few bandits off course.

At that point, the bandits seemed to realise that if Elle could hit them, then they could hit her too. They opened fire with much enthusiasm. Shots started pinging off the ground and rocks around them, much to the dismay of Hamsa who was stepping about in panic.

Elle ducked as a bullet whizzed past her head and she turned to meet her attackers head on. It wasn't much but at this angle she and Hamsa would be a smaller target to aim for. She could see the individual shapes of the bandits clearly now. They would be upon her soon.

'Go. Tell them to open the gates! Get some reinforcements or we'll all be dead in a moment,' she shouted at the cheering Bedouin.

They stopped cheering and swung their camels round.

Elle took aim again. Eight bullets left. Better make them count.

The third and fourth bullet hit a camel. The beast squealed and stumbled. Elle flinched and ducked behind the rocky outcrop in order to avoid the volley of shots that were fired in return. One of the shots hit the ground next to Hamsa's foot and he bellowed in surprise.

Elle fired her fifth and sixth rounds which took the front rider out.

Hamsa let out a low growl and showed the whites of his eyes.

'Easy now. We'll be home in a minute.'

Rounds seven, eight and nine, she fired in quick succession. This took out one of the bandits on horseback.

The last shot missed, the bullet lost in the rapidly growing spray of dust and hooves.

With shaking hands, Elle stowed the rifle and drew out her Colt. All she could do now was try to send the bandits off course. She fired a rapid volley at them, emptying all the chambers except the last.

The bandits were almost upon her. To her dismay, Elle realised that there was no time to run now; she would be shot in the back for sure. She stowed her pistol with a grim determination. She would keep the last bullet in the chamber, just in case – for in this world there were some fates that were worse than death.

With the fort firmly in their sights, the bandits seemed to renew their efforts to cut off the archaeologist's route to safety. Elle watched helplessly as the bandits split into two groups in an attempt to outflank the wagon. If they came within firing range of the fort it would be too late for them to catch Dr Bell.

Elle gritted her teeth. She hated to admit it, but it was time to seek the assistance of the Shadow Realm.

She took a deep breath and closed her eyes. It took only a moment to focus on the metaphysical dimension she sought. Just beneath what we see in this reality, the space between the two worlds of Light and Shadow lay. The 'barrier' opened up for her almost instantly.

'Come on, boy. Don't falter now,' she said to the camel. She nudged Hamsa firmly into the space. Instantly, she disappeared from sight.

Stepping into the space between the two worlds was like being under water. The barrier between the realms lay before her in a glimmering ribbon of golden light.

Touching it was a practice strictly forbidden by the Council of Warlocks. But Elle was the Oracle. She was the force that held the two realms together, and so the barrier was hers to command. And what's more she did not give a fig about the Council or their draconian laws.

Carefully she pushed her hand into the barrier and felt about until she found one of the globules of power that had accumulated against it. The barrier did not only act as a means of keeping Shadow creatures and humans apart. It also acted as a giant net that caught and retained energy. Elle – and those gifted with the Shadow – used this energy as fuel for their powers. But the net had been growing ever more empty over the years so harvesting power without authorisation was strictly forbidden. Only warlocks with permission from the council were allowed to access it. Another stupid law, in Elle's considered opinion.

Hamsa squealed at the sight of the barrier. The poor camel was so terrified that he promptly let out a rather large series of droppings. Evidently, in camel terms, being shot at was one thing, but being ridden into a parallel dimension was beyond the pale.

'Easy now,' Elle said. She reached out and dug her fingers into the globule of energy. This was a trick she had learned from a rather unpleasant nemesis not so long ago. Her fingers split the membrane and instantly she felt the energy flow into her, filling her up in an exquisite fizzing sensation.

As soon as the fizzing stopped, she focused her attention on the side of the Light and nudged Hamsa. The camel did not need much encouragement and they stepped back into the Realm of Light.

The doctor's party was almost upon the spot where Elle had been. One of the archaeologist's guides let out a shout of surprise when she materialised next to him and veered off just in time to avoid a collision.

'Run! Make for the fort!' Elle shouted.

She dug her heels into the high stirrups and turned Hamsa around to face the bandits who were bearing down on them.

She closed her eyes and reached inside herself for the white-hot ball of energy she had stowed. In one swift move she grasped it and hurled it at her attackers. The ball of light hit the ground just in front of the first riders. It exploded like a bomb, sending camels, horses and men flying.

But the energy of the blast was not entirely spent, and Elle stared in amazement as the aether rose up and collapsed in on itself as it fought for somewhere to go.

'Oops,' Elle said as she watched the residual power turn to wind. Bright blue bolts of lightning crackled and clouds swirled, turning and whirling with a deafening rumble. Red-brown dust, thicker than the thickest smoke, churned in the air, obscuring the blue sky above them.

The explosion, together with the force of the wind, sent the bandits reeling. She saw men and camels stumbling about in confusion.

Elle did not wait about to see what would happen next. She knew she had to retreat or face obliteration. 'Go, Hamsa. Go!' she shouted, wheeling her camel about.

Hamsa did not need to be persuaded. He set off at top speed set for the safety of the fort. Soon the gates loomed up from the haze of red dust around them.

'Incoming!' Elle yelled at the top of her voice.

She was met by the sound of cover fire as rifle bullets whizzed over her head from the stone parapets above her. Seconds later she thundered through the gates of the fort.

'To the stables! Take cover!' one of the guards shouted as the heavy doors rumbled shut behind her.

The vast cloud of dust had now all but swallowed the bandits and was spreading, bearing down upon the fort like a huge tidal wave.

Elle urged Hamsa towards the large but rather crowded stable block. People, horses, camels and dogs were all milling about seeking cover from the looming sand. Riders were trying to get their camels to kneel. A horse whinnied and reared up, upsetting a hay trough.

All this confusion was too much for Elle's trusty mount and the instinct that had allowed his species to survive sandstorms over the millennia took over. Hamsa bellowed loudly before sinking to his knees in a terrified crouch, his head slung low. The momentum of his movements threw Elle from her saddle and she landed with a heavy thump on the ground, just as the stable doors rumbled shut behind her. Outside the wind howled as the massive cloud of red dust swallowed everything. It was pitch dark; the light from the sun blocked out by the storm.

'Lady Greychester, I presume?'

She heard a match strike. A flame flickered and flared up as it lit a lamp taper, casting a pool of light around her.

Elle looked up to see a formidable-looking woman in her forties. She was dressed from head to toe in a rather austere khaki-coloured outfit. The only thing whimsical about her was the pair of round blue haploscopic spectacles perched upon her nose, presumably to guard against the glare of the sun. Elle noticed with amazement that the glasses must have remained perched there throughout the death-defying chase across the desert.

'Dr Bell?' Elle wheezed.

The woman smiled and her weather-beaten face cracked into a myriad of lines. She held out her hand to help Elle up. 'The very same. How do you do.'

Elle groaned as Dr Bell pulled her up to her feet.

She gave her jodhpurs a perfunctory pat and winced. Her left shoulder was tender from where she had landed on it. But on the whole she appeared to be in one piece.

'Good heavens, girl, are you quite all right?' said the doctor.

'I am quite well, thank you. Just made a rather inelegant dismount it seems.' She gave Hamsa a dirty look. The camel ignored her. He was now sitting quietly with his legs folded underneath him, the picture of serenity.

Dr Bell peered up at the dark sky, which was just visible from the small windows high up in the wall. 'That's quite a sandstorm you've unleashed upon us. Am I correct to presume that you are blessed with the gifts of the Shadow?'

'In a manner of speaking. It's a trick I learned a while ago, but I fear I may have used a tad more force than needed,' Elle said, evading the question. Discussing her gifts was not something she liked to do with strangers. Even friendly ones.

'Well, I think that was jolly well done. I thought we were done for out there. The blighters came out of nowhere. I think you may have saved our lives and for that I thank you.'

Elle blushed. 'It was nothing.'

'Well, shall we go and find ourselves a cup of tea? I don't know about you, but I am absolutely parched,' Dr Bell said.

As if on cue, a young soldier appeared. He stood to attention, spine straight, arms held stiffly by his side. 'Lady Greychester. Dr Bell. The lieutenant asks that you meet him in his office for debriefing and refreshments at your earliest convenience.' He punctuated his sentence by straightening up further and added 'Ma'am' for good measure.

Elle smiled. 'That is the best suggestion I've heard all day.' She turned to the archaeologist. 'Shall we?'

Dr Bell nodded, looking rather grateful. 'Lead the way my dear. Lead the way!'